Praise for the other
Art History Mysteries

The Raphael Affair

"[As] mystery, *The Raphael Affair* is very good; as cultural explication, it is superlative." —*Publishers Weekly*

"Presents a world the author knows well in the satisfying way Margaret Truman and Dick Francis set their mysteries in milieus they know." —The Associated Press

"Masterful and calls for an encore." —*Houston Post*

The Titian Committee

"Mr. Pears does some lovely brushwork on the minor characters who contribute to the subtle tones of this elegant mystery . . . but the real work of art here is the plot, a piece of structural engineering any artist would envy."
—*The New York Times Book Review*

"Light and sassy . . . Agatha would have loved it."
—*Los Angeles Times*

"Writes with a Beerbohm-like wit."
—*Publishers Weekly*

continued . . .

Death and Restoration

"Gleeful . . . articulate characters and erudite art commentary . . . high style."

—*The New York Times Book Review*

"Pears exhibits quite a masterful touch at suspenseful storytelling . . . [he] writes clearly, persuasively and with a hand guided by touches of sentimentality as well as mischief."

—*Chicago Tribune*

"Enjoyable."

—*The Washington Post*

"Pears again achieves a delicate, sure balance with a book simultaneously witty and instructive."

—*Publishers Weekly*

"It is to Pears's great credit that the textured paths of modern-day mystery, ancient empires, and religious faith collide so effortlessly. Clearly, his training as both journalist and art historian make for a finely tuned duet . . . In the end, once all the dots are connected, *Death and Restoration* leaves a memorable, satisfying imprint. We have Pears's subtle technique of mixing intrigue with intelligence to thank for that."

—*The Boston Globe*

"An exciting mystery."

—*The Dallas Morning News*

"The pleasure of Pears' book . . . lies in its careful . . . revelations of character."

—*The Houston Chronicle*

"Pears' tremendous affection for Rome comes through strongly, making the city one of the most engaging characters." —*The Sunday Times*

"Pears writes delightfully witty, elegant, well-informed crime novels." —*The Times* (London)

The Last Judgement

"Clever and entertaining . . . Pears knows what he is talking about and tells a rollicking good yarn."
—*The Boston Globe*

"A sophisticated, adventurous, and gripping story that is sure to hold wide appeal." —*Booklist*

"The latest (mis)adventure of art historian Jonathan Argyll delivers its plot twists at a rapid clip right up to the closing pages . . . Pears keeps his readers well occupied."
—*Publishers Weekly*

Giotto's Hand

"Fine art, quirky characters and scenes set in Rome and an English country village add to the joys of *Giotto's Hand* . . . A neat twist at the end is the cherry on this fudge sundae of a mystery." —*Minneapolis Star Tribune*

"Pears has a whimsical take on the scruples of the art trade, on English food and plumbing and on Italian bureaucracy . . . A sweet, art world 'cozy'."
—*The Mercury News* (San Jose, CA)

"Art, crime, and Italy mix well . . . Pears masterfully juggles his plot elements while providing delightful diversion in the contrasting manners of his English and Italian characters."
—*Booklist*

THE BERNINI BUST

Iain Pears

BERKLEY PRIME CRIME, NEW YORK

THE BERNINI BUST

A Berkley Prime Crime Book / published by arrangement with the author

PRINTING HISTORY
Harcourt Brace hardcover edition / 1994
Berkley Prime Crime mass-market edition / March 2001

For information address: The Berkley Publishing Group, a division of Penguin Putnam Inc.,
375 Hudson Street, New York, New York 10014.

The Penguin Putnam Inc. World Wide Web site address is
http://www.penguinputnam.com

ISBN: 0-425-17884-6

Berkley Prime Crime Books are published
by The Berkley Publishing Group,
a division of Penguin Putnam Inc.,
375 Hudson Street, New York, New York 10014.

PRINTED IN THE UNITED STATES OF AMERICA

10 9 8 7 6 5 4 3 2

To Ruth

CHAPTER 1

Jonathan Argyll lay contentedly on a large slab of Carrara marble, soaking up the mid-morning sun, smoking a cigarette and considering the infinite variety of life. He was not a sun-worshipper—far from it—he was quite proud of his ultraviolet-free complexion, but needs must, despite the risk of wrinkles; his temporary colleagues looked upon his packet of cigarettes with all the approval of vampires presented with a clove of garlic and were prepared to cite innumerable Los Angeles County Clean Air Acts to force him into the open when his nerves required reassurance and sustenance.

He didn't mind really, although all that moral fervour in such a confined space occasionally made him feel claustrophobic. He would be at the Moresby Museum for only a few days and his stock of moral relativism would last. The when-in-Rome syndrome. A bit longer and he would no doubt be reduced to hanging round the toilets, blowing smoke into air-conditioning vents. But he could survive for a few days.

So he was frequently to be found wandering down the highly expensive, mahogany-coated stairs, through the vast brass and glass doors and into the gentle warmth of California in early summer. And then on to his favourite slab where he performed the joint exercise of having his smoke, watching the world go by, and obscuring the letters which announced to the passerby—not that there were many, this being a part of the world where legs now served mainly a decorative function—that the Arthur M. Moresby Museum of Fine Art was located in the building behind him (9–5 weekdays, 10–4 weekends).

Ahead of him lay what he had come to accept as an almost typical Los Angeles townscape. A broad swathe of luxuriously tended grass—kept going by water piped nearly a thousand miles and then sprinkled in a fine mist—separated the white concrete museum building and the adjacent administrative block from the street. Palm trees sprouted everywhere, doing little but sway in the light wind. Cars drove with painful slowness up and down the wide boulevard ahead. From his well-placed vantage point Argyll could see everything but, apart from himself, there was not another living person visible.

Not that he was paying much attention to the street, the weather or even the palm trees. Life in general was much more on his mind, and beginning to get him down a bit. Success; that was what his presence on the lump of marble signified, and a very mixed blessing it was proving to be. He did his best to look on the bright side; he had, after all, just successfully unloaded a Titian for a client on to the museum behind him for an outrageous sum of money, of which he (or rather his employer) would collect 8.25 per cent. Better still, he had done almost nothing whatever to earn it. A man called Langton had turned up in Rome and said he wanted to buy. Simple as that. Apparently the Moresby considered itself a little short on sixteenth-century Venetian and wanted something by Titian to reinforce its credentials.

Argyll, quick on his feet for about the first time in his professional life, asked for a grossly inflated sum to start off the bargaining. To his immense astonishment, this Langton man had squinted, nodded and said, "Fine. Cheap at the price." More money than sense, evidently, but who was Argyll to complain? Not even any haggling. Pleased though he was, he still felt slightly let down. People should bargain; it was only proper.

The whole sale went through at such lightning speed he was left breathless. Within two days a contract had turned up. All the normal business of examining and testing and humming and hawing was dispensed with. However, one of the terms of the sale was that the picture should be delivered to the museum free of charge, and that Argyll should be on hand to witness the authentication process—provenance checking, scientific tests, and so on—with museum staff. If there was any dissatisfaction, he would have to take the thing back. More to the point, it was strict payment on delivery—or rather acceptance.

As a point of principle he had protested about this, making vague complaints about honour and gentlemen and the like. No deal. The terms were invariable and set by the owner who, in forty years of collecting, had learnt not to trust an art dealer further than he could throw one. In his heart, Argyll sympathised. Besides, the important thing was to get his hands on the cheque. Essentially, he would have dressed up in Greek national costume and sung sea shanties in a public place if that was what they wanted. Times were hard in the art business.

He had arrived a few days back, alarming the museum staff by bearing the small picture wrapped up in a supermarket bag and transported as hand luggage on the aircraft. It was firmly removed from his care, encased in an especially designed wood and velvet box weighing an extraordinary amount, and carried in an armour-plated wagon from the airport to the museum, where a team of six began to study it and another three considered where it might best be hung. Argyll was impressed. He thought one person with a hammer and nail would have done the trick well enough.

But it was the consequences of the sale that bothered him, and cooled off the warm glow of affluent well-being that should, ordinarily, have suffused him. If there was one thing worse than an unhappy employer, it was a happy one, it seemed . . . His thoughts returned yet again to the unwelcome generosity of Sir Edward Byrnes, proprietor of the Bond Street gallery bearing his name, and Jonathan Argyll's employer. But, as he knew that no satisfactory decision was likely to result from thinking any more about Byrnes' offer—instruction, rather—that he return to London after nearly three years in Italy, he was not completely disappointed to be interrupted by the sight of a cab pulling slowly off the street, driving along the driveway of carefully laid, hand-fired terracotta tiles, through the mist keeping the lawn in fine fettle, and finally stopping outside the museum entrance.

The man who emerged was tall, excessively thin and had a carefully cultivated air of aristocratic fastidiousness combined with just a suggestion of aesthetic flair. The first side was indicated by the immaculately fitted suit and watchchain crossing his stomach; the second by a handsome ebony and gold walking stick in his right hand and a lilac handkerchief in his breast pocket.

As the taxi drew away, this man stood still and gazed imperiously about him, very much with the air of someone faintly surprised not to see the full welcoming committee that must be around somewhere. He also looked distinctly annoyed, and Argyll sighed heavily. His day was spoilt already.

It was much too late to escape. The man's gaze, having little else to alight on, fixed on him and Argyll saw the look of recognition spread over the ageing but still handsomely chiselled face.

"Hello, Hector," Argyll said, accepting the inevitable, but refusing to show any form of welcome by budging from his marble slab. "You're the last person I expected to see here."

Hector di Souza, a Spanish art dealer resident in Rome for longer than anyone could remember, walked over and saluted the Englishman with a well-practised wave of the walking stick.

"In that case, I have the advantage," he said smoothly. "I fully expected to see you. Although not, of course, in such a languorous posture. I trust you're enjoying your stay?"

That, of course, was Hector all over. Stick him at the North Pole and he'd act as though he owned the place. Argyll tried to think of a suitably cutting reply, but inspiration failed him, as usual. So he yawned, leant over and stubbed out his cigarette in an inconspicuous corner of the marble.

Fortunately di Souza neither wanted nor waited for a reply. Instead, he resumed his gaze around the landscape, looking with right eyebrow delicately raised to indicate a somewhat contemptuous disapproval of American urbanism. Eventually his eye came to rest on the museum itself, and he sniffed loudly in a fashion that was utterly damning.

"This is a museum?" he asked, squinting at the bland and anonymous building behind Argyll's left shoulder.

"For the time being. They plan to build a bigger one."

"Tell me, dear boy, is it as bad as they say?"

Argyll shrugged. "Depends what you mean. By bad, that is. The truly disinterested might say it's full of tat. But as it's just shelled out a large amount of money for one of my pictures, I am honour-bound to defend it. But I think they could have spent the money better."

"They just have, my dear, they just have," he said with quite unbearable self-satisfaction. "Twelve of the finest pieces of Graeco-Roman sculpture on the market."

"Provided by yourself, I suppose? How old are they? Fifty years? Or did you have them carved to order?"

Argyll's sarcasm was perhaps a little heavy-handed, but to his mind it was perfectly excusable. If not one of the biggest rogues prowling the Roman art market, di Souza was at least one of the more consistent. Not that people didn't like him; far from it. Admittedly, some had trouble with the way he would come over all a-quiver at the very sight of an aristocrat; others found his baroque gallantry with women (the richer the better) annoying. But, on the whole, once you got used to the arrogance, the affected accent and his uncanny inability to find his wallet whenever a bill for a meal arrived, he was quite good company. If you like that sort of thing.

The only trouble was he could never resist the opportunity to make money, and a naïve and inexperienced Argyll had once come into his sights. Not serious, really; a little matter of an Etruscan figurine (fifth-century BC) cast in bronze a matter of weeks before Argyll was persuaded to buy it. It is difficult to forgive that sort of thing. Di Souza had taken it back—more than he had ever done for a real client—and apologised, and taken him out for a meal in recompense, but Argyll still nursed a certain grievance over the affair. The man had, after all, forgotten his wallet that time as well.

Hence his scepticism, and di Souza's wish to brush the matter aside.

"Selling things to you is one thing; selling things to old man Moresby is another," he said airily. "I've been trying to catch him for decades. Now I have, I don't want to lose him again. The stuff I've sent here is perfectly genuine. And I'd much prefer it if you didn't start casting aspersions on my integrity. Especially considering the favour I've done you."

Argyll regarded him sceptically. "And what favour is that?"

"You got that Titian off your hands at last, didn't you? Well, you've me to thank. That man Langton asked about you, and I gave you a marvellous write-up. Of course, a recommendation from myself carries considerable weight in the more knowledgeable quarters. I told him your Titian was superb, that you were a man of great integrity. And here you are," di Souza concluded with a broad sweep of the cane around the landscape which implied strongly that he had personally called it into being.

Privately, Argyll considered that a recommendation from di Souza was no great favour, but let it pass. At least it partly cleared up the point of how Langton had come to him. He'd wondered about that.

"So," di Souza went on, "your career in Italy is now on a much more secure footing. You may thank me later."

Certainly not, Argyll thought. Besides, it looked like his career in Italy was drawing to a close, and he rather resented di Souza for reminding him.

How could he refuse Byrnes' offer? The art market hadn't collapsed entirely, but it was shaky round the edges and even a well-established figure like Byrnes was having to draw in his horns. He needed his best personnel on hand to advise him, so someone, either Argyll or his opposite number in Vienna, was going to be summoned back to London. The sale of the Titian made him choose Argyll. It was a gratifying show of confidence.

But—and it was a big but—to leave Italy? Go back to England? The very idea made him miserable.

The same thoughts again. Di Souza's garrulousness was proving useful for the first time in their acquaintance, taking his mind off matters.

"It's a fairly new place, isn't it?" he was saying, impervious to Argyll's inattention. "Can't say I'm all that impressed."

"Nor is anyone else. That's the trouble. Arthur Moresby spent so much money and this is all he gets for it."

"Poor man," said di Souza sympathetically.

"Indeed. I'm sure it must be terrible. So now they think it's not grand enough to stand comparison with the Getty. They're on the brink of an all-out construction war. You know the Getty Museum is a replica of the Villa dei Papyri at Herculaneum?"

Di Souza nodded.

"This lot are thinking of building a full-size copy of Diocletian's Palace at Split. About the size of the Pentagon, as far as I can see, but more expensive. According to rumour, you'll be able to put the entire Louvre in the thing, and still have enough room left to throw the Olympic Games."

Di Souza rubbed his hands together. "And they'll have to fill it, dear boy. How splendid! I got here just in the nick of time. When do they start building?"

Argyll tried to dampen his enthusiasm. "Don't get too keen. I gather they've got to get Moresby to sign on the dotted line. And he's not someone who's used to being hurried along. Still, you may meet the architect. He wanders around with a fanatical look in his eye all the time, muttering to himself. He's a sort of guru of what he terms the post-modern return to classical tradition. His roofs leak. Awful charlatan."

Argyll had by this time reconciled himself to di Souza's company, and they walked over the lawn together so that the Spaniard could present himself to the appropriate authority. He was still plainly irritated that there had been no one to meet him at the airport.

"What about these priceless objects of yours?" Argyll asked as they ignored the whistles and shouts of a guardian telling them to get off the grass. "Where are they?"

"Oh, at the airport. They arrived a couple of days ago,

I gather. But you know what customs people are like. Same the world over. It's all on account of the other pieces I brought over."

"What other pieces?"

"Langton's. He's been buying stuff all over the place. Nothing important, I gather, but he wanted to get some of it back here. So he asked me to arrange shipment for him. Another healthy fee, and a satisfied customer. One should always be happy to oblige a man with access to so much money, don't you think?"

Still in an effusive mood, Hector babbled on, hopping from topic to topic with the agility of a mountain goat. He burbled away about his important clients—all nonsense as Argyll knew; Hector's career had always been more style than substance—and eventually broke off to point at a small figure emerging from the office block and heading in their direction. "So this place is inhabited, after all," he said. "Who's that odd little man over there?"

"That's the museum director. Samuel Thanet. Pleasant enough, but the anxious type. Hello, Mr. Thanet," he continued, switching to English as the man came into earshot. "How are you? Enjoying life?" It is always a good idea to be nice to museum directors, especially if they command an acquisitions budget bigger than all of Italy's museums rolled together. In this, at least, he and di Souza had a common outlook.

In making the characterisation Argyll was accurate, but a little unfair. If Samuel Thanet looked worried, it was mainly because he had a great deal to be worried about. It is not easy being in charge of a museum, but when it is owned and run in an almost medieval fashion by a man used to having his every whim treated like a heavenly command, life can become well nigh intolerable.

Not that Thanet bore any resemblance to the archetypal laid-back Californian even on his days off. Instead of the tall, lean, suntanned jogging type the outside world is convinced lives in the area, Thanet was short, overweight, much given to highly formal clothes and was restrained to the point of neurosis. He was not one to waste energy on tennis or surfing; such as he had was divided equally between worrying and an almost fanatical devotion to his museum.

For which latter occupation he needed money, and for that he needed to be appallingly sycophantic to the museum's patron and owner. There is nothing unusual about this; all museum directors have to be sycophantic to someone, be it patrons, donors or boards of governors. It's part of the job; some might say the most important part. And everybody else in the museum has to be sycophantic to the director. By the time you make it to the top, you are well practised in the art.

Even for the practised courtier, however, Arthur M. Moresby II was a bit of a handful. It wasn't just a question of telling him how wonderful he was; he knew that already. It was a given, like the sun rising, or the income tax form arriving. Rather, Moresby had whims. For a start, he was a businessman, and liked reality to be presented in terms of development concepts and budgeting proposals. Next he liked those around him to be lean, mean and hungry. And however ambitious Thanet might be for his museum, he was far from lean, could occasionally be mean, but was utterly hopeless at appearing hungry. It made him nervous, and the prospect of an encounter with the great man turned him into a chronic insomniac for weeks ahead.

"I'm afraid I'm having to deal with several crises simultaneously at the moment," he said in reply to the question, sneezed loudly, and whipped out a handkerchief too late. He blew his nose and looked apologetic. Allergies, he said. Martyr to them.

"Really? I haven't noticed any crises. By the way, may I introduce Señor di Souza? He's arrived with your new sculptures."

The comment, innocent enough, clearly added another crisis to Thanet's mental checklist. His brow furrowed mightily and he eyed di Souza with considerable alarm.

"What new sculptures?" he said.

This was more than di Souza's ego could bear. Being ostentatiously ignored was one thing; at least that indicated people knew you were around. But to have Thanet appear genuinely oblivious of his existence was too much. In a clipped and stern voice, marred only by his limited English vocabulary, he explained his presence. Thanet looked even more irritated, although it appeared to be the content of the message, not the style of its delivery, which alarmed him.

"That infernal man Langton again. He really has no right to cut across established procedures like this," he muttered.

"You *must* have known I was coming . . ." di Souza began, but Thanet cut him off.

"What, exactly, have you brought with you?" he demanded.

"Three cases of Roman sculpture, provided by myself, and one case brought for Mr. Langton."

"And what's in that?"

"I've no idea. Don't you know?"

"If I knew I wouldn't ask, would I?"

Di Souza looked perplexed. All he'd done was arrange shipment, he said. He assumed it was other bits of sculpture.

"It's like trying to run a madhouse," Thanet confided to nobody in particular, shaking his head in disbelief. "Do you really give your agents free run to buy things? What about my Titian? Did Langton buy that on a whim as well?"

Thanet shifted from foot to foot, then decided to unburden himself. "It's Mr. Moresby, I'm afraid," he said. "He often decides to buy things on his own account, and instructs people like Langton to go ahead. Then they turn up here."

What he meant, and couldn't bring himself to say, was that, in the past, he had found his employer and benefactor's judgement in artistic matters to be a little shaky. An alarming number of pictures in the museum were there partly because Mr. Moresby was convinced he could spot a masterwork which the dealers, curators and historians of several dozen countries had unaccountably overlooked. And partly for other reasons. There was one picture, and Thanet shuddered involuntarily every time he thought of it, which had almost certainly been painted in the 1920s, probably in London.

But Mr. Moresby had been persuaded it was by Frans Hals when he bought it eighteen months previously, and Frans Hals it was still labelled. Thanet couldn't think of it without remembering the occasion he was walking through the gallery, past a little knot of visitors, and had heard one of them snickering as he read the description. Nor could he forget the awful row that erupted when a junior curator produced proof that the thing was a dud. The Frans Hals was still there; the junior curator wasn't.

"In both of your cases," he said, pushing such thoughts aside, "I'm afraid museum procedure was bypassed. It's no good, you know. Not professional. I shall have to talk to Mr. Moresby—again—when he comes this evening."

Commercial instincts pricked up their metaphorical ears here. This was the first mention of an impending visit by Moresby himself, a figure legendary in equal parts for his excessive wealth, prodigality in art collecting and singular unpleasantness.

"He's coming here?" they said almost in unison. Thanet looked at them, knowing exactly what was passing at high speed through their minds.

"Yes. We're having to arrange a party at short notice. You're both invited, I suppose. You can make up numbers."

A bit graceless, but the man was under pressure. Argyll ignored it.

"Panic in the ranks, eh?"

Thanet nodded sombrely. "That's it, I'm afraid. He likes surprising us with this sort of thing. I'm told he's constantly dropping in at short notice at his factories to see how things are run. Always fires someone, *pour encourager les autres*. So I suppose we can count ourselves lucky we have some warning, even if only a few hours." He sniffed once more, and the two visitors took a step backwards to avoid being caught in the blast. After dithering for some time, Thanet decided not to sneeze after all, and wiped his teary eyes instead. He sighed in a rheumy fashion and sniffed heavily. "I do hate this time of year," he said confidentially.

"It could be worse," he went on. "We're just going to give him a reception, then a tour of the museum. And I think there will be an important announcement to justify our efforts." He looked suddenly smug as he said it, very much like someone nursing a delightful secret.

"I should be delighted to come, thank you," said Argyll. Not that he liked parties particularly, but if the room was going to be positively strewn with billionaires, he couldn't afford to miss it. Even a measly multimillionaire would satisfy. Doesn't do to be fussy.

He was about to make careful enquiries about the guest list when he was interrupted by a semi-sniffle of alarm from Thanet, who whipped out his handkerchief once more and gave a convincing impression of trying to hide behind it.

The focus of his anxiety was a small, brown-haired woman whose immaculately constructed elegance was marred only by a face of steadfast and determined hardness. Early middle age, but fighting back with the best technology money could buy. She had driven up to the museum in a vast car and was now heading their way.

"Damnation," said Thanet, turning to confront the menace.

"Samuel Thanet. I want a word with you," she called as she marched across the lawn, giving the luckless gardener a nasty look as he started to protest once more.

Her eyes swept across the assembled company with all the warmth of a high-pressure water-hose. "What piece of chicanery have you pulled off this time?"

"Oh, Mrs. Moresby . . ." Thanet said desperately, giving the others the only introduction they ever received.

"Oh, Mrs. Moresby," she mimicked in an unappealing fashion. "Stop whingeing. What I want to know is," she paused for dramatic effect and pointed an accusing finger at him, "what in God's name are you up to now?"

Thanet stared at her in bewilderment. "What?" he said in surprise, "I don't know what . . ."

"You know very well what. You've been bamboozling my husband again."

Di Souza, always adverse to being left out of conversations with handsome and vastly wealthy women, spotted his opportunity. "What does bamboozling mean?" he asked, smiling in the way which, he firmly believed, normally made hearts flutter.

Mrs. Moresby added him to her list of people who deserved looks of withering contempt. "Bam-boozling," she said slowly but rather nastily. "From bamboozle. Verb. To defraud. To corrupt. To pull the wool over the eyes of sweet, trusting old men. To buy, in other words, stolen or otherwise illegally acquired works of art for the purposes of egotistical self-aggrandisement. That's what bamboozling means. And this stumpy little creep," she said, pointing at Thanet in case there was any doubt, "is the arch bamboozler. Got it?"

Di Souza nodded slowly, having failed to understand what on earth she was talking about. "Yes, perfectly, thank you," he said in what he always considered to be his most charming fashion. Highly reliable usually, and the prop on which he had built an old but deserved reputation for irresistibility. It singularly failed to work its magic on Anne Moresby.

"Good," said Mrs. Moresby. "Now keep your nose out of this."

Di Souza drew himself up in dignified protest. "Madam, please . . ."

"Ah, shut up." She cut him dead and directed her full attention at Thanet. "Your grasping ambition for this museum is out of hand. I'm warning you, if you keep on manipulating my husband, when he comes this evening you are going to pay a very heavy price indeed. So you watch yourself." She poked him in the chest for emphasis.

She did an abrupt about-turn and marched back across the lawn. Didn't even say goodbye. In the background the gardener threw up his hands in despair and, as soon as the car swept back out into the street, came across to examine the damage.

Thanet watched her go impassively. He almost looked pleased.

"What on earth was that all about?" Argyll asked in astonishment.

Thanet shook his head and declined the invitation to hand out confidences. "Oh, it's a long story. Mrs. Moresby likes to take on the role of the dutiful wife protecting her husband from the outside world. And looking after her own interests into the bargain. I'm very much afraid she likes to practise on me. It may well indicate that Mr. Moresby will indeed be making an important announcement tonight."

Clearly, much remained unsaid here, but Argyll had no opportunity to pursue the matter. Thanet fended off further questions, apologised profusely for the unorthodox way in which di Souza had been welcomed, and sniffled his way off to the solitary splendour of his office in the administrative block. The two Europeans watched him go in silence.

"Can't say I'd like his job," Argyll ventured after a pause.

"I don't know," di Souza said. "Whatever Moresby's faults, I have heard that he pays well. Are you going to go this evening?"

Argyll nodded. "Seems so."

Di Souza waved his hand dismissively. "Good. The place will probably be littered with artistically starved wealth. All wanting genuine works of art imported direct from Europe. Could make your career, if you oil your way around the clientele properly. And mine, come to think of it. If I can only unload my stock on some of them I'll be able to retire a happy man. I just hope that dreadful woman won't be there."

"The trouble is, I've never been very good at parties . . ."

Di Souza tut-tutted. "You're the only art dealer I know who feels embarrassed about selling things to people. You must get over this disgusting reticence, you know. I know it's the mark of an English gentleman but it's bad news here. The hard sell, my boy. That's what's needed. Get the bit between your teeth, the wind in your sails, the eye on the ball . . ."

"And trip up?"

"And make money."

Argyll looked shocked. "I'm most surprised to hear you talking in such blatantly materialistic terms. And you an aesthete, too."

"Even aesthetes must eat. In fact, we spend a fortune

on food, because we're so fussy. That's why we're such expensive friends. Come now, this is your big chance."

"But I've just sold a Titian . . ." Argyll protested, feeling his professional acumen was being called into question a little.

Di Souza looked unconvinced. "Many a slip," he said supportively, and Argyll glared at him. The last thing he needed at the moment was something else to worry about. "After all, you've not cashed the cheque yet."

"I haven't even got the cheque yet."

"There you are. It's amazing the things that can go wrong. Take Moresby, now. I remember, just after the war . . ."

Argyll did not want to hear. "That Titian is as sold as you can get," he said firmly. "Don't go around putting ideas into people's heads."

"Oh, very well," di Souza replied, annoyed to be interrupted in mid-anecdote. "If you restrain yourself over my sculpture. All I was trying to say is that the good dealer never misses an opportunity. Think how much your stock will rise with Byrnes if you unload something else while you're here."

"My stock is quite high already, thank you," Argyll said primly. "I've been asked to go back to London. Perhaps become a partner."

Di Souza was impressed, as well he might be. Argyll, after all, left out the bit that it was more of an order than a request, and the result of a cutback rather than a promotion.

"You're leaving Rome? I thought you were settled permanently."

That, of course, was the rub. Argyll had also thought

he was settled permanently. But it seemed that, in reality, he had no real ties to the place at all. Not when it came to the test.

He shrugged miserably. Like Thanet, he was not in a confiding mood at the moment. Di Souza, ever insensitive, assumed he was thinking about money.

CHAPTER 2

For all Argyll's misgivings, the party was an impressive affair, especially for a scratch effort. However nasty an employer Moresby might be, clearly parties were an area where blank cheques ruled. And whatever the inadequacies of the museum itself at least its entrance lobby was a good place for a bash. Centre stage was a vast table covered in ice and half an ocean full of miscellaneous shellfish; nibbles there were aplenty; a jazz band blasted away in one corner, a string quintet in another, to emphasise the museum's mission to unify high and popular culture. No one paid much attention to either. The drink situation, while not generous, was adequate if you worked at it.

In short supply, however, were all those multimillionaires slavering at the chops to buy up Argyll's small (but select) stock of goods. Perhaps they were there and he just didn't know how to spot them. You couldn't, after all, just sidle up to someone and ask for a quick peek at their bank statement, though some people did seem to have a sixth sense for this sort of thing: Edward Byrnes instinctively headed towards people with excess cash burning a hole in their pockets. Argyll had never worked out how he did it. Nor had he ever grasped how to manipulate a conversation so that it imperceptibly came round to the question of, say, nineteenth-century French landscapes. Of which, by chance, you happened to have a fine example . . .

On his own little ventures into this complicated territory he generally found himself trying to sell Flemish genre pieces to waiters. When he did manage to latch on to the right person, he ended up demonstrating at length how his pictures weren't really that good, and recommending something currently owned by a rival.

So it was this evening. Almost subliminally, he managed to convey the notion that he found the idea of selling something faintly distasteful. While he had the distinct impression that Hector di Souza was unloading his fakes on every wealthy woman in the area, Argyll scarcely even managed to tell anyone he had anything to sell. His one substantial conversation was with the architect, a flamboyantly casual man with a pronounced tendency to middle-age spread, who lectured him on the synthesis of modernist utilitarianism and the classicist aesthetic as expressed in his own *oeuvre*. To put it another way, he talked about himself non-stop for twenty minutes. The fact that he was one of those people who constantly look over your right shoulder for someone more interesting didn't make him any more endearing.

But the conversation was not entirely without interest: in a fit of self-satisfaction, the architect confided that this was a big evening for him. Old man Moresby had finally committed himself to the Big Museum (known to all staff as the BM), and was going to announce it tonight. Hence the panic, hence the sudden visit, hence Thanet's vague air of smugness to counter the more general worry, and hence, presumably, Anne Moresby's pre-emptive strike a few hours earlier.

"The biggest private museum commission for decades," he said with excusable satisfaction. "It's going to cost a bomb."

"How much is a bomb?" asked Argyll, who loved hearing of other people's folly.

"The fabric alone will be about 300 million."

"Dollars?" Argyll squeaked, appalled at the very thought.

"Of course. What do you think? Lire?"

"Dear God. He must be crazy."

The architect looked upset that anyone might query the idea of entrusting him with so much money. "Museums are the temples of the modern age," he intoned sonorously. "They enshrine all that's beautiful and worth preserving in our culture."

Argyll gazed at him quizzically, trying to discern whether he was joking. He came to the depressing conclusion that the man was serious. "Bit pricey, though," he objected.

"You have to pay for the best," the architect insisted.

"And that's you?"

"Of course. I am by far the most significant architect of my generation. Perhaps of any generation," he added modestly.

"But doesn't he have anything better to spend it on?"

Evidently for the first time, the architect considered the

possibility for a moment. "No," he said firmly after a while. "If he abandoned the museum, everything would go to his godawful son. Or his godawful wife. If they weren't so dreadful, I doubt this project would ever have got off the ground."

Then he saw a more important person on the other side of the room and whisked himself off. Argyll, offended at being abandoned but relieved he was left alone, shot like a bullet in the direction of the drinks section to recover himself.

Business was not brisk; the waiter had a slight air of underemployment. One person, however—and Argyll warmed to him the moment he saw him pointing a shaky finger at the whisky—seemed to be doing his best to make the poor soul feel wanted.

"Great," said this stranger, a man in his late thirties with long fair hair of an antique cut. "Thought I was the only person here drinking something other than Perrier. What you having?"

This wasn't so generous, considering all the drinks were free, but as an invitation to conversation it was adequate. Argyll refilled and they leant back on the table, companionably side-by-side, and watched the world go by.

"Who're you?" the man asked. Argyll explained. "Thought I'd not seen you around before," he said. "You here to unload fakes and curios on my old man?"

Argyll was both affronted and intrigued in equal measure. This, it seemed, was Arthur M. Moresby III, known as Jack, although he did not know why. So he asked. Jack Moresby looked pained.

"To distinguish me from my father. My middle name, I hate to say, is Melisser."

"Melissa?"

"Melisser. My mother's maiden name. Father reckoned that being his son gave me too many advantages, so he thought he'd give me something to struggle against. You know, he sort of thought that being beaten up at school for having a cissy name would give me an edge."

"Goodness."

"Yeah. I can't be called Arthur, as I refuse to be mistaken for him, and being someone who drinks a pint of whisky a day, I naturally can't accept being called Melisser. Jack seems more writerish, I reckon."

"You write books?"

"Just said so, didn't I?"

A direct manner, just this side of being rude. Argyll began to understand why he was not held in high esteem by architects and people like that. To change the subject he assured him that he did not sell fakes. He was here to deliver a small but exquisite piece of unquestioned value.

Jack was not convinced, but seemed content to let it pass. Argyll asked if he spent much time at the museum. He nearly choked on his whiskey and said he would ordinarily not be seen dead in the place.

"Look at this bunch," he exclaimed, sweeping his arm across to include the entire room. "Have you ever seen such a collection of creeps gathered into a room before? Eh? What you think?"

Legally, this is known as a leading question and was one which required a careful answer. Besides, as Argyll could assure him, in his line of business a whole room full of creeps was nothing unusual. Who else was he meant to sell his pictures to?

Jack conceded the point, and refilled. Argyll proffered a bowl of peanuts by way of return. Jack shook his head. Never touched them. The salt made his ankles swell up. Argyll regarded the peanuts with new respect. Which creeps did he have in mind, in particular? he asked, pointing out that, being new to the country, he was not so good at spotting them yet.

So junior gave a quick guided tour. He was surprisingly knowledgeable, considering that he said he avoided his family and its associates as much as possible.

Samuel Thanet, he said, pointing ostentatiously to the director, who had been cruising around the room being hospitable ever since they got there. He had a very definite party technique: regulation one minute of conversation then on to the next person. Some people do this well, but not Thanet; he managed to make everything seem an unwelcome chore. Not surprising, really, Jack commented. Thanet didn't really care about people; he was wedded to the idea of going down as founder of the greatest private museum in North America. Using other people's money, of course. Mousy, quiet, nervous, but utterly poisonous. A man who would never do a mean trick—as long as he could get someone else to do it for him.

"Look at him there," he said. "All tweedily a-twitter, waiting for my father to turn up so he can give his boots a good lick."

The characterisation seemed a little unfair. Argyll was prepared to agree about the mousy and nervous side, but so far at least had seen nothing resembling venom. On the other hand, he was prepared to admit he did not know the man very well. In any case, his technique clearly worked, whatever it was, if Moresby was on the verge of shelling out over $300 million on a new museum.

Jack didn't seem very impressed. "You don't know my father," he said. "I'll believe in this new museum when I'm invited to the opening ceremony."

He got tired of contemplating the director and moved on. "James Langton," he said, pointing at the white-linen-clad man in his late fifties who had been so gratifyingly keen on Titian. "English slimebag."

Argyll raised an eyebrow.

"Sorry. But you know what I mean. Supercilious, disdainful, mocking, dishonest. Wouldn't you say those are national characteristics?"

"Not really," Argyll said, a host of English people fitting that description swarming into his mind.

"Well, I do. Used to be chief leech, until Thanet came along. Since then he's become an international parasite. Paris, Rome, London, New York, as they say on the perfume bottles. Devoted himself to searching out every overpriced fake in the world for my father's collection, buying it and taking a hefty cut for his services."

Argyll felt aggrieved, and mentioned his Titian once more. He was beginning to develop a complex about it.

"So we all make mistakes," Jack said with no discernible interest. "Even a man of Langton's huge talent couldn't get a hundred percent success rate. He must slip occasionally and buy something genuine."

On he went. "Mummy dearest," he said, pointing at the petite, expertly dressed woman Argyll had encountered earlier that afternoon. She had arrived twenty minutes earlier. "She's my stepmother, but she doesn't like to be called that. On the make. Quite assiduous about it. She has a vague southern accent but in fact comes from Nebraska. Do you know where Nebraska is?"

Argyll confessed he didn't. Jack nodded as though this proved it.

"Nor does anybody else. She hit the jackpot with my old man, and will stick with him until he croaks and she can get her hands on his money. Unless the museum gets it first." He regarded the woman with apparent indulgence, then dismissed her abruptly from his mind and switched to another target.

"David Barclay," he said firmly, pointing to an excessively groomed personage talking to Anne Moresby. "His signature will be on your cheque—if you ever get it. My father's lawyer and personal factotum, on permanent secondment from some law firm. The *éminence grise* of the family. Handsome little bastard, don't you think? The sort that works out before going to the office. So many designer labels on him he resembles the advertising section of *Vogue*. Drop him in a sewage plant and shit would become fashionable. My father," he went on in a loud stage-whisper, breathing a whisky fragrance into Argyll's face from close range, "is a bit of a sucker for up-and-coming professional types. That's why I'm such a disappointment to him. He can't resist someone like Barclay. Nor can my beloved stepmother."

"I beg your pardon?" Argyll said, caught a little by surprise.

"Little David is connected to my family most intimately," Jack said, speaking ever more loudly. "All services, legal and otherwise, rendered with equal skill."

He sniggered, and Argyll regarded the lawyer with increased interest. He expressed surprise that the man kept his job.

"Discretion is a wonderful thing. The trouble is, it's not that easy to keep up. Even the best-kept secret is apt to leak out eventually. Given a helping hand, anyway. That's why I'm here, in fact," Jack went on elliptically. "I love firework displays, and are we going to have one tonight."

"Are we, indeed?" Argyll said, thinking that perhaps this party might turn out to be more fun than he'd anticipated. "You don't seem to rate your father's judgement of character very highly."

"Me? The grateful son, not respect one of the richest men in the world? I have the highest opinion of his judgement. After all, he spotted me immediately as a drunken, ill-disciplined bum who'd never make a go of anything. And I can assure you, he was right. I have never disappointed him in the slightest."

There were distinct signs by this stage that Jack was teetering on the brink of self-indulgence. The last thing Argyll wanted was a detailed account of life with father, so he caught di Souza's eye as the Spaniard wafted past. He barely had time for introductions when there came the sound of Samuel Thanet trying to get the attention of the assembled gathering. Silence gradually fell, and Thanet's high-pitched, reedy voice eventually began to be heard. As everybody knew, he said, this party was in honour of Mr. Moresby's visit to the museum.

A respectful silence greeted this news, with the museum staff pondering their sins as though Thanet had suddenly upped and announced the second coming. It was a rather soupy speech, to Argyll's way of thinking, a bit over-reverential in the almost hushed way in which he referred to the Great Man. Had the said Great Man been there, this would have been almost understandable. But Moresby hadn't even arrived yet. Being nice to people behind their backs was going too far.

Apart from dropping heavy hints about what Moresby was going to say when he arrived, the speech did little except satisfy one small item of curiosity, which was the contents of the box which di Souza had brought over with him for Langton. In fact Argyll had been too busy pondering the implications of the proposed move back to London to wonder very much about this, but he listened with due care and attention as Thanet said he had a preliminary announcement to make about the museum's latest acquisition.

As he was sure everybody knew, he said, the Moresby's growth strategy—detestable term for a museum, thought Argyll, but let it pass—was to target specific areas of western art, and become world leaders in them. Impressionism, neo-classical, and baroque were high on the agenda, and much progress had been made to date.

Argyll shifted from foot to foot and leant over to di Souza.

"So what are they doing buying twelve priceless works of Roman sculpture?" he asked sarcastically. Di Souza gave him a nasty look.

"And what are they doing buying a Titian?" he countered.

Then the Spaniard held up his hand for silence. Thanet was at last getting to the interesting bit. Particularly, he was saying, they had decided to give new emphasis to baroque sculpture, and he was proud to announce that, in accordance with the Moresby's tradition of excellence—di Souza snorted—their latest acquisition in this field was a piece of unsurpassed importance. Although it was still in a packing case in Thanet's office, he was happy to announce that the museum would shortly be putting on display a masterpiece by that superlative artist of the Roman Baroque, Gianlorenzo Bernini. The museum now had in its possession the master's long-lost portrait bust of Pope Pius V.

Both Argyll and Jack were standing next to di Souza, glass in hand, when this announcement was made, and were thus in a position to hear the sharp intake of breath and gargling sound which erupted from the Spaniard's throat as he choked in mid-martini. They also witnessed the rapid change of expression—from surprise, to alarm and on to anger—which flitted across his face as he digested this announcement.

"Don't worry," said Jack, patting him on the back. "This place has that effect on everybody."

"What's the matter?" Argyll asked. "Jealous?"

Di Souza downed his drink in a gulp. "Not exactly," he replied. "Just heart failure. Excuse me a moment."

And with that he shot off in the direction of Samuel Thanet. Argyll's curiosity was piqued so, with as much subtlety as he could manage, he sidled over to see what was going on. Quite a lot, evidently, although most of the conversation seemed to be coming from di Souza. While clearly angry about something, he was at least in sufficient control to keep his voice down, otherwise the cheery atmosphere at the party might well have been severely damaged.

Argyll didn't catch it all, but the words "worrying" and "alarming" wafted in his general direction as he drew near. Di Souza seemed to be demanding to speak to Mr. Moresby.

There was a lot—especially of Thanet's attempts to pacify—that Argyll didn't pick up. Also in earshot, Jack Moresby was shaking his head with sheer enjoyment. "Christ, these people. How do you stand them?" he asked. "Hell, I've had enough. I'm off home. It's not far. D'you want to come around for a drink sometime?"

He gave Argyll his address and wandered out into the pure air of a Santa Monica evening.

Meanwhile Thanet was rocking back on his heels due to the unexpected assault, but not giving ground. Initially he seemed to be doing his best to reassure the indignant Spaniard then, as the battering continued, resorted to the reliable technique of stonewalling. He had nothing to do with the bust, Thanet insisted; and di Souza knew that perfectly well.

Hector was unimpressed, but could do little. He retreated in good order, muttering furiously. Argyll was, naturally, curious about this display, but knew di Souza's volubility well enough to realise that all would be revealed in good time. Hector was legendary for never being able to keep anything to himself.

"What are you looking at?" the Spaniard said rather sharply in Italian as he returned to the bar.

"Nothing at all. I was just wondering what you're so upset about."

"A great deal."

"Go on, then," Argyll prompted.

Di Souza didn't reply.

"You've been smuggling again, haven't you?" he said in a confiding tone. It was relatively well known that di Souza supplemented his income by arranging for works of art to be spirited across the Italian border before the authorities could refuse export permission. They would certainly have refused an above-board application to export a Bernini: there would be thermonuclear detonation if they ever found out that one had been *smuggled* out of the country.

"Don't be ridiculous," di Souza snapped back, with enough uncertainty in his voice to convince Argyll he was on the right track.

Argyll sucked in his breath and tutted with wholly hypocritical sympathy. "Wouldn't want to be in your shoes if the folk at the *Belle Arte* get their fangs into you. Nasty, that'll be," he said with an uncontrollable grin. Di Souza gave him a very unpleasant look. "Serious offence, smuggling . . ."

"It's no smuggling I'm worried about."

"Oh, go on, Hector, spill it."

But there was no persuading him. Di Souza was panicked and adopting the tactic of saying as little as possible. You could see his point, Argyll thought. A public announcement, and reporters here as well. Had Thanet stood up and thanked di Souza for smuggling the bust out for him, it couldn't have been more awkward. All it needed now was a little whisper, a little looking, and Hector would be in big trouble back in Italy. Standing up in a court and saying that he hadn't known what was in that case would merely be greeted with hearty guffawing from the prosecutor. Argyll found it hard to believe himself.

"Hmm," he said thoughtfully. "You'll just have to hope that no one notices too much. All I can say is you're very lucky Flavia isn't here. She'd have your guts."

He shouldn't have said that. Flavia di Stefano had been greatly on his mind all afternoon, all week, in fact, and he had only just succeeded in thinking of other things. If he put his hand on his heart and confessed what it was that most attracted him to living in Rome, he would have had to say that, splendid though the buildings, the art, the streets, the food, the weather and the people were, what he really liked most was Flavia di Stefano, old friend, investigator in the Italian polizia art squad and a woman with a long-standing disapproval of those who smuggle the Italian heritage out of the country.

Flavia, alas, did not return his feelings. She was a wonderful companion and a perfect friend, but though Argyll had worked hard to persuade her to be something more his labours had produced remarkably little result. He was fed up with it. That was why he was able to reconcile himself to going back to England.

What more could he do? He'd mentioned Byrnes' proposal to her one evening as they came out of the cinema—with what result? Oh, don't go? Please stay? Even, I'll miss you, would have been a start. But nothing. All she'd said was that if his career would benefit then of course he should go. And changed the subject. Not only that, since then he'd barely seen her.

"What was that?" he said, coming out of his reverie and realising that di Souza was still talking.

"I said that when I have sorted everything out with

Moresby not even your Flavia will have any interest in me."

"If you can. Besides, she's not my Flavia."

"I've already told you I can. Simple to prove."

"What is?" Argyll asked, puzzled. Evidently he'd missed more of di Souza's conversation than he'd thought.

"If you can't listen I'm not going to repeat it," he said crossly. "It's the second time you've spurned my anecdotes today. Besides, judging by the way the crowds are beginning to practise doing obeisance, I'd guess Moresby is arriving and I need an urgent talk with him. I'll fill you in later, if you can pay attention for long enough."

Argyll followed in the slipstream of the guests heading for the main door where they could get a decent view of the proceedings. Di Souza was right. Moresby arrived with all the sense of occasion of a medieval potentate turning up to visit some minor province. Which he was, in a way. Compared to the vast range of his interests—Argyll vaguely remembered they stretched from oil to electronics, miscellaneous weaponry to financial services and just about everything in between—the museum was a fairly minor operation. Unless, of course, Thanet managed to prise open the old man's very tight fist and keep it open long enough to build his big museum. It was an odd experience, halfway between being impressive and slightly ludicrous. The car was one of those stretched limousine affairs, about forty feet long with a small radio telescope on the back, all black tinted glass and shiny chromium. It swept up to the entrance and a host of nervous museum folk swept down to it, competing for the honour of opening the door. Then one of the richest men on the western seaboard emerged in the fading light of evening and everybody gazed at him reverentially.

From Argyll's standpoint, there wasn't much to be reverential about. From the purely visual, or aesthetic, point of view, Arthur M. Moresby II didn't amount to much. Tiny little fellow, peering myopically around him through thick round glasses, dressed up in a heavy suit much too thick for the weather and which, in truth, did little for his general appearance. He was almost completely bald and slightly pigeon-toed. A thin mouth, mottled complexion and ears that rose up to conclude with a very definite point at the top. He looked, indeed, a bit like a malevolent garden gnome. Putting himself in Anne Moresby's position, Argyll began to see the appeal of a narcissistic concoction like David Barclay.

Had it not been for the bank balance, it was difficult to imagine anyone gushing over him. On the other hand, he reflected as he scrutinised Moresby more closely, maybe that was unfair. The face indicated a man to reckon with. Entirely expressionless, it nonetheless radiated an air of chilly contempt for the clucking hordes gathered around him. Whatever his possibly innumerable faults, Arthur Moresby knew exactly why people were so keen to welcome him, and realised it had nothing to do with his loveable personality or exciting physique. Then he disappeared into the museum to get on with business, and the excitement was over.

CHAPTER 3

Looking back on events later, Argyll viewed the following couple of hours with profound embarrassment. It was just like his luck that, whenever something interesting happened, he would be elsewhere. It was simple enough; he was hungry and, no matter how many virtues oysters possess, no one can call them filling. Not like a burger and french fries, anyway, so after a few moments' indecision, resolved when he decided that hanging around in the hope of shaking Arthur Moresby by the hand was a demeaning way of spending an evening, he sloped off in search of a halfway decent restaurant and sat feeling miserable for an hour or so.

Indeed, he regretted not latching on to Jack Moresby to spend the night getting drunk together. He also regretted agreeing to have breakfast with di Souza. He'd had enough of the man already, what with spending much of the afternoon booking him into the same hotel he himself was staying at, carrying his luggage around, and listening to him at parties. Quite apart from the fact that he knew who was going to end up paying for breakfast.

And he also regretted his choice of restaurant. The service was interminably slow. The waitress (who introduced herself as Nancy and was most keen that he enjoy his food) did her best, but it was one of those places where the cook evidently begins by grinding his own wholemeal. Alas, he shouldn't have bothered. The end result wasn't worth the effort.

It was nearly eleven o'clock by the time Argyll set out for his hotel, after two hours spent all on his own with ample opportunity to feel sorry for himself. Apart from that, completely uneventful, except for narrowly avoiding being run over by an ancient truck painted with purple stripes. It was his own fault, he crossed the wide boulevard which led past the Moresby and on to his hotel in the cavalier fashion he had adopted for dealing with Roman traffic, and discovered that drivers in California, while generally slower, are not nearly as accurate as their Italian counterparts. A Roman shaves past your legs and makes your trousers billow in the wind but disappears over the horizon with a triumphant hooting of the horn, leaving no real damage behind. The driver of this particular vehicle either had clear homicidal tendencies or little skill; he flashed past, saw Argyll, blew his horn and swerved at only the last moment, very nearly consigning Argyll to the hereafter in the process.

As he reached the opposite sidewalk and his heart—boosted by alarm and the remarkable turn of speed he put on to reach safety—calmed down once more, he reflected that it was quite in keeping with life as it was currently progressing.

Heaving self-indulgent sighs at regular intervals, his

thoughts meandered in a haphazard fashion as he ambled mournfully towards the hotel. Such was his mood that he was nearly past the museum itself before it penetrated his consciousness that all was not quite as it was when he'd left to search out nourishment. The floodlights still illuminated the building with ostentatious discretion, cars were still parked all over the place. But the number of people engaged in wearing the lawn down to waste land had grown enormously, and Argyll was fairly certain that the place had not been surrounded by fifteen police cars, four ambulances and a large number of helicopters when he left.

Strange, he thought. Prompted mainly by the pessimistic view that, knowing his luck, something untoward must have happened to his Titian, he changed direction and headed up the driveway.

"Sorry. No entry. Not 'til morning." This from a policeman of impressive dimensions blocking the way in a fashion that brooked no argument. Even without the heavy weaponry strewn about his person, Argyll would not for a moment have contemplated disagreeing with his pronouncement. On the other hand, the scene had tickled his curiosity somewhat; so he announced firmly that the museum director had asked him to come round immediately. Samuel Thanet. The director. You know?

The policeman didn't, but wavered a little. "Little fat guy? Wrings his hands?"

Argyll nodded. Thanet to a tee.

"He's just gone with Detective Morelli into the administrative block," he said, uncertainly.

"And that's just where he told me to meet him," Argyll said, lying through his teeth in a fashion which made him feel rather proud. He generally wasn't a very good liar. Even fibs gave him a hard time. He beamed at the policeman and asked most politely to be let through. So convincing was he that, seconds later, he was climbing the stairs in the direction of a faint hubbub of noise.

It came from Samuel Thanet's office, a carefully designed piece of upmarket administrative chic; whatever the museum architect's limitations on exterior appearance, he had worked overtime on getting the office space right. A slightly anonymous room to Argyll's mind, he preferring a more cosy and cluttered look, but expensively tasteful, nonetheless. White-washed walls; off-white sofa; beige-white woollen carpet; tubular modern armchairs covered in white leather; black wooden desk. The whorls and lines of two harshly illuminated modern paintings from the museum provided the only colour in the whole room.

Apart from the blood, of course, of which there was an appallingly large amount. But that was obviously a very recent addition rather than part of the decorator's overall design concept.

And on the carpet lay the prostrate and immobile form of Samuel Thanet. Argyll stared horror-struck as he came through the door.

"Murdered?" he said aghast, eyes unable to tear themselves away from the sight.

A scruffy, tired-looking man, dressed in a casual fashion that would have been entirely unacceptable in the Italian polizia, and even in the carabinieri, looked up at him, wondering for a moment who this interloper was. He snorted contemptuously.

" 'Course he's not been murdered," he said shortly.

"He's fainted, that's all. Came in, took one look at that and keeled over. He'll be all right in a few minutes."

"That" being a man-sized mound behind the desk covered, appropriately enough, by a white cloth, part of which was stained crimson. Argyll peered at it and felt a little queasy.

"Who the hell are you?" the man, apparently Detective Morelli, went on with perhaps forgivable directness.

Argyll explained.

"You work for the museum?"

Argyll explained again.

"You don't work for the museum?" he said, proceeding inexorably towards the truth. Argyll agreed this statement summed the matter up admirably.

"Get out, then."

"But what is going on?" Argyll insisted, natural curiosity overcoming him completely.

The detective made no answer at all except to bend down and casually flick back the white sheet from the mound on the floor. Argyll stared at the figure underneath, wrinkling his nose in disgust. No mistaking those ears: seen once, never forgotten.

The sudden and unexpected demise of Arthur M. Moresby, President of Moresby Industries (among other things) had clearly been caused, as the unemotional language of officialdom would put it, by a shot in the head from a pistol at close range. It was not an appealing sight, and Argyll was heartily glad when the detective replaced the cloth and made the object once more a fairly unobtrusive shape under a sheet.

Morelli was in a bad mood. He had just been turned down for a promotion and felt a summer cold coming on. He'd been on duty for eighteen hours and badly wanted a shave, a shower, a decent meal and some peace. On top of that he had chronic gum inflammation and dreaded the prospect of a visit to the dentist. It wasn't the pain; that he could cope with. It was the bill that would follow that alarmed him. As his dentist kept on telling him, fixing gums was an expensive business. The man collected antique cars, so it must be profitable as well. Detective Morelli wasn't sure whether his gums were really going, or whether the dentist merely wanted a new carburettor for his 1928 Bugatti.

"Do you need any help?" Argyll asked, thinking it was a supportive thing to say. No harm in offering, after all.

The detective looked scornful. "From you? Don't trouble yourself."

"No trouble at all, honestly," he said brightly.

Morelli was halfway through indicating that the Los Angeles homicide division, having managed without Jonathan Argyll for more than half a century, could probably stagger on without him for a bit longer when a pained groan came from the other recumbent form on the floor. Thanet, when he collapsed, had done so inconsiderately, straight in front of the door, causing a major bottleneck to traffic. The groan was caused by a large police boot inadvertently kicking him in the ribs.

"Oh, the Sleeping Beauty," Morelli said, then turned to Argyll. "You really want to be useful? Bring him round and get him out of the way. Get yourself out of the way while you're at it."

So Argyll did, bending over the director and slowly helping him to his feet. Propping him up uncertainly, he called to Morelli that they'd be down the corridor, if needed. Then he steered Thanet in that direction, settled him on a sofa and fussed around vainly trying to open windows and, more successfully, to provide glasses of water.

Thanet was no great shakes at conversation for some time. He stared at Argyll owlishly for several minutes before the power of speech returned.

"What happened?" he asked, with a striking lack of originality.

Argyll shrugged. "I was rather hoping you'd tell me that. You were on the scene. I'm just a nosy passerby."

"No, no. Not at all," he said. "First I knew was when Barclay came running back to the museum, telling people to phone the police. He said there'd been some sort of accident."

"He must be a bit thick if he thought that was an accident," Argyll commented.

"I think he was concerned not to let on too much to the newspaper men around. They always turn up. Can't keep anything secret from them, you know."

"He found the body?"

"Mr. Moresby said he was going to use my office to talk to di Souza . . ."

"Why?"

"Why what?"

"He could talk to him anywhere, couldn't he?"

Thanet frowned disapprovingly at the Englishman's concentration on irrelevancies. "Di Souza wanted to talk about that bust and it's in my office. Anyway, later on . . ."

Argyll opened his mouth to ask how much later on. This concentration on detail was a habit he'd picked up from Flavia over the years. But he decided it might throw Thanet off his stride, so shut it again.

". . . later on, Mr. Moresby used the internal phone to call Barclay and told him to come over. He went, and found . . . that. We called the police."

Argyll had about two dozen questions he wanted to ask, but made the grave mistake of pausing briefly to arrange them in order of importance. What was the conversation with di Souza about? Where was di Souza? What time was this? And so on. Unfortunately, Thanet took advantage of the momentary silence to wander off in pursuit of his own thoughts.

These came across as almost entirely selfish, although this was perhaps forgivable under the circumstances. Samuel Thanet had never liked Moresby; no one had. While it was dreadful that the man should be shot, to Thanet's way of thinking it was much more terrible that such an event should take place in his office and in his museum. The worst thing of all was that it should take place before Moresby had made his announcement about the Big Museum. Had all the relevant documents been signed? He'd be frantic with worry until he found out.

"I assume that all the papers were drawn up and signed in advance," he said. "But it really couldn't have come at a worse time."

"You mean to tell me that Moresby was topped just before he publicly committed himself to this project? Doesn't that strike you as odd?"

Thanet stared at him blankly. Clearly, everything struck him as odd at the moment. But before he could reply, the door opened and Detective Morelli, hair ever more rumpled and rubbing his inflamed gums in a thoughtful fashion, walked in.

"Case in your room," he said flatly. "What is it?"

Thanet paused a moment while he collected his thoughts. "Case?" he asked.

"Big wooden thing."

"Oh, that. That's the Bernini. It hasn't been opened yet."

"Yes, it has. It's empty. What's a Bernini, anyway?"

Thanet's mouth flapped around uncertainly for a while before he stood up and rushed out of the room. The other two trailed after him, and reached his office just in time to see him bent over the large wooden box scrabbling around desperately among all the packing inside.

"Told you," Morelli said.

Thanet re-emerged with little bits of plastic padding in his thinning hair, white with shock.

"This is terrible, terrible," he said. "The bust has gone. Four million dollars, and it wasn't insured."

It occurred to Morelli and Argyll simultaneously that Thanet was more obviously upset about the Bernini than he was about Moresby.

Argyll suggested that it was a little careless not to insure it.

"The insurance came into operation tomorrow morning, when we were going to move it into the museum. The company won't cover stuff in the administration building. It's not secure enough for them. Langton had it put here temporarily so Moresby could inspect it if he wanted. We didn't feel he should have to go down to the storerooms."

"Where is Hector di Souza?" Argyll asked, finally deciding that this was the central point that needed to be answered.

Thanet looked blank. "I've no idea," he replied looking around as though he expected to see the Spaniard emerging from a cupboard.

There was a brief interlude as Morelli asked who di Souza was and Argyll explained.

"Señor di Souza brought the bust over from Europe. He was upset about something and wanted to talk to Moresby. They came over here to discuss it in Thanet's office. Some time later, Barclay discovers the body and presumably by then the bust had gone as well."

Morelli nodded in a fashion which communicated understanding and profound irritation in equal parts. "And why didn't you mention this di Souza before?" he asked Thanet. It was clearly a rhetorical question as he didn't wait for an answer. Instead, he picked up a phone and gave instructions that di Souza was to be found as fast as possible.

"If you ask me . . ." Argyll began, thinking that Morelli would undoubtedly want the benefit of his experience.

"I'm not," the detective pointed out kindly.

"Yes, but . . ."

"Out," he said, pointing helpfully to the door, lest there be any confusion about where the stairs were situated.

"All I mean . . ."

"Out," he repeated. "I'll talk to you later to see if you have any relevant information. Now, go away."

Argyll was displeased. He liked constructing theories, and generally found the Roman police receptive to them. Well, Flavia sometimes was. Evidently the Los Angeles police were less sophisticated in their approach. He glanced at Morelli, saw that he meant it, and reluctantly left.

Morelli breathed a deep sigh of relief, and scowled at the quiet snicker from a colleague who'd been listening to his attempts to restore control.

"Right," he said, "Let's start again. From the beginning. Can you identify this man?" he asked formally.

Thanet swayed once more, but managed to stay perpendicular. This, he said, was Arthur M. Moresby II.

"No doubts?"

None whatsoever.

Morelli was deeply impressed. Northern Los Angeles, while not the battle zone of other parts of the city, undoubtedly had more than its fair share of mayhem. Generally speaking, however, the victims were not enormously illustrious. Only rarely did a member of the social register get himself disembowelled. Hollywood directors, television magnates, noted authors, fashion models and all the other exemplars of local industry were usually remarkably adept at keeping themselves alive.

It also made him rather nervous. He could not remember the figures, but he was willing to bet that the percentage of homicides where he successfully fixed the handcuffs on the guilty party was pretty small. Ordinarily, this was distressing but had few other consequences. People—and that meant his superiors—understood that a conviction was unlikely and didn't for a moment attach any blame to him. He arrested people often enough to have earned himself a respectable reputation for general professionalism. He did his best and that was that. Better luck next time.

But he already had a strong feeling that a very large number of people were going to be keeping their eyes on him over this one. This time, doing his best was not going to be good enough.

"I was wondering," he went on, "about the alarm system. You do have alarms, don't you?"

Thanet snorted. "Oh yes. This place is wired like Fort Knox."

"So can we check if any doors except the main entrance were used?"

"Sure. In theory the murderer should have been caught on film in the corridor. Although personally, I'm dubious."

Thanet explained that their enormously complicated alarm system included concealed cameras in every room of the museum. Although the administrative block was less well endowed, it was still a bit like a maximum security prison. So they trooped off to the central security office, a room on the third floor crammed with enough electronic equipment to equip a small film studio. While they were eyeing it up and wondering where to start, a tall, balding man in his late thirties came in, radiating nervous excitement.

"Who are you?" said Morelli.

The man introduced himself as Robert Streeter, chief security executive, and his curiosity turned to alarm when he was brusquely told that his much vaunted system, responsible both for museum security and his salary, had not so far impressed the police.

"To put it another way," the detective informed him, "it was a dead loss. If that man Barclay hadn't discovered the body, no one would have known anything had happened until a hell of a lot later. What good is that?"

Streeter was also concerned, perhaps even more so than was the detective. After all, his job could depend on this. He had been brought in originally as a consultant when the museum was expanding, to give advice about how to protect the collections. However, as he had discovered, consultancy work was merely an elaborate way of being unemployed, and Streeter's income had been somewhat erratic at the time. So, spotting his opportunity, he went for it. His report was disdainful, if not devastating. The place was, he concluded, about as secure as the average doll's house. Not only did he set out a bewildering array of electronic necessities, he accompanied the report with elaborately printed flow diagrams of responsibility structures and integrated fast-response networks to demonstrate how, in the event of a break-in, the felony could be interdicted and the threat neutralised.

It was all Greek to the museum staff, who accordingly concluded that an integrated fast-response network was an absolute must for anyone who wanted to be on the cutting edge of the museum business. Besides, the man was recommended by Moresby. A college friend of his wife's or something. So they did the only thing possible, that is, set aside a vast budget, created a new security department and gave Streeter the job of presiding over both. Who began by using the entire allotment to hire secretaries, administrative assistants and liaison personnel in order to lobby for more money. He now had a staff of twelve, another six to patrol the museum, enough electronic gadgetry to make the CIA jealous and was beginning to insist on having the final say on where pictures were hung. In the interests of security. He had even restarted his consultancy business on a sounder footing, and travelled the country giving lectures on "Museum security in the modern age" for hefty fees. It also meant he had less time to spend in Los Angeles, so he was currently bidding for a deputy to take care of day-to-day operations.

Some people didn't approve of what they considered Streeter's imperial tendencies, and Thanet, sensing the growth of an alternative source of power to his own, was one of them. There was no need at all, he suggested, for either Streeter or the vast bureaucracy he had conjured into being. Streeter, not surprisingly, had disagreed quite strongly with this view, and the two men had been at loggerheads ever since. Clearly, a showdown was now in the offing. Recent events would either demonstrate the utter uselessness of all the security systems (victory for Thanet), or indicate the need to work even harder to turn the museum into a cross between Stalag Luft VI and an electronics factory (victory for Streeter). Or, of course, the museum could collapse entirely, and both would find themselves on the breadline.

Going instantly on the offensive, the security man took a perverse pleasure in pointing out that, in fact, he didn't really have quite the equipment he had wanted.

"I did indicate at the time the dangers of cutting corners on security. For optimum coverage . . ."

"Please. That's not what we're here for," Morelli said, rubbing an inflamed gum and too tired to get involved in domestic squabbles. "Why don't you just show us what you've got, not what you wanted."

Not before the guided tour. As Streeter set it all out, each room in the museum was covered by a camera system whose lenses swept across a minimum of eighty-two per cent of the area every minute. Equally, they could be automatically directed to particular spots when pressure pads were activated or light-beams cut. The entrycard system automatically logged the entry and exit of everybody employed by the museum, correlated their personal codes to the telephone system so the administration knew where and when they were dialling. More sensors picked up the cards as people moved from room to room, permitting a read-out of their movements. Finally, microphones in every gallery could pick up conversations, in case any visitors were planning a break-in. And, naturally, all the rooms were fitted with smoke detectors, metal detectors and explosives sniffers.

"Christ," said a surprised Morelli as this explanation finally came to an end. "You're all ready for Doomsday here. You seem more intent on watching the staff than anything else."

"You may sneer," said Streeter, affronted. "But because many of my recommendations were ignored, our employer has been murdered. And now my system is going to tell you who did it."

Even Thanet thought that Streeter's voice lacked its normal conviction as he said this, but Morelli paid no attention, being too busy watching the man manipulate an extraordinary system of controls on the central console. "Naturally, the administrative block is less comprehensively covered, but we have adequate visual coverage. I've directed the image outputting to this VDU unit," he said, pointing a finger.

"He means the picture will be on that television screen," Thanet explained helpfully. Streeter glared at him, then turned disdainfully to watch the screen. It remained resolutely blank.

"Ah," he said.

Director and detective looked at him inquisitively as he rushed over to his console again and began scanning buttons and levers.

"Damn," he added.

"Don't tell me, let me guess. You forgot to put a film in?"

"Certainly not," Streeter said, manipulating wildly. "It doesn't use film. A visual recording node seems to have malfunctioned."

"Camera's bust," Thanet said in a loud stage-whisper.

Streeter rolled back a video, explaining as he did so that the image should come from a camera in the corridor leading to Thanet's office. Still nothing. Careful checks revealed that it had stopped working at a little after 8.30 p.m. Subsequent investigation revealed that the cause of the problem was nothing more hi-tech than a pâté sandwich stuck over the lens.

Morelli, who had a deep-seated distrust of all gadgetry, was not in the slightest bit surprised. He would have been much more amazed—pleasantly, admittedly—had the video shown some miscreant trotting down the staircase wiping bloodstained hands on his handkerchief. Fifteen years in the police, however, had taught him that life is rarely so kind. Fortunately, there was always good old-fashioned police procedure to fall back on.

"Who did it?" he asked Thanet, who looked taken aback by the question.

"I've not the faintest idea," the director said after a moment to gather his thoughts.

"What happened, then?"

"I don't know."

Morelli paused, standard procedural techniques having proven less than immediately effective, and thought a moment.

"Tell me what happened when the body was discovered," he said, thinking this might be a good place to start.

Thanet, with the occasional interruption from Streeter, gave his account. Moresby had arrived at the party, circulated awhile, then was approached by Hector di Souza, who insisted on talking to him.

Streeter put in that di Souza seemed agitated and had insisted on privacy.

"What were his exact words?"

"Ah, now, there you've got me. Ah, he marched up to Mr. Moresby, and said something like 'I understand you've got your Bernini.' Then Mr. Moresby nodded and said, 'At last,' and di Souza said was he sure? And Moresby said he—di Souza, that is—was going to have to do a lot of explaining."

"Explaining about what?"

Streeter shrugged, closely followed by Thanet. "No idea," he said. "I'm just telling you what I heard."

"Time?"

"I'm not entirely certain. Shortly after nine, I'd guess."

Morelli turned to Thanet. "Do you know what it might have been about?"

Thanet shook his head. "No idea. I had words with di Souza earlier myself. He was upset about the bust, but wouldn't tell me why. Just said he urgently wanted to talk privately to Moresby about it. Maybe there was some dispute over the price."

"An odd time to start having second thoughts."

Thanet shrugged. No accounting for art dealers.

"You didn't by any chance have a microphone in the director's office, did you?" Morelli asked.

Streeter looked thunderstruck for a moment, then switched to being outraged. "No," he said shortly. "I did once suggest that office space be monitored more closely, but Mr. Thanet here said he'd take me to the Supreme Court if necessary to stop me."

"A monstrous, unconstitutional and illegal idea," Thanet huffed. "How anyone can so lose sight of basic civilised . . ."

"Oh, shut up, both of you," Morelli said. "I'm not interested. Can't you keep your minds on the fact that Arthur Moresby has been murdered?"

As they clearly couldn't, he told them he'd take statements properly later, and got a junior officer to usher them out. Then, taking several deep breaths to calm himself down, he ran his fingers through his hair and began to organise his investigation. Press to be talked to, names to be taken, statements to gather, bodies to be moved, someone to go round immediately and find di Souza. Hours of work stretched before him. And he couldn't really face it. So, instead he settled down and watched the video of the party, to see if that produced any real leads.

It didn't help him, nor did it greatly illuminate more professional analysts who looked it over later. The multiple interaction patterning, as the experts termed it, concluded that Thanet was having an affair with his secretary; that no less than twenty-seven per cent of the guests departed with at least one piece of museum cutlery in their pockets; that Jack Moresby drank too much, that David Barclay, the lawyer, and Hector di Souza, the art dealer, both spent extraordinary amounts of time looking at themselves in mirrors and that Jonathan Argyll was a bit lost and ill at ease most of the evening. They also noted that Mrs. Moresby arrived with David Barclay, and didn't speak to her husband once all the time he was there. Finally, they saw with disappointment that the pâté sandwiches were singularly popular, although no one was seen secreting one about his person for unorthodox purposes.

They also watched Moresby talking to di Souza and leaving the party with the Spaniard at 9.07 p.m. and later on saw Barclay be summoned to the phone, talk into it, and walk out of the building at 9.58 p.m. The body was discovered moments later and Barclay came back to phone the police at 10.06 p.m. After that, everyone hung around and waited, with the exception of Langton who could be seen on the phone at 10.11 and again at 10.16. Simple enough, he explained later, he was phoning Jack Moresby and then Anne Moresby to inform them of the disaster. He was, it seemed, the only person who even thought of telling them. All the rest were too busy panicking.

Apart from that, they came up with a list of people who, at various stages of the evening, conversed with Moresby. Surprisingly enough there weren't all that many; almost everybody greeted him in one way or another, but he responded in such a frigid manner that few had sufficient courage to pursue the dialogue further. The party may have been thrown in his honour, but Arthur Moresby did not look as though he was in a party mood.

To put it another way, dozens of expert man-hours and all the techniques of advanced social-scientific investigation devoted to analysing the tape produced no useful information whatsoever. And Morelli had known they wouldn't, all along.

Jonathan Argyll tossed and turned in bed, his mind churning over recent events with a degree of manic obsessiveness. He had sold a Titian; he hadn't been paid for it; he had to go back to London; the prospective buyer had just been murdered; he wasn't going to get paid for it; he was going to lose his job; he had nearly been run over; the cheeseburger was in violent dispute with his stomach; Hector di Souza was the likely candidate for gun-toting connoisseur; the Spaniard had smuggled a bust out of Italy.

And he had no one to talk it all over with. A brief conversation with di Souza himself might have cleared his mind enough for him to get some sleep, but the infernal man was nowhere around. Not in his room, anyway; policemen there were aplenty, but Hector himself had, apparently, come back to the hotel, then left again shortly after someone phoned him. The key was with the reception. Maybe he would turn up for breakfast, unless the police got to him first, in which case he might be otherwise engaged.

Argyll rolled over in the bed for the thirtieth time, and looked at the clock with eyes that were not in the slightest bit weary, try as he might to convince them that they needed a rest.

Four in the morning. Which meant that he'd been lying in bed for three and a half hours, eyes open, brain rotating.

He switched on the light, hesitated and finally took the decision he'd been wanting to take ever since he got back to his hotel room. He had to talk to someone. He picked up the phone.

CHAPTER

4

While Argyll was wide awake in the middle of the night, Flavia di Stefano, sitting at her desk in the Rome headquarters of the Italian art squad, was half asleep in the middle of the day. Like him, however, she was in a disturbed frame of mind, and her colleagues were beginning to notice.

Ordinarily she was an exceptionally good-humoured person to have around. Cheerful, charming, relaxed. A perfect colleague to spend an hour chattering to over a cup of espresso when the work load flagged a bit. In the four years she'd worked for Taddeo Bottando as a researcher, she had successfully established a reputation for all-purpose amiability. She was, in short, well-liked.

But not at the moment. For the past few weeks she had been grumpy, uncooperative and a complete pain in the neck. A very junior and pimply-faced lad who had just joined had his head almost bodily ripped off for a trivial mistake that, usually, would have elicited nothing more alarming than a patient explanation of how to do it properly. A colleague asking for a swap on the work rota so he could take a long weekend was told to cancel the weekend. A plea for help from another, bogged down in a mass of documents from an art gallery raid, was told he would have to sort it out himself.

Not herself at all. General Bottando even made cautious enquiries after her health, and wondered whether she was, perhaps, overworking a little. He got short shrift as well, and was told, in effect, to mind his own business. Fortunately, he was a tolerant man, and more worried than annoyed. But he was beginning to find himself watching her more carefully. He ran a happy department, so he liked to think, and was disturbed at the effect she was beginning to have on morale.

Doggedly and persistently, though, Flavia plugged on with the work; forms in, forms annotated, forms out again. No one could fault her work, or the amount of time she spent doing it. She just wasn't much fun anymore. The bad mood seemed an almost permanent fixture, and was approaching high tide when, at 5.30, the phone rang.

"Di Stefano," she snapped, rather as though the instrument was a personal enemy.

The voice at the other end bellowed through the receiver at a volume which suggested the owner was shouting loudly into it. He was; Argyll had still not fully accepted that the audibility of phone lines varies in inverse proportion to their length. His voice came through as clear as a bell, while a call across Rome was frequently incomprehensible.

"Wonderful, I've got you. Listen, something awful's been going on."

"What do you want?" she said crossly when she realised who it was. Typical, she thought. Don't see him for weeks on end, then, when he wants something . . .

"Listen," he repeated, "Moresby's been murdered."

"Who?"

"Moresby. The man who bought my picture."

"So?"

"I thought you'd be interested."

"I'm not."

"And a Bernini's been stolen. It was smuggled out of Italy."

This was, of course, more in Flavia's line of business, as much of her time in the past few years had been devoted to stopping smuggling, and recovering at least some of the works of art which were smuggled. Generally speaking, no matter what sort of mood she was in, she would have picked up pen and paper and begun listening. However . . .

"In that case it's too late to do anything about it, isn't it?" she said shortly. "What are you ringing about? Don't you know I'm busy?"

There was a two dollar fifty-eight cent pause from California until the slightly aggrieved voice returned for another try. "Of course I know you're busy. You always are these days. But I thought you'd want to know."

"Don't see what it's got to do with me," she said. "It's an American affair. I haven't noticed any official requests for our assistance. Unless you've joined the local police or something."

"Oh, come on, Flavia. You love murders and thefts and smuggling and things like that. I rang you up just to tell you. You could at least sound interested."

In truth, she was, but was damned if she was going to let on. Argyll and she had been close friends for a couple of years. She had long given up any notion that they would be anything else. Until he came along she had tended to think of herself as the sort of person who, if not irresistible—she was not sufficiently vain to think that—was at least generally attractive. But Argyll didn't notice. He was companionable, friendly, evidently enjoyed trips round the countryside and to movies and dinner and museums with her, but that was it. She had provided the openings, had he been so minded, and he had not taken them. He just stood there, looking awkward.

She'd eventually got used to that and settled for his company. It was the blithe way he announced he was leaving Italy that finally made her lose patience. Just like that. A career to be made, so he was off.

And what about her? she'd felt like asking. He was just going to go and forget her? Just like that? Who was she meant to go to dinner with?

But if that was what he wanted to do, he could go, as far as she was concerned. So she said, in a chilly, angry voice, that if his career needed it, he should go. The sooner the better, in fact. Then she'd got on with her work.

Now here he was again, with problems.

"I'm not interested," she said shortly. "I don't care if the whole of the National Museum is scattered along the Pacific Rim, and I don't have any time to waste talking to you, you . . . Englishman."

And slammed the phone down and made chuntering

noises as she tried vainly to remember what it was she'd been doing before he'd rung.

"Jonathan Argyll, I assume," came a deep, reassuring voice from the doorway behind her as General Bottando walked in clutching a sheaf of papers. "What's he up to these days? I heard he was in America."

"He is," she said, turning round and hoping he hadn't heard too much of her conversation. "He just rang me up to tell me about a murder."

"Really? Whose?"

Flavia told him, and Bottando whistled in surprise. "Good heavens," he said. "I'm not surprised he rang. How extraordinary."

"Fascinating," she said shortly. "Is there anything you want? Or is this a social visit?"

Bottando sighed and looked at her sadly. It was perfectly obvious to him what was wrong, but it wasn't at all his job to say. And even if he had tried to give her the benefit of his advice, he was fairly certain it would not have been well received. She was touchy that way, and had no respect for the wisdom of age.

"I've got a little job for you," he said, confining himself to business. "Needs tact and delicacy, I'm afraid." He looked at her doubtfully before proceeding. "You remember that little drinks party we had a few weeks back?"

It had been a small celebration for Bottando's fifty-ninth birthday. A date and a number shrouded in secrecy, but the office had weasled it out by dexterous spying on the personnel returns. They'd all clubbed together to throw a surprise party in his office, and presented him with a little Piranesi print and a large plant to replace the one that had died because he always forgot to water it.

"Well," he went on a little nervously. "That plant. Someone watered it to show me how to do it, and water spilled over the desk and I grabbed a piece of paper to mop it up."

Flavia nodded impatiently. He did ramble sometimes.

Bottando produced a stained, crumpled and almost illegible document and handed it to her shamefacedly. "Been under the pot ever since," he said. "Carabinieri report about a burglary in Bracciano. Should have followed it up weeks ago. You know the remarks they'll make if they ever find out. Could you go and do something about it?"

"Now?" she said, glancing at her watch.

"If you could. Damned man's a curator at some museum. Influential. The sort who complains. I know it's getting late . . ."

With a long-suffering look she got up and stuffed the report in her bag.

"Oh, all right," she said. "Got nothing else to do. What's the address?"

And, radiating disapproval of her boss's inefficiency, she marched out of the office. The Alberghi family inhabited a castle—a small one, but a castle nonetheless—rather handsomely sited overlooking the lake. The area has gone downhill in recent years; the nearest bit of fresh water to Rome, it is swamped by people desperate to get away from the heat and dust and pollution of the capital. So they come to the heat and dust and pollution of Bracciano instead. It makes a change, and also means the water is no longer quite as fresh as it once was. Those local residents who bought their houses some time ago are not pleased at the disturbance that thousands of noisy Romans bring with them; others make a small fortune out of them and are perfectly happy about it.

The Alberghi were firmly in the former category. Their castle looked basically medieval with lots of modern conveniences added in the sixteenth century, like windows. The owners were not the sort of people who rushed out to sell Coca-Cola and popcorn to the tourists. The place was more than a little secluded; from the road the only indication that it was there at all came from the signs at the gate warning of ferocious dogs and announcing that you were entering private property so go away.

If the gateway was unwelcoming, the owner was even less hospitable. It took some time for the door to be opened, and even longer for the appropriate person to put in an appearance. They were the sort who still had servants; indeed, they were clearly the sort who, without a cook, would starve to death. Flavia handed her card to an ancient woman who opened the door, and waited for results.

"And about damn time too." The voice of the owner preceded his actual appearance. He came limping down the stairs shortly afterwards, bristling with indignation. "Pretty disgraceful, I call it."

Flavia looked at him in a cold manner. It seemed the best way to deal with the situation; to adopt a general air that implied that Alberghi was at fault himself and should count himself lucky he was getting any attention at all.

"Pardon?" she said.

"Four weeks," he said, glaring at her. "What do you call that? I call it appalling, myself."

"Pardon?" she repeated frostily.

"The robbery, woman, the robbery. Good God, we have thieves swarming all over the house and what do the police do about it? Nothing, that's what. Absolutely nothing. Can you imagine how my dear wife . . ."

She held up her hand. "Yes, yes," she said. "But I'm here now, so why don't we get on with it? I gather you were meant to be drawing up a list of everything that was stolen. Have you got it?"

Still grumbling and stroking his moustache with fury, he grudgingly led the way in. "Waste of time, I suppose," he complained as they passed through a dusty entrance hall into a dark, wood-panelled study. "Can't imagine you'll get anything back now."

He flung open the top of a desk in the corner and extracted a sheet of paper. "There you are," he said. "Best I can do."

Flavia looked at it and shook her head despairingly. The chances of getting anything back were always fairly small, even when the descriptions were complete and photographs appended. Any burglar with even half a brain knew that it was imperative to get stolen goods over the border fast.

But this thief needn't have bothered. The list was about as useful as an old sweet packet. On the other hand, it did provide a useful cover for the department's tardiness. No one could blame them if Alberghi's goods were never seen again.

" 'One old landscape. One silver pot, an old bust, two or three portraits,' " she read. "Is that all you could manage?"

For the first time she got him on the defensive, and his moustache twirling switched from aggressive to defensive mode. "Best I could do," he repeated.

"But this is useless. What do you expect us to do now? Go round and examine every portrait in Europe in the hope one might turn out to be yours? You're meant to be an art expert, for heaven's sake."

"Me?" he said scornfully. "I know nothing about it."

In the circumstances, Flavia thought that the tinge of pride in his voice was misplaced. A small amount of expertise would have greatly increased his chances of recovering his family possessions. Mind you, now she thought about it, he did not look much like a museum curator to her.

"I thought you worked for a museum," she said.

"Certainly not," he said. "That was my uncle, Enrico. He died last year. I'm Alberto. Army man," he said, chin jutting up and chest popping out at the very mention.

"Isn't there a list or inventory or something? Anything would be better than this."

" 'Fraid not. Uncle had it all in his mind." He tapped the side of his head as he spoke, in case Flavia was uncertain where his uncle's mind might have been located. "Never got around to writing it down. Pity, but there it was. Would have done." He lowered his voice as though revealing a family scandal. "A bit—you know—in his last years," he said confidingly.

"What?"

"Ga-ga. The old brain box. Not what it was. You know." He tapped his head again, a bit mournfully this time. Then he cheered up a little. "Still," he went on. "Eighty-nine. A good run. Can't complain. Hope I last so long, eh? eh?"

Flavia agreed, although privately thinking that the

sooner the old fool dropped dead the better, then wondered if there were any insurance documents that might provide a bit of help.

Colonel Alberghi shook his head again. "None," he said. "I know that, because I went through his papers when he died and looked again after that fella came."

"What fella?"

"Chap turned up, wondering if I wanted to sell anything. Damned impertinence. Sent him away with a flea in his ear, I can tell you."

"Hold on a second. You didn't mention this to the carabinieri."

"Didn't ask."

"What man was this?"

"I told you. He turned up and knocked on the door. I sent him away."

"Did he look around the house?"

"Damned silly maid let him in here to wait for me."

"And what did he look like?"

"Didn't see him. Maid phoned me, and I told her to chuck him out. Didn't give up, though."

"What do you mean?"

"He rang a couple of days later. I told him I hadn't the faintest idea what my uncle had owned, but I did know I didn't want to—didn't need to—sell any of it."

"I suppose it's too much to hope that you got his name?"

"Sorry."

Flavia had thought so, somehow. "And what was stolen from here?"

"Ah, now. Let me see."

"A painting," she hinted, pointing at the patch on the

woodwork that had evidently been covered by something.

"Yes, yes. Perhaps. A portrait? Great grandfather? Or may be his father. Perhaps it was my great grandmother? Do you know, I never paid much attention to it."

Evidently. "And what about that empty pedestal there?"

"Ah, yes. A bust. Big damn ugly thing, it was. I was going to grow a pot plant over it."

"Too much to hope for a description, I suppose?"

"Just given you one," he said. "I'd recognise it if I saw it."

Not much chance of that, she thought. "I'll put out a search request for a big, damn ugly bust, sex indeterminate, then," she said sarcastically. "Can I see this maid of yours?"

"Why?"

"It's quite usual for thieves to case a place before they burgle. Posing as an art dealer is a good way of going about it."

"You mean he was looking the place over? The cheek of it!" Alberghi said, puffing up with righteous indignation. "I shall call that maid immediately. Who knows? She may well have been part of the gang."

Flavia did her best to turn him away from the idea of international conspiracies of burglars that was clearly forming in his mind, and pointed out that the robbery—a simple brick through the window when the house was empty—hardly required an inside hand to succeed.

Nor was the maid, a woman of at least eighty years and almost bent double with arthritis, the archetypal gangster's moll. The moment she saw the old biddy, Flavia had the feeling she was going to be as blind as a bat. It was one of those days.

A youngish man, the maid said, which was a start, but then she pointed to the colonel, a man in his late fifties, and said that maybe he was the same age as the master. Tactically acute though; Alberghi was quite pleased.

After much patient questioning, Flavia established that the purported art dealer was between thirty and sixty, medium height, and had no distinguishing features she could remember.

"Hair?" she asked.

That's right, she said. He had some.

"I mean, what colour?"

She shook her head. No idea.

Marvellous. Flavia snapped her notebook shut, stuffed it back in her bag and said she was going to go.

"Frankly, Colonel, I think you can wave goodbye to your pieces. We pick stuff up every now and then, and when we do, we'll give you a call. Apart from that, the only thing I can recommend is that you keep your eye on auction sale catalogues, in case you see something you recognise. If you do, let us know."

Alberghi, with a sudden spurt of regimental courtesy, swept ahead to open the door for her as she left. The gesture was spoilt by a noisy yapping sound and a heart-felt, military style stream of cursing as a tiny dog ran in and almost swept him off his feet. This was evidently the ferocious animal advertised on the gate.

"Get that beast out of here," he instructed the maid. "Which one is it, anyway?"

The old woman, with remarkable agility, pounced on the animal, swept it into her bosom and cradled it gently.

"There, there," she said, and patted it on its head. "This one is Brunelleschi, sir. The one with a white spot and the clouding eyes."

"Horrid little things," he said, eyeing it like someone wondering how it would do as a pot roast.

"It seems quite sweet," Flavia said, noting that the old lady's hearing and eyesight weren't so bad after all. "Odd name, though."

"My uncle's," he said mournfully. "Otherwise I'd get rid of them. Arty type, as you know, so gave his dogs stupid names. Other one's called Bernini."

"Oh, good," said Bottando as Flavia arrived back in the office at slightly after nine. She was planning to dump her notes on the desk for typing up the next morning, then go home for a long bath and an evening's self-indulgent misery in front of the television. There was never anything worth watching, which made it an even more appropriate way of wasting time. "I was hoping you'd come back. Got something for you."

She looked at him with cautious disapproval. He had on his air of amiable benevolence, which generally meant having to do something she'd rather avoid.

"What is it now?"

"Well, I thought of you, you see," he said. "Because of your friend Argyll. Just the person, I thought."

There was, at the moment, no surer way of irritating Flavia than to think of her because of Jonathan Argyll, so she sniffed loudly, got on with rearranging papers on her desk and tried to ignore him.

"This murder, and theft. The one in Los Angeles. It's

causing quite a stir, you know. Even made the evening news. Did you see it?"

Flavia pointed out that she'd spent the last few hours wasting time talking to military idiots in the countryside, not idling away in her office with her feet up. Bottando brushed the comment aside.

"Quite. The point is that the police there have been on the phone. A man called Morelli. Speaks Italian, surprisingly. Just as well, otherwise I'd have had enormous difficulties understanding him . . ."

"Well?"

"They want us to pick up their prime suspect. A man called di Souza, do you know him?"

As patiently as possible, Flavia said she didn't.

"I'm surprised. He's been around for years. Awful old fraud. Anyway, it seems he and Moresby were having a row about a Bernini that di Souza smuggled out of the country. Moresby dead, Bernini gone and di Souza, so they reckon, on the next plane back to Italy. It gets into Rome in about an hour, and they want us to grab him and bung him back."

"Not our department," she said shortly. "Why not try the carabinieri?"

"Paperwork. By the time all the international liaison departments had finished organising it, the plane would have been sold for scrap. So your friend Argyll recommended us. Good idea. Quick thinking. Could you, er . . ."

"Miss dinner and spend the night hanging around Fiumicino? No."

Bottando frowned sternly. "I really don't know what's got into you these days," he said. "What on earth is the matter? It's not like you, all this bad temper and uncooperative attitude. You used to spend most of your time begging me for jobs like this. But if you insist, you can get back to being a simple researcher. Full time. I'll get a proper member of the polizia to do it."

Flavia sat down on the desk and looked at him mournfully. "I'm sorry," she said. "I know I've been a pain recently. I just don't seem to have much enthusiasm for anything these days. I'll go to the airport for you. I suppose it might perk me up a bit, arresting someone."

"What you need is a holiday," Bottando said firmly. It was his universal remedy for all ills and he took one himself as often as was decent. "Change of air and scenery."

She shook her head. A holiday was the last thing she wanted at the moment.

Bottando eyed her sympathetically for a moment, then patted her gently on the shoulder. "Don't worry," he said. "It'll pass."

She looked up at him. "What will?"

He shrugged slightly and waved his hand about airily. "Whatever it is that's putting you in such a bad mood. Anyway, nice though it is to talk . . ." He looked at his watch in a significant fashion.

She got up wearily and brushed her hand through her hair. "OK. What shall I do with him when I get him?"

"Hand him over to the airport police. They'll hold him until all the paperwork's in order. I've arranged everything. You'll just be there to identify him and deal with formalities. I've got all the bits of paper you'll need, and a photograph. Shouldn't be any real trouble."

• • •

In making this statement, Bottando was almost entirely wrong, but for reasons which were not his fault. Getting to the airport was a trouble, due to a large pile-up on the stretch of motorway which leads from the city to the patch of reclaimed marshland which tries its hardest to be an international airport. Silly place to put it, but there was some story about a deal with the Vatican which had all this useless land and a friend in the planning department . . .

Flavia got to the terminal at ten, parked in a Strictly No Parking area—she was lucky there was a space left, but it was late in the evening—and marched in to find the airport police. Then they took up their stations and waited until someone had the bright idea of checking the board, and discovered that the plane was half an hour late due to a longer than anticipated stopover in Madrid.

Madrid? she thought. No one ever said anything to her about Madrid. The day had started off badly, got worse, and now looked as though it was going to go out in appropriate style.

There was no alternative but to wait, knowing with that utter certainty that sometimes descends, that she was wasting her time.

She was. The plane finally touched down at 10.45, the first passenger appeared through the gate at 11.15 and the last emerged at five minutes to midnight.

No Hector di Souza. Flavia had sacrificed her evening and had nothing to show for it except a protesting stomach and a foul temper.

What was more, she knew full well she could not just go home and forget about it. International protocol demanded you at least put up a show of being co-operative, especially when, somehow or other, you may have made a mess of things.

So she went back to the office yet again, and settled down to the phone. Calls to the airline, to Rome Airport, to Madrid Airport. They'd ring back, they said; and she had to wait. Couldn't even go out and search for a sandwich, not that there were many places open at that hour.

The final call-back came at nearly three in the morning. Madrid Airport, just like Rome and the airline, confirmed what she basically knew already. No di Souza. Didn't get off in Madrid, didn't get off in Rome, didn't get on the plane at all, as far as anyone knew.

One final call, and that was it. Fortunately—and it was the one good thing that had happened all day, although the fact that it was now tomorrow may have had something to do with it—Detective Morelli was in his office. Bottando said he could speak Italian, and so he could, after a fashion. But Flavia's English was better.

"Oh, right," he said. "Yeah, well, we sort of knew that," he added laconically as she announced her failure. "We checked here. He phoned and booked himself on to the flight, left the hotel, but never showed. Sorry if we put you to unnecessary trouble."

A couple of hours earlier and Flavia would have been capable of a most impressive speech, outlining the need for consideration in international endeavours and concluding with an impressive paean of praise to the continuing value of simple courtesy in human relations. But she was too tired to manage, so she simply said, not at all, not to worry, think nothing of it.

"I would have rung," he went on. "Should have, in fact. Sorry. But you just can't believe what's going on here. Talk about a circus. I've never seen so many cameras and reporters. Not even at a superbowl. Then there was that English guy nearly killing himself . . ."

"What?" she said, suddenly alert. "What English guy?"

"Man called Jonathan Argyll. The one who put me on to your Bottando. Do you know him? He rented this ancient car, went out and crashed it. Comes of renting rubbish. They save money on the servicing costs, you know. That's how they keep the prices down. I reckon . . ."

"What happened?"

"Eh? Oh, simple enough. Straight through a light and into a designer clothes shop. He made a real mess . . ."

"But how is he?" she cried, noticing that her heart was thumping wildly as she tried to interrupt his flow of inconsequentialities. "Is he all right?"

"Oh, sure. He'll be fine. Cut up a bit. Bruised. Broken leg. I talked to the hospital. Doctor says he's sleeping like a baby."

"But what happened?"

"I've no idea. Nearly got run over last night as well. Seems a little accident-prone."

Flavia agreed. He was just the sort of person who'd drive into a shop selling designer clothes, or get run over, or fall into a canal, or something similar. He did it all the time. She got the number of the hospital from Morelli and rang off. Then sat and looked at the phone for half an hour, contemplating the degree to which the news of his mishap had alarmed her, and the relief she'd felt when Morelli had said he'd survive.

And it was all his own fault, as well. That, at least, was predictable.

CHAPTER 5

Argyll's car accident may not have come as a surprise to Flavia but it did to Argyll. Like most people, his vision of himself differed markedly from that of others. While Flavia, in a good mood, saw an amiable soul prone to tripping over his shoelaces, he preferred a slightly suaver, more sophisticated image in which the occasional mishap was the exception rather than the rule. He was always rather hurt and surprised when she had an attack of the giggles every time—on the rare occasions, that is—he walked into a traffic bollard.

Until the accident took place, he'd had a rather good day, even though his lack of sleep made him a little less alert than usual. But his insomnia did at least lead to his meeting Detective Morelli once more. When the American turned up early the next morning and banged on the door of the room next to his, Argyll was already awake and functioning.

"Oh, it's you," he said, sticking his head round the door. "I thought it might have been Hector. I was meant to be having breakfast with him. I'm dying to find out what he's been up to."

"You don't say. I reckon quite a lot of people feel the same way." Morelli looked at the door of di Souza's room rather like someone hoping it would suddenly open and reveal that the occupant had been there all along. Eventually he gave up, rubbed his eyes and yawned.

"You look awfully tired," Argyll said sympathetically. "Why don't you come and have a coffee? It might keep you going for an extra couple of hours."

Morelli, who'd also missed most of his night's sleep, although for different reasons, accepted gratefully, thankful for the prospect of sitting down for a while. He could also get some museum gossip, and as he was going to have to talk to Argyll sometime, he might as well combine the two tasks. You never knew when stuff like that would come in handy.

Argyll recounted his evening, up to and including the quality of his cheeseburger and his brush with the hereafter, and Morelli in return gave him a warning about the dangers of jaywalking. Then the Englishman passed on titbits of gossip he had picked up in the very short time he'd been around. Not much use; as far as Argyll had been able to find out, everybody in the museum disliked everybody else. "Are you all right? You look in pain," he broke off and looked at Morelli with concern.

Morelli stopped rubbing his gum for a moment and looked up. "Gingivitis," he explained.

"What?"

"Gum. Inflamed."

"Ooh, nasty," Argyll said sympathetically. He considered himself something of an expert in this field, having spent much of his life sitting in a chair having dentists peering into his mouth and shaking their heads in distress.

"Cloves," he added.

"Eh?"

"Cloves. And brandy. You make a solution and rub it on the gum. Very effective. My mother's recipe."

"Does it work?"

"I've no idea. But the brandy tastes nice."

"I don't have any cloves on me," Morelli said regretfully, patting his pockets just to make sure.

"Don't worry, leave it to me," Argyll said brightly. "You just drink your coffee. I'll be back in a minute."

About ten minutes, in fact. He went down to the lobby and then realised that, no matter how devoted to the ideals of old-world service American hotels might be, the chances of them keeping a stock of cloves handy were small.

But then Argyll recalled that Hector di Souza was notorious throughout central Italy for being almost a professional-level hypochondriac. Argyll had never heard him complaining about gums before, but that proved nothing. On top of that, there was no one behind the desk, the key to Hector's room was dangling invitingly on its little hook . . .

He returned to his room to find Morelli making free with his telephone. Did he have any idea how much extra hotels charged for calls?

"Did you search Hector di Souza's room?" he asked in a tone which had a decidedly critical edge.

"I didn't, no. But I sent some people over to pick him up, and I'm sure they had a look around. They wouldn't have searched it, though. We'll do that later. Why?"

"That room's an awful mess. It looks as though a bomb has hit it."

Morelli was not impressed. "How do you know?" he asked.

Argyll explained the reasoning which had led him to di Souza's portable medicine cabinet.

Morelli went slightly pale. "You broke into a suspect's room?" he said aghast, thinking of all manner of unpleasant consequences.

"Certainly not," he said robustly. "I used a key. I took it from the desk. There was no one there, and I couldn't think anybody would object. Anyway, the point is . . ."

Morelli held up his hands and shut his eyes. "Please," he protested with real anguish in his tone. "Don't say any more. That's probably a felony. More importantly, if there is any useful evidence there, you've just compromised it. Can you imagine what a defence lawyer would make . . ."

Argyll looked gravely offended. "I was only trying to help," he interrupted. "But judging by the mess your people made, I don't imagine anyone will find anything. They disturbed it far more than I did."

"What are you talking about? They barely touched it," said Morelli firmly. "Whatever the state of di Souza's room, it's the way he left it. Now, give me that gum ointment."

Argyll handed it over and watched as the detective gingerly applied it.

"I don't think so, somehow," Argyll ventured after Morelli had stopped grimacing at the foul taste. "The thing about Hector is that he is, shall we say, an aesthete."

"Eh?"

"Fastidious. Punctiliously, even fanatically, neat, tidy and proper. Obsessed with appearances. The sight of a crooked tie or speck of dust makes him feel faint. I once had dinner with him in a restaurant and he was served coffee in a cracked cup. He had to retire to bed to recover, and spent an hour gargling with antiseptic in case he'd picked up any germs."

"So?"

"So, Hector does not make his room untidy. He even makes his own bed in the morning because he doesn't trust chambermaids to get the folds straight."

Morelli turned pale as horrified realisation dawned. "You broke into the wrong room," he stated flatly.

"Of course I didn't. What I am trying to say is either that your people made a right mess, or someone else did. Or, I suppose, Hector left so fast that he made the place untidy. If so, he must have been in a very great hurry indeed."

"Personally, I'd go for the last option," Morelli replied. "Seeing that I've just been told he was on the 2.00 a.m. flight back to Italy. That's what they were telling me on the phone. Why else do you think I'm still sitting here rather than running around looking for him?"

An idea crossed his mind and he glanced at his watch and calculated furiously. "Damn," he concluded. "Won't be enough time to pick him up at the other end."

Argyll was not impressed by this, having had recent and all too memorable experience of the length of time it takes to fly between Rome and Los Angeles. Weeks, as far as he could remember. He pointed out that there was at least six hours. All they had to do was get someone to trot down to the airport . . .

It was not, Morelli assured him, like that at all. There were procedures. Quite apart from the business of getting hold of extradition orders.

"But why do you want an extradition order, anyway? Obviously you want to talk to him, but this is going a bit far."

Morelli gazed at him. "Why do you think we want one? I want to arrest him for murder, of course. I would have thought that was obvious."

Argyll considered this carefully, then shook his head. "Hector wouldn't kill anyone. Not by shooting them at close range, anyway. Might get blood on his jacket. I see him more of a poison man. Not that he's the murdering sort, really; certainly not clients."

Morelli didn't find this line of argument at all convincing. "I'm sorry, and I know he's your friend, or colleague, or something, but we want him. The evidence so far is pretty convincing."

"And that is?" Argyll asked.

"One, he was angry during the party about that bust; two, the bust was later stolen; three, he went off with Moresby moments before the murder; four, he was the only person with Moresby at the time; five, he immediately tried to leave the country. To me—and remember I'm only a homicide man with fifteen years' experience—it looks suspicious. Not that it's any of your business."

It wasn't, of course, except indirectly, and Argyll was beginning to get the glimmerings of an idea. On the whole he disliked crime: his occasional brushes with it always seemed to involve, at some stage, police mentally measuring his wrists and wondering how a nice pair of handcuffs would look dangling around them. Similarly, as long as he got his cheque for the Titian, he didn't really care two hoots about Moresby, or Hector di Souza, or stolen Berninis.

His main aim, in fact, was to sort out his fragmenting friendship with Flavia, whose hostile tone in the middle of the night had upset him enormously.

And perhaps this overworked and frowzy homicide man sitting in front of him provided an opportunity. Flavia was avoiding him like the plague. She was going to have to be forced into contact, whereupon she could be made to see the error of her ways, or at least he could find out what was upsetting her so much.

Simple. So he made the suggestion that led to Flavia wasting her evening at Fiumicino and recommended an informal approach to the Roman art squad, which would be much faster and more co-operative if Morelli promised to pass on any information about the odd Bernini that might come into view. Phone General Bottando and say that he, Jonathan Argyll, had suggested it.

Morelli considered the suggestion. There would, certainly, be advantages, like the possibility of actually catching di Souza. Going by officially prescribed procedures would be hopeless.

"What's his name?" he asked.

"Bottando," Argyll said, looking up the phone number in his book. "It would be a good idea to play up the importance of this bust. If it was smuggled out of Italy—and it probably was—he'll love to help."

"We don't know it was."

"All the more reason for him to find out."

Morelli nodded. It was quite a good idea.

"Somebody else other than di Souza could have stolen it, of course," Argyll went on. "After all, there are other reasons for stealing busts. It would be a pity to neglect them."

Morelli, who was in essence a simple soul and certainly unprepared for the extremes of deviousness that come as second nature to the true scholar, could think of no others. Argyll listed them, one by one.

"First, for the insurance, although Thanet reckons it wasn't insured. Second, for ransom. Wait for the demands. If a large lump of marble ear comes through the post, with a promise that a nose will follow in due course, you know where you are. Third possibility, to stop people looking at it too carefully."

"Why?"

"Fakes."

Morelli snorted. He was a man with little time for idle speculation, and pointed out that this was all it was.

"It's not idle. It's scene setting. The product of years of experience in the nether world of art connoisseurship. Just trying to help."

"Gives no practical help, though. Phoning this Bottando character might, and for that idea, my thanks. Then I suppose I'd better go and get on with my work. Have to talk to the press, as well. Like flies round a honeypot already."

"Good idea," Argyll said. "And I shall go off and visit people as well."

Morelli looked uncertain again. "Don't you do anything of the sort," he said. "You've made your contribution. Now keep out of it."

"Surely I don't need authorisation from you to pay a visit of condolence to a grieving son who invited me to stop by for a drink? Do I need police permission to see Thanet to finalise details about the sale of his picture?"

Morelli agreed, with great reluctance, that such bureaucracy was unnecessary. But repeated that he thought Argyll would be better occupied trading pictures, or whatever he did for a living.

Being naïve in such matters, Argyll had imagined that he would get around Los Angeles by public transport. For him trains were the height of civilisation, and by far his preferred means of transport. Failing that, a bus would do. Both, however, were notable for their absence. Buses were in almost as short supply as pedestrians. Trains seemed to be as extinct as the brontosaurus. So, after anxious enquiry, nervous indecision and much research to find something inexpensive, he had hired a car. The rental place was a bit like a scrapyard, full of old, rusting machines that looked as though merely staying in one piece was as much as they could manage. The selection was not great, but, as the salesman—he shook Argyll warmly by the hand and introduced himself as Chuck, by which name Johnny was to call him on all occasions—pointed out, the prices weren't so big either. Argyll hated being called Johnny.

But at least there was one car that he instantly fell in love with. It was a pre-oil-crisis Cadillac. 1971. Light blue. Open topped. About the size of the Queen Mary, and used as much fuel.

Well why not? Argyll thought when he saw it. He'd never drive anything like it again. This was a moving piece of cultural history. The first thing he did when he got back was to get the doorman of the hotel to take a photograph of him resting against it, wearing sunglasses. So he could show his grandchildren, who might not otherwise believe such machines had ever existed.

So after Morelli left, Argyll went round to the parking lot behind the hotel. The car started, eventually, and in a billowing cloud of lead-laced petrol fumes he navigated slowly out. It had the acceleration and the manoeuvrability of a supertanker, but otherwise was in reasonable condition, apart from the rust patches. The main thing was that it went forward when requested, and stopped when asked. And traffic regulations in California are such that an ability to accelerate from nought to sixty in under five minutes is a bit redundant, anyway.

The machine roared along, backfiring periodically, and having to stop every 150 yards for traffic lights. Argyll tried admiring the scenery, and found himself wondering how any place could support so many car dealers.

It took him about half an hour to drive the six miles to Venice, Jack Moresby's part of town, although he reckoned he could have done it faster had he known where he was going. Once he'd found the place, it took considerable imagination to see why it was called Venice at all; though a rather stagnant patch of water and a sort of piazza-thing that might have been impressive had it been finished, gave a clue as to the original intentions of the developers.

Still, it looked like being a much more appealing part of the world than the rather obsessive bit of town which housed the museum. In Venice the residents' main occupation seemed to be sitting around not doing very much; and Argyll was only too glad to see it. Despite their reputation for being relaxed, everybody else in the city seemed to be constantly hurrying. On the rare occasions that they stopped working, they still bustled manically. Even on the beach they insisted on running around, throwing things at each other and jumping in and out of the ocean for no obvious reason. It was agreeable to see that some people liked just to lie about, immune to their fellow-citizens' frantic desire to prolong their lives forever. The place was scruffy, fly-blown and charming, or so it seemed. Perhaps that was how it got its name.

It was also almost as difficult to get your bearings as in its Italian namesake. Finding the abode of Jack Moresby was harder than he'd anticipated, and he was very surprised when he did eventually track it down. Not what he'd anticipated at all. He knew that Moresby had retreated from the consumer society to write the Great American Novel—a common failing in this part of town, he'd been told—but he'd anticipated that the son of a multi-billionaire would have hung on to some of the vestiges of the good life. He'd met many alternative types in Italy, and they all seemed to find handmade Versace clothes, Rolex watches and nine-room apartments overlooking the Piazza Navona perfectly compatible with the principled rejection of the consumerist tyranny.

Young Moresby, however, seemed determined to do it properly. His home was not the stereotypical millionaire's residence and bore little resemblance to a Beverly Hills mansion. Millionaires' houses have roofs, with windows in the side. And when windows break, millionaires have them replaced; they don't patch the holes with old newspaper. When a tile falls off the roof they replace it, rather than leaving the rare downpour of rain to come in. Millionaires have gardens, complete with gardeners; Jack Moresby's equivalent bore more than a passing resemblance to the depot where Argyll had hired his car. Nor, in general, do millionaires sprawl on the floor of the little deck at the back, smoking a cigarette with a most unusual aroma, drinking from a half-empty bottle.

Moresby regarded him passively as he approached, then half-waved a hand in casual and unenthusiastic greeting.

"Hey," he said, a term Argyll had learnt was the local, all-purpose way of indicating hello, goodbye, surprise, alarm, warning, interest, lack of interest, and do you want something to drink. The American looked at a seat by his side, pushed an old and mangy dog off and gestured for him to sit. Argyll eyed the clumps of dog hair warily, then reluctantly eased himself down.

"Come to commiserate about the old man, I suppose," he said absently, squinting up at the weak sun through the clouds.

"When did you hear?"

"Langton phoned me last night. And everything else I picked up from the police when they woke me up at dawn to ask me to account for my movements. I suppose it would be far too much to expect my stepmother to come a whole twenty miles to pass on the news. Too busy celebrating, I guess. What d'you want?"

A good question. Pertinent and to the point. The trouble was Argyll didn't really know. After all, he could hardly say he wanted to dig something up about the bust so he could get back into more amicable contact with Flavia. Wouldn't sound right. Heartless, in fact. Besides, initial questioning made it clear that Moresby knew nothing about the Bernini—or any bust, for that matter. Nor did it seem appropriate to enquire why Jack Moresby couldn't be bothered to drive the few miles back to the museum himself to find out what was going on. All families have their ways of going about things.

"I thought you might want company," he said rather lamely. "You struck me as being the only tolerably sane and normal person involved with the museum."

It provided no reason at all, but it seemed to do. Moresby gave him an odd look, but it seemed more prompted by surprise that anybody could act humanely than suspicion at his motives. He proffered the bottle by way of welcome. Bourbon was the last thing Argyll wanted at that time of day, but he felt it was uncivil to refuse. He took a long suck and, while he was getting his voice back, and trying to stop his eyes watering, Moresby rambled on about his old man.

They were not close, Argyll divined. It appeared that old Moresby had cut the aspiring author out of his will a year or so ago—depriving someone of a couple of billion dollars does sometimes make relations a little frosty.

"Why did he do that?"

"Let's just say he had a really weird sense of humour. He wanted me to follow him and make more money. I reckoned he'd made enough already. So he said that if money was so unimportant to me, he'd leave all of his to someone who appreciated it more."

"Like his wife?"

"She adores the stuff."

"And the museum?"

"A virtual money sink."

"And this was meant to make you mend your ways?"

"I guess. But, here I am, penniless. Likely to stay that way, as well. Too late to change his mind now."

"But he didn't really cut you out, did he?"

"Not specifically, no. Just didn't leave me anything. Same thing. 'To my dear son I leave my very best wishes.' Or some such. No one can accuse him of inconsistency."

"I suppose that's lucky, in a way," Argyll commented.

"Why's that?"

"Well, the police are looking for whoever killed him. You had a perfect motive for keeping him alive."

"Yup. And an alibi, too, as Langton phoned me after the body was found and I was here."

Argyll did some quick calculations. That fitted. No way he could have got back that fast. What a suspicious person you are, he thought.

"And where were you?" Moresby asked.

"Me?"

"Yes. You. After all, if you're going to check up on me, it's only fair I should check up on you."

"Fair enough. I was in a restaurant until an hour after the murder. Lots of witnesses. No trouble there."

"Hmm. OK, I'll believe you. That's us out. That leaves that Spaniard, doesn't it?"

Argyll wrinkled his nose to indicate disapproval of police thought patterns. "So the police seem to think, but I don't rate him as a murderer. He wanted to sell your father too much sculpture. Killing the goose is one thing, but a sensible person would wait until it laid an egg or two. Besides, Hector's always appallingly polite to clients. Shooting them is not in his book of etiquette. On the other hand, I must admit that until he turns up he's likely to be the front runner."

"You reckon?"

"Yes. But I'm sure he'll reappear. He hardly seemed homicidal when I talked to him just before the murder. Did he?"

Moresby confessed he didn't really know how homicidal tendencies manifested themselves in party conversation.

"I rather suspected your stepmother, myself," Argyll confessed, not sure whether this was a good thing to say. Jack didn't seem to mind. "But Morelli tells me she'd already left and has an alibi from her chauffeur. Are you sure she was having an affair?"

"Oh, sure. Lots of absences, extended shopping expeditions, weekends away with girlfriends. Easy enough to work out."

"And your father knew?"

"He did after I'd rung his office to tell him, yes." Jack looked at him curiously. "I suppose you reckon that's pretty disgusting, eh? And you're right. But that bitch poisoned his mind to get me cut out, and all I was doing was fighting back. Fair's fair.

"I guess it's sad I didn't see the old man before he died," he went on meditatively. "I shouldn't have left so soon. Hadn't seen him for, oh, must have been six months or so. Call me an old sentimentalist, but I would have given a lot just to have called him a mean old bastard one more time. By way of farewell. You know."

Argyll nodded understandingly. "Well, I'm glad you're taking it OK. Just came to see."

"Appreciate it. Come up for a proper drink sometime."

Argyll considered it. "Thanks. Maybe I will. But I think I'll go back to Rome in a few days. If I stay here much longer I'll probably get run over."

"Safest drivers in the world, we Californians."

"Tell that to the driver of the purple truck that nearly took my kneecaps off."

Moresby looked sympathetic.

"Of course, it might have been my fault," Argyll said, determined to be fair. "Partly, at least."

"Don't say that," Moresby advised. "Never admit fault. Then you can sue the driver if you find him."

"I don't want to sue him."

"But if he finds you, he might sue you."

"What on earth for?"

"Emotional distress caused by the closeness of damage to his fender. Sort of things courts take seriously out here."

Only just convinced that Moresby was joking, Argyll took his leave, first asking for directions back to his hotel. His sense of direction was such that he could well have landed in the Rockies without guidance at every turn. Right, right and left at the bar, Moresby said. Then follow your nose. Yes, it does serve food. Argyll didn't want any, really, but thought it would be a good place to stop, so he could get more directions and soak up the whisky. Just in case.

He did. Ate a vegetarian hamburger of mind-boggling awfulness, drank a cup of coffee so weak you could see through it, and proceeded to round off a perfect day in a hospital bed with a broken leg.

It was perfectly simple. He drove all the way back to the hotel without making a single wrong turn, had a shower and then headed up the freeway to pay his respects to Mrs. Moresby. No mishaps or problems whatsoever. Except that, technically speaking, he didn't need to take a freeway at all, but got wedged in an entry lane and had no choice. Even, miracle of miracles got the right exit. Well, more or less. Down the ramp to the lights and right turn at the end, put on the brakes to slow down in the officially approved manner, and nothing happened.

Or rather, everything did. His vast and unwieldy Cadillac sailed majestically through the red lights, narrowly missing an assortment of cars, buses and trucks coming across at him. Mounted the sidewalk, still travelling at a decorous twenty-five miles an hour and scarcely jolted by the bump due to the formidable suspension, then proceeded inexorably through a twenty-foot-square plate glass window of, as Morelli mentioned, a designer clothes store, causing considerable damage to their stock.

Fortunately it was a very expensive shop, catering only to the seriously wealthy and, at the time of his entry, had no customers whatever. Indeed, there had been no customers at all so far that day. Business was so bad that the one saleswoman felt it perfectly safe to go out the back for a few moments for a quick smoke. Regulations forbade her to smoke inside the building and neither the owner nor the few customers approved.

It was just as well that she did, as when she returned the shop was not in the tidy condition in which she had left it. Argyll's left leg was jammed hard down on the brake pedal, even though the mechanism refused absolutely to respond. And, in a habit picked up from too much time in Rome, he indicated his pique at developments to curious spectators by throwing both hands above his head in the archetypal Italian gesture that indicates a cosmic despair at the bizarre absurdity and unfairness of life.

And he was in this posture when the front end of the car, fortunately several yards ahead of him, hit a brick wall in the centre of the building. Argyll was pushed forward, but his left leg, wedged against the brake pedal, tried to keep his body in place and gave way under the strain. A sizeable portion of the rest of him crashed against the steering wheel, unrestrained as it was by his hands which had still not completed their gesture, and broken glass coming in the other direction completed the damage.

Damn it, he thought as he lost consciousness. I'll never be able to criticise Flavia's driving again.

CHAPTER 6

Flavia arrived at the office at ten in the morning, feeling very much the worse for wear. She had, after all, been up until the early hours chasing phantom art dealers, and had spent what little remained of the night in bed, strangely disturbed about Argyll's likely condition. An expensive phone call to the hospital yielded only platitudes and a point-blank refusal to let her talk to him. He was as fine as could be expected and asleep; and anyway, who was she?

A friend, she said. If there was any change in his condition would they call immediately. They said they were not authorised to make overseas calls. So call Detective Morelli, then. This they agreed to do.

It was mere habit that brought her into the office, combined with the simple realisation that there was not much else to do. She was summoned immediately to Bottando's office when she arrived.

"Good God, you look awful," he said as she staggered in. "Anyone would think you'd been up all night."

She tried, but failed, to stifle a yawn and did her best to focus on him properly. "I suppose you want to hear about di Souza," she said. "He wasn't on the plane."

"I know," he replied. "I've been having another long chat with that Morelli. He's launched a request—official this time—for our help."

"If his murderer's not here, I don't see what we can do. What sort of help?"

"This bust. May have come from here, probably smuggled, certainly stolen from a packing case next to the body. Perhaps a connection. They want to know what it is. So do I. As you've looked into this already, I thought you'd better continue with it. If you're up to it."

She was halfway to protesting that she'd wasted enough time on this already, but Bottando's implied reference to female frailty swung her decision the other way. Of course she was up to it. Just a little woozy, that was all.

Bottando, of course, who'd known her for several years now, had been certain that the comment was just the deft little touch that was required. For himself, he was largely of the opinion that the matter could wait, certainly until the Americans actually recovered the thing, and they could find out whether it was worth trying to get back.

But international co-operation was always prestigious, and he was quite pleased that his department was getting involved rather than the carabinieri. It looked good on the annual report, that sort of thing, and his fiefdom was small enough and vulnerable enough not to be able to turn its nose up at high-profile activities, no matter how futile they were likely to prove.

On top of that, of course, Morelli had mentioned that Argyll had suggested the contact, so he owed him one. Putting Flavia on to it, he reckoned, paid the debt promptly and generously. Judging by what Morelli had said—the Englishman with a broken leg and liable to be sued for enough money to restock an entire shop full of French lingerie, quite apart from hospital bills—he needed all the help he could get at the moment.

"So," she said, yawning again and overcoming a reluctance to get involved in anything concerning Argyll, sorry for him though she felt, "what do you want me to do?"

"First," he said, listing the points on the fingers of a pudgy little hand, "Go out, and buy yourself several of the strongest coffees you can lay your hands on. Second, drink them. Third, get the paper—*Herald Tribune* would be the best—and see what it says about this whole business. Then see what you can find out about this bust. Finally, go and see the man who bought it. Man called Langton, apparently. He lives in Rome, and is flying back today."

"He bought Argyll's Titian," she said absentmindedly.

"Hmm. Find out where he got the Bernini from, how much he paid for it, how it left the country, what di Souza's gripe was. You'd better dig out di Souza's file as well. There must be one somewhere around here. I really must get our filing system sorted out. Go and see his friends, search his apartment. Usual stuff."

"And then?"

"Then," he said, smiling slightly as he noticed that she was beginning to revive a little. Got her, he thought. Stage one complete. "Then you can stop for lunch." Of course, it took longer than that; drinking coffee and reading newspapers can't be hurried. A couple of hours later, Flavia had learnt what there was to know about the case from the fulsome reports in the papers, drunk the better part of a litre of coffee and then decided to go straight into lunch to consider matters.

She was feeling very much better. For all her reluctance, the case had tickled her fancy a little, and Argyll's mishap had done something to soften her hostile thoughts. He was still an idiot, of course, but he was manifestly a bigger danger to himself than he was to anyone else.

As for the case itself, she could not see any clear explanation for what had happened. This was not surprising—if it had been obvious to her then undoubtedly the Los Angeles police would have leapt to the same conclusion. However, it seemed that Moresby and di Souza had gone to the office to discuss the Spaniard's gripe about this bust; and that it must have been fairly important for a man like Moresby to interrupt his evening to talk to a mere art dealer.

Now, if you are going to talk about something, it helps to see it. So, it was reasonable to suppose that the first thing they did was peer inside the case containing the bust. Moresby then summoned his lawyer or aide or whatever he was, and moments later he was shot and di Souza legged it.

As far as she was concerned, this indicated that the bust was pretty central to proceedings.

She finally located the office record on Hector di Souza—filed under "H" for some reason—and read it carefully. A bit of a lad, our Hector, she thought. Even though the file was thin—the department had only existed for a few years and early material had been begged, borrowed or stolen from somewhat inadequate carabinieri archives—it was clear that di Souza was one of that breed who couldn't help pulling a fast one on gullible clients. He'd been in operation since about 1948, when he'd been washed up in Rome after the war. A lot of people got into the art business then, in a period when tens of thousands of works of art were drifting around the continent, their owners dead, or lost or forgotten. A lot of money to be made if you knew what you were doing and didn't mind cutting a few corners.

Di Souza was a master corner-cutter. For some reason he had never been prosecuted for anything, but he had sold some dodgy stuff, and almost certainly fobbed newly made fakes on to the unsuspecting for high prices. There was, in fact, the name of a sculptor in Gubbio who had worked for him occasionally. Many years ago, certainly, but old habits . . .

She noted that down thoughtfully. Pity the information was so scanty. Of course, if you open a box and find you have paid four million dollars for a fake, you might get annoyed. Demand your money back.

James Langton, the Moresby agent in Rome who had assiduously plundered the galleries and collections of the country for the past few years to stock the museum, was clearly the place to start. Flavia checked her watch, and reckoned that he should have got back by now. Then she picked up a phone book, found the address and summoned a taxi.

Langton, however, was hard to get hold of; he had gone straight to bed and was evidently reluctant to get out of it again. She had to lean on his doorbell before he appeared, frowsy, ill-humoured and very much the worse for wear. That was his problem; she had a job to do. So she pestered him with officialese until he agreed to get dressed, and then took pity on him and steered him off to get some coffee in him. The fresh air seemed to do something to wake him up.

"Terrible thing, terrible," he said as they walked across to a small piazza that contained a dingy bar. "I'd known old Moresby for years. Imagine, being killed like that. Have you heard anything new? Have they arrested di Souza yet?"

Flavia said they hadn't, and asked why he thought they would. Couldn't see who else might have done it, he said.

Langton broke off to order a coffee. Decaffeinated, he insisted. Caffeine made his heart race. "Bit outside your area of operations, isn't it?" he said. "I thought you dealt with art thefts?"

"We do. There's been one. Your Bernini," she went on. "Quite apart from the fact that it was material to the murder, we have reason to believe it may have left this country illegally. If so, we'll want it back. You know the laws about exporting works of art as well as I do, I'm sure."

"So what do you want to know?"

"First routine details, if you don't mind. I'll read, stop me if I go wrong. James Robert Langton, nationality British, born 1941, educated London University, worked as a dealer until employed by Arthur Moresby in 1972. OK so far?"

He nodded.

"Curator of Moresby collection in Los Angeles until

three years ago, then chief buyer in Europe based in Rome."

He nodded again.

"A few weeks ago you bought a bust said to be by Bernini . . ."

"It was."

"Said to be of Pius V."

"It is."

"Where did you get it from? What was it like?"

"It was perfect," he said. "Undoubtedly genuine. Excellent condition. I can let you have my written assessment, if you want."

"Thank you. I'd like to see it. Where did it come from?"

"Well, now," he said. "That's a bit tricky."

"Why's that?"

Langton adopted the look of someone whose sense of professional propriety was coming under strain. "Confidential," he said at last. She waited for him to go on. "The owners were most insistent. Family matter, I gather."

Flavia assured him that, while she was ordinarily very aware of the difficulties of families, she wanted to know where that bust came from. Discretion assured. He still didn't seem convinced, so she also told him that, in order to continue his career in Italy, he'd need to get his residence permit renewed in a few months. And smiled sweetly in the way you do when you have the power to make the Interior Ministry get awkward. Not that she had, and anyway it didn't seem to have much effect. He said he anticipated leaving the country to go and live in America again soon. Having him deported wasn't much of a threat. So she tried the all-buddies-in-this-together approach.

"Listen, Mr. Langton," she said in her kindest of voices, "You know as well as I do that an unknown seller is the oldest trick in the book for covering up smuggled goods. Unless you want us to go all the way back until we get to the marble dust underneath Bernini's fingernails, you'd better tell us where that thing came from. Because we'll be after you until we get it back."

Oddly enough, it didn't work. What more could she possibly do? All he did was smile at her and shake his head slowly. It seemed that the more she pushed, the more relaxed he got. Strange.

"I can't stop you investigating," he said smugly. "But I'm absolutely certain you won't find anything at all to incriminate me. I bought it fairly, and the museum paid for it when it arrived in America. As far as smuggling goes—well, you're right, it was. No harm in admitting that. Di Souza took it out of the country, and the previous possessors owned it until it arrived at the museum. Di Souza and they bear the responsibility, not me. That's why I'm not going to tell you who they are. And, frankly, there's not much you can do about it now."

The statement made Flavia twitch with anger. Because Langton was essentially correct. The most they could do was fine the owner for smuggling—if they ever worked out who it was—and perhaps di Souza for complicity, if he also turned up. As the bust was not paid for until it arrived in America, it remained the old owner's property until then. The museum had done nothing at all that was actionable. It was enough to make her hope they didn't recover it.

"You will at least confirm that Hector transported it?"

This Langton was happy to do.

"But he didn't know what it was. You can't blame him."

"A contract's a contract," he said. "Besides, you don't really believe that Hector was such an innocent, do you?"

Flavia drummed her fingers on the table with frustration and tried one last time. "Look," she said. "You know very well we're not interested in you, or in this family, or in prosecuting anyone. We want that bust back, but more importantly we're trying to help the Los Angeles police sort out Moresby's murder. Your employer, after all. His death had something to do with that bust. So why don't you just tell us where you got it from?"

Langton shook his head slowly. "Sorry," he said, again with the slight glimmering of a smile on his face. "Can't. And you're wasting your time pressing me."

"You're not being very helpful, you know."

"Why should I be helpful? If I thought incriminating this family might be of use I would be bending over backwards to help. But there's nothing I can do or say. That's why I'm back here. The police there didn't want me for anything. I told them I'd bought the bust, that di Souza had transported it, I'd been at the party and hadn't seen anything unusual. They confirmed from the video cameras that I was sitting on a lump of marble smoking a cigarette at the critical moment so couldn't have killed anyone. That's all I have to tell you as well. Telling you where the bust came from is entirely irrelevant and would achieve nothing but compromise my reputation for integrity."

"You have one?"

He smirked at her. "I do. And I intend to keep it. So mind your own business."

He dusted a fleck of ash from his jacket and stood up. "Nice to meet you." With this sardonic comment he walked off, leaving Flavia to pay the bill.

That settles it, she thought, leaving the money on the table and stumping out. I'll have him. And that bust.

Back to basics. Flavia went straight to the office and started ringing old friends, people who owed her a favour and some other people to whom she was prepared to owe a favour.

What she was after was any official mention of either Moresby or Langton. There was very little to be had, except for a file on Moresby held by the security forces who, as usual, were not all that keen on letting outsiders see what they had. She only began to make progress when he solicited Bottando's help. He remembered a senior civil servant connected with Intelligence had once illegally sold a Guardi through a London auction house and the department had buried the affair under a pile of paper.

"Ring him up and remind him," he said complacently, noting that there was a bit of colour back in her cheeks and her sense of purpose was returning. "You see, you're always so critical when I do that sort of thing. Now you see how helpful it can be."

Hmmph. Flavia still thought the civil servant should have been prosecuted, but who was she to complain at the moment?

On the second attempt, security promised the file for that afternoon.

That accomplished, she leant back in her chair and thought. Bernini. How to find out about Bernini? Answer, ask an expert on Bernini. And where do you find an expert? Answer, in the museum that owns lots of Berninis.

Flavia picked up her coat, walked out into the sunlit piazza, and grabbed another taxi.

"Borghese Museum, please," she said.

The Borghese, one of the nicest museums in the world, not so grand it causes indigestion but every piece in it a marvel, is based on the collection of the Borghese family, one of whom, Scipione, was the first and most enthusiastic patron of Bernini. So keen was he, indeed, that the museum has Berninis coming out of its ears. It's a bit of a shock to discover that the cutlery in the tea room wasn't hand-sculpted by the man as well.

Like all museums, the Borghese houses its employees in a less stately fashion that it does its pieces. Lumps of marble get the full stucco and gilt and painted-ceiling treatment, staff occupy grubby little shoeboxes formerly inhabited by lesser domestic servants. In this respect, at least, museum priorities are pretty much the same the world over. Flavia ended up in a tiny, grim and dark little office, asking her questions.

As might have been expected, the resident Bernini man was on sabbatical in Hamburg for the year, although no one was entirely certain what he was doing there. His deputy was at a seminar in Milan, and the third under-deputy had disappeared at eleven and not come back. In fact, the nearest they had to a resident expert at the moment was a young foreign intern called Collins, working his passage for a year before using the experience (and patronage) as leverage to get a job which actually had a salary attached.

And he confessed after the introductions were performed that he was more of a seventeenth-century Dutch man himself and didn't really know much about sculpture. He was just filling in while everyone else was on holiday. Sorry, on sabbatical. But he was willing to do what he could, as long as it wasn't too complicated.

"Bernini," Flavia said, resigning herself.

"Oh," he replied.

"I think a bust of Pius V may have been smuggled out the country. I want to know as much about it as possible. Owners. Where it's been. A photograph would be nice, as well."

"Pius V?" he said, suddenly interested. "Has this got something to do with the Moresby murder that's all over the papers?"

She nodded. Of course it had.

This information galvanised Collins into action. He got up from his seat and headed out the door. He was going into battle with the filing system and would be back as soon as possible.

"This could take time," he said as he disappeared. "There's so many Berninis around. And those files . . . well, let's just say they could be organised a little better. The man who set them up preferred to keep everything in his head. And he died last year without passing his system on to anyone."

So Flavia sat and admired the view, after deciding that yet another cup of coffee might not be such a good idea. She had a tolerant stomach, but it could be pushed too far.

Collins came back remarkably quickly, triumphantly waving a thin brown file. "Stroke of luck. Got something for you," he said. "More than I expected, in fact. It's a bit out of date, but all there is."

Flavia was twitching with anticipation. "Doesn't matter," she said. "Anything will do. Let's have a look."

He opened the file, and Flavia saw it contained only a couple of pieces of paper, musty with age and covered in tiny crabbed handwriting that was almost indecipherable. "Here you are. It's all rather curious, in fact. It seems to have passed through the museum very briefly in 1951. This sheet is an assessment of a bust, said to be of your Pope Pius by Bernini. Brought in by the customs police for examination."

He glanced up at Flavia, who was staring at him blankly. "Dated September 3, 1951," he went on. "Great enthusiasm, detailed description. Conclusion, that this work was undoubtedly by the Man Himself, and a work of national importance. OK?"

Flavia virtually snatched the document from his hands and studied it with the intensity of someone who scarcely credited it.

"Now, as you will see, there is this strange note at the end."

Collins turned the paper over and pointed out a line, written in the same crabbed hand. Flavia read it.

" 'Discharged from the museum by E. Alberghi. September 9, 1951.' And signed. What does that mean?"

"Just what it says. In essence, the museum decided it didn't want it and Alberghi authorised it leaving the museum."

"But Alberghi?"

"Enrico Alberghi—keeper of sculpture here for years. The man who set up the files. He was a very great authority. A nasty man by reputation, but the best. Never made a mistake and used to terrify everybody. One of the old breed; a collector as well as a connoisseur. Nowadays we're all too poor, but . . ."

"Hold it. What did he collect?"

The young man shrugged. "I've no idea. Before my time. But he was an expert on baroque sculpture."

"Tell me about this report, then. What does it mean?"

He shrugged. "Not a clue. This really is outside my area of expertise. All I can tell you is the obvious: Alberghi concluded it was genuine, and the museum didn't keep it."

"Could they have done?"

He groaned slightly. "I'm really not the right person to ask," he repeated. "But as far as I understand Italian law, yes. If it's caught being smuggled out, then it can be confiscated. Museums can then try and acquire it, or it gets sold off."

"Wouldn't this museum have wanted another Bernini?"

He shrugged. "I would have thought so. But evidently not. This document is a little vague. Alberghi might have bought it for himself for all I know. But at least it wasn't returned to the owner."

"What owner?"

He picked up the file and handed her the other piece of paper. It was a carbon copy of a typewritten letter, dated October 1951, saying that in the circumstances, of which the owner was only too aware, the bust would not be returned and there would be no further communication on the subject.

The letter was addressed to Hector di Souza.

"Well, how very interesting," Bottando said, as he scratched his stomach and considered what Flavia had just told him. "So you reckon this Alberghi character liked the bust so much he stuck it in his briefcase and took it home, where it stayed until it was pinched a month or so ago?"

"I don't know, but there's a remarkable connection there," she said. "All I know is that di Souza owned a Bernini in 1951 and it was confiscated. What happened after that I've no idea. He may even have got it back eventually and been waiting for another chance."

"Hardly seems likely, though, does it? I mean, a character like di Souza. A real Bernini is a goldmine, and he wasn't so rich. I can't see him sitting on a potential pile of money like that for forty years or so."

"Unless he was afraid to attract attention by selling it," she said. "That would explain it. He might have been waiting for Alberghi to die."

"True, but you don't think that's what happened, do you?"

"Not really. Morelli reckons di Souza was surprised when he heard the director's announcement. It seems more likely that this awfully confidential family was a blind and the bust came from Bracciano. The point to be cleared up, of course, is who pinched it."

"Chronology? Does it all fit?"

She picked up her notes and proffered them. Bottando

waved them aside. He was prepared to take her word for it.

"Very well, I think," she said. "As far as I can work out the burglary took place a few weeks before the case left the country. Perfect timing."

"If di Souza either owned it or stole it, it's hardly likely he would be surprised about its appearance in the Moresby Museum."

"He might have been simply alarmed at it being announced publicly, with Argyll there to hear. After all, the first thing he did was ring me up to tell me about it."

Bottando thought about this for a while, looking out of his window at the big clock on the church of San Ignazio opposite. "And if your Argyll wasn't there, we might never have been put on to it. There's a coincidence for you. The trouble is," he added, "Alberghi's heir can't confirm what was stolen. We'll have to wait until the Americans recover it before there's any chance of identifying it."

Flavia nodded. "What this doesn't clear up, of course, is why it got stolen a second time. That doesn't make any sort of sense. Now, if it had been a fake . . ."

"Do we know it wasn't?" Bottando asked idly, still watching the clock. "I mean, the only real indication we have is a report written forty years ago by someone who died—very conveniently if you ask me—last year. Didn't you say di Souza had a long-standing connection with a sculptor?"

"Man called Borunna, in Gubbio. That's right. It's what the file says, anyway."

"Go and see him. It'll be worth examining all the angles. Meantime, I'll put someone on to checking auction catalogues and dealers. See if anything stolen from Alberghi has surfaced. Waste of time, I think, but you never know."

Flavia got up to go. "If you don't mind, I'll go up tomorrow. I'm a bit whacked at the moment."

He peered at her, then nodded. "Fine. No great rush. You might go and give di Souza's apartment a going over, though, if you feel like it. Don't want you getting bored."

"Is there anything else going on in America?"

Bottando shook his head. "Not really, no. I had another word with Morelli, but he didn't have much to add. Your Argyll is coming along nicely. The accident wasn't his fault, apparently. The brake cable of his car dropped off, simple enough. Do you, by any chance, have a passport?"

"Of course I do. You know that. Why do you ask?"

"Oh, nothing, nothing. It's just that I've booked you on to a plane for Los Angeles tomorrow. You'll have time to go to Gubbio first. But I thought you ought to pop off and recover this bust yourself. Get you out of the office for a bit."

She gave him a suspicious look, and he smiled sweetly and innocently back at her.

Flavia directed her third taxi of the day to an apartment block in a street off the via Veneto. No missing art dealers were in residence, and the apartment was as well defended as the American Embassy down the street.

But the caretaker had a set of keys, and it didn't take long to persuade him to hand them over, even though he was not at all impressed by the warrant Flavia had written out for herself in the back of the taxi. She also relieved him of the mail, to give herself something interesting to read in the elevator.

Di Souza's letters were not enlightening. Flavia learnt only that he was in danger of having his electricity cut off for non-payment, was being asked to tear his American Express card in two and send both halves back to the organisation, and had unaccountably failed to settle an outstanding bill with a tailor.

When she finally got through the formidable array of locks and metal plating on the door, she began to search. Initially not knowing where to start, she employed the impressionistic method, flitting about and inspecting whatever took her fancy, particularly satisfying her curiosity about what lay under the bed. Not even fluff. A tidy man, she decided. The cavity under her own bed resembled a full-blown dust storm.

Then she settled down to a more methodical approach, beginning at the inlaid Empire writing desk, moving on to the filing cabinet before the more whimsical business of investigating down the sides of gilt Venetian sofas or peering behind baroque history pieces on the walls.

Neither fancy nor professionalism produced much to justify her diligence. The only thing Flavia was sure of at the end was that Hector di Souza was no businessman. His accounting procedure was more than a little quaint. Notes of purchases were written on the back of cigarette packets which were then crushed and filed. Most of his assets—except for those which were used for sitting on or hung on walls—seemed to be in a moderately sized bundle of bank notes stuffed in a drawer. His bank statement revealed wild and inexplicable fluctuations, but nothing so grand as to suggest that several million dollars had recently come his way. That, indeed, tallied with the checks Bottando had instituted with assorted banks. He had found no trace of surreptitious Swiss accounts and the bank manager in Rome, asked if di Souza had recently made an enormous deposit, guffawed heartily. Any deposit at all, he indicated, would have been a bit of a novelty. Apart from that, there was a small file labelled "Stock" but it contained no note of a Bernini. Not even an Algardi.

So, what did the apartment tell her? Di Souza was not in the big league of dealers. The apartment was fairly small and the furniture not of the highest quality. You can tell an art dealer by the chairs he sits on. Argyll's, she remembered, had the stuffing coming out of them. Di Souza made a reasonable income, assuming that most of it was hidden and never appeared in his account books. No one could live off the tiny sums entered officially for taxation purposes. A purveyor of middle-ranking stuff to middle-ranking collectors. In all, not the sort of man you'd expect to find selling major works of art to places like the Moresby. No more than Argyll was, really.

But there they both were, selling stuff to the place. Was this relevant? Probably not, or at least, not yet. But it was a coincidence, as Bottando had noted. She put the thought to the back of her mind, in case it came in handy later on.

CHAPTER 7

Jonathan Argyll woke up with a splitting headache and spent some fifteen minutes staring at the ceiling and wondering where he was. It took a long time to retrieve his thoughts, put them all in the correct order and reach a satisfactory conclusion to explain why he wasn't tucked up in bed in his apartment in Rome.

He proceeded by association. First he remembered his Titian, then the imminent return to England that it implied. The search for the cause of this brought back the memory of the Moresby, which led straight on to di Souza, the theft and the murder.

His head punished him for the gruelling early morning exercise with a sudden stab of pain, and he groaned quietly.

"You OK?" asked a voice, out of his field of vision, somewhere to the right. He thought about it for a while, trying to place it. No, he decided, he didn't recognise it.

So he grunted, vaguely, in response.

"Nasty crash you had," the voice went on. "You must be pretty mad about it."

He thought about that as well. A crash, eh? No, in fact, he wasn't pretty mad about it. Or at least, he wouldn't be if his headache went. So he murmured he was fine, thanks for asking.

The voice tut-tutted disapprovingly, and said that was the posttraumatic shock syndrome talking. When he woke up a bit more, he really would be mad. Argyll, who rarely managed to get even slightly upset about anything, didn't bother to contradict him.

"And then," continued the voice, "I bet you'll want to do something about it."

"No," he murmured. "Why should I?"

"It's your public duty," the voice explained.

"Oh," he said.

"Cars like that on the road. It shouldn't be allowed. These people have to be stopped, or they'll kill us all. It's a disgrace, and you can help make California a safer place. I'd be happy to help."

"That's very kind of you," Argyll said, wondering where he could get coffee, aspirin and cigarettes.

"It'll be a privilege," said the voice.

"Say, who are you?" came another voice, from the left this time. It was slightly more familiar. Argyll considered opening his eyes and turning his head to see, but decided it was much too ambitious.

There was a restful muttering of voices, and he considered going back to sleep again. Splendid stuff, sleep, he thought as the voices began to increase in both pitch and volume.

One voice, he noted—voice two, so to speak—was protesting, and accusing voice one of being a vulture. Voice one identified itself as Josiah Ansty, attorney at law, specialist in auto damage claims, and said it was looking after the interests of injured citizens. If voice two hadn't rented out badly maintained vehicles, it wouldn't be sued. He was going to have to pay for this.

This gave Argyll a lot to think about. Voice two he identified as the man called Chuck who rented him his nice 1971 Cadillac, which, he now remembered, had gone through the window of that shop. The other point was the bit about suing. Whoever said anything about that?

The conversation was continuing, meanwhile, over his prostrate body. The voice of Josiah Ansty, attorney, was saying that the brake cable had been badly maintained.

Chuck interrupted here, and said that was a pile of crap. He himself had serviced the car only last week. That brake cable was screwed on tight with a double screw. No way could it have come loose. No way.

Ansty said that merely proved how culpably incompetent he was, and went on to request that he not be poked in the chest like that.

Chuck then called Ansty a little creep, and there drifted into Argyll's slumbering consciousness the vague sound of grunts and scuffling followed by a shout from a long way away saying to stop that immediately and that this was a hospital not a place for a barroom brawl.

Oh, he thought, as a loud cry of pain accompanied that tinkling sound that results when a shelf of surgical equipment crashes to the ground, that's where I am. In hospital.

That's all right, then, he thought, as he drifted off to sleep to the sound of people calling for the police. Now I know.

"You OK?" came a voice as Argyll surfaced again, hours later.

Oh, God, not again, he thought.

"Hear you've been causing a bit of excitement."

This time he placed the voice. Detective Morelli. For the first time his eyes opened, more or less focused, and he turned his head without regretting it.

"Me?"

"People fighting over your body all morning. A lawyer and a car rental man; nearly wrecked the place. Didn't you notice?"

"Vaguely. I remember something. What was a lawyer doing here?"

"Oh, them. Jackals. They turn up everywhere. How are you doing?"

"Fine, I think. Let's see." He quickly checked to see that everything was where it ought to be.

"What's wrong with my leg?"

"You broke it. Clean snap, so they say. Nothing to worry about. You'll have to give up jogging for a bit."

"That's a pity."

"No permanent damage, anyway. I thought I'd come and see how you're getting on. So I can tell your girlfriend."

"Who?"

"That Italian woman? She been ringing up every few hours for the last couple of days, driving the entire department nuts. The whole homicide squad's on first name terms with her now. She's pretty gone on you, isn't she?"

"Is she?" Argyll said with grave interest. Morelli didn't bother to reply. Seemed pretty obvious to him.

"So, now I see you're OK, I'll leave you in peace."

"Double screw," Argyll said, a vague memory coming into his mind.

Morelli looked surprised.

"The brake cable couldn't have come undone on it's own. So I'm told."

"Yeah, well, I was going to mention that . . ."

"Which means," he went on, thinking hard, "what does it mean?"

Morelli scratched his chin. Amazing. The man never seemed to shave. "Well," he said, "it sort of struck us, down in the department, that maybe someone gave it a tug."

"Seems a bit silly to me. I might have been hurt. I can't imagine who'd do something like that."

"How about the person who killed Hector di Souza? And Moresby? And stole that bust?"

"What do you mean?"

"Di Souza's body was found this morning. He'd been shot."

Argyll stared at him. "You're not serious."

Morelli nodded.

A long pause followed. "You OK?" he asked eventually.

"Umm? Oh, yes," Argyll began, then stopped and reconsidered.

"In fact, no. I'm not. It never occurred to me that something might have happened to the poor old sod. He's not the sort who gets killed. Why on earth would anybody want to kill Hector? I didn't like the man much, but he was part of the landscape, and pretty harmless. Unless you bought something from him, that is. Poor bugger."

Morelli, of course, was scarcely upset at all. In his career he had seen the murdered remains of nice people, nasty people, old ones, young ones, rich and poor, saints and sinners. Di Souza was just one more, and he had never even met him.

Argyll stirred from his mournful reflection and asked for more information. Morelli kindly spared him most of the details. He'd been up early to go to the bit of woodland where the body had been found in a shallow grave, and could remember it all far too well to share with someone in Argyll's delicate state of health.

"It's a bit difficult to tell, but the experts reckon he must have died less than twenty-four hours after he vanished. One bullet, in the back of the head. Never felt a thing."

"They always say that. I can't say I've ever found it too convincing. Personally, I suspect being shot hurts. Do you know where the gun came from?"

"No. A small pistol. We found it thrown into some scrub nearby. They don't know any more yet, except that it's almost certainly the gun that killed Moresby as well. We'll find out something about it eventually."

"And I suppose it'll be up to me to get him back to Rome," he said reflectively. "Typical."

"Do you think that's a good idea?" Morelli rubbed his gum with his finger again, in an exploratory fashion.

"Still hurting?"

He nodded. "Hmm. It seems to be getting worse, damn the thing."

"You should go to a dentist."

Morelli snorted. "When? I'm swamped with work because of this murder. Besides, do you know how far ahead you have to make an appointment with dentists? It's easier to get an audience with the Pope. Why do you feel responsible for di Souza?"

Argyll shrugged. "I don't know. But there it is; I do. Hector would never forgive me if I left him here. He was a professional Roman and an aesthete. I don't think a graveyard in Los Angeles would please him at all."

"We have very good cemeteries."

"Oh, I'm sure. But he was very fussy. Besides, I don't know of any relations or anything."

Takes all sorts. Morelli was very much less sentimental. Argyll, on the other hand, reckoned that the least he could do was give the old man a decent send-off in the style to which he was accustomed. Full requiem with all the trimmings in a church of suitable magnificence, weeping friends at the grave, all that.

"Very clever of you to find him," Argyll said, not being able to think of anything else to keep the conversation going.

"Hardly. We got a tip-off."

"Who from?"

"Someone hunting out of season, I reckon. It often happens. They want to report a body, but don't want the risk of being prosecuted." Morelli said it as though illegal hunters tripped over corpses every day.

"Sort of lets Hector off your list of suspects, doesn't it?"

"Maybe. Maybe not. But we're certainly short of at least one murderer at the moment. You were one of the last people to talk to him at that party, weren't you?"

Argyll nodded.

"Can you remember what he said?"

"But I've told you, more or less."

"Exactly. Word for word."

"Why do you want to know?"

"Because if someone at some stage loosened the brake cable of your car, then it stands to reason they wanted to kill you. With all due respect, why would anyone want to kill you? Unless you know something that you haven't told us."

Argyll thought hard, and could come up with nothing that might, somehow, solve the problem.

"He said that he could sort everything out with Moresby," he said eventually.

"Did he say how?"

"Yes."

"Tell me, then."

"Well, you see, the trouble is, I didn't listen. I was thinking of something else. And Hector does tend to go on. I asked him to repeat it but he wouldn't."

Morelli gave him a nasty look.

"Sorry."

"And who may have overheard this?"

Argyll scratched his head as he thought. "Lots of people, I suppose," he said eventually. "Let's see. Streeter, Thanet, Mrs. Moresby, that lawyer man were all there. Young Jack had gone, Old Moresby hadn't turned up . . ."

"But who was close enough to hear?"

Argyll shrugged. No idea.

"You're not a dream witness, do you know that?"

"Sorry."

"Yeah, well, if you remember . . ."

"I'll call. I don't know that it would do much good though."

"Why not?"

"Because we were speaking in Italian. Langton speaks Italian, but he wasn't anywhere near. Hector was looking for him. I suspect that none of the others speak it."

Morelli looked even more disappointed in him, so Argyll switched the subject.

"Have you found the bust yet?"

The detective shook his head. "No. And I don't imagine we will. It's probably been thrown in the sea."

"That's daft," Argyll said with conviction. "Why steal something and throw it away?"

Morelli snorted. "Don't ask me."

"But somebody must have seen something."

"Why?"

"Because marble is bloody heavy, that's why. You can't just stick it in your pocket and stroll off. If you stagger down the street with a Bernini in your arms, somebody should notice."

Morelli smiled cynically. Just goes to show how little people know. "Just as somebody should notice a murderer trotting about the administrative block, or hear a shot. And no one did. Nobody ever sees anything in this city. Nobody's ever around and if they are they're too busy going somewhere. I sometimes think you could steal the city hall and there'd be no witnesses.

"Anyway," he went on, getting up to leave. "This bust is not really my main concern. Your friends in Rome are taking that one on. They think it's the genuine article and they've lodged an official complaint with the Moresby about illegal export. They're going to harass the museum until they get it back. Don't blame them, either. This friend of yours is coming over to try and recover it."

"Flavia?" Argyll asked with surprise.

"That's the one. That Bottando told me. That'll cheer you up, won't it?"

Argyll thanked him for the news.

"You OK, there?"

Oh, the limits of conversational gambits in this part of the world, Argyll thought, and turned to look at the new visitor.

"Mr. Thanet," he said, with real surprise. The director did not seem the sort to go running around hospital wards bearing bunches of grapes. But, there he was, standing by the bed looking anxiously at him. "How nice of you to come."

"Least I could do. I was most distressed to hear of your mishap. Most upsetting for you. And for us, of course."

"It's not your week, is it?"

Thanet opened his mouth to say something, then changed his mind and sat down instead. Argyll looked at him carefully. Clearly the man had come with good intentions, to cheer and console. But equally clearly it wasn't going to work out like that. Thanet had a captive audience—with his leg sticking up in the air there was nowhere for Argyll to run—and it looked as though he wanted to unburden himself.

"What's up?" Argyll asked, inviting the man to get on with it. "You look worried."

This was something of an understatement. In fact, Thanet looked dreadful. His normally anxious-looking face had developed vast bags under the eyes indicating he had had little sleep in the past few days. Everything about him, from the tired and creaky way he moved, to the almost random gestures of exhaustion, indicated a man on the edge. Hadn't lost weight, though.

"We're in an appalling situation. You wouldn't believe what's been going on."

"Sounds bad," Argyll said sympathetically, turning cautiously to rearrange his pillows and make himself comfortable. This could be a long haul.

Thanet sighed the sigh of the almost deranged. "I fear the museum might close. And we were so near to clinching the most exciting project. It's terrible."

It sounded a bit like exaggeration, and Argyll suggested Thanet might be overreacting. Whoever heard of museums closing, after all? They just got more expensive in his experience. By the time he died, he reckoned that the whole of Italy would have come under the aegis of the National Museum.

"This is America, and this is a private museum. Whatever the owner decides happens. The new owner of the Moresby Museum is, it seems, Anne Moresby. And you have witnessed for yourself how high we rank in her regard."

"I thought that there was meant to be a trust fund or something set up to guarantee your future?"

"So there was. But Mr. Moresby hadn't signed the papers yet. He was going to announce it at the party and sign at a little ceremony the following morning. He never signed. Never signed."

Clearly, this omission was weighing on Thanet a little.

"But the museum administrators have money anyway, don't they?"

Thanet shook his head. "No."

"None?"

"Not a cent. Not of our own. Everything was paid for by Moresby personally. It was awful—we never knew from one year to the next what our budget would be. We didn't even know whether we would have one at all. We had to ask him personally every time we wanted to buy something. It was his way of making sure we knew our place."

He sighed heavily as he contemplated what might have been. "Three billion dollars. That's what we would have got if he'd lived another twenty-four hours and signed those papers."

"But he might have changed his mind anyway, mightn't he? His son said he was always doing that."

The very thought of Jack Moresby made Thanet look pained, but he conceded that it was accurate. "But not this time. That's the good thing about trusts. Once it was set up, it couldn't have been dismantled without the agreement of all the trustees. And I was going to be one of them."

"So what's the situation now?"

"Disastrous. Anne Moresby inherits everything."

"And what about his son?"

"I can't say I've thought about him much. There will be a monumental legal squabble, of course, but considering that he was legally and properly cut out of the will and has little money to pay lawyers, I doubt he'll get much. If anything. At least his position hasn't changed because of all this."

"And what about you?"

Thanet looked heavenwards for support. "What do you think?" he said bitterly. "Mrs. Moresby has made it clear over the years that she thinks this museum is a complete waste of time. It's such a tragedy. After five years, I thought we could finally get on with building a great collection. And on top of that, the police in Italy are breathing down my neck about this bust. Do you realise, they've made a complaint about illegal export?"

"What I'd like to know is where it came from."

Thanet shook his head. Minor detail, to his way of thinking. "I don't know anything about it. You know that. You'll have to ask Langton. Of course, he's made himself scarce."

Argyll looked at him incredulously. "Do you really expect anyone to believe a director of a museum saying he doesn't even know where his pieces come from?"

Thanet gazed at him sadly with a slight tinge of despair. "People don't, but it's true nonetheless. You must know the history of the museum?"

Argyll shook his head. Always willing to learn something new.

"Mr. Langton used to be in charge of Moresby's private collection, before the old man had the idea of founding a museum. When the museum project came up, he naturally expected to be made director. I can't say I blame him.

"That, of course, was not Moresby's way of doing things. He decided it was going to be a prestige project and so he wanted a prestigious person to head it."

"You?" Argyll asked, trying hard to keep a tone of slight incredulity from seeping in at the edges.

Thanet nodded. "That's right. Yale, Metropolitan, National Gallery. A glittering career. Langton had never worked in a major museum; so, in short, he was shunted aside. Naturally I wanted the job, but I thought it was unfair, the treatment he got. So I created a post for him in Europe."

"Nicely out of the way," Argyll commented. Thanet gave him a disappointed look.

"I could have got him a lot further out of the way, you know, had I put my mind to it. But despite that, I'm afraid he's never really forgiven me for occupying his chair."

"Did Moresby like him?"

"Did Moresby like anyone? I don't know. But they went back a long time, the pair of them, and the old man realised that Langton was a useful person to have around. Langton stayed in the hope of easing me out one day, and he took great pleasure in organising acquisitions direct with Moresby, not telling me what was going on. Hence this bust turning up—and your Titian."

"So was this thing paid for?"

"Yes."

"Why?"

"What do you mean, why? Why do you think?"

"Well, it's just that you haven't paid for my Titian. And when I even raised the possibility, everybody was very sniffy at the idea."

Thanet looked at him pityingly. "And you gave way. What do you expect? The owner of this bust was evidently better at bargaining than you were."

"You mean that song and dance about museum policy was just guff?"

"Obviously we prefer to delay payment as long as possible. But if we can't get a piece otherwise . . ."

"And what about Hector? Has his stuff been paid for?"

"Certainly not. Nor is it going to be. I had our sculpture people go over the contents of those cases. Utter garbage, the lot of it. Langton must have taken leave of his senses. This is why I get annoyed about him flouting acquisitions procedure . . ."

"Yes. Indeed. But what I'm trying to get at, is who was the legal owner of the bust when it was stolen?"

"Oh. We were. A guard met the case at the airport and signed for it and Barclay authorised transfer of the money. From that moment it became the property of the museum."

"As I see it, then, Hector was persuaded—knowingly or not—into smuggling it out of Italy. And when you announced what it was, he saw a prosecution looming up before him. No wonder he was angry."

Thanet continued to look discomforted.

Argyll closed his eyes and thought. "He complained to Moresby, went back to the hotel, received a phone call and booked himself on a flight to Rome immediately. Why did he do that, I wonder? But someone got to him first. Did he see something, or was it important to make sure he didn't get back to Italy? How strange. Do you happen to know where Mr. Langton was between eleven and, say, one in the morning?"

Thanet looked startled, not so much at the question but at the implication behind it. He also seemed vaguely disappointed at the answer he felt morally obliged to give. Langton, he said, had not left the museum from the moment that the body of Moresby was discovered. He was certainly in the museum until three in the morning, and may well have been there until he left to catch a plane back to Italy. There was not the slightest possibility that he could have been responsible for either death. Had Samuel Thanet bowed his head in sorrow, he could not have made his feelings more plain. He would have been delighted to have had Langton locked in a cell.

Argyll digested this and looked at Thanet. "What about this infernal Bernini, then? What did you think of it? Did it seem the real thing to you? None of this makes sense unless it all centres on the bust."

Thanet shrugged again. "I couldn't even begin to hazard a guess," he said. Helpful today.

"Oh, go on. Educated amateur. If you had to put five dollars on it, which way would you bet? True or false?"

"Honestly, I don't know. After all, I never saw it."

"What?"

"I never saw it. I was going to have a look, but it was an appallingly busy day preparing for Moresby's visit. If we ever get it back, I'll happily venture an opinion. Judging by the noise the Italian police are making, they clearly think it's genuine."

"Odd way to run a museum."

Thanet didn't even bother to reply; simply gave Argyll a look to indicate that he didn't know the half of it.

CHAPTER 8

The next morning Flavia headed off for Gubbio at around ten. She was not entirely sure what purpose the visit to di Souza's sculptor-friend was supposed to serve; there was so far not a shred of evidence that the Bernini was a fake. Indeed, such small fragments as she had collected so far strongly indicated that it wasn't. On the other hand, the sculptor knew di Souza, evidently from way back, and all help was gratefully received. Whatever had been going on in 1951 was at least one starting point in this business.

It's a three-hour drive from Rome to Gubbio, four and a half if you are the sort who insists on an early lunch before getting down to business. And there is also some of the most delightful scenery in the country. Not that Flavia spent too much time admiring the landscape. In about ten hours' time she'd be stuck on a plane heading for California. It was reasonable to send her, she thought. But she did rather suspect that Bottando was interfering in her private life again.

The man in charge at the local police station, where she presented herself for reasons of protocol, was agreeably welcoming, but most surprised to hear Flavia had come to interview Alceo Borunna, a veritable pillar of local society. A foreigner, of course; the commandant believed he hailed from somewhere around Florence. But he had lived in the little town for years, and was presently working with an architect to restore the cathedral, which, believe him, needed restoration very badly. Shocking the way the government and the church neglected the national heritage.

Flavia nodded sagely and agreed. Borunna, it seemed, was a fervent churchgoer as well as restorer, was somewhere in his seventies, as hale and hearty as ever, had lived as a devoted husband for decades and had so many grandchildren only he could even begin to count them. He was also held in awe by the architect because of his enormous facility both with the stonework he was restoring and with the men in his charge. The only slight worry was either that he might retire or that the architect at Assisi might poach him. But it was well known he had already turned down one offer of a better-paid job, saying that he wasn't interested in money.

It all sounded too good to be true, but it was always possible. Saints do still walk the earth and one runs across them just often enough to restore faith in mankind. It would be sad if this trip showed that Borunna was not as perfect as his reputation.

Too late to worry about that, Flavia thought as she walked through the steep, narrow streets towards the cathedral and asked for the workyard. There was, she reckoned as she walked in, probably little difference between this sight and the workyard of the original masons and carvers who had decorated the place in the middle ages: large wooden tables set out in the open air, with a small group of large, untidy workmen gathered round them; blocks of marble, stone and wood stacked all over the place, and tools which had changed little in half a millenium. They did things properly here; no shortcuts using electric drills and sanders.

Borunna was standing on his own, chin resting in his hand, looking peaceably and with concentration at a large, half-finished madonna that was slowly emerging from a block of limestone. He came out of his reverie as Flavia introduced herself and greeted her gently with all the innocence of a child.

"That's very fine workmanship. I congratulate you," she said, studying the madonna.

Borunna smiled and stretched himself. "Thank you. It'll do, I suppose. It's going in one of the niches on the façade, so it doesn't have to be perfect. I must admit it's coming out better than I thought. We don't really have time to do a perfect job."

"Nobody will be able to tell, though."

"That's not the point, not the point at all. The old masters didn't care whether anyone could see their flaws or not. They wanted to do as well as they could, because their work was a gift to God, who deserved the best. That's all gone; now what's important is whether any German or English tourists will notice the difference, and how much it will all cost. It changes the spirit of the building for ever."

He stopped, and shot her a half-whimsical, half-apologetic glance. "My obsession. It makes me sound very old-fashioned. I do beg your pardon. You must be here for a more important reason than to listen to the meanderings of an old man. How can I help you?"

"Eh?" said Flavia, dragging her eyes away from the statue and back to the present. "Oh, yes. Not so important, but I am a bit pressed for time. It's about some—ah—work you may have done."

Borunna looked interested. "Really? When was this?"

"Well, we're not sure," she said, feeling a little embarrassed. "Sometime in the last half century. For Hector di Souza."

This made him think. "Hector, eh? Is he still around? Goodness, that does take me back. I've not seen him for years. Let's see now . . ."

Without a doubt, the police chief was right; Borunna was not quite of this earth. His soft voice and kindly eyes were of the variety that made you feel entirely comfortable in his presence. Not one of the get-rich-quick mob who infest the world of art dealing. Saintly, indeed.

"You must come home," the old man said firmly. "It's nearly lunchtime, and while you eat I could find my papers. My wife would never forgive me if I went home this evening and told her I had received a beautiful visitor from Rome and didn't let her cook for her."

As they walked, Borunna explained that he had known young Hector, as he called him, for years; ever since the Spaniard washed up in Rome in the aftermath of the war. Times were hard then. He himself, a married man in his thirties, had been working as a mason for the Vatican, going around repairing war damage. Often had to go away for days on end. Hector did his best buying up works of art and trying to sell them to the few people left in Europe who had any money. Swiss and Americans mainly. But even so, it was difficult.

Borunna himself was relatively secure; at the Vatican he had a steady job and a regular income—and not many people in the capital could say that at the time. But everything was in short supply—food, clothing, heating, oil—whether you had money or not. He and di Souza had helped each other as much as possible. He lent money, and Hector reciprocated with gifts.

"What sort of gifts?" she asked.

Borunna looked a little embarrassed. "Hector was a bit of an entrepreneur, if you see what I mean. He had contacts, and friends and business arrangements with lots of people."

"You mean the black market?"

He nodded. "I suppose. Nothing large scale, mind. Enough to live off and supply the necessities. You're too young to realise what antics we'd get up to then to get hold of half a litre of olive oil."

"And you bought this stuff from him?"

He shook his head once more. "Oh, no. Hector always gave what he had freely. He was always a little naughty in business matters, but an enormously generous friend. What was his, was ours. I'd often come home and he and Maria would be there . . ."

"Maria?"

"My wife. She and Hector were like brother and sister. In fact, it was through her that I got to know him. We were all such good friends. And he'd have brought bottles of wine, and salami, and a ham, and sometimes even fresh fruit and he'd lay it all on the table and say, 'Eat, my friends, eat.' And believe me, young lady, we did.

Sometimes in return I'd get him to accept a little money. And sometimes I'd do some work for him. I'm afraid desperation led both of us into temptation."

"You faked stuff for him?"

Borunna looked very awkward at the statement. Even now, he clearly felt guilty about the whole period. Flavia could hardly see why; she'd heard enough stories from her own family to understand what conditions had been like in the post-war débâcle. A little light forgery to get some bread or oil or meat seemed hardly a great sin to her.

"Improved. That's the term I prefer. Restored. Hector would occasionally acquire a haul of nineteenth-century sculpture; wood or marble, and I would—ah—add a couple of hundred years on to their age. You know, I'm sure. Turn parts of an 1860s fireplace into a *cinquecento* madonna, that sort of thing. Here we are. Welcome to my humble home."

They'd been walking along the cobbled streets in the warm afternoon sun as they talked, turning from one narrow lane into others even narrower. Flavia was lapping up Borunna's reminiscences with enthusiasm. It was almost like a snapshot of a vanished and innocent age. The two young men and the woman, carousing over a black market salami, a little work here, a little faking there. And who could possibly blame them? Nowadays smuggling and forgery has largely lost its romantic and bohemian air. Like most other forms of crime it's become big business with millions of dollars involved. The rewards are no longer a treasured bottle of chianti, and the motives no longer simple hunger.

But that was all a long time ago. It didn't look as

though Borunna had been raking in a small fortune by forging Berninis for di Souza—his home certainly showed no sign of it. To call it humble was an understatement. It was shabby, with only poor sticks of furniture, but the air of modesty was mitigated by an alluring smell of fresh cooking. And dozens of the most beautiful carvings Flavia had ever seen in her life, scattered around like diamonds in a refuse dump.

"Maria. A distinguished guest. Coffee, please," Borunna called as he ushered her through the heavy green door into the cool, dark interior. By the time he had found the papers, his wife had appeared, about ten years younger than her husband, a woman with an oval face, sparkling eyes that were truly lovely, and a manner of open and total welcome. She set down the tray and gave her husband the sort of embrace you normally give to someone you've not seen for years. How sweet, Flavia thought. Decades of marriage and still devoted. There's hope for us all.

She thanked the woman profusely for the coffee, apologised for disturbing her and declined—with ever growing reluctance—the repeated invitations for lunch.

"This is all yours?" she asked, studying some of the pieces scattered around the room.

Borunna looked up from a small mountain of papers in his desk. "Oh, yes. Practice work, mainly. I did them to get the style before I worked on pieces that would be put on display."

"They're extraordinary."

"Thank you," he said with simple, genuine pleasure. "Please, take one you like. There are dozens, and Maria is always complaining how they collect dust. I'd be happy, and honoured, if you gave one a good home. As long as you always remember how young it really is."

Flavia was sorely tempted, but eventually shook her head with equal parts vigour and regret. She would have loved to take one or two for her apartment. Indeed, she already could visualise a small polychromatic Saint Francis sitting on her fireplace. But Bottando, a stickler for such matters, would quite rightly have disapproved. On the other hand, if this case was sorted out fast, with Borunna as uninvolved in this affair as she hoped and increasingly expected, she could come back . . .

"So there you are," Borunna said when his wife had once more retreated into the aromatic kitchen. "I knew I'd find it sooner or later. 1952; that was the last time I did any work for him. An arm and a leg. Roman, I think. Perfectly nice but not at all remarkable. It only took me a day or so. Nothing dubious, I assure you; merely patching a few cracks and chips."

"You have records going that far back?"

The old man looked surprised. "Of course. Doesn't everybody?"

Being someone who never had the faintest idea how much she had in her bank account, Flavia was frankly astonished.

"I take it you're looking for something in particular?"

"That's right. A bust, purportedly by Bernini. Of Pius V, which Hector was apparently connected with in some way."

"In what way was this?" There was a sudden caution in his tone, which Flavia instantly noticed. There was something here after all, she thought. The difficulty was going to be getting it out of him.

"We're not certain," she said. "One of several possibilities. He bought it, sold it, stole it, smuggled it or had it made. Any, or all, of the above. We just want to know, that's all. Mere interest, quite apart from the fact that the new owner has been murdered. It crossed my mind that maybe Hector . . ."

". . . was up to his old tricks? Is that what you think? That I forged a bust for him?"

Flavia felt guilty even though Borunna's admissions made him a legitimate suspect. "Well, that sort of thing. Could you have done it if he'd asked?"

"Fake a Bernini? Oh, yes. Very simple. Well, not so simple, in fact, but perfectly possible. It's the design that's the thing. Get that right and it's simple. Pius V, you say?"

She nodded.

"Of course, you know there's a bronze copy in Copenhagen. So it would mainly be a copying job. Sculpting it would be straightforward, the only difficulty would be getting marble from the right quarry, and ageing it so it didn't look too new. Again, not that difficult."

It was curious, she thought later; he took on board the praticality of forging a Bernini with no surprise at all. Very knowledgeable, as well. Not even Alberghi's report in the Borghese had mentioned a bronze copy in Copenhagen.

"Why do you think it was faked?" he went on.

"I don't; we don't know. It's a possibility. We don't know where it came from, that's all. It just turned up."

"Why don't you ask Hector?"

"Because he's disappeared."

"Is he in trouble?"

"Potentially. In very deep trouble if the American police ever catch up with him. There's quite a lot of people who want to ask him a question or two."

"Dear me. That's the story of Hector's life, I'm afraid." Borunna paused, evidently considering a series of possibilities. Had Flavia only known what they were, she might have been able to help him make up his mind. He walked over to the mantelpiece and examined a sixteenth-century cherub for a while. The effort seemed to help him reach a decision.

"Well," he said. "I'm afraid I'm not going to be of much help to you. As I say, I haven't seen Hector for years; I'm afraid we had a little argument. Years back. A misunderstanding."

"About forgeries?"

He nodded reluctantly. "Among other things." He hesitated, and then hurried on. "Times were changing. Getting easier. I never really approved. It was necessary, back then, but as soon as it was possible I stopped, and told him he was going to get himself into big trouble if he didn't see sense. Eventually even he and Maria fell out. But Hector—well, he was always a little reckless, and always convinced his charm would see him through. I'm afraid there was some bad blood about it, and we gradually drifted apart.

"As for your Bernini, he did own one. Very briefly, alas, and it did him no good at all. But I very much doubt that he has sold it recently."

Aha, Flavia thought. A brief flicker of light at the end of what had turned out to be a long and dark tunnel. It was a pity that Borunna immediately snuffed the brief glow out again.

"He lost it, you see," he went on implacably.

"Lost it?" she said incredulously. "How on earth could you lose a Bernini?"

A stupid question, really. Recent events seemed to demonstrate that it was the easiest thing in the world. The damn things just keep vanishing.

"Well, lost is not perhaps the best word. I do hope you will keep this to yourself. It was a grave shock for him, and he did his best to forget it . . ."

Flavia informed him that discretion was her middle name. Reassured, he told the story.

"It was very simple," the old man began. "Hector bought a bust at a house sale; about 1950, or '51, if I remember rightly. He identified it in a job lot of miscellaneous pieces. A priest's family, I think it was. Lovely piece. And sold it to a buyer in Switzerland, who asked him to deliver it."

"Smuggle it out, you mean."

Borunna nodded. "I fear so. It was a lot of money, and the risks of being caught were tiny. So he got hold of a car and went. It wasn't his lucky day. The border police were holding a day of spot checks looking for people taking out goods, currency, escaping fascists, and Hector got caught up in the net. They found the bust and discovered Hector could not prove ownership, had no export papers, nothing. For once his charm let him down. They arrested him and impounded the bust until it could be examined by an expert at the Borghese. That happened all the time in those days; so many works of art had gone missing during the war and there was an enormous effort to get everything back to the rightful owners."

"And what happened?"

He shrugged. "Hector never saw it again, as I say."

"But he must have wanted to know what had happened to it."

"Of course. He drove everybody crazy. The Borghese confirmed it was genuine, then went very tight-lipped about it. He was convinced they were going to keep it."

"They didn't. We know that."

Borunna dismissed the comment as though it was of no importance to him. "Perhaps not. So what do you think happened to it?"

"We don't know."

He nodded thoughtfully at this, then continued. "Well, Hector didn't get it back, that I do know. It was a great blow; he was so excited to start off with. And, of course, he didn't have enough money to absorb a loss like that. He resented it for some time, because he reckoned he'd bought it fair and square. But there was nothing he could do about it."

"Why not? I mean, if it was his . . ."

"Ah, but was it? I really don't know where he got it from. Perhaps it was at a house sale. Perhaps—well, perhaps it wasn't. But legal or not, a poor foreigner fighting something like the Borghese? He wouldn't have had a chance; if he'd persisted he might have been charged with theft, war looting, who knows what. There was a lot of that going around at the time.

"You're too young to know anything about that, but Italy after the war was chaotic. Thousands of works of art wandering around the country, and fakes being produced at an extraordinary rate, exploiting the situation. No one knew where anything came from, or where anything had gone. The authorities were doing their best to restore order, and occasionally they were a little harsh, perhaps. Anyway, that was the situation, and Hector got caught in it. I advised him to forget it, and eventually he did. Frankly, he got off very lightly in the circumstances. I'm not sure the buyer was very happy, though. I'm not entirely certain that Hector ever gave him his deposit back."

"This was the Swiss man?"

"He lived in Switzerland."

"You can't remember his name, can you?" Flavia asked, for form's sake.

Borunna looked a bit bemused. "No, not really. Foreign name. Morgan? Morland?"

She looked at him, light dawning. "Moresby?" she suggested hopefully.

"Could have been. It was a long time ago, you know."

Borunna's wife came into the room again, and beamed at Flavia happily as she cleared away the cups. Flavia reminded her, she said, of their own daughter when she was young. Borunna agreed there was a resemblance.

"And you have no idea at all of the movements of this bust over the past few decades."

Borunna looked fondly at his wife as she bustled about, then shook his head. "I know it went into the Borghese. Hector was certain it never came out again. I'm afraid that's all the help I feel able to offer you."

She finished jotting down her notes, then stood up and shook them both by the hand. Come again, they said. Stay for lunch. Perhaps Alceo will persuade you to take one of his statues off our hands next time.

With a last regretful look at the carvings all over the room, Flavia promised she'd be back, as soon as she had a free moment. Meanwhile, she had a plane to catch.

CHAPTER 9

Argyll, still confined to his bed, was occupying himself by doing battle with the nurses, having nice shiny new plaster poured over his leg, and plotting how soon he could discharge himself. Not that he was one of these get-up-and-go types who twitch with frustration if they are immobilised; on the contrary, the idea of a few days in bed normally delighted him. But a few days in a non-smoking hospital was a bit much to bear. Morelli had kindly left some cigarettes behind him, but these were rapidly removed by the nurses, all of whom seemed to be equipped with smoke-detectors, and the symptoms of withdrawal were building up.

On top of that, Argyll reflected, there was a lot going on out there: di Souza was dead, Moresby was dead, someone had tried to murder him, Flavia was on the way. He had heard that she had been ringing Morelli every few hours with anxious enquiries after his health and reports of her alarm did more to make him feel better than all the somewhat brusque ministrations of the nurses, whose bedpan technique was another very good reason for getting out of hospital as soon as possible.

While Argyll spent the day hopping around evading the enema merchants, Flavia was wedged in great discomfort in seat 44H of an overstuffed 747 heading west.

She liked her job; she liked the relative smallness of the department, the collegiality which this bred. But the department's status as a sort of investigatory annexe had its problems. And the main one, as far as she was concerned at the moment, was the size of the budget. In particular the inability of expense allowances to allow personnel to travel anything other than steerage class on aircraft.

But the flight had some interesting moments. The secret service file on Moresby had come through and, contrary to all regulations, she'd photocopied it before sending it back. As she read, her contempt for the intelligence of Intelligence grew. The file, protected by so many rules and surrounded by the aura of omniscience, was little more than a collection of press cuttings and the occasional jotting, set down at the time that Moresby Industries was competing for a defence electronics contract. The most interesting was a cutting from *Who's Who*, and the fullest account of Moresby's life a clipping from a *New York Times* profile. Three hours in a public library and she could have dug up more herself.

For all its amateur flimsiness, however, the file yielded some intriguing points for her to ponder.

First of these came from the newspaper account of Moresby's career. Not a self-made man, by any stretch of the imagination, unless you are prepared to be generous and say that inheriting five million dollars from your family counts as being self-made. Something of a playboy in his youth (although from the attached photograph that seemed to be stretching it as well) but interrupted in mid-party by World War Two. Administrative duties in the safety of Kansas, then dispatched to Europe just as the fighting died down.

There, as the profile said obliquely, he laid the foundations of his career and collection. Reading between the lines, it seemed to Flavia that he was little more than an upmarket speculator, importing scarce goods from the United States and selling them at outrageous prices to Europeans who had to pay anything to get them. So time-consuming was this business that in 1948 he left the army, and spent four years organising his trading networks from Zurich before returning to California. Having spent some years selling radios, toasters, and other electrical goods, he turned to making them as well, before branching out into television, hi-fi, and then on to computers. Moresby Industries effectively stirred into life in a little office in Zurich.

And Zurich was in Switzerland, and that was where the original buyer of the Bernini was said to be. That confirmed old Borunna's vague recollection very nicely . . .

Detective Joseph Morelli also spent a day hunched over files of papers, carefully, painstakingly and with much furrowing of the brow going through vast reams of documents that had been accumulating on his desk almost since the moment that he had been called on to investigate Moresby's death.

Had he ever met Taddeo Bottando, the two men would probably have got along quite nicely. However different their outlook on life—Bottando's idea of a quiet Saturday was to spend it in a museum while Morelli preferred beer and ball games—they shared a similar approach to policing.

Thoroughness, in a word. No stone unturned. Combined with a joint belief nurtured by years of experience that crime was a pretty shabby business with money generally to be found at the bottom of it all somewhere. The bigger the crime, the more money, so Morelli was looking for a hefty stash of it.

Like Flavia, he had pulled favours to get his hands on papers, particularly Moresby's tax returns for the past five years. He had also borrowed a large number of files from Thanet's cabinets and persuaded Moresby's factotum, David Barclay, to hand over more.

Then he set to work, and a dull and painful business it was. He thought his taxes were complicated. The only potentially useful piece of information a couple of hours furrowed brow produced was a note, in Barclay's hand, authorising the release of two million dollars to pay for the bust. That he found curious, in a passing fashion.

Then innumerable lists of where people were and what they were doing at the critical moment. Thanet, at the party, confirmed by the evidence of the camera. Langton outside having a smoke, also confirmed. Streeter nowhere to be seen but claimed to be in the toilet, seeing to his piles. That had a ring of truth, somehow, but he put a little asterisk by his name anyway. Barclay got a big asterisk, di Souza an asterisk and a question mark. Anne Moresby was in her car going home, confirmed by the chauffeur. Jack Moresby was telephoned at home by Langton about ten minutes after the murder was discovered, and that let him out.

The confirmation that the pistol found near di Souza matched the bullet in his brain distracted him only briefly; he'd expected that. He'd also expected that it would prove to be the gun that killed Moresby. He did not expect the information that the gun was registered in the name of Anne Moresby. That made him think about her with renewed interest. And he added another asterisk to the name of David Barclay.

It was a major tribute to American notions of hospitality, the importance of the case and Morelli's inherent helpfulness, despite his worsening dental crisis and resultant hostility to just about everyone, that he was at the airport at one o'clock in the morning to meet Flavia staggering off the plane.

The past few days had not been pleasant for him, after all. Quite apart from the built-in problems of dealing with a case that was remarkably hard to get at, his attention was constantly distracted by other unfinished cases, the anxious enquiries of supervisors and the silly speculations of newspaper reporters. And his gums were killing him.

He was working long hours, his wife was starting to protest and, although he was rapidly accumulating masses of pieces of information, until this afternoon he had made little progress in fitting them together. The fact that they were now slotting together made him feel no less tired. And however much he welcomed international co-operation, he could not really see how the arrival of

Flavia di Stefano was going to help. She would undoubtedly use up more of his precious time, and contribute little in return.

On the other hand, as those further up the greasy pole had pointed out, it was something to throw to the press as a way of distracting their attention for a while. The arrival of this woman had already sent the reptiles into paroxysms of speculation. The prospect of a connection with Europe (a place indelibly associated in all right-thinking West Coast minds with deviousness and decadence) was a useful red herring. Mention the word Italy in connection with a crime and by morning half a dozen pundits will be intoning gravely about the Mafia.

While they chewed on that, and Moresby's possible links with organised crime, Morelli and his comrades could get on quietly with their business.

He saw her first, wandering around in a daze heading for the enquiries desk. Even at that time in the morning he could feel a touch of envy for Argyll. Being of Italian descent, Morelli still had a patriotic preference for women from the Old Country. Bashed and battered though she was from the flight, she was still pretty beautiful, and the fair dishevelled hair and rumpled clothes somehow made her look more so. Nor, he thought as she wandered in his direction, was she just a pretty face. There was something which gave an impression of sturdy competence.

"Signorina di Stefano?" he asked as she gave another enormous yawn and rubbed her eyes.

She looked at him suspiciously, slowly worked out who he was and gave a smile.

"Detective Morelli," she replied, thrusting out her

hand. "It's very good of you to meet me here," she added as he shook it.

She spoke good English, with a heavy accent that Morelli found so unbearably appealing he could hardly stand listening to it, and gave him an account of the flight as they walked to Morelli's car. Miserable. What else?

"I've booked you into the same hotel as Argyll. I hope that's OK. It's near the museum, and is pretty comfortable."

"I suppose it's too late to go and see Jonathan?" she asked. "I've spoken to the hospital a couple of times, but I've never got through to him direct."

"You'd be wasting your time," he said, pulling out on to the freeway and heading north. "He discharged himself this afternoon."

"Was that wise?"

"Not according to the doctors, no. But doctors are like that. I don't suppose it matters really. He apparently said that if he stayed in the hospital he'd die out of boredom and he was going home. So he called a taxi and hopped out. I haven't heard from him since."

"Oh, dear, and he's so careless."

"So it seems. He's only been here five days and he's nearly been run over, had a major car crash, destroyed a shop, broken his leg and been the cause of a brawl in the hospital. People like that are dangerous to be around. Besides, I wanted to give him protection, until the case is properly wrapped up. But as I don't know where he is . . ."

"What do you mean, 'protection'? What for?"

"In case someone tries to kill him again."

All news to Flavia. Until then, she'd been assuming

that Argyll's mishap was one of the inevitable and normal parts of his life-cycle. Morelli's account of loosened brake leads, of the party, of something he must know but couldn't remember, was the first she'd heard of any of it. She was also a little bit irritated by the American's confident explanation of how the noose was, metaphorically speaking, tightening around David Barclay and Anne Moresby. What was the point of her coming all this way if the case was going to be all over in a matter of hours?

On the other hand, at the moment she was more concerned with Argyll. Now she really did want to see him. Which was fairly easy, as he was back in his hotel room. Flavia discovered him, leg propped up, sitting on the bed reading, with a glass of whisky and an ashtray by his side. Freedom.

Had he been more mobile, he would have leapt up, raced across the room and taken her in his arms when she came in. As it was, he did the best he could, waving enthusiastically, beaming with welcome and beginning to apologise for not moving.

He was not allowed to finish the explanation. Flavia had intended to make some sardonic remark about his carelessness before sitting down for a civil conversation about this bust. Cool and distant. She still hadn't forgiven him for planning to leave Italy.

Somehow or other it all went wrong. She had been angry with him, worried about him and thoroughly alarmed by the news that someone had tried to kill him. The fact that she was able to walk straight through his unlocked door, that he was so dimwitted he was taking no precautions at all, simply pushed her over the edge, and she let rip with a veritable torrent of abuse which completely erased his cheerful welcome.

Briefly summarised, she informed him that he was stupid, inconsiderate, reckless, selfish, a danger to himself and others, blind as a mouse (here her command of English idiom let her down) and thoroughly irritating. Except that she took longer to deliver her opinion, which came complete with innumerable examples stretching back over many weeks, accompanied by much wagging of the finger, elaborated with many baroque turns of phrase—Italian when the supply of English ran out—and was finally spoiled by ending with a lower lip that was beginning to tremble with relief that, after all that and despite his best efforts, he was still in one piece.

For Argyll it was a critical moment. He had two choices; either to pick up the gauntlet and shout back, at which point the reunion he'd been looking forward to would degenerate into a slanging match; or try to calm her down, and run the risk of receiving another torrent based on the thesis that he was, in addition, pompous and condescending.

This he knew very well, as well as he knew Flavia. A ticklish choice, and he took so long trying to make up his mind that he said nothing at all, just looked at her wistfully. Oddly, it was the right thing to do. You can stand, hand on hips, looking pugnacious, for only so long. Sooner or later you have to shift stance, and when she did, he reached out, took her hand and gave it a squeeze.

"I'm so very glad to see you," he said simply.

She sat down, sniffed loudly and nodded. "Yeah, well. Me too, I suppose," she replied.

CHAPTER 10

"The trouble is," Argyll said next day when Flavia's mental faculties had returned to something approaching normal, "that I'm a bit stuck, you see. The deal was that if I sell this Titian, I keep my job and go back to London. And I've sold it."

"Can't you just say you don't want to go?"

"Not really, no. Not without resigning or being fired. Besides, Byrnes has done an awful lot for me, and he wants someone there he thinks he can trust."

"He trusts you?"

"I did say *thinks* he can trust."

"Can't you say you need more experience, or something?"

"I've just sold a Titian for a client for a handsome fee. He seems to think that indicates I'm doing quite well."

"Cancel the sale."

"But the deal's going through. I can't cancel it. How would I explain to the owner. 'Sorry, but I want to stay in Italy so you'll have to accept only half the price in a year's time?' That's not the way to get ahead, you know. Besides, the real point is that Byrnes wants to draw in his horns a little. Basically, the choice is promotion in London, or unemployment in Rome. And I'm lucky to have the choice."

"Hmm. Do you want to go to London?"

"Of course not. Who in their right mind would want to live in London if they could stay in Rome? I could stay on and work to commission . . ."

"Do that, then."

"Yes, but you're missing the point. My big secret."

"What's that?"

"Essentially," he confided, "I'm not a very good art dealer. Without a regular salary, I don't know that I could earn enough to survive. Not at the moment. And on top of that, you didn't seem to care one way or the other."

"That's not my fault," she protested. "Is it my fault your way of declaring undying affection is to offer someone a cup of tea?"

Argyll brushed these details aside. "The point is, I've now given up the lease on my flat. I will have nowhere to live and nothing to live on."

"But," she said, "what if the museum cancels the sale?"

"They won't."

"They will if the museum closes. Then you can call Byrnes, say the whole thing was a flop, you're a disaster as an art dealer, and insist that your presence in his London gallery would ensure bankruptcy in a matter of months."

"And lose my job. Very helpful."

"But you could sell the Titian to someone else and keep all the commission yourself."

"If I could sell it. If the owner wanted me to sell it. This place is paying far more than the picture is worth and the market's in a right mess at the moment. I could be sitting on it for months. Besides, I don't know what's going to happen to the museum at all yet. Thanet's worried about Mrs. Moresby, but it's all in the hands of lawyers."

"Fine. So let's go and find out what the situation is."

The Moresby seaside retreat, one of the many homes where the happy and united family spent the summer months, was not at all what Argyll had imagined, and certainly far from Flavia's experience. But almost everything in Los Angeles was far from her experience. She had a very traditional notion of cities; cathedral, museum, town hall and railway station telling you where the centre was, historic district, modern suburbs wrapped around separating town from country. Los Angeles is not like that and from the moment she arrived to the moment she left she had not a clue where she was. Only by keeping the Pacific Ocean in view could she tell if she was going north or south, east or west. And it was unexpectedly difficult to tell where the ocean was. Flavia associated beaches with public access but Californians, in this as much else, evidently did things differently. As far as she could see, most of the Pacific had been commandeered for private use, with houses built along the coast specifically to obscure the view for everyone else.

At first sight, *chez* Moresby was not much to look at. That at least was Flavia's excuse for driving past the first time; turning round and coming back again was not easy, so it was doubly unfortunate that she overshot again heading south. From the road, the place could have been the back end of a seedy restaurant, and the site straight on to the road was not what either of them would have associated with enormous wealth.

Convinced that they were in the wrong place, they walked cautiously round to the front, and changed their minds. It was an extraordinary house, if you like twentieth-century architecture, plate glass windows thirty foot long with uninterrupted views of the Pacific Ocean, and a hand-carved beechwood sundeck about the size of a tennis court.

Of course, it would have helped if the architect had provided an easily findable door, so they could have knocked on it, but fortunately they didn't need one. A man, evidently a servant of some sort, emerged from somewhere and shouted at them. Argyll cupped his hand over his ear and tried to understand what he was saying.

"He's telling us to go away," Flavia said.

"How do you know that? I can't understand a word he's saying."

"That's because he's speaking Spanish," she said, and bellowed back a stream of verbiage in his direction.

He came over, eyed them suspiciously and a lengthy conversation ensued. Argyll was impressed. He didn't know Flavia spoke Spanish. Very irritating; she could do things like that. He had laboured long and hard to acquire his smatterings of language, and had sweated blood over the most regular of imperfect subjunctives. Flavia, in contrast, seemed to pick up the most abstruse grammatical points as casually as someone buying a bar of chocolate. She didn't put any effort into it at all, as far as he could see. There's no justice in life.

"What are you talking about, then?" he asked as the conversation petered out into mutual smiles.

"I've been winning his confidence," she said. "He has orders from Mrs. Moresby not to let anyone into the house and, because I am such a particularly nice person, he is going to make an exception on our part. He's from Nicaragua, and doesn't have any work permit, and the Moresby's pay him virtually nothing and threaten to have him deported if he complains. He has to clean the house, do the shopping and the cooking, act as a chauffeur and doesn't like working here at all. The only compensation is that they have lots of houses and aren't here very often. On the other hand, the awful son uses the place occasionally when they are away and he has to clean up his empty bottles. He is certain that Mrs. Moresby is having an affair, he doesn't know who with and, very regrettably, he is her alibi for the time of the murder. He wishes he wasn't."

"And how is his family doing back in Nicaragua? Or didn't you have time to get to that stage?"

"Wasn't necessary. Let's go in."

They advanced into the house before Alfredo could change his mind, as he was clearly beginning to do. The inside was disappointing, as Moresby had filled it, most incongruously, with eighteenth-century French furniture, which looked as out of place as a tubular steel sofa would in the Palazzo Farnese. Not only that, there was an awful lot of it, and the dozens of chairs, sofas, pictures, prints, busts, and miscellaneous knick-knacks seemed to have been chosen more or less at random. Occasionally the junk-shop approach to home decorating works and produces a pleasing confusion, but not here. Arthur Moresby's beach house, designed for clean, uncluttered, fresh-air modernism, looked as though it had been furnished by an unusually acquisitive magpie.

But despite that, the decor was effective in conveying the impression that the owners were not short of ready money. Even the ashtrays were of baccarat crystal. Argyll suspected the toilet rolls would turn out to be of the finest water-pressed Venetian paper. All the commodes, bureaux, Louis Seize sofas, Chippendale tables had been restored, revarnished, reupholstered and regilded. It looked like the lobby of an international hotel.

Argyll was only halfway through a mental inventory and estimation of the furniture and fittings—an occupational hazard of art dealing that Flavia found profoundly irritating—when Anne Moresby came in. If she was grief-stricken she disguised it well. Nor had trauma softened her vocabulary.

"Bullshit," she said after Argyll had performed the introductions, explained why his leg was in plaster, and Flavia got things rolling by muttering something about condolences.

"I beg your pardon?" Flavia replied a little taken aback. Seeing through one's little ploy was one thing; mentioning it quite another. On the other hand, vocabulary was vocabulary, and Mrs. Moresby looked like proving a rich vein.

"You're snooping. You have no authority, so I don't have to tell you anything. In fact I could just throw you out. Right?"

"On the nail," said Argyll cheerfully. "No fooling you.

But we would still be grateful for a brief talk. After all, you were upset about that bust, and so are we. If the museum has been indulging in any illegal activities, we want to know. Then Flavia here can take appropriate action. Against those responsible, if you see what I mean."

What this speech did, quite neatly to Flavia's way of thinking as she considered it afterwards, was offer a little alliance. You want to put the knife into the museum—so Argyll—why not let us help you? Rather acute, for him.

Mrs. Moresby was no fool. Her eyes narrowed as she thought of it, weighed the pros and cons. Then she gave him a quick and surprisingly charming half-smile and said: "Oh, all right. Makes a change from the police. Come and have a drink; then we can talk this over."

She walked over to the fireplace—what possible function it served in this climate Flavia could not imagine—opened a delicate ivory box and took out a packet of cigarettes; then lit one. Took a deep breath and the pair of them saw of a look of extraordinary satisfaction come over her face.

"It's an ill-wind," she said. "Do you realise I can now smoke in this house for the first time since I got married twelve years ago?"

"Your husband disapproved?"

"Disapproved? He threatened to divorce me. Even had it written into the marriage contract that any divorce settlement would be void if I was caught smoking in his presence."

"Just a joke, though," Argyll suggested.

She gave him a stern look. "Arthur Moresby did not joke. Never. Any more than he forgave, forgot or oozed the milk of human kindness. When the good Lord made him there was a temporary shortage of humour; so he was sent forth with an extra dose of self-righteousness instead. Didn't drink, didn't smoke, didn't do anything except accumulate. Used to, of course, but when he stopped enjoying himself he wanted everybody else to do the same." Here she waved her hand around the room to indicate what she had in mind. She may have had a point. "Do you realise that for the last twelve years I've been married to the most boring man ever to walk the face of the earth?"

"Liked art, though."

She snorted. "You must be kidding. He bought it because he thought that's what multi-millionaires did."

"You weren't keen on his museum project?"

"Damn right I wasn't. It was all right to start off with, when it was just a straight tax write-off. Then he got the immortality bug and Thanet got his hooks into him."

"Tax write-off?" Flavia asked. Really, this woman was a walking dictionary of idiom.

"You know, the IRS."

She shook her head blankly, and Anne Moresby gave her a stupid-foreigner look she rather resented.

"Internal Revenue Service," she went on. "A sort of Spanish Inquisition redesigned for the consumer society. Trying to put one over on it is a national sport rivalling the baseball. Arthur regarded it as a civic duty to try and pay as little tax as possible."

"What's the museum got to do with it?"

"Simple. Buy a picture and hang it in your house, and you get no tax relief. Hang it in a museum and you become a public benefactor, entitled to deduct a huge chunk of the price off your income tax."

"So what changed?"

"The little creep had a heart attack."

"Who?"

"Arthur. It started him thinking about the future, or lack of it. Arthur's great weakness was a desire to be remembered. It's a fault with a lot of egomaniacs, so I'm told. Once upon a time, people built almshouses or had monks say Mass for them. In the US they found museums. I'm not sure which is the more stupid. The more money, the bigger the ego, the larger the museum. Getty, Hammer, Mellon, you name it. Arthur caught the bug.

"He was getting old. Thanet and his crew were beginning to convince him that a small museum was nowhere near enough for a man of his stature. They were touting plans for a museum the size of a football stadium and Arthur was getting hooked."

"And Thanet knew all about this tax relief scheme?"

"Of course; nothing wrong with it. Not as far as I've been able to find out, anyway, and believe me I've looked. And even if there was, that slimy ball of fat would do anything to keep on Arthur's right side."

"When I met you briefly before the party you described your husband as a sweet old man," Argyll reminded her. "That doesn't fit too well with all this."

"So, sometimes I exaggerate, for appearances' sake. He was a mean old bastard. Please don't get me wrong; I'm sorry he's dead. But I can't deny that life will be much more pleasant without him. And that goes for everyone who worked for him or was related to him. Not just me."

"So what happens to the museum now? I mean, if I understand rightly, your husband died before transferring most of his money to the museum trust and you inherit the entire estate."

She gave a stiff little smile. It seemed pretty obvious what was going to happen to the museum, if she had her way.

"I hope you don't mind me asking, but if the transfer had gone ahead, you wouldn't have been left penniless, would you? Not like your stepson."

Anne Moresby seemed to think this a bizarre question, one which she had never considered before.

"No, not penniless," she replied reflectively. "No, not at all. I gather that I would have inherited the residue of the estate. About five hundred million."

"That's quiet enough to make ends meet, isn't it?"

Evidently, she didn't follow Flavia's line of reasoning. "Well, yes. So what?"

"So why battle for all the rest?"

"Oh. Because it's mine. As the woman who put up with him and his meanness for all these years. You're right—it's far more money than I can spend. But that's not the point. If the museum continues, it'll enshrine his name in perpetuity. The great art lover, the great philanthropist. The great man. Phooey. And all those leeches, hanging around him, just to get their hands on his wallet, to aggrandise themselves. Phooey again. All conceit and fraud and dishonesty. That's why I want to stop it. Because, dammit, I married that man because I loved him, once upon a time. And nobody believed me. Not Arthur, or his son, or Thanet, or Langton. I hated them all for that. And eventually I stopped believing it myself. If they insisted I married him for money, then so be it. But in that case, I want it all, and I'm damn well going to get it."

An awkward pause followed this. Argyll, never comfortable with other people's outbursts, frowned heavily and pretended not to be there. Flavia, less typically, was also thrown off-balance and temporarily forgot what her line of questioning was. Eventually she retreated back to safer, less complex ground.

"I see," she said. "Yes. Well, about this bust, then. I don't understand. I mean, you turned up and shouted at Thanet about it, but how did you know it was coming, and why did you reckon it was stolen or something?"

"Oh, hell. There's no secret about that. I overheard Arthur talking to Langton about it. Arthur was exultant, punching his fist into his palm with those childish gestures businessmen have."

"He said it was stolen?"

"Oh, no. But it wouldn't have been the first time things turned up in unorthodox circumstances, and it was obvious something fishy was going on."

"Why?"

"Because Arthur had that gleeful look on his face that he only got when he'd shafted someone."

"And when was this, exactly?"

"Christ, I don't know. Couple of months back. I was drunk at the time. I often am, you know."

"And what did they say?"

She shook her head. "I didn't hear. Just that Langton was to get that bust and was to use someone or other. That man whose body they found. The one at the museum."

"Use him for what?"

She shrugged to indicate that she hadn't heard.

"You knew about the trust for the museum?"

She nodded.

"And you knew it was unbreakable once it was set up?"

"No such thing as an unbreakable trust."

"But if Thanet was a trustee and could veto . . ."

"The director of the museum is a trustee," she corrected. "A new director might see differently."

"Like Langton, for example?"

"Oh, no. Not him. He's as bad as Thanet in his way."

She smiled as sweetly as she could manage.

"How do you know all these details?"

"David Barclay told me."

"That was kind of him," Flavia said. The comment got no reaction. "When was this?"

"Oh, last Wednesday, I reckon. Typical of Arthur; intimate family business and I get filled in by a lawyer."

So to speak, Flavia thought. "And you protested about it," she went on.

"Christ, no. That wasn't the way to get anywhere with him. No, I told him it was a wonderful idea; but I did want to undermine Thanet, and the museum, to make Arthur disenchanted with the whole scheme."

"Who did have a reason to bean him?" Argyll asked.

She shrugged again, as though the murder of her husband was a minor detail in the overall scheme of things. "Dunno. If you wondered who would *like* to kill him, then the list is endless. I can't think of anyone who liked him at all, and an enormous list of people who didn't. But I suppose you mean who had a good reason to do it. No idea. That slug of a son was at the party, wasn't he?"

Argyll nodded.

"A bum," she said with a sneer that indicated that she had almost as low an opinion of junior as she had of senior. "Pure and simple. Beer, checked shirts and bar-room brawls. And the traditional Moresby knowledge of the value of money. I'd put my money on him."

She saw Flavia calculating dates. "Oh, he's nothing to do with me. Arthur's third wife. The third of five. Anabel, her name. Wilting ninny. She died, typically. Junior has the worst characteristics of both of them. The only thing going for him was the simple fact that Arthur loathed the very sight of him."

"Happy family," Argyll said.

"That's us. The all-American nightmare."

"Were you, ah, happily married?"

She looked at him suspiciously. "And what does that mean?"

"Well . . ." he began.

"Listen. I'll tell you once, and once only. I'm sick to death of people prying into my life. That unshaven creep from the police department has been insinuating nonsense as well. My private life is none of your business, and it certainly isn't connected in any way with the death of my husband. Got that?"

"Oh, right-ho," he said, wishing he hadn't asked.

She stubbed out her cigarette with ferocity. "I reckon I've spent enough time talking to you. See yourself out." And with that she rose uncertainly from the sofa and ostentatiously opened the door for them to go.

"Well done, Jonathan. Soul of tact and discretion as

usual," Flavia said as they emerged into the sunlight once more.

"Sorry."

"Oh well, it doesn't matter. I don't suppose she would have told us anything useful, anyway. Besides, we're late for lunch."

CHAPTER 11

As far as Argyll was concerned, lunch epitomised why he preferred the company of detective Joe Morelli to that of someone like Samuel Thanet. The latter would have opted for some tastefully constituted French affair, all candles, expensive wine list and a somewhat unctuous atmosphere, but Morelli, coming from a very different background, had a very different notion of food. He took Argyll and Flavia to a run-down shack called Leo's Place.

It looked a bit like a truck stop, and most of the clientele were as big as their trucks. The sort of people who, if they had ever heard of chloresterol, dedicated their lives to ingesting as much of the stuff as possible. Not a candle in sight, except when the power failed. A wine list commendable in its brevity, waiters who neither introduced themselves nor sneered at you during the entire meal, and some of the best food Flavia had ever tasted. Oysters and ribs, washed down with martinis, perhaps make up America's greatest contribution to western civilisation. Martinis certainly do. Argyll's enthusiasm made Morelli warm to him a little. Not many people drank martinis anymore, he said gloomily. Country was going to hell.

While Argyll dug his beak into a second and beamed happily, Flavia ate and questioned. What were the police going to do now?

"Looks as though we're going to arrest Barclay and Anne Moresby, I guess," he said.

"But will you manage to convict them?"

"I hope so. Of course, I would prefer to wait a bit. . . ."

"Why?"

"Because I'm not convinced we have enough. Persuading a jury is going to require more work. But those above me are getting alarmed. They want something to hand to the press. Did you know we live in a pressocracy in this country?"

"Pardon?"

"Pressocracy. Everything is run by, and organised for the convenience of, the press. Television, rather. They need an arrest to keep interest up, so I'm put under pressure to give them one."

"Hmm. So, what's the line? Ooh. How nice. More oysters."

Morelli leant back in his chair, wiped his mouth daintily with his napkin and reeled off his reasoning. And very good it was too, to Flavia's way of thinking. Motive was simple; Moresby probably knew his wife was having an affair, and was not the sort of person to take that lying down. He'd got through five wives already, and could easily go on to number six. Combined with setting up the trust for the museum, Anne Moresby's financial future was crumbling before her very eyes.

"Now we know that Anne Moresby herself could not have killed him, if your Alfredo is telling the truth and she was in her car heading home at the time. But she must have talked it over with Barclay and given him her gun. The opportunity came when Moresby summoned Barclay to see him in Thanet's office. He went over and was told that a) he was fired and b) Anne Moresby was out as well. Barclay was within a heartbeat of getting his hands on billions—he only had to wait for Moresby to drop dead, then he could marry the grieving widow, and it's party time. What does he do? You could never talk a man like Moresby round when his mind was made up, so it was now or never. So Barclay shoots the old man, and runs back to say that when he got there he discovered the murder. No trust—and Barclay must have been one of the very few to know that the papers had not in fact been signed—so Anne Moresby inherits the lot. Success."

There was a pause as Argyll finished off the oysters and Flavia looked uncomfortable.

"What's the matter?" Morelli asked.

"Quite a lot of things," she said reluctantly.

"Such as?"

"The camera, for one thing. That was knocked out sometime before. Before anybody could possibly have known Moresby might go to Thanet's office. So your notion of a sudden decision on Barclay's part doesn't hold up."

"If I remember correctly," Argyll added uncertainly, "people at the party reckoned there was only about five minutes between Barclay getting his phone call and rushing back."

"That's very approximate. It was actually eight minutes."

"Well. The point is," Argyll said, taking over for once, "that it was a busy few minutes, in your account. To walk over, have an argument, shoot Moresby, plan to do something about di Souza—why? for heaven's sake—steal the bust—why again?—run back and raise the alarm. I mean, is that really possible? I suppose it could be done, but only if it was rehearsed. Quite apart from the fact that Langton was outside the museum most of the time and should have seen all this coming and going, and I don't see how either Anne Moresby or Barclay slipped off to shoot Hector and dump his body. And on top of that. . . ."

"Yeah, OK. I got the point." Morelli shifted uneasily in his seat as he mentally visualised a defence lawyer in court saying the same thing, with the jury nodding sagely in agreement.

"And there's something else," Flavia went on, disregarding the American's baleful look in her effort to refocus attention on the matter which concerned her. "If the theft of the bust was planned in advance, it would have to have been by someone who knew where it was. At the time the camera was knocked out only Thanet and Langton knew that."

"And Streeter, of course," Argyll chipped in. "As security man. Didn't you say he was out of sight when the murder took place?"

"Can't we keep this goddamned bust out of it for a while?" Morelli asked a little plaintively. Much of what they had said had passed through his own mind in the past hour or so, but he'd decided that the only way of proceeding was to tackle the two elements of the events separately.

"It's a very big thing to forget. I think I'd leave Anne Moresby alone for a bit, if I were you."

"Hmm. That's going to go down well with my superiors. They'll crucify me."

"You'll be saving them from a nasty mistake."

"What's that got to do with it?"

"Can't you tell them you're on the verge of getting hundred percent proof evidence?"

"We're not."

"No, but we could try a little harder. I think we should go and visit Mr. Streeter."

To say that Robert Streeter lived in a small, whitewashed house in a quiet, palm-lined street would say nothing about his accommodation. There was scarcely a single house in the whole area which wasn't whitewashed and almost no streets that weren't quiet and lined with palm trees. Not in the respectable bits, anyway. The expert would have noticed a few details that might have indicated something about his way of life. The absence of a basketball hoop on the garage indicated that he had no adolescent children in the house; the lack of a manicured patch of lawn out front suggested he was no gardener and that his more fastidious neighbours, who snipped—or had someone snip—each blade of grass as it poked its well-watered head above two-eighths of an inch, might have regarded this as a sign of rampant bohemianism. But apart from that there was almost nothing to indicate the character of the occupant, and neither Flavia nor Argyll would have picked up the signs even had they been present.

Streeter took a long time to answer the doorbell, and appeared in a bad mood when he finally opened the door. This, they assumed, was because he'd been having an afternoon siesta, but in that they were wrong as well. Despite living in a Mediterranean climate custom-built for afternoon siestas, Californians don't waste their time in this fashion. Besides, he was much too engrossed in an earnest, not to say frantic, discussion with Langton when the doorbell went to have much peace of mind left over for such frivolities.

Indeed, he and Langton had just got around to the central issue. Streeter, who was thoroughly upset about the performance of his camera system and feeling that, as a security expert, he ought to do a little amateur investigation of his own, had just popped the question. In fact, as Morelli's tireless investigators had realised, he had been trotting around interrogating just about everybody in the museum with varying degrees of subtlety. As had everybody else. Neither he, nor anybody else had much to show for the effort, but it made them feel a lot better. Besides, nobody was much in the mood for real work.

Streeter's own investigation had left him feeling a little vulnerable. Having laboured so tirelessly to secure his position, he had this impression that recent events threatened to undermine it all. He had been thinking and plotting furiously and the general aim was now clear; that is, to make sure he was on the right side of whoever it was that emerged triumphant at the end. In order to achieve this, he had to know who was responsible. And strong suspicions were forming rapidly. In the course of several sleepless nights in the past week, he had constructed innumerable nightmarish scenarios, all of which ended in unemployment—and some where the outcome was much worse.

So, with a good deal more directness than was his custom, he set about Langton when the latter flew back from Rome. Had it occurred to the Englishman, he asked, who stood to benefit from the death of Arthur Moresby? And who were the only people who could have killed him?

Not perhaps the most sophisticated way of approaching a potential witness who had demonstrated, in Rome at least, his complete unwillingness to answer questions. Langton, a man who had spent much of his time travelling the world and negotiating the purchase of pictures, was much too self-possessed to be caught out answering questions gratuitously.

He reacted with a lightly amused smile. Yes, he replied indulgently. As far as he could see, only Anne Moresby benefited. And only three people could have killed him, that is, di Souza, who was with Moresby before the murder, David Barclay, summoned over at about the time it took place, and himself, sitting outside the museum and in a fine position to nip over and do the deed. But, he went on, unless someone connected Mrs. Moresby's motive with everybody else's opportunity, there was not much chance of any progress. He did not presume to speak for the rest—although Hector di Souza's own murder seemed to indicate a possible degree of innocence there, but he saw no connection with David Barclay. As for himself, Streeter's own cameras picked him up sitting placidly outside the museum. Whatever else he might have done, he had not murdered Arthur Moresby. Or anyone else either, he added as an afterthought. Just in case someone might start worrying about loopholes.

It didn't get him much further, Streeter thought as he walked to the door to answer the sudden peal of the bell. But if the more obvious suspects were knocked out, the police would start looking at alternatives. He was very aware—having checked himself—that he had, quite fortuitously, been in the toilet at about the time of the murder. For reasons of human dignity, there were no cameras in the toilets. A grave mistake, that. His movements were thus unaccounted for. Which left his final defence; it was just a pity it was such a dangerous weapon.

"Sorry if we've come at a bad time," Flavia said brightly as the door swung open and she introduced herself.

If Langton was never caught on the hop, Streeter was. He mumbled something that sounded like not at all, do come in, and was indicating the way to the little plot of concrete out the back before it had properly dawned on him that he should have told both of them to go away because they had no authority to ask anybody questions.

"Well, what a surprise," Flavia said as she saw Langton and started drawing exactly the sort of conclusions that Streeter so much feared. "I thought you were in Rome. You do get around, don't you?"

Both she and Argyll sat themselves down and accepted the offer of a beer. It was a hot afternoon, and this knocked Argyll out of most of the conversation. While Flavia began round two of her battle with Langton, he concentrated on trying to get at a profoundly annoying itch five inches down from the top of his plaster cast.

Langton explained that, with such a crisis in full blossom, he naturally thought that his place was right here, in case he could be of any assistance.

"So you come all this way to visit your old friend Mr. Streeter to spend a quiet Saturday sitting in the garden," she observed. Langton nodded and said that was about it.

"I'm very glad to see you. We have so much to discuss."

If Langton was wary about what was coming next, he didn't show it. Instead he just leant back on the chair with a look of complete indifference and waited for her to continue.

"About the mysterious people who sold you the Bernini."

Langton looked benignly at her and raised an eyebrow. "What about them?" he asked calmly.

"They don't exist. The bust was stolen from Alberghi's house at Bracciano, and transported across the Atlantic."

"I admit the family didn't exist," he said with surprising readiness and an even more alarming smile. "More than that I couldn't say."

"You knew it was stolen."

"On the contrary. I knew nothing of the sort."

"How did you hear about it?"

"Simple enough. I was looking at some of di Souza's other stuff and found it shrouded in a bedsheet. I made him an offer, there and then."

"Without checking what it was, without even getting permission from the museum?"

"Of course I checked what it was afterwards. But I

knew in my bones without really having to. And I asked Moresby if he wanted it."

"Not the museum."

"No."

"Why not?"

"Because Moresby took all the real decisions. Just wanted to save time."

"And he wanted it?"

"Obviously. He leapt at the chance."

"You knew he'd already bought it once. In 1951?"

"Yes."

"From di Souza?"

"That I didn't know at the time," he said blandly. "All I knew was that for years Moresby had disliked art dealers. And as an example of their perfidiousness he used to say that he had once—only once—been cheated out of a Bernini by someone who had sold it to him, taken some money and then never delivered. Moresby felt he'd been made a fool of, and he didn't like that. It was obvious he'd leap at the chance to get it."

"So you then got di Souza to ship it over. Why?"

"What do you mean?"

"Why were you both prepared to use the same man who had cheated Moresby all those years ago?"

"He had the bust. Moresby wanted the bust in California, and there was no way we could have got export permission. Somebody not connected with the museum had to smuggle it. We made up a story about another owner to cover him, so he wouldn't get into trouble. That's why he was leaping around and looking so concerned and complaining about his good name. All an act."

"And you paid him?"

Langton smiled. "I'm sure that Detective Morelli has discovered that already. Yes. Two million dollars."

"Moresby told Thanet four million."

"Two."

"And this was when?"

"When what?"

"When was he paid?"

"On delivery. Moresby wasn't taking any chances this time."

"And when did you see this bust and make him an offer?"

"A few weeks back."

"When?"

"Oh, lord, I don't know. First week in May, perhaps. The whole deal was done very quickly. I assure you that I had not the slightest doubt about the fact that di Souza was the legitimate owner of that bust. If you can prove otherwise, I'm sure the museum will insist on sending it back to the rightful owners. And bear any other costs.

"I'm sure it will be found," he went on. "Large busts like that don't go missing for long."

"This one has already been missing for forty years."

Langton shrugged and repeated that it would turn up.

Flavia thought it time to try another line of approach. Langton had nettled her badly back in Rome, and she was convinced that everything concerning this bust was crooked, and that he knew it. His calm confidence that they would never pin anything on him was spoiling her afternoon. Especially because, as far as she was concerned, he was probably right.

"You disliked Thanet for taking your job and were

hell-bent on sabotaging him and getting him out of the museum."

She was proud of that. Hell-bent, that is. It was a word she'd picked up from a movie she'd watched on television while wide awake from jetlag at three o'clock in the morning. She'd tackled Argyll about its meaning later on. Langton, not impressed by her linguistic skill, at least seemed prepared to concede the general thrust of the statement.

"Sabotaging is going too far. And it wasn't personal. I just think he's a dangerous person to have in a museum. You know."

"I don't. From everything I've heard he sounds fairly meek and mild."

"In that case you don't understand anything about museums. The Moresby was a nice museum, once. Small and friendly, despite Moresby's awful presence hanging over it. He loathed arty types; he was always saying how they were thieves and swindlers. Then he brought in Thanet and these ideas for the big museum began to surface."

"So?"

"A big museum isn't just a big building and collection. The first thing you do is develop a big bureaucracy worthy of it. Steering committees, hanging committees, budget committees. Hierarchy, interference and plans. Thanet is making the museum about as much fun to work for as General Motors."

"And you weren't happy."

"No. And it wasn't working either. To start off, the collection was quirky, individual and interesting. Now it's just like every other museum; a boring plod through the Great Schools of art, from Raphael to Renoir. The trouble is all the good pictures are already in museums. All Thanet can do is get the leftovers. The place is becoming an international joke."

"So why don't you leave if you dislike it so much?"

"Firstly, because the pay is OK. Secondly, because I like being the lone voice of sanity in the wilderness. Thirdly, because I like to think that at least I buy stuff worth having, most of the time. I haven't given up hope yet."

"You may have to, if Mrs. Moresby goes ahead and shuts the place down," she said.

Langton's eyes narrowed as he listened. "When did she say this?"

Flavia told him.

"Long time before we get to that point," he said. "A lot can change by the time lawyers have finished with it all."

"Is it true Anne Moresby was having an affair?" she asked, this being, to her mind, one of the crucial questions.

Langton almost seemed to have been expecting the question, and he smiled slowly, a bit like a teacher when a particularly stupid pupil gets something right for once. Streeter seemed properly shocked and appalled by the very idea; he sucked in his breath in a most disapproving fashion.

"Probably," Langton said. "I would, if I was married to someone as repulsive as Moresby. They virtually lived apart anyway, you know. But she would have to be discreet. The consequences would have been horrendous if old Moresby ever even suspected."

"He may well have done more than suspect."

"In that case she's a very lucky woman. She's a multi-billionaire, and she's fortunate she's not a penniless divorcee." He paused and considered awhile before making his next comment. "So lucky, in fact, that it makes you wonder."

"That fact," she said, "had occurred to us as well."

"But," he went on, half talking to himself, "she had an alibi. Which means she needed an accomplice. So, the big question is, who's the lucky man?"

She shrugged. "Work it out for yourself, if you don't know."

Argyll looked up for a moment, temporarily distracted from his by now manic hunt. Then the itching gave another twinge and he resumed the assault, bashing the plaster, sticking little twigs and cocktail stirrers down the top until Streeter was looking at him with appalled fascination.

"What are you doing?"

"Preserving my sanity," he replied. "What you might call an itch hunt." He looked up for applause, but nobody seemed to be in the mood for little jokes. "You don't have any knitting needles do you?" he asked helplessly. Streeter said there was not a single one in the house. Argyll looked pained until he offered to search the kitchen for something suitable. Half crazed with desire, Argyll hopped after him.

"Do the police know about Anne Moresby's lover?" Streeter asked once they were out of earshot inside the house.

"Seems so. Lots of extended shopping trips, weekends away. And Moresby knew, which provides a very good motive for murder. It's the awkward business of proving it that seems to be slowing them all down. Very unlike Italy, you know. There the police could have simply arrested everyone and sat on them until they confessed. Pity about your camera," he said casually to Streeter as they searched. "It would have made life so much easier if it had been a bit more difficult to get at."

Streeter seemed suddenly gloomy. "Tell me about it," he said.

"I suppose it makes your job a bit less secure, doesn't it?"

Streeter looked at him mournfully.

"Just as well we can call on that microphone in Thanet's office."

"What?"

"A bug in Thanet's office."

"Listen, I've already told . . ."

"I know. But you've such a reputation for being a hitech snoop, who will believe that?"

"Bugging offices is an offence, you know. The very idea . . ."

"So if a murderer was suddenly *told* that a tape existed, I mean, they'd believe it. It might make them nervous. Just as they thought the coast was clear, all of a sudden a piece of evidence turns up. Not that any one has heard what's on it. Destroy that tape, and you're safe, he might tell himself. Desperate circumstances make for desperate actions. Which might lead to a mistake. And you'd get full marks and thanks for co-operating with the police."

At last the penny dropped. Argyll didn't have a very high opinion of Streeter. A bit slow, he thought.

"I see," he said.

"My leg feels so much better now. I suppose we ought to go back outside. Flavia and I are meant to be having dinner with Detective Morelli and it's time we were off. I'll tell him about our little chat, if that's all right by you."

"Oh, yes," said Streeter. "Sure."

"Did Mr. Streeter have all that much to say for himself?" Flavia asked after they had extracted themselves, she'd levered Argyll into the car—she had rented a small but practical machine which was not designed for people with plaster casts—and they'd begun the lengthy process of crossing much of the city in search of Morelli's house.

"Oh, yes," he replied smugly. "He was a bit slow on the uptake. I had to drop so many heavy hints I thought he'd sink under the weight. But he got the idea eventually."

"And?"

"We can go ahead and tell people that he was tapping Thanet's office. Isn't that nice? It's a pity he wasn't, but I suppose you can't have everything."

Flavia had assumed that the meatballs Detective Morelli had invited them to eat would be prepared by his wife. She was wrong. Morelli was proud of his meatballs. They found him in the kitchen with a pinny around his middle, though the air of domesticity would have been enhanced had he taken his gun off. A large bottle of Californian Chianti was on the kitchen table, the pasta was ready to go into the water, and the tomato sauce was approaching that pitch of absolute perfection which only true Italians can recognise.

"What you think?" he said, caressing his creations with

a wooden spoon as though they were made of finest gold. Argyll poked his nose into the pot, gave a long sniff and nodded appreciatively. Morelli grunted and poured the wine. They settled down; the wine, the smell of cooking, the noise of the children, and the informality all combined to produce an atmosphere of easy relaxation. The only difficulty—for Argyll, if not Flavia—was in eating the vast portions that Morelli poured on to the plates. But after two years in Italy he was getting better at that, and knew how to prepare himself mentally before settling down to a long haul.

"So what did you two do while I was plugging through my paperwork? Find your bust?"

Flavia provided a succinct summary of Langton's remarks, which brought a frown from Morelli.

"He's changed. He never said anything about di Souza supplying that bust before. Why not?"

"He's shedding his defences. The first line was that everything was legal and any impropriety was due to this anonymous seller. That was obviously nonsense, so now he's blaming di Souza—who can't answer back. The trouble is, it's much more difficult to disprove. Might even be true, for all I know. But I'm not inclined to trust him all that much. Jonathan here thinks he's putting a cloth in our eye."

"What?"

"That's it, isn't it?" she asked, slightly hurt and turning to Argyll for reassurance.

"Close, but not quite. Pulling the wool over our eyes."

"Ah," she said, repeating it a couple of times to lodge it in her memory. "Right. Anyway, that's what he thinks."

"So what about this bust?"

"It exists, was owned by di Souza in the 1950s, was sold to Moresby, was confiscated before it reached him, and then was stolen from Alberghi's house a few weeks back."

"And turned up here?"

She nodded. "A pretty convincing provenance, if you think about it, if a little unorthodox. The more we look, the more genuine it gets."

Morelli chased the last trace of tomato sauce round the plate with a piece of bread, popped it into his mouth and chewed thoughtfully.

"Have you asked the customs people at the airport if they examined the thing?" Argyll asked.

" 'Course we have. And no they didn't. No reason to. The Moresby is perfectly respectable; the case was sealed so tight that it would have taken ages to unpack. It was built like a tank; weighed in at around a hundredweight and it was all they could do to move it, let alone unpack and examine it. They reckon they're overworked and understaffed. All they did was check the paperwork."

"So, the story seems to be that di Souza goes over to the office with Moresby. They inspect the bust, and for some reason or other the Spaniard leaves with it, and prepares to go straight back to Italy. Not a theft, obviously, as it must have been done with Moresby's approval, as he wasn't dead then. Why could that have happened? No matter. Barclay goes over after di Souza leaves. Argument with Moresby, pop. He comes out, raises the alarm."

They refilled the glasses and thought about that for a while, realising this was a seriously flawed explanation.

So Morelli turned to his wife, Giulia, sitting placidly by his side, saying nothing but looking a little contemptuous of their mental meanderings. He always turned to her when there was a problem. She was so much better at them than he was.

"It's obvious," she said calmly as she gathered the plates and took them over to the sink. "Your Spaniard didn't take it. The bust had already been stolen. If it was so heavy and there was no time to take it out after Moresby and di Souza went over to look at it, it must have been taken before."

Well, of course. Silly of them not to have thought of it themselves. Unfortunately, there Giulia Morelli's inspiration dried up. As she pointed out, she hardly knew all the details; so they were once more thrown back on their own, inferior, intellectual resources.

"Can't you swear her in as a deputy, or something?" Argyll asked. "You do that here, don't you?"

"Nah," he said. "That went out with Jesse James. Besides, the police committee would start an inquiry if I gave my own wife a job. We're on our own."

"Pity. We'll have to do some work ourselves. This pâté sandwich. When was it stuck over the lens of the security camera?"

"The camera picture stopped at about 8.30."

"Can we assume that was when the bust was stolen?" Flavia persisted.

"We can assume it. But we can't prove it."

"What about the gun used to kill him? No fingerprints?"

"As you'd expect, wiped clean. No hint of anything on it at all. But bought and registered to Anne Moresby."

"And still no witnesses to anything at all?"

"No. Not that anyone is saying, anyway. But the way that all of them are manoeuvring and playing little games with each other, they may be just too busy to tell us everything they know."

With all the sense of achievement of someone reaching the top of Everest, Argyll stuffed the last fragment of meatball in, swallowed and considered the state of his stomach a while.

"There is, of course, the problem of the date," he said, uncertain whether this little detail was going to win an appreciative audience.

"What date?"

"The date Mrs. Moresby said she heard her husband and Langton talking about the bust. A couple of months back, she said."

"So?"

"According to my calculations, if Langton saw it for the first time at di Souza's, as he said, that was a couple of days after the robbery at the Alberghi's."

"So?"

"That's only about four weeks ago. I think someone's fibbing."

CHAPTER 12

By Monday morning, Joe Morelli was more and more convinced that he had been wrong not to arrest David Barclay and Anne Moresby. After all, everything pointed in their direction. Motive there was aplenty; adultery, divorce and several billion dollars was sufficient reason for anyone to lose control of themselves, as far as he was concerned. Opportunity again was there, and the whole operation became practical once his wife had pointed out that there was no reason why the bust should not have been stolen an hour or so before the murder. The alibi of everybody else seemed to be moderately adequate. And besides, everybody else needed Moresby alive; at least for another twenty-four hours in Thanet's case, and indefinitely in the son's case.

However, there were little problems still. Flavia, who dropped into headquarters to fax a report to her boss, wanted a better explanation for the murder of di Souza before all her reservations could be laid to rest. And she still wanted to know where the bust was.

He looked at her impatiently. "Listen, I know you're sore about the Bernini. But this is pretty unshakeable. Moresby was alive just as Barclay was leaving to go and see him. He was dead less than five minutes later. Everything fits. What more do you want?"

"Completion, that's all. Just a feeling in my bones that everything is explained."

"Nothing is ever completely explained," he said. "And in my experience it's rare we get this far. I'm surprised you're not satisfied with what we've achieved."

And so she should be, Flavia told herself as she wandered off to the museum to find Argyll once more. He had vanished earlier on, to take care of business in the museum. By common consent—mainly due to the lack of anyone else willing to take on the grisly task—he had been appointed impromptu executor to Hector di Souza, in charge of taking the man's body back to Italy and, in a regrettable piece of meanness on the museum's part, also delegated to remove his three boxes of sculpture.

She tracked him down eventually in the storeroom under the building, rummaging around in the boxes.

"I've got a good mind to leave everything here," he said. "The cost of transporting it all is going to be enormous. I don't want to be mean about poor Hector, but taking care of him is going to use up a lot of my commission for selling that Titian. Which makes it even more difficult to stay on in Rome."

"You could always have di Souza buried here."

He groaned with dismay at the fastidiousness of his conscience. "Don't think I haven't considered it. But Hector would haunt me for ever. Oh, well. Do you think

I could commandeer this box?" He gestured at a particularly large crate. "It's empty."

She looked at it. "You can't move corpses in packing cases," she said, slightly shocked.

"It's not for Hector, it's for his carvings. The museum's decided they don't want them. Thanet said Langton should never have bought them. Junk, in his opinion."

He held up a lump of arm and showed it to her. "Frankly, he's right. Surprises me that they ever considered them."

"Me, too. And your Titian."

"Nothing wrong with that," he said defensively.

"Except that it's the only piece of Venetian painting in the place. It doesn't fit with the collection at all."

Argyll grumbled away for a few moments about what a good picture it was, then changed the subject. "So, what do you think? About this case?"

"Don't see why not. Unless it's used for something."

She bent down to examine a piece of paper encased in plastic stapled to the side. "It's the case the Bernini came in," she observed. "You can't just take it. We'll have to check with the police to make sure it's not needed for something."

Argyll looked around to see if there was anything else suitable for the task; apart from a few woefully inadequate cardboard boxes, the room was virtually empty.

"It's going to be one of those days," he said. Then he came over and peered once more into the box. "And it's perfect, as well. Just the right size, enormously strong and even got lots of padding in it, all ready."

He stood back. "I don't see why we can't use it. I mean, if it was vital evidence the police would have taken it, wouldn't they?" Then he made up his mind. "Come on, give me a hand."

He grabbed the packing case by the top and pulled. "Jesus, this is heavy. Push. Come on. Harder."

Straining away on all three legs, between them they shifted the wooden box about ten feet across the concrete floor of the storeroom to di Souza's statuary. Argyll liked to think that, fully functional, he could have done it himself. But it was still absurdly well built, even by the Moresby's standards.

Puffing and blowing, they leant back on it to recover themselves.

"Are you sure this is a good idea?" Flavia asked anxiously. "It's going to cost a small fortune just to shift the crate back to Italy. It's ridiculously heavy."

"They're like that here," he said. "Don't believe in taking risks. Everything is packed, repacked and double packed. You should have felt the weight of the box they put my little Titian in at the airport. Better take the Bernini label off, in case people get confused."

He reached down and pulled off the old shipment label, scrumpled it up and tossed it into the corner.

Flavia wandered over, retrieved the sheet of paper he had so carelessly thrown away, and carefully flattened it out again.

"Jonathan?" she said.

"What?"

"How heavy do you think this thing is?"

"Search me. About five tons?"

"Seriously."

"Don't know. Over a hundredweight? Something like that."

"And how much do you reckon the bust weighs?"

Argyll shrugged. "Seventy pounds? Maybe more."

"But this shipping label records the case's weight as 120 pounds. So what does it mean if the box weighs the same now as when it came through customs with a Bernini in it?"

"Um."

"It means that the bust wasn't stolen from Thanet's office at all. Which, of course, means that . . ."

"What?"

"It means that you're going to have to find another box to ship di Souza's statues in. And Mr. Langton has got some explaining to do."

The last person she had to see was David Barclay, whom she tracked down in his office high in the skies over the city. Awfully chic—thick pile carpet and secretaries and high-technology bits all over the place. All in white again; strange how the local population didn't seem to like colour in their rooms.

Flavia tried hard to remember that personal antipathy did not, in law, constitute grounds for conviction. But Barclay was not her sort. Something about the hair, and her strong suspicion that his character and opinions had been so carefully groomed over the years that they had almost ceased to exist, made her dislike the man. Blandness, as universally acceptable as his white sofa, carefully adopted to offend no one.

Not that spending a fortune on clothes and haircuts and shoes and little gold knickknacks offended her; she was Italian, after all. But Italian men were more open about being incurably vain; delighted in it, in fact. They dressed to impress themselves, often succeeded and didn't really care what other people thought. But any vanity in Barclay was a secondary matter; he constructed himself to impress others; there was nothing of him on show at all.

Questioning him was difficult. The best way of loosening him up would have been to inform him that, all things considered, he was lucky he wasn't already in jail. But this strictly wasn't her business, and she was a touch nervous about saying the wrong thing. Other people's legalisms are often very difficult to understand. So she started off with generalities, asking for his opinion about the murder.

"Can't help. Even in abstract I can't think of any reason to kill Moresby."

It was extraordinary how obtuse people were about their own advantage, she thought. Anne Moresby was inheriting billions; he might well share in it, Langton was after Thanet's job, Thanet was gunning for Streeter, Moresby junior was resentful about being penniless, they were all neurotic about what the old man was about to do with his money, and this lawyer couldn't think of any reason for what had been going on. Extraordinary.

"As far as the bust is concerned, all I know is that I authorised the transfer of money to an account in Switzerland to pay for it."

"You took no part in the acquisition process?"

"Apart from that, no. The first I heard about it was when I got a call from Moresby telling me to rustle up the money. Buying art is not my business. Paying for it is. Was, rather."

"And there was nothing unusual about it? Nothing in the process that struck you as odd?"

"Not at all."

"So you transferred two million dollars on the day the bust was stolen? Or was it four? People seem oddly hazy about this."

Barclay hesitated. Flavia caught the change in mood and wondered about it. It was, after all, merely a routine question; hardly a penetrating thrust to the heart of the matter. A random sentence designed merely to give her time to think up the next line of enquiry. So she couldn't really take any credit at all for the result.

Which was that, coming at a moment when Barclay was feeling more than a little alarmed at his prospects, the enquiry made him take a leap and open up about a little matter which, he considered, could make him look very bad indeed should he ever be hauled into court. Much better to mention it now; try it out on someone unofficial and see what the result was.

"I wondered when you'd find out," he said.

"Hmm," she replied, not being able to think of anything better.

"It was both, of course."

"Pardon?"

"Both."

It meant nothing at all to Flavia, but the grave and confiding look on Barclay's face clearly indicated that he regarded the matter as being of some significance. So she nodded in the way you do when you want to suggest that the anomaly was just the little detail that you'd been expecting to find.

"I see," she said slowly. "I see."

Barclay was reassured that she dealt with the revelation in such a matter-of-fact way. Leaning back in his chair and looking at the ceiling, he elaborated on the theme, while Flavia tried to work out what on earth he was talking about.

"It's been going on for years," he said. "I should never have agreed; but Moresby was a man you did not say no to. Now I imagine it's only a matter of time before someone starts going through columns of numbers and totting up figures and finding my name on every authorisation. And Thanet's of course."

"Thanet?"

"Of course. Couldn't have worked without him. He had to provide the valuations, saying these things were worth the amount Moresby wanted to claim. At the start I think he took it on trust, same as I did. Moresby would say he'd paid a certain amount, and Thanet would say Moresby had donated a piece *worth* that amount. I don't suppose it ever crossed his mind there was anything wrong. Nor did I; I just did as I was told.

"Of course, Thanet reckoned the old man was paying far too much, but that was his prerogative. Then he mentioned to me that those crooked Europeans were taking him for a ride, and I looked around. By that time it was too late. We could imagine all too easily an IRS inspector staring at us: 'Mr. Moresby has been consistently evading taxes for years by claiming to pay three or four times what he in fact paid, and you expect us to believe you knew nothing about it?'

"Of course they would never have believed it. Both of us were naïve, and then both of us, I guess, were too concerned about keeping our jobs. So I transferred money and hid it all over the place, and Thanet kept on making our fraudulent assessments of value for presentation to the taxmen."

Flavia had at last caught up with him. But just to make sure, she said: "So you transferred four million to Europe. Two million of that went to pay for the bust itself, and the other two is still in a Moresby account somewhere?"

Barclay nodded. "That's right. From there on, the process would have been the same. Moresby would have presented a bill saying the bust cost four million, Thanet would have said it was worth four million, and I would have filled out Moresby's tax form to that effect claiming an income tax deduction. The result would be that he got the bust almost free."

"But where did the two million which paid for the bust go?"

"Automatic transfer to the owner from the Moresby account in Switzerland."

"Yes, but who? Tell me, is there any chance that the money went into Langton's bank account?"

He shook his head with a quiet smile. "Oh, no. One thing about Mr. Moresby, he was not the trusting type. Not where the art world was concerned. He always kept tabs on his employees. I've been checking; the money did not go to Langton. And the police tell me it didn't go to di Souza either."

Nor to anyone else, as far as Flavia could make out. How strange. "Tell me, all this was just a bit illegal, wasn't it?"

Barclay nodded. "You could say that."

"And the total saved in this fashion?"

"I added it all up this morning. Spent about forty-nine million, claimed eighty-seven million. Working it out exactly is hard, but at a rough guess I reckon he avoided tax of about fifteen million dollars."

"And that's what? Over the last five years or so?"

Barclay looked at her in faint surprise. "Oh no. The last eighteen months. Of course, the outlay began to go up fast once he began to warm to the idea of the Big Museum."

Even at the uninflated prices it was pretty impressive stuff; certainly more than any museum in the Italian system ever got. Barclay, however, was more concerned with other matters.

"Pulling a fast one on the IRS . . . Well, I mean, they're vengeful. I'd rather upset the Mob, myself. Only real brutes work as IRS investigators."

He gave an involuntary shudder, and Flavia considered what he had said. "Who knew of this? Presumably it was the sort of thing that was kept relatively quiet?"

He nodded. "Oh yes. I imagine quite a lot of people suspected—Anne Moresby certainly did; she even asked me to pass on material to incriminate Thanet. Of course I refused, because it would have incriminated myself as well, but she seemed to get hold of material anyway. I don't know how. Langton may well have had a notion of what was going on. But I think probably only Thanet, myself and Moresby knew precisely. That's why there was such a fuss over Collins."

"Who?"

"A curator that Langton brought in. He mentioned he was a bit doubtful over a Hals that Moresby bought. There was a bit of alarm that there'd be an investigation and the real worth—and the real price—of the picture would emerge. So he was got rid of, pronto. Thanet came up with some reason for accusing him of incompetence and he was out. There was a hell of a fight about it in the museum; it brought out the long-standing enmity between Thanet and Langton a bit too clearly for comfort."

Flavia nodded again. Another complication. Moresby in the centre of things, as a sort of hole in the middle. She realised suddenly that she knew nothing about the man at all. Many opinions, all of them unfavourable, but no real sense of what made him tick. Why, for example, did a man worth so much work so hard to cheat the tax man out of so little? Relatively speaking, anyway.

Barclay, who she was coming to think of as not nearly as facile as initial impressions suggested, scratched his chin and tried to think of an explanation.

"Just the way he was, I guess. He was a miser. Not in the classic sense of living in a slum and hiding it under the mattress, but a psychological miser. He knew the value of money and would do anything to hang on to what he considered was his. It was a religion. He would work as hard to save one dollar as a million. Or a billion. The sum wasn't important; the principle was the thing. He was a man of principle. Anyone who took his money was an enemy, and he'd do anything to stop them. And that included all taxmen.

"That doesn't imply he was mean; he wasn't. When he wanted to be he could be very generous. As long as he decided. Not someone else. Does that sound convincing?"

She supposed so. But having never met anyone like that she'd have to take it on trust.

"Was he a vengeful man?"

"In what sense?"

"I mean, if someone wronged him, in his eyes. Did he bear a grudge?"

Barclay threw back his head and laughed. "Did he bear a grudge? Ha! Yes, I think you could say that. Indeed. If someone trod on his toe Moresby would follow him to the end of the world to get his revenge."

"For forty years?"

"Into the next world and the one after that, if necessary."

"So," she said, finally manoeuvring for the kill, "anyone having an affair with his wife might kill him first, if he found out. For fear of the consequences."

That stopped the lawyer in his tracks. His mouth opened wide and shut again, and then he whistled softly. "Well, I'll be."

And stopped. Despite the risk of losing the psychological advantage here, Flavia could not help herself. She held up her hand.

"You'll be what?" she asked.

"Pardon?"

"You said 'I'll be,' and then stopped," she prompted.

Barclay frowned, and then grasped what she was talking about. There followed a brief interlude as he explained the meaning of the phrase. Flavia noted it down.

Then she decided it was time to go. Only her little message to deliver. She merely hoped she could make it sound convincing enough.

"Fortunately the case is nearly closed, so I'll be able to get back home in a day or so. Pleasant though it is here, I'm looking forward to getting back to Italy," she said in what she hoped was a cheerfully inconsequential fashion.

Barclay eyed her suspiciously. "What do you mean?"

"The murder. It was all taped."

"I thought all the cameras were out?"

"They were. But Streeter had also installed a bug in Thanet's office. He was another one who suspected that there was something fishy about the financial dealings in that museum. He reckons it probably taped the whole thing. You know, someone saying, 'Die, Moresby!' followed by a clump. He's going to hand it over to the police at his house this evening."

CHAPTER 13

Argyll, having slightly pulled a muscle in his one remaining leg, had decided not to accompany Flavia on her little trip to Barclay's office. Instead he'd stayed in his hotel, resting his plaster cast and watching the television in the morning; he rather enjoyed it, although the choice of fare was a little meagre.

So meagre, in fact that he eventually settled on a long sermon from what appeared to be a fundamentalist preacher intoning about sin and money; the general line being that you could cancel out the former by giving him the latter. Engrossing stuff; he'd never seen the like before, and was almost annoyed when a knock on the door distracted his attention.

"Come in," he called. "Oh, hello, there," he went on as Jack Moresby stuck his head round the door. "How nice to see you."

Moresby grinned sheepishly as he came into the room. "How ya doin'?" he asked. "I heard you'd taken a tumble."

He peered at Argyll's leg and tapped it. "Only one? Pretty lucky, from what I heard."

"Better luck next time, I suppose."

"What does that mean?"

"Eh? Nothing. It was lucky. I can't say I'm that happy about it, mind."

Moresby nodded. "Hmm. Still, you're still here, that's the important thing. Just thought I'd check."

"That's very good of you. Get yourself a drink, if you want."

"How's the great search coming along?" Moresby grabbed a beer and sat down.

"For the bust?"

"I was more concerned about my father's murderer."

"Oh. Yes. Well, I suppose you would be. The answer to both is the same, though. Something is coming together."

"And who's the front runner?"

"Your stepmother and Barclay. I suppose that comes as no surprise to you."

Moresby digested this along with the beer and nodded sagely. "I wondered. I did wonder. Seems a wild gamble to take on."

"Lot of money. People have done more for less."

"But she would have been so rich even if he'd gone ahead with the bigger museum."

"Not if she'd been divorced for adultery. And you're likely to be a witness for that."

"She been asked about that?"

Argyll nodded. "She denies it. But Morelli's lot have been digging away. There's considerable evidence she's having an affair. His little posse of searchers has tracked her going away for weekends, staying in hotels with someone else under assumed names. But how did *you* find out?"

"Easy to work out. She's the sort, it was obvious she was having an affair, and her servant at the beach house hinted at it. And I heard she was remarkably well informed about the workings of the museum. My father never told her anything, so it had to be Barclay. Add it all up . . ."

"Ah. I see."

"And it won't be just my word against hers?"

"Seems not."

"Doesn't look good for her, then?"

"No. But there's nothing solid enough, I gather. I don't know what the rules and regulations are here, but Morelli seems to want something unchallengeable. Reckons he'll soon have it, too."

Moresby's interest brightened. "Oh? How's that?"

"Streeter is telling everybody he has just recovered a tape. From a bug hidden in Thanet's office."

"Oh yeah? And has he?"

Argyll smirked significantly. "OK, so it's not such a good story. But we think it might smoke out the murderer, if you see what I mean."

"The tape, or the news of it?"

"There's going to be a little gathering *chez* Streeter, this evening. At about nine," he said, ignoring the remark. "To listen to the tape he's got there."

Moresby nodded thoughtfully and stood up. "Hey," he said quietly. "I brought you a little present."

Argyll loved presents; always had. It was almost worth getting sick for. He had the fondest memory of measles and mumps and all those childhood diseases. He was halfway through thanking his visitor when there was another knock on the door.

"Oh, hell," he said. "Come in, then."

A mousy grey little man came in and nodded nervously. "Mr. Argyll, sir? Perhaps you don't remember me?"

He walked towards the bed, holding out a card.

"Well, I'd better leave you," said Moresby reluctantly, downing the last of his beer in one great swig.

"You don't have to go. Wait a bit."

"No, it's OK. See you."

And he left, quite abruptly. Argyll turned his attention to the stranger standing expectantly before him. He was a little annoyed. Moresby had forgotten to give him his present.

"My name's Ansty, sir," the man said, sitting himself down. "We met at the hospital."

Argyll looked at him blankly, then consulted the visiting card. Josiah Ansty, attorney-at-law. Then he remembered.

"Oh, right. You're the one who got into a fight with the car rental man."

Ansty nodded. "Pig," he said. "Aggressive pig. He attacked me."

"Well, anyway. What can I do for you?"

"It's more what I can do for you. I gather that you have several legal problems hanging over your head . . ."

"No, I don't."

"Oh, but you must."

"I don't. And if any turn up, I shall get on the plane

and go back to Italy. If anyone wants to sue me, they'll have to find me first."

Ansty looked properly shocked at this cavalier approach to the law. How was a man expected to earn a living with clients like that?

"How did you find me, anyway?" Argyll went on. "I never called you."

"Well, I happened to be listening to the police broadcasts when the first report of your accident came in. And the hospital gave me your address. So I thought . . ."

"You're a bit of a ghoul, aren't you? Is this how you find all your clients?"

"Some of them. It's no good waiting for people to come to you these days. You've got to get out there. So many people could launch suits, but don't even think of it."

"Well, I have, and I still don't want to. Go away."

"Surely . . ."

"No."

"But the car maintenance . . ."

"It had nothing to do with maintenance. Someone loosened the brake cable. It was attempted murder. Not an accident."

Ansty looked grieved as he saw a lucrative piece of business slipping away forever.

"Still," he said, clutching at straws, "you could always add a civil suit for damages, parallel to any criminal charges."

"There's no one been arrested, yet," Argyll pointed out. "Who am I meant to sue? Besides, the car rental place says the insurance is perfectly adequate. And I don't want to sue anybody. Not even Anne Moresby; assuming that she was behind it all."

"Is that what the police think?"

"It seems to be their current theory, yes."

"In that case, sir, as a professional I must advise you to start drawing up a suit against her immediately. Otherwise the opportunity will be lost."

"What *are* you talking about?"

"If I remember correctly, Mrs. Moresby has no personal money of her own; I remember the stories in the papers when they got married. She comes from a modest family. Any money she has will come from her husband's estate."

He looked up at Argyll who was gazing at him with an exasperated expression on his face, evidently not grasping the point he was driving at. This, Ansty told himself, is why people need lawyers. Sooner or later, professional expertise shows its true worth. And this was a classic example.

"Is that not true, sir?"

Argyll shook his head. "Probably. For all I know. So what?"

"In that case the chances of you winning any damages will be slight unless you launch a suit against her prior to charges being preferred."

"I'm not with you."

The lawyer laid it out, logical step by logical step, as though instructing an infant; or at the very least a first-year student in law school.

"I assume that the prosecution case will be to argue that she killed Moresby . . ."

"She didn't. Conspiracy to commit, or some such. But let it pass."

". . . That she was involved in the murder of Moresby," he said pedantically, "to gain control of his fortune. If convicted she will automatically be debarred from inheriting his estate under the law that criminals cannot benefit from their crimes. I can quote you . . ."

"Please don't bother," Argyll said. "I'm still not interested in suing anyone."

He leant back on his pillow and thought about it all, though. And suddenly had a very nasty idea. So unpleasant, in fact, that he broke out in a cold sweat merely thinking about it. If something he was supposed to know was putting a gigantic inheritance like that at risk, he could see the urgency of getting rid of him. Didn't help him work out what it was he'd heard or seen, but still . . .

"Hold on, there," he said. "Tell me, are you busy today?"

Ansty looked at him sadly as he prepared to go, and in a sudden fit of honesty confessed that he hadn't been busy for several weeks. No cases and no clients at all, at this precise moment in time.

"Good," said Argyll. "I want you to stay here with me. Just hang around for a few hours, will you? We can have lunch sent up, if you want."

Ansty settled himself down again. "That's very hospitable of you," he said. "I'd be delighted."

"I've never seen anyone eat so much in my life," he complained four hours later when Flavia finally returned in the company of Morelli. "The man was a walking food processor. Even you don't eat that much."

Argyll's temper was a little frayed. Putting up with the lawyer had been a sore trial, and the fact that it had been necessary didn't ease the pain at all. Had he known that Flavia was going to be such a long time, or that Ansty had such an appetite, he might have simply taken the risk.

Still, he couldn't really grumble, as he had not told the man why he so suddenly desired his company. And the latter part hadn't been so bad; sitting on the bed, drinking beer and having the rules of baseball explained was not such a bad way of passing the time. He'd never realised it was so complicated. Fascinating, really. He just couldn't understand why the players dressed in their underclothes, and Ansty was unable to enlighten him.

So when Flavia and Morelli arrived, they found Argyll and this middle-aged man in a grey suit sitting on the bed, laughing uproariously at a badly timed spitball (when tackled about this, Argyll had to confess he could not for the life of him remember what a spitball was, nor could he differentiate between a well-timed and a badly timed one) the room littered with empty cans of beer and plates, the curtains tightly drawn.

"No joke," he said as he finished explaining. "I've had the most awful day. The trouble was, I couldn't decide whether it was simple paranoia or not. But with murderers wandering around at will, it struck me that I was an easy target, if anyone had thoughts in that direction. I still don't know why they might, but the evidence seems to point that way. Of course, had I known you were with Barclay all the time, I would have been less concerned about the possibility of him leaping through the door, gun in hand."

"Well, it's best to be certain about these things."

"And we'll look after everything from now on," Morelli said, with a little frown of anxiety. "The trouble is, it doesn't really take our case any further. Evidence is evidence, and we still don't have it."

"So you'll have to pin your hopes on this meeting, won't you? Have you seen everybody?"

Morelli nodded. "They've all been told, as subtly as we could manage. Streeter will be working late, so he won't get back home till just before nine. We've been saying the tape is stored in his house. Very tempting."

Argyll grinned. "Good," he said. "I suppose you ought to have something to eat before we go. More sandwiches? Then we can go and lay the phantom bust."

Morelli looked puzzled. "What do you mean?" he asked.

"Didn't you tell him?"

Flavia looked sheepish. "Sorry. I forgot. We've worked it all out, you see. I hope you don't mind."

Morelli had the air of someone who did mind very much, and suggested that, seeing that this was Los Angeles and he was in the Los Angeles police and they were little more than tourists here on sufferance, perhaps they would try to keep him better informed.

"I did mean to tell you. But I only put the last few pieces together when I saw Barclay . . ."

"And?" Morelli prompted.

"Langton," she said firmly. "It's obvious. That's because of the case, you see. It was empty."

"Empty?" Morelli said, thinking he was spending much too much time uttering one-word questions.

"Empty. It's in the basement of the museum. Weighs 120 pounds. Which is what the shipment label said it weighed when it contained the Bernini. Conclusion, it was always empty. There was no theft from Thanet's office. No bust was smuggled out of the country and, whatever was stolen from Alberghi's place in Bracciano, the haul did not include a bust of Pope Pius V by Bernini. In fact, I'm beginning to doubt Alberghi ever had it."

"So what in God's name was all this about? Just a way of confusing us? If it was, it worked very well."

"For that we'll have to ask Langton. All I know is that the whole thing was a fraud, and Langton was the only possible person who could have done it. D'you want to hear the reasoning?"

Another tray of sandwiches and beer arrived, which delayed her satisfying their curiosity for a few moments. Then, when the delivery boy had vanished and she had downed a pastrami sandwich, she recommenced.

"There were three characteristics to Moresby which made him a target in this. One, he was a collectomaniac, if that's the right word. Two, he did not like anyone getting the better of him, and three, he disliked paying taxes."

"Everybody dislikes paying taxes," Morelli put in, speaking from the heart.

"Anyway, in 1951 he bought a bust on the Italian black market from Hector di Souza. Paid a deposit, and that was that. It was never delivered. We know it was confiscated, maybe di Souza even told him that as well, but I doubt very much he believed it. After all, it was never heard of again; had it been taken into the Borghese collection it would have been easy to find out. He couldn't do anything about it without letting everyone know he was conspiring to smuggle works out of the country, so he had to forget about it.

"After that, Moresby was a little cautious about dealers, which is only sensible. Anyway, the next stage was the Frans Hals affair."

Morelli frowned. Must have missed that; at least, he couldn't remember interviewing this Hals man.

"Everybody knew there was something wrong with the painting, but only one person, a junior curator called Collins, had the temerity to say so. He suggested it be investigated with more care, and implied that the price had been far too high. Uproar. The curator is out on his ear.

"If you think about it, this was very curious. On the whole—the Moresby may be an exception but I don't think so—museums don't like owning fakes. If anyone can prove an acquisition is a bit dicey, they should get a pat on the back. The curator in question was an expert on seventeenth-century Dutch painting. And, of course, he was a protégé of Langton's.

"That the picture is a dud I don't doubt for a minute. That the whole business was an early attempt to nobble Thanet seems equally likely."

Morelli, who'd been staring at the ceiling, nodding to himself and wondering whether she was ever going to produce any evidence, stirred into activity. "How do you reach that conclusion?" he said as he leant forward, surveyed the sandwiches and selected another beer.

"It was not bought by Langton, so exposing it wouldn't hurt him. It would hurt Thanet, who OKed it, Barclay who paid out the money, and in turn could well lead to an investigation of Moresby himself. A full investigation would have revealed that, while the picture only cost

200,000 dollars, Moresby claimed on his tax form that he paid 3.2 million. Barclay gave me the figures. Further investigation would undoubtedly have shown up that over the years millions of dollars had been saved in taxes by the process. Moresby would have been in deep trouble and could only have got out of it by blaming Thanet and Barclay. Overzealous servants. You know the routine."

"Didn't work, though," Morelli pointed out.

"No. Thanet acted with more determination than anyone thought possible and booted the curator out fast. So Langton tries again. Collins ends up as an intern at the Borghese and uncovers this document about the Bernini. Cogs click over. Langton has heard the story many times about Moresby being defrauded of a Bernini. It can't be hard for him to work out that Moresby might be very pleased indeed if he got hold of it.

"There are difficulties, not least the problem of getting hold of it and getting it out of the country. They decided on di Souza as the poor unfortunate who will have to take any blame for smuggling, so that the museum will be in the clear. That will satisfy Moresby's desire for vengeance and add to his temptation to get hold of the bust.

"So Langton goes to Bracciano to enquire but is thrown out. Collins tells him that old Alberghi has recently died, he phones Colonel Alberghi and finds out that no one has the faintest idea what is in the house. So Langton knows that if there is a Bernini there, he is the only person who is aware of the fact. So there is a robbery to get hold of it, and this comes up with nothing. No Bernini. A bit of a snag.

"But Langton isn't the sort of person to let a minor

detail like this get in his way. He realises that if he came to the conclusion that there was a Bernini there, then so would anybody else. Langton hooks di Souza by buying some of his antiquities and then paying him to transport the case across the Atlantic; money is transferred under the normal scheme, with two million dollars, I suspect, making an unscheduled stop in Collins' bank account until it can be made to disappear properly.

"Langton is close not only to defrauding Moresby of a large amount of money, but also to gaining his thanks into the bargain and to ousting Thanet. The snag is to make sure that no one looks into the case. Having brought stuff for the museum before, he can be fairly certain the customs won't waste too much time over it. But just to be on the safe side, he delays picking the case up until he hears that Moresby is coming for his unscheduled visit. It was he, after all, who arranged for the case to be put in Thanet's office, partly opened, and suggested that there was no time to examine it. Then all he had to do was stick a sandwich over the camera lens and wait for everyone to start leaping to conclusions."

Morelli wrinkled his nose with dissatisfaction. "He didn't really expect anyone to believe that, did he?"

"But we did. The trick was to convince everyone that the bust was genuine after it supposedly vanished from Thanet's office. And for that he needed the active, if unknowing, collaboration of the Italian police. Me, in fact damn him. He knows we'll investigate the robbery at Bracciano, and all we need to do is link that theft and the Bernini. That link was provided by Jonathan Argyll, who immediately rang me up to rabbit on about smuggling in such a way that we were bound to look into it.

So I went to the Borghese and only an idiot could have missed the connection."

Argyll looked up at this, somewhat surprised to hear himself described as a virtual accomplice in wholesale fraud.

"Langton brought that Titian very late on, after he had set up di Souza. Then he insisted that Argyll come to Los Angeles. That Titian scarcely fitted in at all with the museum's collection. It stuck out like a sore finger . . ."

"Thumb."

"A sore thumb, amongst the other paintings in the building. If you assumed the museum had a coherent acquisitions policy, it made no sense at all. No more than the purchase of di Souza's sculpture made sense.

"It was bought simply to make sure Argyll was present when the issue of smuggling came up. His friendship with me and the art squad was no secret in the Italian art business, after all. The moment the bust vanished, Argyll rang me up, and I started following the trail so conveniently laid out for me."

Full of idioms, that spurt. Must be a mistake somewhere. She paused, and looked at Argyll inquiringly. He nodded approvingly.

"Langton's careful planning successfully created the illusion of a convincing provenance. Careful investigation would trace the bust to Alberghi, di Souza, the 1951 sale. And when added to the enthusiastic account of Alberghi in 1951, pretty convincing.

"The result was that a couple of days later, the polizia sent an urgent message attesting to the national significance of the bust, its undoubted authenticity, and demanding its return.

"What better way of convincing anyone that the theft had been real and the bust genuine than to have international warrants flying around wanting it back? From the start, the police were being manipulated to convince people that the bust was a lost masterpiece.

"The trouble is not that di Souza starts grumbling, but that he gets to talk to Moresby so quickly. He has told Jonathan that he can prove he didn't smuggle the bust out and presumably tells Moresby as well. Emergency action is called for. The rest is straightforward."

She looked up at them complacently, content that the whole thing was wrapped up barring an arrest. Morelli did not look as admiring as she'd expected; he was still concerned about evidence, and said as much.

"Oh, that," she said airily. "Simple enough; he's bound to turn up this evening at Streeter's. We just collar him then. Besides, I've rung Bottando; he's going to go round to the Borghese and nail Collins' head to the floor until he confesses."

"Talking of Mr. Langton," Argyll said. "I was thinking about those phone calls he made after the murder."

"Nothing fake there," Morelli said. "Both recipients confirm them, and Streeter's patent telephone tapping system also confirms the times and the numbers dialled."

Argyll looked disappointed, so Morelli moved to block off what seemed to be another trivial quibble from the other side of the Atlantic.

"Here," he said, opening up his briefcase and pulling out a sheaf of computer print-out. "Check for yourself, if you don't believe me."

Argyll took the proffered sheet of paper. "External PABX Utilisation," it was called. Who used the phone, in other words. And not greatly informative in the matter of these calls, either. 10.10 p.m., a phone call to a number identified as Jack Moresby's. 10.21 p.m., another to Anne Moresby from the same phone. All distressingly truthful. He sighed.

"Oh, well. Just an idea. What's this, by the way?"

With his finger, he indicated the previous line on the print-out, a record of a call to the same phone, timed at 9.58 p.m.

"That's the call from old man Moresby," Morelli said after he'd looked at it briefly. "The one that summoned Barclay over. It checks out."

Argyll scratched his head, then re-examined the sheet. "Hang on a second," he said. "Are you sure?"

"Oh, yes. We've got it on video."

"I know that. But, unless I'm mistaken, this came from outside."

"So?"

"An external call."

Morelli looked at him enquiringly.

"Aren't all the museum's phones linked up to an internal network? I mean, a hi-tech, go-ahead place like this . . ."

Morelli seemed decidedly upset. "Of course they are," he said thoughtfully. "Offices as well. Thanet's office phone too. And this was external. Damnation . . ."

Argyll smiled. "Another good reason for going over to Streeter's. Come on."

CHAPTER 14

The trouble with Robert Streeter's house was that it was so open, light and airy. The sort of residence that makes real-estate agents and potential homeowners lick their chops with excitement can be profoundly annoying to policemen eager to go about their business with discretion. Joe Morelli had not seen the house before, and was profoundly disappointed.

"Couldn't you have chosen somewhere better than this?" he asked, rubbing his gun with annoyance. Damn thing was getting worse. Much worse. Tomorrow, he'd do something about it. "This is a nightmare. It's much too exposed. I can't even park my car in the street without risking someone noticing it."

He puffed up his cheeks and let the air out slowly as he thought how to proceed. "Tell you what. I'll go and leave it in the next block. You go and wait in the house, I'll be with you in a few minutes. All the backups will have to make themselves scarce as well. Damnation."

He walked back to the car.

"It's amazing how comforting a policeman can be," Argyll said a few minutes later as they were settling down in the kitchen. "I feel quite nervous with him not here."

Flavia nodded. She also was feeling a bit nervous. This was, after all, potentially quite a dangerous business. While it was clearly the right way of proceeding, she had been loosely attached to the police for long enough to know that nothing ever goes to plan. There was no reason to think that the first basic rule of police work operated any differently in California than in Italy. Morelli could, and had, called on resources far beyond the capacity of her own department—as far as she could see he could rustle up almost anything from attack helicopters to anti-tank missiles, if needed. Nonetheless, she had a horrible feeling in the pit of her stomach . . .

"Do you think this is going to work?" he asked.

"It should do."

"You really reckon that he'll fall for this tape story? I don't know that I would. It seems so heavy-handed."

"It was your idea."

"I know. That doesn't mean I think it was a good idea, though."

Morelli came in; he didn't seem to be standing up to the strain quite so well either, all things considered. Bit strange, considering that he was meant to be used to this sort of caper. But there he was, sweating visibly, pale in the face. And trembling; visibly trembling.

"Are you all right?" Flavia asked, brow furrowed with sudden concern. The first basic law seemed about to swing into operation.

Morelli nodded. "Fine, fine," he muttered. "Just give me a minute."

He sat down uncertainly at the table, supporting himself by leaning on the table.

"You don't look well," Argyll observed.

Morelli looked up at Argyll, gave a sharp cry and sank to his knees. Both Europeans stood looking at him flabbergasted. Flavia bent down.

"I think it's his tooth," she said after listening to an incoherent mumble.

"Hurts, does it?"

Another mumble, longer this time.

"He says he's never felt anything like it before."

"Sharp, stabbing pain, a bit like having a red hot pin stuck in it?"

Morelli indicated this was about right.

Argyll nodded. "Abcess," he said firmly. "Very unpleasant. They sometimes do explode like that. Had one myself once. If it's bad it's a devil to sort out. Do you know, they often can't give you an injection? Just have to pull the nerve out straight. Use a little wire with hooks on."

Morelli gave an anguished cry and rocked back and forwards. Flavia suggested Argyll might keep the details to himself and, in the meantime, what were they going to do?

"I think he needs a dentist."

"But we're chasing a murderer. We can't stop to go to a bloody dentist."

"Painkillers, then. Strong ones, and lots of them. That might hold it. 'Course, he won't be at his perkiest."

Morelli mumbled. Between them, they grasped he was saying that his car had a first-aid kit in it. Police Department issue, complete with painkillers.

"That's simple, then," she said. "I'll go and get them."

"You're not going out there on your own."

"We can't leave him here. And he can't go."

"Take him with you, then."

"And leave you? Absolutely not."

"We can't all go. This is meant to be a covert entrapment—that was the term, wasn't it?—not a May Day parade."

She looked uncertain.

"Look, it's very simple," Argyll said firmly. "Go out the back, walk him to the car, leave him and come back. I will stay here, and if anything untoward happens I'll be out the door as fast as my crutches can carry me. And believe me, I can really move on these things now. It'll only take a few minutes."

Flavia was unconvinced, but could think of nothing better. Morelli's tooth had transformed him from a competent, reliable man into a quivering moaning wreck, more beast than human. On top of that, he was making quite a lot of noise.

"Oh, all right, then. But remember, no clever stuff."

"Don't be silly. Go on, go. We can't stand here all evening discussing it."

Between them they lifted Morelli up and pointed him out the back door. He seemed slightly better; it was the initial explosion of pain that had caught him unawares; now it had settled down into steady, consistent agony he could cope. As long as he wasn't required to do anything.

"Don't open the door while I'm gone," she said as they lumbered out.

"I won't," Argyll promised.

Courage is all very well, he thought, as he considered

his situation a few minutes later, but was this entirely wise? If he was honest with himself, he had to admit that he was only hanging about here to impress Flavia. And wasn't there a distinction to be drawn between the courageous and the merely foolhardy? If, for example, Morelli had thought of leaving his gun, that would have been different. Not that Argyll knew what to do with one, but he supposed he could blast away like anything if necessary.

But the point is, he reminded himself, Morelli *didn't* leave his gun. And Argyll wouldn't be much use even if something did happen. Not with only one leg operational.

And the conclusion of that, he thought as he headed for the door and reached for the handle, is that being there on his own was asking for trouble.

The door opened easily, in fact it opened faster than he pulled it. This was because, as he reached for the handle, so did someone else on the other side. As he turned the knob, so did someone else; and as he, on the inside, pulled the door open, someone else, on the outside, pushed.

Both were equally surprised when the manoeuvre was completed and each saw the other standing there.

In Argyll's case, instant automatic responses took over. Ever since he was tiny, people had instructed him in the virtues of politeness and hospitality.

"Gosh, hello. What a surprise. Come in, do. Make yourself at home."

Well, how else do you talk to your murderer?

Despite the first basic rule of police work, all could still have gone according to plan had not Morelli been forced to park his car in a different street, for the sake of discretion. The little area of houses was arranged in a grid; and a lot of people had more cars than there was space to garage them. A common problem; Rome is the same, if not worse. Morelli had only been able to find space for his vast machine some streets away and it took several minutes to walk back to it. Once they arrived, he slumped in the front seat and Flavia began rummaging through his first-aid kit.

"I'm still not happy about leaving Jonathan on his own, you know," she said as she tossed a packet of band aids on to the floor. "He'll probably electrocute himself making tea. He does have a knack of getting himself into trouble. How about this?"

She held up a tube. Morelli looked at it and shook his head. Useless. Like using a peashooter on a battleship.

She searched again. "I mean, just think. Accidents, attempted murder. Can't even cross the road without being run over by purple trucks. This?" she asked.

"No good either," Morelli said indistinctly. "What do you mean, purple truck? Who said that?"

"He told you, didn't he? It'll have to be this then," she went on, holding up a small syringe with a slightly sadistic glint in her eye. "A bit strong but all there is. Open up."

"Not the colour," Morelli said. "No one mentioned the colour. Ever. Not to me."

"Well, so what?"

"So," he replied, concentrating hard so the words came out comprehensibly. "There was a purple truck behind us for a while as we drove here. I didn't think anything of it. And it's parked in the next street down."

She stared blankly at him, syringe in hand.

"Oh, my God," she said.

"And, what's more, if you'll get the registration number and hand me that file on the back seat, I think I can tell you who owns it . . ."

But Flavia didn't wait for the details. She thrust the syringe into Morelli's hand, reached under his jacket and grabbed his gun. Then slid towards the door.

"Wait for me," he called after her.

"No time," she called back.

And she ran as though her life depended on it. It didn't, but Argyll's did, and she flew around the corner, jumping over hedges, nearly tripping over hosepipes, trampling flowerbeds, anything to cut a second, even a fraction of a second, from the time it would take to get back to the house.

What could Argyll possibly do to defend himself? He wouldn't stand a chance. He had no weapon, he had a leg in plaster and, in truth, violence was not his forte.

It wasn't hers either, but she scarcely thought of that. She would have surprise and a gun. They would have to do. What did they tell her in that self-defence course Bottando had sent her on? Damned if she could remember. Shows how useless these things were.

An expert would probably have counselled a cautious approach. Reconnaissance, as the military would have it. Sneak up to the window, see what's going on, locate your target, plan your mode of attack. A second's calm reflection can save lives.

But Flavia was proceeding by instinct, and would almost certainly have disregarded an expert's advice even had she remembered it. Rather than the calm approach, she ran up the little driveway and round the back of the house as fast as her legs would carry her. Instead of cautious reconnaissance, she charged at the back door with all her force, crashing into it with her shoulder at such speed that it sprang open.

And instead of patient situation assessment and target location, she slid to the floor on her knees, swung the gun up in both hands and pointed it at the figure standing over the inert form by the living room door.

"Get off him," she screamed at the top of her voice.

And pulled the trigger.

"All I can say," Argyll said heavily when he recovered from the fright, "is thank God for safety catches. Although killing me by nearly scaring me to death is almost as effective."

When Flavia put in her appearance he'd been feeling quite pleased with himself. But the sudden apparition and the gun—particularly the gun, as it was rather long and pointed at him—made his self-congratulatory mood ebb a little. He hurled himself to one side, and cracked his elbow on a side table as he did so. Just at that point where the funny bone is particularly vulnerable. Brought tears to the eyes.

He lay there gasping and clutching his elbow and Flavia, thoroughly winded from her sprint, her shoulder hurting damnably from the way she'd crashed through the door, and speechless from terror over so nearly blowing Argyll's head off, collapsed on the sofa and panted. That was the other thing they'd taught her on the course, she remembered. Take the safety catch off. Just as well she hadn't paid much attention.

"So what happened?" she asked eventually.

He thought for a moment, trying to choose between the paths of honesty and dissimulation. In the circumstances, he thought that a little light editing might be permissible. So he left out the bit about being on the verge of bolting after them because he was too frightened to be on his own.

"I was in the kitchen and heard someone outside the door. So I hid behind it; I thought it was probably you, but wasn't sure. Anyway, in he came. Saw me, pulled out a gun."

"And?"

"So I kicked him. When in doubt, you know. Probably wouldn't have done much good except for the plaster cast. It must have been like being hit by a train. Down he went, but began crawling after the gun. So I hopped after him and brought him a sharp crack over the head with my crutch.

"I was a bit worried that he might come round while I was looking for something to tie him up with, and I didn't feel like leaving him alone. So I was just standing, wondering what to do when you came in and nearly killed me."

"Sorry."

"That's OK. It's the thought that counts."

"A small detail," she went on.

"What?"

She pointed at the recumbent form. "Who is it?"

"Oh, him. I'm sorry." He pulled the figure over so she could see his face. "I forgot, you've never met. Flavia; meet Jack Moresby."

CHAPTER 15

By the time all the other invitees had drifted along, the atmosphere in Streeter's living room was almost jolly. Well, not quite. Anne Moresby, causing a local stir by arriving in her absurd limousine, was no more charming than usual. Samuel Thanet had bags under his eyes the size of full suitcases, James Langton had the look of someone prepared for a fight and even David Barclay looked concerned about the on-going situation.

Morelli had turned up only a few minutes after Flavia burst in, doing his best to give support. Quite admirable, really; he had taken the syringeful of painkiller, and injected the whole lot into his gum. All on his own. The very idea gave Argyll the quivers. It's bad enough when a dentist does it. Then he'd grabbed his regulation-issue shotgun and come after Flavia. His run along the street was observed by a back-up car, and they had followed him. Another back-up summoned reinforcements, and that turned the street outside into something resembling a battlefield. Grim-faced men in camouflage talking into radios and marching around with machine-guns; the works. That of, course, alerted the vultures, and within half an hour the press had arrived in full force as well. You could see local residents didn't approve. The neighbourhood watch committee was going to have something pretty severe to say about this at the annual meeting.

They were all a bit late, as well. By that time all the excitement was over. But as Morelli said, it would look great on the news, and he had a promotion to worry about.

Not that he was very talkative; in his haste and enthusiasm he had rather overdone the painkiller, and the lower part of his head felt like a large block of ice. But his tooth had stopped hurting. However, it did curtail his conversational powers.

So, when explanations were demanded, all he could do was mumble incomprehensibly and ultimately indicate through sign language that Flavia would have to do the talking. He thought it better to preserve his strength for the reporters outside.

"It's all quite simple, really, once you think about it," she said. Personally, she would have preferred to have gone back to the hotel and thought it out at leisure. It was, after all, not very long since her careful exposition of what had happened had been revealed as a bit wrong. She was thinking furiously to find out why.

"It was two separate cases, operating in parallel. Once you see that, it becomes easy. The problem was that we tended to assume that the two parts—the bust and the murder—were connected.

"Let's start with the murder of Moresby. As you know, we've just arrested his son; we laid a trap by spreading a story about a fictitious tape. Unfortunately, he didn't fall for it; but he knew that Jonathan Argyll would be here. He followed us, saw Morelli and I leave to get painkillers, and spotted his opportunity to get Jonathan alone. He needed to kill Argyll, but fortunately he was equally keen on staying alive himself.

"Why kill Argyll? Simple. After he left the party at the museum, Jonathan went to eat, then began walking back to his hotel. He must have left the restaurant about forty minutes after the murder, and was crossing a road about ten minutes later. His head was in the clouds as usual, and he was nearly run over.

"As he lives in Rome and constantly dices with death in this fashion anyway, he didn't pay much attention to it. A minor incident, but he mentioned it to Jack Moresby, to whom he had taken a liking at the party. Typical, he said, to be run over by a truck. A purple one, to boot.

"Moresby, I discover, drives a purple truck, and his alibi for the murder was that he went home and stayed there. And it was clearly damaging if anyone could say they saw him in the area of the museum fifty minutes or so afterwards. What was he doing there? He was sitting on a time bomb. The least comment might forge a connection and that might start people thinking. A small risk, but any at all was too big. So he loosened the brake cable while Argyll was eating at a restaurant in Venice. I always had trouble imagining Anne Moresby under a car with a spanner in her hands. It's not her style, somehow. Anyway, the result was one broken leg, and he was lucky it wasn't his neck."

Argyll glared indignantly at Moresby. Moresby shrugged.

"Prove it," he said simply.

"Back to the point. How did son kill father, and why? We assumed he had nothing to gain from his father's death. But he would have had something to gain, if his stepmother was convicted of the murder.

"Criminals cannot benefit from their crimes. If Barclay and Anne Moresby were convicted of conspiracy to murder in order to get their hands on the old man's money, then she could not inherit. The money would go to the next of kin, which was Jack Moresby. The will didn't say he was not to get anything, it just left him out. As it was clear his father would never change his mind, it was the only possible way he could ever become the heir.

"The murder of Arthur Moresby had clearly been decided on, and some of it planned, in advance. The day comes more rapidly than Jack anticipates because he discovers that his father is about to set up the trust for the Big Museum. He comes to the party at the museum—the sort of function that ordinarily he would not be seen dead at—to find out what is going on. He discovers, through Argyll and others, that his father plans to finalise the arrangements very soon—Moresby junior needs to act that same night, or wave goodbye to several billion dollars.

"So straight away he starts laying the groundwork. To Argyll, for example, he drops the information about his stepmother having an affair with Barclay, and says his father knows about it . . ."

"But I wasn't," Barclay interrupted.

"So you say," replied Morelli.

"But look . . ."

Flavia raised her voice, lest she lose her tenuous grip on events. "Jack Moresby," she said, and waited until she had everybody's attention again. "Overhears di Souza saying he wants Moresby to inspect the bust in Thanet's office, and spots an opportunity.

"So he leaves, saying goodbye so everyone knows he's going. Back to his truck, gets the gun, then waits. When di Souza leaves he walks up the stairs to the office, kills his father, then gets in his car and drives home."

"Hold on, there," said Thanet, raising a tentative hand in protest. "This is all very interesting, but I don't think it fits."

"And why not," she asked, a little annoyed to be interrupted in mid-peroration.

"Because of the camera. If, as you suggest, Jack decided to kill his father in my office only about half an hour before he did it, how come the camera was knocked out about two hours before? That suggests much more advanced thought."

"No, it doesn't," she said. "I'll deal with that later. You'll see. Anyone else have any points they want clearing up?"

Silence.

"Good. Where was I?"

"You've just shot Moresby," Argyll prompted.

"Yes. Anyway, everything else," she resumed, "happened as the various statements said. Summoned by a call from Arthur Moresby, Barclay makes his way over to the administration block, discovers the body, rushes back to call the police and everybody stands around waiting for them to arrive, except for Langton who, considerate and caring man that he is, goes and makes his phone calls."

This was a weak spot; Flavia knew it, and so did Jack Moresby. "Yeah, but my alibi," he said. "Langton called and I was home. Ten minutes after the body was discovered—and the murder can only have been committed a few minutes before that. Because of that call my father made to Barclay."

Flavia frowned at him, and so did Argyll.

"Of course," he said. "And if your father had indeed made the phone call to Barclay, then you could not have killed him, because you couldn't have got home in time to take Langton's call. But he was already dead by then. You made that call. Easily done, after all. It's not hard for children to be mistaken for parents—they often have the same accent, mannerisms and intonations. You shot your father, went home, then phoned. The records prove it. The call summoning Barclay came on an external line. Therefore it couldn't have come from Thanet's office. Therefore it couldn't have been your father."

Flavia looked at him thankfully. A concise explanation, she thought. Nicely put.

"From there on, the police go into action," Flavia continued calmly, as though she'd been clear on this point all along. "They hear about the trust not being signed; they hear about this affair; they hear that Moresby had been told; they hear he is a vengeful man; they can assume he would not be at all happy; and eventually they find and identify the gun.

"Careful planning has given Anne Moresby and Barclay means, motive and opportunity to kill Moresby. Jack Moresby, seemingly, had none at all.

"The trouble was that it all immediately began to go wrong, because of the missing bust. When the police turn up, one of the first things they discover is the empty case. They assume, reasonably enough, that there is some link between murder and robbery, and everybody wastes a huge amount of time trying to work out what it is. The camera is knocked out too early, as Mr. Thanet noted; the bust vanishes. Query, where is Hector di Souza?"

Here again, her narrative was interrupted by a contemptuous snort from Moresby who was leaning back in his seat with a passable smile of amusement. Indeed, he looked very confident; sufficiently so to make Flavia feel uncomfortable. She would have much preferred him to be quivering with fright and offering to make a confession. Evidently he was made of sterner stuff.

"You expect anyone to believe this garbage? You're planning to take this to a jury?"

She gave him as nasty a look as she could manage, and tried to resume her story. But she was feeling rattled; this was so far an exercise in creative speculation, undertaken in the hope that something would turn up in time so that they wouldn't be forced to let Moresby go. She, as well as anyone, was aware that the evidence so far wasn't that good. It wouldn't even stand in Italy, let alone in America. What was worse, Moresby clearly realised this as well.

"For reasons which need not detain us here, we have already established that the bust was not stolen, and that the appearance of a theft was a scheme by Langton to unseat Thanet and enrich himself in the process."

This was the stage at which Langton joined Jack

Moresby in scowling ferociously and sniffing contemptuously.

"It wasn't difficult for Langton to work out what was going on. Clearly, Jack Moresby wanted police attention to focus on his stepmother, and equally obviously Hector di Souza was going to be prime suspect."

"Very flattering," Langton commented drily. "Although I must say I don't see how I'm so clever if the combined resources of two police forces had such trouble."

"Firstly," she replied tartly, "because you knew the bust business was mere piffle. Secondly, because you were outside the museum, captured on the camera, at the time when Moresby went over to the office and when Jack Moresby must have left. Jonathan used to sit on the same lump of marble for his smoke as well. If he could see all comings and goings in the administrative block very clearly, so could you."

"Prove it," he said. Jack Moresby gave him an understanding smirk.

"Langton saw Jack Moresby leave the administrative block, and was smart enough to realise what was going on," she continued doggedly. "He also knew that the existence of di Souza meant it was going to go wrong. That is to say, Hector di Souza was going to be the main suspect. It had also dawned on him that Hector knew more about this bust than he'd thought.

"What about Hector? Somehow he knows that whatever is in that case, it isn't the bust he once owned in 1951. Old Moresby, I imagine, tells him to go back to Rome and get the proof. He has no love of di Souza but this looks like a fraud by a close associate. Hector runs back to the hotel and prepares to leave, booking himself on a two a.m. plane.

"Both Langton and Jack Moresby have a great interest in getting di Souza out of the way. Killing Hector meant that he couldn't say what he knew about the bust and also that Anne Moresby and Barclay would again become the main suspects."

More speculation, of course. Any lawyer would make mincemeat of it.

"In essence, I suspect the telephone conversation said either you will be arrested or di Souza will be; but certainly neither Mrs. Moresby nor Barclay will come under suspicion unless you do something fast. Will you confirm that, Mr. Langton?"

"No," said he uncooperatively. He and Moresby exchanged comradely smiles. Flavia ploughed on.

"Hector meanwhile, not knowing old Moresby is already dead, is packing his bags in a hurry—leaving the room in an uncharacteristic mess—and preparing to leave. Jack Moresby, alerted by Langton, calls di Souza, hears he is going to leave the country and offers to take him to the airport. Any favour for a friend of his father's. Especially in the circumstances. He drives like fury to get to the hotel before the police arrive, and is in such a hurry that he almost runs over Argyll near the hotel. Di Souza is probably dead within the hour, and buried in the patch of waste ground within two."

"The trouble for Moresby is that di Souza's disappearance merely convinces the police even more that di Souza is their man. A heavy hint is required. So he plants the gun near the body and phones the police to tell them where it is.

"Obvious, really. Whoever heard of any sensible murderer leaving an identifiable gun by the side of the victim? But at long last, and after much prodding, the police take the hint.

"Everything is coming along swimmingly. Moresby dead, di Souza converted into evidence against Anne Moresby, the bust safely vanished, with the police in Italy daily increasing their estimate of its importance. And, I imagine, a tacit understanding between young Moresby and Langton that in return for silence he will continue to fund the museum with Langton as director. Or maybe it's just a cash deal.

"And just to be on the safe side, Langton heads back to Italy as quickly as possible in case Moresby decides to dispose of another possible witness. As long as he is immune from attack, Moresby will have to keep to his side of the bargain.

"Perfect and delightful. But it all slowly comes unpicked. How? Firstly because the attempt to kill Jonathan fails and my arrival means that he hangs around rather than taking the first plane back to Italy as any sensible accident victim threatened with being sued should."

Moresby had kept calm throughout this narrative, and seemed barely perturbed. "Entrapment," he said. "Won't get very far on that without anything else. And you don't have much else, to my way of thinking. I may have stolen the gun, but you have to prove it. I may have nearly run Argyll over, but again you have to prove it. I may have imitated my father, but so might someone else. There are lots of trucks painted all sorts of colours in Los Angeles. I may have tried to kill Argyll, but the cable might have come loose on its own. I may have killed my father, but I may not. A bit flimsy."

"And this evening?"

"I was invited, got here early. Walked through the door and was kicked in the stomach."

"Carrying a gun?"

"Lots of people in Los Angeles carry a gun."

Morelli's frown by this stage was clearly caused by more than his tooth. His anxious glance at Flavia indicated that he was seriously concerned that his case was falling to pieces. He was sure that Moresby had tried to kill Argyll; and that Argyll had little choice but to hit him first; but it undoubtedly weakened the case. A serious provable attempted murder would have been so much more satisfactory, however distressing Argyll might personally have found it.

"And now, I think, I'll go home," Moresby continued with quiet confidence. "If you'll undo my handcuffs. And I wouldn't take the risk of harassing me any more. There are laws about that, and I reckon my lawyer will be telling you about them tomorrow morning."

If it hadn't been so risky, Morelli might have ground his teeth in frustration. Moresby was right; they'd have to let him go, sooner or later. He even started, reluctantly, to fumble in his pocket to get out the keys.

"What the hell have you done to my house?" came an outraged voice from the door. They looked up and saw a red-faced Streeter standing, open-mouthed and surveying the devastation. It was, indeed, a bit of a mess; the lawn had been churned up by cars driving over it and policemen marching up and down; much of the crockery had been broken in Argyll's self-defence exercise; the doors were not on nearly as securely as previously; the furniture had been disarranged, books and furnishings all over the place.

Even before he'd parked his car, a neighbour had marched up and protested.

"Mr. Streeter," said Morelli, glad of the distraction. "You're late."

"Of course I'm late. You could work that out for yourself, couldn't you? Obviously, I couldn't come before Thanet."

Morelli squinted in the attempt to understand what he meant.

"What are you talking about?"

"I had to wait until he left his office. I couldn't just walk in and take it with him there."

"Take what?"

"The tape."

"What tape?"

"The one you asked me to bring. From Thanet's office."

A long silence, as Morelli, Flavia and Argyll all shook their heads in disbelief.

"You mean to tell us that you *were* tapping his office?"

"Of course; I don't know how you found out. I put it in several months ago; I have grave concerns about some financial matters . . ."

"But why the hell didn't you say this before?"

"Well, it was illegal," he said, lamely and unconvincingly.

"I don't believe this," Morelli said thickly through the painkiller. "Are you really such a . . . Oh, what's it matter? What's on this tape, then?"

Streeter, with some considerable air of self-importance, handed it over.

"I should say . . ." he began, but Morelli waved him to silence.

"Shut up, Streeter," he said as he borrowed a Walkman from a patrolman, stuck the earphones in his ears and listened. The silence was interminable, and Morelli didn't help alleviate the tension by the way he occasionally snickered, grinned, frowned, and looked at members of the museum with suspicion, disapproval and a hint of scornful malice. Evidently it was an interesting tape. Eventually he switched it off, pulled out the earphones, and looked around with an air of profound satisfaction.

"Right," he said cheerfully to two policemen standing in the corner. "Take him off and charge him with the murder of his father. That'll do for the time being. We can add di Souza later. And him"—here he pointed at Langton—"you can book for attempted fraud and conspiracy to commit murder."

Getting Moresby out of the house and into a police car took longer than it should. He didn't want to go, and he was a big man. Overcoming his reluctance took an awful lot of pushing and shoving from the police, but it was clearly work they enjoyed. Eventually Moresby exited, pursued by a television crew.

"Why are you charging me with murder?" Langton asked with understandable alarm when attention finally turned to him. "I didn't do anything to anybody."

"That's the law. That's the way it is."

"This is ridiculous. You can't prove anything."

"If you were defrauding Moresby about the bust then all the rest follows naturally."

"If," he replied. "But I stand by my story. I bought it from di Souza, and di Souza stole it, as far as I'm concerned. You can't prove that case was empty."

Flavia smiled sweetly. "Oh, yes we can."

"How?" he said scornfully.

"Because we know where the bust is."

"Do you?"

"Yes."

"Where?"

"Still in Italy. And, of course, we've arrested Collins."

"But in return for a co-operative attitude . . ." said Morelli, striking while the iron was hot.

Langton thought it over. "Do you think I can have a talk with you for a moment, Detective?"

He and Morelli went into the kitchen to discuss matters. Despite the rather strained circumstances, Langton clearly entered into the spirit of the occasion. Once a dealer, always a dealer; it gets into the bloodstream. And he evidently believed that, once you had reached a decision, you should go ahead with it as quickly as possible. As the bargaining went on, voices were raised, both of them flounced about, positions were stated, withdrawals were made.

And the upshot was that Langton would testify about seeing Jack Moresby leave the administrative block, that he would give full details of the phone call that led to the death of di Souza and would refund the two million dollars that he had absentmindedly transferred into a bank account in Switzerland.

In return Morelli would do his best to arrange matters

so that the court looked sympathetically on his genuine sense of remorse and contrition and would not overstress the argument that Langton had incited Moresby to murder di Souza. Jail was likely, but not for very long. All very satisfactory.

While this was going on, Thanet and Barclay were in another corner, staring out of the window and also doing a certain amount of hard bargaining. They suddenly had a lot to talk about.

"I'm glad to hear about the Bernini," Thanet said, crossing the room with a satisfied look on his face. "Now we won't have the embarrassment of having to send it back."

"No. But you can send di Souza back if you want," Argyll said. "It is the very least you can do, in the circumstances."

"I suppose we should. I'm sure Barclay will oblige with the money. We don't have a penny at the moment. Not until this is all settled."

"You're not going to have a penny, anyway, settled or not," Anne Moresby chipped in from her lonely position on the sofa. "I'm still going to close you down." Despite being saved from innumerable years in jail by the efforts of others, the experience did not seem to have softened her much.

Oddly, the remark did not have the usual effect on Thanet's demeanour. He looked at her with interest, then glanced at Barclay.

"I don't know that this is a wise move, Mrs. Moresby," Barclay said.

"Why not?" she asked.

"Because of the circumstances. If you go to law over

this, the museum will fight. There is a more than fair chance that it will win."

"It doesn't have a leg to stand on."

"I think that if it came out in court how you persuaded your lover to bug Mr. Thanet's office to get material for blackmail . . ."

Morelli and Flavia exchanged glances. *Streeter?* Well, why not. She was having an affair, they were old college friends, she had got him a job, he was useful as a spy in place. No wonder he'd looked so upset when the subject was raised the other day. Another mistake, they thought simultaneously. Anne Moresby looked furious and Streeter had an air of almost childish sheepishness about him.

"Go on," she said.

"Mr. Thanet has made a suggestion . . ."

"Which is?"

"A billion to the museum and the rest to you. Even you should be able to rub along on that. And you give up your place as a museum trustee."

A silence greeted this remark.

"You'll abandon the Big Museum?" she asked eventually.

Thanet nodded regretfully. "No choice, really. Not much you can do with a billion these days."

"Well, at least that's a blow for sanity."

She thought carefully, calculating risks, costs and options. Then she nodded. "OK. Done." Also a decisive person.

Thanet smiled, and so did Barclay. Both were highly concerned that their role in the income tax affair should be kept under wraps. This seemed the best way of doing it. Admittedly, preserving their careers had just cost Anne

Moresby a fortune she would otherwise have undoubtedly won, but nothing's cheap these days.

"Get it settled as quickly as possible," she went on. "Then I can wash my hands of the entire place."

"That will take time, of course," Barclay said, thinking of his fees.

"Which, I'm afraid, is the other thing I have to say," Thanet added apologetically, his face looking concerned once more.

"What's that?" Argyll asked, as the statement seemed to be addressed to him.

"Money. It's all frozen, you see."

"Pardon?"

"Until the estate is settled. It's held by administrators. We can't get at it too easily."

"So?"

"So, I'm sorry to say that we won't be able to buy your Titian. No way of paying for it. I'm afraid we'll have to cancel the deal."

"What!"

"It's off. We don't want it. Or rather, we do, of course, naturally, but can't afford it. Not at the moment."

"You don't want that Titian?" Argyll said, astonishment growing as understanding seeped in.

Thanet nodded apologetically, hoping he wasn't about to be thumped.

"I know it will set back your career . . ."

Argyll nodded. "Certainly will," he said.

"And I know your employer won't be at all happy . . ."

"No. Indeed not. He'll be most upset."

"We will of course pay a cancellation fee, as per the contract. When we get some money again."

"That's kind of you," he said, feeling strangely elated.

"And I'd be happy to explain things to Sir Edward Byrnes and the owner, so that there is no misunderstand . . ."

"No!" Argyll said sharply. "Absolutely not. Don't you explain anything. Leave that to me."

Then, overcome, he gripped Thanet's hand and pumped it up and down. There is a lot to be said for having decisions taken out of your hands. It is so much easier to accept the inevitable without regret or doubt. "Thank you," he said to the bewildered director. "You've taken a great weight off my mind."

"Really?" Thanet said cautiously.

"Yes, indeed. Of course, I have made a proper mess of this . . ."

"*You* didn't mess it up," Thanet said, trying to console.

"Oh, yes I did. Dreadful. What a waste of time."

"Well, I really wouldn't go that far . . ."

"Of course you would. And Byrnes will think, do I really want someone like that running my gallery? Much better to have that fellow in Vienna. He may be boring, but at least he's reliable. Don't you think?"

Thanet had given up by now, and just stared at him blankly.

"So I'll just have to rot away in Rome. Unemployed, homeless, no money, and the market in a mess. How awful." And beamed happily.

Flavia had watched all this with interest. It is not everyone who watches their careers disintegrating with such contentment. And the fact that she understood perfectly why he was so happy made her come over all funny.

Sentimentality apart, though, it did seem a high price to pay for her company. Flattering though it was. Argyll's trouble was his lack of finesse. He often missed a neat flourish because he was, essentially, much too nice to be really determined.

So she thought she'd provide that extra touch herself. As a mark of affection.

"Of course, in six months time you might come along and decide you want that Titian, after all," she said gently. "For a bit more than you offered this time, taking into account all Jonathan's time and trouble. Risking life and limb to save your museum, and all that."

Thanet agreed this might be possible, but privately doubted it. Six months was a long time in the future. Amazing what you could forget. It was not as if he ever wanted the picture in the first place.

"But it would have to be with no funny business this time," she continued, half talking to herself. "I mean, no income tax fiddles. Jonathan here has his reputation with Sir Edward to think about. Did you know that people say Byrnes is the only honest dealer in the business? Hates shady stuff. If he ever heard of any of this . . . I mean, he's the sort of person who just might tell the IRS, just to safeguard his good name. It is the IRS, isn't it?"

Thanet nodded thoughtfully. IRS it was. And the last thing he needed now was to be hauled over the coals by them. The very thought of those flinty-eyed hatchet men going through the books made him shudder. It might give Anne Moresby fresh ideas as well. So, recognising an in-built transitional overhead cost when he saw one, he nodded.

"Ten per cent over the original price?" he suggested.

"Fifteen," Flavia corrected gravely.

"Fifteen, then."

"Plus a ten per cent cancellation cost now, to go direct to Jonathan."

Thanet bowed in agreement.

"Plus interest, of course."

Thanet opened his mouth to protest, then decided it wasn't worth the effort. Flavia was smiling charmingly at him, but he could see her eyes glinting with what looked like a very nasty combination of merriment and determination. She was, he decided, perfectly capable of paying a visit to the IRS before she left the country.

"Very well, then. I think we understand each other. Is this satisfactory, Mr. Argyll?"

Argyll, standing there and feeling that life's infinite variety was too kaleidoscopic this evening, could do little more than indicate that it seemed just about OK.

"By the way," Flavia continued absently. "Who is going to keep an eye on the market in Europe for you? Now that Langton seems unlikely to be in any position to keep his finger on the pulse, so to speak?"

Thanet was getting used to her now, and could see where she was heading. So he stood, feeling resigned, and waited for it.

"You really need an agent, just to keep you informed. Nothing permanent, or full-time, simply someone to be your eyes and ears on the continent. On a retainer basis. Don't you think?"

Thanet nodded, and sighed.

"Indeed," he said, giving way gracefully. "And I was rather hoping that Mr. Argyll . . ."

"Eh? Oh, yes," said he. "Delighted. Delighted. Anything to help."

"Drink," Morelli said after everyone had finally gone. He'd sneaked them out of the back and into his car, over the fence and across the neighbour's garden so the waiting press didn't see them. Pity about the neighbour's cactus collection, though. It would take years before Streeter won communal forgiveness. But then he probably wouldn't be living there much longer.

"You shouldn't. Not with all that junk in your bloodstream."

"I know. But I need one. And I owe you one."

A dingy bar, full of dingier people. Very nice.

"Your health," he said from behind a beer.

"Salute," she replied raising the glass. "Pretty odd about Streeter tapping the office after all. Sneaky little sod."

"Yes, interesting, that. Another example of museum politics at work."

"How so?"

"Well," the detective began, "as you heard, he was Anne Moresby's lover. More than anyone he knew the Moresbys weren't a tender loving couple, and he suspected that Anne was behind the shooting somehow. Naturally, he was concerned that she not be arrested, so he did his best to keep what he assumed would be incriminating evidence under wraps.

"The trouble was that we started going after her anyway, and then all this business of the lover as accomplice came up. Streeter wasn't in the camera's view at the time of the murder, he knew that Anne Moresby had a perfect alibi and began to think that he was being set up.

"So he swapped sides. Instead of trying to protect her, he decided to incriminate her before she got him. Any indecision vanished when Argyll suggested he produce his tape. He thought Argyll had discovered it really existed. I'm not too sure who was more dimwitted, him or us."

"If you think about it, none of them are exactly paragons, are they?" Argyll said. "I mean, tax fiddles, murder, fraud, adultery, theft, framing each other for crimes, eavesdropping, firing people. They deserve each other, I reckon."

There was a long pause as they considered this. Then Morelli smiled at the thought, and raised his glass once more. "My thanks. I don't know whether we would have got him eventually without your help. Maybe we would. But your comment about the bust made Langton tell all. How did you find out where it was?"

She shrugged. "I didn't. I haven't a clue."

"None?"

"Not the foggiest. I made it up. I wanted to annoy him."

"In that case it was lucky."

"Not really. After all, not much depended on it. You could convict Moresby on the taped evidence alone."

Morelli shook his head. "Maybe, but every bit helps."

"What were you grinning at when you were listening to that tape, by the way?"

The American gurgled with sheer pleasure. "I told you we thought Thanet was carrying on with his secretary?"

Flavia nodded.

"Well, he was. In his office. Very passionate. I was

just thinking how much I will enjoy myself when that tape is presented at the trial and is played to the entire courtroom."

Argyll looked at them both with a rueful grin. "This hasn't been a very impressive display, has it?"

"How do you mean?"

"We pointed the finger at the wrong murderer three times. We got Anne Moresby's lover wrong. Someone tried to murder me and I didn't even notice. Out of all of them Moresby was the only one I thought was basically OK. We invented a theft that didn't happen, and in the end only have a chance of getting a conviction because Streeter completely misunderstood me and Flavia told a whopping lie to Langton. And we still don't know what happened to that bust."

Morelli nodded contentedly. "A textbook case," he said.

CHAPTER 16

Hector di Souza was buried twice; once after a requiem Mass in Santa Maria sopra Minerva with full choir, dozens of attendants—including a real cardinal archbishop, the sort he'd always had a weakness for—and more cloth-of-gold vestments than you could shake a stick at. Friends, colleagues and enemies turned up in full force, dressed in their best, and the incense was burned like it was going out of fashion. Hector would have loved it. The march to the grave was appropriately solemn, the grave itself suitably verdant and the requiem dinner afterwards agreeably fine. No gravestone, yet. Enormously expensive, gravestones.

The second time he was buried in the accounts of the Moresby Museum; Argyll sent them a combined bill for transporting di Souza and his antiquities back to Italy and he heard no more of the matter. The beechwood coffin with brass trimmings got lost under the heading of post and packing for unwanted goods and the Mass went down as administrative expenses. All true, in a way, but not exactly poetic.

However sneaky they may have been in the past, the jolt of recent events seemed to reform the museum somewhat. The removal of Langton, and Streeter's decision to develop his consultancy on a more full-time basis lightened Samuel Thanet's universe to such an extent that he became almost obliging. Certainly, as far as Argyll was concerned, the director kept his word; Argyll got a cheque for his cancellation fee and a post-dated contract for the Titian within a fortnight. He and Byrnes came to an arrangement regarding future commissions and thankfully put aside any thought of his returning to England. And, within three months, the cheques for his retainer started arriving with commendable regularity. Not big, by the standards of art dealing, but more than sufficient to live off and have money left over.

There was a problem of accommodation, of course; the housing shortage in Rome has been chronic since the days of the Renaissance popes and there is no sign of that changing before the end of the next millenium. In the end, he lodged with Flavia until he got organised. But the practical solution was largely disingenuous; both were primarily concerned to see what happened. To their mutual amazement, the arrangement worked extraordinarily well and he eventually gave up even the pretence of looking for anything of his own. Domestically speaking, she was a complete pig, having developed not a single housewifely skill in her entire life, but that was OK; Argyll was not exactly houseproud either.

Domestic matters sorted out, Flavia got back to work with a vengeance and a cheery insouciance that made Bottando both relieved at the change and complacent about his original diagnosis of her ill humour. Among more routine matters, she interrogated Collins at the Borghese, took a statement from him about his involvement with Langton, got him to admit burgling Alberghi, picked up the other oddments he'd stolen from his flat, sent them back to their rightful owner—together with a stern recommendation that he look after them this time—and packed the young and foolish man off to California for a little chat with Morelli. For her own part she persuaded Bottando not to bring any charges against him. No point in being vindictive; it just created paperwork and she doubted whether he'd ever do the like again. Not in Italy, anyway; not with a passport stamped like that.

And then it was truffle season, one of the highlights of any thinking person's year. Black ones, white ones, and spotted ones. Cut thin and scattered as liberally as you can afford over fresh pasta. Worth travelling several hundred miles for, so you can eat them fresh. And to one restaurant in particular, which is so good that it appears in no guides, no gazettes and is scarcely known to anyone outside the Umbrian hilltown where it has been seducing tastebuds for a generation.

Flavia was even reluctant to tell Argyll where it was, but he got the information out of her eventually, and he decided that it was time to celebrate his return to full mobility by taking her to lunch. And en route, she had the brainwave of what to get him for his birthday. He was thirty-one and beginning to feel his age. It is the time of life when even the most optimistic get their first glimpse of senile decay looming up over the horizon.

A fine lunch of truffles, mushrooms and Frascati did something to reconcile him to the vale of tears through which he was passing at such alarming speed, however, and he was in a much more benevolent mood by the time he loaded himself into the passenger seat of Flavia's car and they set off erratically on the road once more.

True to his Californian decision, he not only refrained from criticising the speed at which she drove, he even managed to avoid flinching every time she overtook. But as far as he could see there was no absolute ban on asking where they were going, even if it was a surprise.

She just smiled, and kept on driving. Only as they swept on to the road to Gubbio did he begin to have an inkling and even then he kept his conclusions to himself. It would be a pity to spoil it by guessing.

He was right though; she parked near the main square, led the way down the side streets and knocked on a door. Signora Borunna answered, and smiled as Flavia apologised for disturbing them.

The smile was not as gentle as before; rather there was a sad tinge about it which she found disconcerting. But they were invited in and Flavia explained that she wanted to take up the offer of a piece of sculpture. To buy, of course.

"I'm sure Alceo would be honoured, my dear," she said quietly. "I shall go this minute and find him. He's in the café up the road."

She walked to the door and then hesitated.

"Signorina, please," she said, turning round to face them. "I need to ask you something."

"By all means," she replied, a little puzzled by the woman's manner.

"It's Alceo, you see. He's not been the same—since he heard about poor Hector. He feels, well, he feels a little guilty."

"Why on earth should he feel guilty?" Flavia asked, even more surprised.

"Well, that's it, you see. I was wondering if you would listen to him. Tell him he did nothing wrong. I know it was unforgivable, but it was with the very best intentions . . ."

"Signora, I don't understand a word of what you're saying."

"I know. But it would be good if Alceo would unburden himself. And if you could find it in your heart to forgive him . . ."

"I can't imagine what there is to forgive. I'll gladly listen, though."

She nodded, apparently reassured, and went off to fetch her husband. While she was gone Argyll slowly went round examining the man's handiwork. They were, he said, wonderful. Even though they were new, he would love one of these. And what a marvellous present, he added, giving her an appreciatory squeeze.

"I wish I knew what's got into Signora Borunna," she said as Argyll held up a madonna and indicated that his life would be complete if he were to be given that. "Seemed such a jolly person last time I was here."

"Soon find out," he replied as the door opened once more and the pair of them came in, the wife leading and the sculptor dragging in behind.

Borunna was greatly changed; grey and haggard, he looked as though he had aged a decade in a couple of months. He now looked old, and didn't look happy. The tranquil contentment had vanished.

Flavia had been brought up to believe that telling people in their seventies that they looked awful was insensitive, so she confined herself to greeting him cautiously and introducing Argyll. She omitted to mention the madonna; that would have to wait until later. But what exactly was she meant to say to him?

Fortunately Borunna helped her out. Eyes cast down, he slumped into a battered armchair, took a deep breath and began for her.

"I suppose you want a full confession," he said heavily.

Both of them were completely bemused by now. So she sat down and decided it would be best not to say anything at all.

He took that as agreement and began again. "Well, I'm glad. Especially now. I've felt so dreadful since I heard about Hector being killed. I should have told you everything then. But I wanted to protect him, you see. When I think I could have saved him . . ."

"Perhaps you ought to start at the beginning?" Flavia prompted, hoping that this would enable her to make some sense of it.

"I was only acting for the best," he said. "I knew that Hector would lose the bust, but compared to being put in jail, or deported, that seemed to be getting off lightly. I thought he'd approve, you see. And he would have done, if I hadn't made such a fearful mess. I provoked him, you see. It was my viciousness that caused all this."

"And how, exactly, was that? In your own words, that is," she said, looking up for inspiration at Signora Borunna.

He sighed heavily, rubbed his eyes, thought long and deeply and eventually brought himself to begin his tale. "Hector came round to our house when he got back from the Swiss border. He was in a dreadful state. Absolutely panicked. His life was coming to an end, he said. The bust had been confiscated, he'd already spent the money he'd been paid for it, he would be prosecuted for smuggling."

"This is 1951, you mean? Right?"

"Of course."

"Just making sure. Carry on."

"He was worried that was just the beginning. What if they searched out where it had come from? I reminded him that he'd claimed to have bought it at a sale. He had, he told me. But he didn't know how it got into the sale in the first place. What if it *had* been stolen? He didn't know, but he knew who was going to get any blame.

"It took us an entire evening to calm him down. He was completely distraught. Never, he said, would he do anything so stupid again.

"It looked as though he wasn't going to get away with it. About a week later he received two letters. One was from the Borghese saying that their examination of the bust was complete, they were convinced it was genuine and would he come round to discuss it. Another from the police, saying that papers in his case had been passed on to the public prosecutor's office which would inform him in due course of any action to be taken. That, as you know, meant that some action *would* be taken.

"Hector was crazy with worry. And, to be frank, he was driving us crazy as well. He was not a bad man, you see. If he'd been a real crook he would have handled it much better. He was careless and got caught out, that was all.

"I felt sorry for him. We both did, my wife and I. She

was particularly keen that we try and help him. They were such good, old friends. Then I got the idea . . ."

Here he lapsed into an introspective and depressed silence again. Flavia sat impassively, waiting for him to come out of it and continue the story.

He did eventually, looking at her properly for the first time with an almost defiant look.

"It was a good idea. I went to the local library and found a picture of the bronze copy of the bust in Copenhagen . . ."

"So that was how you knew about that," she said, speaking for almost the first time.

"Yes, that's right. And I studied it carefully, and made drawings. Dozens of them. Then I went to my workshop in the Vatican.

"I didn't have much time, so the workmanship was not my best, but it was passable. I used old fragments of marble that were left over from a job we'd done repairing bomb damage. In three days I had enough to pass muster. I made an appointment at the Borghese and went round, with my notepad and my fragments.

"I was shown into the office of a little man in the museum. I must say, I didn't like him. One of those cold, arrogant, snobbish little men you come across sometimes. The sort who rhapsodise about sculpture but sneer at sculptors. I was a communist in those days, and perhaps a bit more sensitive to these things. It made me all the more determined, especially when it came out that he was the man who'd been assessing Hector's Bernini.

"So I ask him, 'Are you finished?'

" 'Oh, indeed,' says he.

" 'And what do you think?'

" 'I don't see how it concerns you. But, if you're interested, it's a very fine piece. One of The Master's best early works. It would have been scandalous had it been lost to the country.'

" 'I'm sure Hector didn't mean . . .'

" 'Signor di Souza is a scoundrel and a crook,' he says, in a nasty tone. 'And I intend to ensure personally that he pays the price. I had a word with the prosecutor only this morning, and he is in full agreement. This sort of behaviour must be stamped out. An exemplary punishment will warn others.'

"So you could see, that it didn't look good for Hector at all. This man was out to get him. I hated him, I must confess. There he was, all sleek and well-dressed. He didn't have to search around for food or worry where the next meal was coming from. He, with his family and his connections and his money, didn't have to concern himself with making a living. And he was so sure of himself. So self-righteous.

" 'You're impressed by the bust, then?' I ask him.

" 'Yes,' he replies. 'Bernini has been my life's work, and I have never seen a better example.'

"So I say: 'Well, I'm flattered. Thank you. I must say I was pleased as well. Though I say it myself.'

" 'What do you mean?'

" 'What do you think I mean? I sculpted that bust. Me. In my workshop. It's not Bernini at all.'

"Now, that rattled him good and proper. But he wasn't having it. 'You?' he says with a nasty sneer in his voice. 'A common labourer? You expect me to believe a cock-and-bull story like that.'

" 'Common labourer I may be,' I say, proper mad now.

'But an uncommon sculptor, if I might say so. Good enough, it seems, to make a fool out of a man who's spent his life studying The Master, as you put it.'

"You see, signorina, I'd all but forgotten Hector by now. I didn't like being called a common labourer. Originally I just wanted to get him to leave Hector alone. But now, I was determined to humiliate him. He still didn't believe me, so I whip out my drawings, and show them to him. Then I bring out my little pieces. A nose, an ear, a chin. You know. Practice pieces, I say. To get it just right on the finished marble.

"You could see him getting uncertain, all his arrogance draining away. He looked at the drawings—I'm a good draughtsman—then at the lumps of stone I'd carved, and you could see him worrying. Maybe, he was thinking. Just maybe. You must remember what turmoil the art world was in. It wasn't long since the Van Meegeren business in Holland, where the greatest experts had authenticated the most awful fakes. And everyone had a good laugh at their expense. This Alberghi man was not the sort to take a joke.

"So I ploughed on with my story. I did my very best to convince him that I'd made the bust for Hector to sell to a foolish collector in Switzerland, who thought it was a great bargain. There was nothing illegal in it; you didn't need a permit to export modern works. And then the Borghese comes in and authenticates it. Thank you very much, says I. Greatly increased in value now, I tell him. Hector will be pleased.

"This was where I went too far, wanting to rub his nose in it. He snaps his head up and says, 'What?'

"And I say, 'Well, in the letter you wrote to Hector

you say it's genuine. So, a bust with an authentication by you . . .'

" 'You will not use that letter . . .' he says, furiously.

"And I smirk at him. 'Try and stop us,' I say. 'I will,' he replies.

"So he calls a guard from the museum, and they go into the next room. Where the Bernini was. The first time I'd seen it, and it really was beautiful. Everything Alberghi and Hector said was true. Obviously the real thing. I could tell, just by looking. A lovely, lovely piece . . ."

He stopped again for a while before restarting, clearly hating every word that he uttered.

"Anyway, Alberghi gestures at the bust, and tells the guard to pick it up. He does, even though it's heavy, and Alberghi leads the way out. They go all the way through the museum, out to the back, to a little courtyard where some builders are doing work, and the guard puts it on the ground. I followed after them, you see. And Alberghi goes up to a workman, and takes a heavy sledgehammer from him. It was before I could do anything to stop him, you see . . ."

"What happened?"

"What do you think? He hit it just once, with enormous force. Right on the head. The blow spread straight through the marble, and the entire bust broke into pieces. A dozen, maybe more, and hundreds of shards. Irreparable damage. I just looked at what he'd done, and Alberghi threw the sledgehammer down and came up to me.

" 'Well, sculptor,' he says, all the nastiness back in his voice. 'So much for that. That's what you get if you try to pull a fast one on me. Now take your work and go.'

"And he dusted off his hands and walked off. If I hadn't goaded him, it might never have occurred to him to destroy it. I don't know why I did it. I collected a few fragments, the least damaged bits, but there was nothing to be done with them."

There was a long pause, during which Borunna didn't feel like talking and Flavia could think of nothing to say.

"How very unfortunate," Argyll put in rather lamely. Borunna glanced at him.

"Unfortunate? Yes. But the trouble is . . ."

"Yes?"

"I don't know how to tell you. You'll think I'm a monster . . ."

"Just try us."

"I felt happy."

"Happy?"

"Yes. When that sledgehammer came down and that beautiful work was smashed into pieces, I was exultant. Triumphant. I can't explain it. I've felt guilty about it ever since."

He looked at her as though she could confer some form of absolution for his feeling. Which she felt unable to offer.

"And Hector wasn't prosecuted?"

"Oh, no. There were no charges. Alberghi thought that any defence would have involved saying the bust was a copy and that could have made him a laughing-stock. Hector still had the letter. So all Hector heard was that the bust had been confiscated. And that was it."

"And you never told him?"

"How could I? It would have broken his heart. I was destroyed by it. And Maria said it was best forgotten. So

I forgot it all, until you turned up. I should have told you everything then. But as I knew that the bust in America couldn't be genuine, I assumed Hector had been forging again. But if I had said something, at least he would still be alive."

"Is that what worries you most?"

He nodded.

"Well, you can set your mind at rest there," she said gently. "By the time I saw you he was already dead."

"I think he did know," Argyll added. "It was why he wanted to examine the bust. And that was why he was killed, in fact. If he hadn't known, he would never have insisted on talking to Moresby alone, and wouldn't have been in the way. He was going to come back to Italy to get you to corroborate what had happened."

"But how could he possibly have known . . ."

Flavia glanced up, beyond Borunna, and saw his wife, framed in the doorway. She remembered everything she'd heard. Di Souza's reputation as a bit of a womaniser. The younger woman alone with him while her older husband was off working. How he had got to know di Souza through his wife, how the sculptor often came home and found them together, how they were so close, how she was so keen that Hector be helped out of trouble. And she understood perfectly why Borunna had felt so happy when he had seen Hector's head smashed into bits by that sledgehammer. Perfectly natural.

And she also saw the look of fright on the old lady's face that she might bring it all up, and remembered the look of sadness and devotion when she'd said how worried she was about her Alceo's fit of depression.

"He must have found out through contacts in the

Borghese," she said hastily. "I don't know when, but as far as I can see he dealt with the blow well enough. He certainly didn't seem to bear you any grudge."

"So you don't think my not telling you made any difference?"

"None at all," said Flavia robustly. "If that's all that's worrying you then you can put your mind at rest. Even the little you told me was crucial and the full story wouldn't have made the slightest difference. I confess it's a shock to find out about the bust, but it was a long time ago. What happened to the bits?"

Borunna was reluctantly and slowly coming out of his gloom, encouraged along by her reassuring comments. Full rehabilitation would take some time, and the ministrations of a doting wife. Still, he at least began the process of coming back to normality. The bits of the bust, he said, were in a box down in his workshop by the cathedral. If they wanted to see them, he'd show them. But only after they had selected and taken a piece of his carving.

"From both of us," his wife added. "With our thanks."

As Argyll had already made up his mind, and Flavia was more than happy with the choice, that bit was easy. So, clutching the madonna wrapped in a piece of old newspaper, and with the old couple holding hands like a pair of adolescents, they walked slowly through the narrow streets to the workyard.

The box was covered in drawings and tools and a thick layer of dust, the lid was formidably heavy, and the contents were covered by old sheets. But underneath them all was the source of their recent problems. One by one, Borunna pulled them out and laid them on a bench, organising them to show how the bust had looked.

Most of the face was there, but he was certainly correct in saying that the piece was irreparable. About half had vanished, and much of the rest was badly chipped.

All four of them looked at it in silence for some time.

"What a pity," Flavia said, a statement so self-evident that it needed little comment from the others.

"The trouble is I've never known what to do with it. It would be criminal just to throw the pieces away, but I don't know what else to do."

They stared a while longer, and Argyll got the glimmerings of an idea. Properly set in an upright piece of marble, the face would look almost unblemished. If restored by an expert. A nice bit of lettering . . .

"Do you still want to make some apology to Hector?" he asked.

Borunna shrugged. A bit late now, he said, but yes. How?

Argyll held the face up until it glinted in the autumn light.

"Don't you think this could be turned into a wonderful gravestone?"

Have you ever struggled through a time when you questioned the reality of your faith in Jesus Christ? Perhaps you're going through inexplicable darkness right now. Your prayers seem to be ignored. You've cleansed your heart of unconfessed sin. But while listening to an exuberant singer or minister extolling the joy of the Lord, you feel no joy—only numbness and frustration.

In *The Thomas Factor,* Winkie Pratney digs deeply into the Bible to uncover practical teaching on the actual benefits of doubt. He writes, "What you are going through is not new.... It came to the prophets and they wept. It came to the godly and they humbled themselves. One dark day it even came to Jesus, the Son of God Himself. And if you set your heart to seek God, this darkness will come also to you. You are not exempt. You will not escape it. It is the essential factor in a deep and thorough Christian experience."

Don't let the experience of spiritual doubt or darkness discourage you any longer. Let Winkie Pratney show you God's purposes and help you find biblical answers through *The Thomas Factor.*

"This teaching has been neglected for so long, it's like a missing piece of the puzzle! In this book, Winkie has reaffirmed the principle that God does allow us at times to walk in darkness in order to move us higher in Him. This book will minister to so many people...anyone struggling with his or her Christianity."

Jackie Mitchum, Guest Coordinator, "The 700 Club"

THE
THOMAS
FACTOR

WINKIE
PRATNEY

FLEMING H. REVELL COMPANY
OLD TAPPAN, NEW JERSEY

Library of Congress Cataloging-in-Publication Data

Pratney, Winkie, date
The Thomas factor / Winkie Pratney.
p. cm.
ISBN 0-8007-9154-1 : $6.95
1. Faith. 2. Belief and doubt. I. Title.
BV4637.P728 1989
234′.2—dc20 89-37259
CIP

A Chosen Book

Chosen Books are published by
Fleming H. Revell Company
Old Tappan, New Jersey
Printed in the United States of America

For that solitary seeker
who braves the darkness
and dares believe.

In His favor is life . . .
"Weeping may endure for a night,
but joy comes in the morning."
Psalm 30:5

This special Billy Graham Evangelistic Association edition is published with permission from Chosen Books.

Contents

Introduction

"For You are my lamp, O Lord; The Lord shall enlighten my darkness."
2 Samuel 22:29

What in the World Is Going On?

We have been chosen by Jesus. We're walking with Him. Being His follower. Committed to doing what He says, being what He wants, going where He leads. But now, after all the years, we ask: Is it *real*?

"There has never been a time when it has been more difficult to be a Christian," says William Barclay, "and there has never been a time when it has been more necessary." At the edge of the new millennium, we now embark on what seems at once the most challenging, frightening, and exciting decade of contemporary history. Vast changes are taking place around the world. Russia. China. The Middle East. Entire political, economic, and military systems are shaking and altering before our very eyes. As we accelerate into the twenty-first century, we all face a time of major decisions. What is going to happen in our world? What is going to happen to us? If a caring, sovereign God is indeed in charge of the future, how can we best prepare to follow Him into it?

We are not the first to ask these questions. The early disciples also came to a time of great crisis and darkness. Jesus said He was going to die, that the Shepherd would be struck and all the sheep would be scattered. And then just when they most needed a sense of closeness, of common purpose and courage to face together what was coming, Jesus spoke to them about betrayal in their own ranks, about denial, about an immediate future they would all apparently have to face alone. And like us now on the edge of an incredible age, they were filled with questions.

"Thomas said to Him, 'Lord, we do not know where You are going, and how can we know the way?' "(John 14:5).

What did Jesus mean? Where was He going? What were they supposed to do now? They had general assurances from the Lord before, but this time was really serious; and the person who dared voice to Jesus his unspoken questions was not satisfied with a general promise.

We all know Thomas, don't we? The disciple who doubted. Thomas, the born skeptic with the heart of a scientist, the man who said even after the miracle: "Unless I can put my hand in the hole in His side I will not believe."

There has never been a time in contemporary Christianity when the temptation of Thomas was so prevalent and widespread at all levels of the Church. We, especially of the Western world, live in a period of deep uneasiness in the Christian Church. While some is obviously fallout from scandals, the failures of well-known people, ministries, and institutions, there is another factor at work deeper than this. Even our culture currently reflects a mood of pessimism, malaise, and disenchantment.

The Church is experiencing a time of great change; a "whole lot of shaking," forsaking, and breaking is going on. There is an inability in most people to get a handle on what is happening personally or globally. The questions of Thomas are ours as we face the immediate future: What is God up to? What is happening to me? What can I do in the midst of all this?

The River Is Rising—Toward 2001 A.D.

Our answer may be found in a vision given to the prophet Ezekiel. In the vision a man took him out into a river, farther and farther until he could no longer stand on his own.

> In the twenty-fifth year of our captivity . . . [the Lord] took me into the land of Israel and set me on a very high mountain. . . . There was a man whose appearance was like the appearance of bronze . . . a measuring rod in his hand. . . . The man said to me, "Son of man, look with your eyes and hear with your ears, and fix your mind on everything I show you."
> Ezekiel 40:1–4

There followed lengthy and specific instructions for the reconstruction of the Temple and the city of Jerusalem. Then this:

> He brought me back to the door of the house; and behold, water was flowing from under the threshold of the house toward the east, for the house faced east. And the water was flowing down from under, from the right side of the house, from south of the altar.
>
> And he brought me out by way of the north gate and led me around on the outside to the outer gate by way of the gate that faces east. And behold, water was trickling from the south side. When the man went out toward the east with a line in his hand, he measured a thousand cubits, and he led me through the water, *water reaching the ankles*.
>
> Again he measured a thousand and led me through the water, *water reaching the knees*. Again he measured a thousand and led me through the water, *water reaching the loins*.
>
> Again he measured a thousand; and *it was a river that I could not ford, for the water had risen*, enough water to swim in, a river that could not be forded. And he said to me, "Son of man, have you seen this?"
> Ezekiel 47:1–6, NAS

This vision is not only a promise of God's inheritance for Israel; it is also a metaphor of increasing risk, of inevitable major changes in our Christian life, the "passages" of spiritual growth. The Church especially in the West is in what seems perhaps the most difficult and frightening level. We have learned to live in comparative security with water around both our ankles and our knees, but now things are getting serious. God is bringing us into life and healing, but first we have to get where we no longer move in the water but the water moves us. This is the task of the man with the measuring line; this is the intention of God for our time.

A Prelude

And he showed me a pure river of water of life, clear as crystal, proceeding from the throne of God and of the Lamb. In the middle of its street, and on either side of the river, was the tree of life, which bore twelve fruits, each tree yielding its fruit every month. And the leaves of the tree were for the healing of the nations.

Revelation 22:1–2

The Waters of Life

To understand the changes God is bringing to our lives—and to find answers to our doubts—we need first to see how much of life from creation to the present day has to do with water.

Scripture speaks of water as a life-giving stream:

> These waters issue out toward the east country, and go down into the desert, and go into the sea: which being brought forth into the sea, the waters shall be healed. And it shall come to pass, that every thing that liveth, which moveth, whithersoever the rivers shall come, shall live: and there shall be a very great multitude of fish, because these waters shall come thither: for they shall be healed; and every thing shall live whither the river cometh. Ezekiel 47:8–9, KJV

It is significant that much of life in creation, in the Scriptures, and in our current physical existence has to do with water. Earth, of all the planets in our solar system, perhaps in all God's universe, is the dominantly water-rich world. Oceans cover two-thirds of our planet. Rain feeds the fertilization cycle and keeps the multiple billions of plants and trees alive. Snow caps our poles and puts some of our world to sleep in winter; rivers, lakes, and streams become a source of refreshment and joy in the heat of summer.

Water is in Scripture a symbol of both life and death. Take Christian baptism, for instance; the image of water signifies both burial and resurrection (new life). During my early years of ministry I had so many backsliders and dropouts as a result of my ineffective witnessing that I thought, *Well, perhaps I should baptize them. I'll hold them under twice and take them out once! I won't get to heaven, but they will.*

Water dominates our whole lives. We commence our physical birth when "the waters burst." A large percentage of the physical body is made up of water. Every major cell, tissue, and lean muscle mass is replete with water. We can go weeks without food but only a few days without water; dehydration invariably means death.

The birth and death of early earth is likewise filled with references to water; the Bible speaks of the waters "above" and "under" (Genesis 1:7) and of God's gathering the waters together (Genesis 1:9–10). God even speaks to the waters in the creation of life (Genesis 1:20–22).

Some creation scientists postulate that before the early earth was destroyed, it had both a water layer in its upper atmosphere and perhaps another modulating water layer around its core. This early earth may not have been struck by the directly unscreened rays of the sun. It may instead have been warmed from its core, an energy source something like a perfectly balanced breeder reactor, gently moderating its heat to the surface.

According to these creation scientists the destruction of the world took place like this: God spoke in judgment to the center of the earth and unbalanced that reactor. It overloaded; sections of earth cracked like a microwaved egg. That water-moderator shell shot up in places under tremendous, intense pressure. Huge, violent explosions of water cracked the floating granite substructure layer of our planet. Fountains of water as high as two or three miles devastated an upper firmament shell loaded with electromagnetic energy and it in turn discharged onto the surface of the doomed early world.

If this is the way it happened, can you imagine how utterly scary it was? In places like the Paluxy River you can still see authenticated dinosaur tracks and what appear to be apparently large human tracks trapped in the same disaster together. The prints are stretched out. There is a human handprint still left of a scrabbling, panicky attempt to get up after a fall. The tracks sometimes cross, but the lizards are apparently not after the people. Everybody's running . . . going in different directions. Everyone is running from something that is scaring the living daylights out of them.

Can you imagine what it would be like to see for the very first time the utter blackness of space and the discharge of lightning like at no other time in earth history? And then, for the first time in the record of mankind, rain. Rain that washed down out of the skies along with subterranean explosions of water that sent giant tidal waves sweeping over the shallow land masses in the awful judgment of the first world. Water: life and death. It was true in the days of Noah. That first flood that destroyed the wicked ancient world also preserved eight people, carried by the waves in the shelter of God.

And so it goes throughout Scripture. There is Moses, the greatest of the Old Testament Law-giving figures. His life is marked, both life and death, by water. Pharaoh commands all Hebrew parents: "Throw your male babies into the water" (Exodus 1:22). Moses has parents who, besides being law-abiding Hebrews, are somewhat imaginative. Fearing God, they look for a creative alternative way to carry out the king's command, and come up with a literal interpretation of the law that certainly meets with God's approval. After all, Pharaoh didn't say *how* to throw the baby into the water . . . so they put him into a little boat (Exodus 2:3) and you know the rest of the story.

The life of Moses is spared by the same water that means

death to so many other babies. Later, he meets his wife through water (Exodus 2:16–21). The spared child becomes a wanted, hunted man; and that man is at last called by God to lead the children of Israel through the waters of the Red Sea, which close down on pursuing Egypt and drown Pharaoh and his hosts (Exodus 14:21–31).

Water: life to Israel, death to Pharaoh. Water also marks the end of Moses' earthly ministry. On the edge of the promise, he strikes the rock of symbol in anger instead of speaking to it. Unable to enter the Promised Land during his lifetime, Moses is buried by God in the desert to await the fulfillment of His original promise. Moses has to wait to enter the Promised Land thousands of years later, when in his resurrection he joins Jesus on the Mount of Transfiguration (Matthew 17:1–5). Life and death by water.

In Ezekiel's vision, we see a rising river of water. He is taken out farther and farther; and level by level the water encompasses him. Four areas this water touches: the ankles, the knees, the loins, and, finally, everything.

There is the man with the measuring line. Did you ever notice in some sections of the Bible how much space is given to apparently useless and boring measurements? Chapters of it! When I first began to study it, I couldn't see the sense of it. I thought, *What a waste! Why didn't God put in more verses like Psalm 23 and John 3:16 instead of all this cubits stuff?* But then I never did like measurements much.

Yet it is obvious that God is a Counter, a Measurer. He not only measures things like this river, the Tabernacle, and the great City to come; He counts the days, the people, the tears, the sins of the world. In Psalm 147:4 we read that God numbers the stars. He even names them all. In Matthew 10:30 we read that even the hairs on your head are numbered! God seems to be into numbers.

Now there are some missionary people who are not only good at speaking or singing or writing; they are also good at engineering and carpentry and building. They can build both a church and a place to put the church. I find such people embarrassing. I can't even put a shelf up straight on the wall!

In my more rational moments between smashed thumbs and wasted materials I think about the factors that make people good builders. I know at least one thing they have that I don't. They habitually think of precise measurement; the first thing they pull out is a tape measure, while the first thing I reach for is a saw. They measure six times and cut once; I measure no times at all and have to cut 150 times! The difference between me and my kinds of attempts and a real carpenter, builder, or craftsman is called measurement and attention to detail.

We have a God who counts stars and comes to the funeral of every sparrow and this God is *infinitely detailed.* We tend to think of the general greatness, immensity, and compassing power of God, but He is also precise. The same God who has upheld the galaxies effortlessly for light-years both knows and cares how many hairs you lost this morning.

So that man walks in the vision and measures. See how slowly the water rises. Only to the ankles after a thousand measures! Nothing very fast. Some things change very slowly. And in this vision, the man walks out a thousand cubits before the river rises to his ankles. A thousand cubits. If we consider a cubit eight inches long, we're talking about 15,000 feet! That's a long way to walk to have water just reach the ankles.

We are perhaps unaccustomed to this kind of slowness. Most of us grew up to like, to prefer instant things. We belong to a generation used to watching T.V. programs with anything slow and boring edited out. We like things to happen fast. We eat fast, drive fast, live life in the fast lane. We want our miracles of provision, healing, or restoration to happen instantly.

Thus, we are not so sure of supernatural things that happen very gradually. How can we see them unless they move quickly?

We may be in a terrible situation and want things changed

immediately. Of course, the same God who turned water into wine instantly can do it again, but a lot of times He moves much more slowly. After all, He turns water into wine all the time. He does this millions of times all over the world every year through His creation, grapes, but we often fail to appreciate that this, too, is a work of God. It is only when He accelerates time and shrinks His power to our level of perception that we are compelled to notice His help and intervention. George MacDonald said, "The miracles of Jesus were His Father's normal works, wrought small and swift that we might see them."

The slow change can be a miracle, too. Someone can look back and say, "That was a mess a year ago. Back then I had no idea how it could ever be any different." But little by little, things changed. It *is* better now than it was before. He has been at work even when we have not been looking. Fractionally the tide has risen, and now there is water where once there was only mud and sand. God has made all these changes in us and we have cause to be thankful for the slow miracle as well as the fast. As the old lady said, "Well, I ain't now what I *should* be, and I ain't yet what I'm *gonna* be, but praise God, I at least ain't *what I was*!"

And you, too, need never be the same. It is time to begin the scary, costly change. Come with me now. We are going to a place of both life and death. We are going down to the river.

THE
THOMAS
FACTOR

Level One
Water to the Ankles

"Lord, we do not know where You are going; how do we know the way?"
—Thomas questions Jesus

When the man went out toward the east with a line in his hand, he measured a thousand cubits, and he led me through the water, water reaching the ankles. Ezekiel 47:3, NAS

1

Healing from Chaos

The first miracle of the early Church after Pentecost had to deal with the healing of someone's ankles. It centered around a man who had been *born* lame; he had never walked in his life (Acts 3:1–16). When the disciples met him, he was at the Beautiful Gate begging for alms. He looked at Peter and John, expecting something from them. "I do not possess silver and gold," said Peter, "but what I do have I give to you." And the power of the Resurrected Christ touched the lame man in the ankles; God healed him instantly. He called out for "alms" but in the name of Jesus, Peter and John gave him "legs" instead!

In our spiritual journeys, all of us begin at the bottom. There really has been a "fall," not only in our world but in us, too. We both bear the consequences and reinforce the choices of our first sinning parents, and the devastating harvest that has resulted over the centuries is now the current tragedy of our world. No one who knows the meaning of the Bible word *lost* needs any illustration of this primary truth; our first and greatest need is to be *found,* at the deepest and most basic levels of our being.

In M. Scott Peck's probing book on community and peacemaking, *A Different Drum,* he refers to an excellent recent university study on six stages of spiritual experience. These stages are not only apparently universal; they seem also to me to have peculiar relevance at this time to the Church in the Western world. Peck reduces these various stages to four ascending levels of experience: what he calls *chaos*, *tradition*, *doubt*, and *mystery*.

The four basic transitional stages or passages of spiritual experience bear a natural correspondence to the four rising levels of Ezekiel's vision of the river: waters first to the ankles (chaos), then to the knees (tradition), to the loins (doubt), and to swim in (mystery).

Let us examine each stage of our spiritual growth as a parallel to the vision of the river. In our lives, too, there will be a river of God from the Temple; at each measure we will come to see and touch a whole new level of spiritual experience. You can think of these if you like as passages of the spirit, necessary levels through which we all must pass in our adventure with God.

Peck calls the first stage of our lives before conversion *chaos*. It's a pretty good description, if we take it in its common meaning and not confuse it with "randomness." Within the last few decades the word *chaos* has become the term for a whole new science, a term to describe patterns discovered in the underlying complex simplicity of nature. The science of chaos has become a way of seeing structure in the apparent disorder of different things like clouds and coastlines, waves and leaves, a dripping tap in your bathroom or a swirling storm on a planet like Jupiter millions of miles away. Chaos in nature is now a study of unity in diversity and order in disorder, replete with odd names like *Koch Curves*, *Lorentz Attractors*, and *Mandelbrot Sets*.

Put simply, this recent discipline says that nothing in life is as simple as it seems. The complex diversity of things is often at heart the result of tiny changes in initial conditions on which the result is sensitively dependent. The new science of chaos has shown that in life, randomness is death; that small things can make a big difference later; and that a complex system can be turbulent and coherent at the same time.

Coherent, yet turbulent. Like you, like me. *Chaos*. All of us know what it is like to live a life that, for all its apparent order, is nevertheless antisocial, adult autistic, and devotedly self-centered—another word for what Barry McGuire called his early life without Christ: "Insanity."

Chaos is a good description for a life in which we have become dangerously irresponsible, so captive to sin and self-deception that we become pawns of our own choices, circumstances, or conditions. In a life of willful rebellion against God, we like to think of ourselves as free. But look closely and you see we are locked into repeating patterns, not truly random, but endlessly repeating. Like the man at the gate of the Temple, we see no real way out of our situation. Maybe we are frustrated, immobilized, helplessly locked down into our own intensifying, recurring patterns of guilt, blame, and self-pity, really wanting something better but wholly unable to get up by our own strength. Crippled, unclean, demeaned, and demoralized, we fight having to admit the final truth: We can do nothing at last but perhaps humble ourselves enough to beg for help and mercy.

This is the place of need for the first stage of spiritual growth. It involves the "waters to the ankles." What is the significance of water that begins at the feet? It means that God will come first to restore in our lives the following things:

(1) *Purity:* He makes us clean.

(2) *Dignity:* He gives us a real self-worth.

(3) *Responsibility:* He restores to us a sense of commitment and care.

(4) *Mobility:* He empowers us to reach out to help others.

Purity

The river of God washes first at our ankles. There is a key significance of that first water contact with the feet in Scripture, one we tend to forget in the world of paved roads, carpets, and socks and shoes. Our feet are the parts of us that are most in touch with the earth. We take off our shoes when we draw near the bush that burns with fire, because we are on holy ground. That's why the footwashing ceremony of Bible times was such an important part of honoring a guest at your home; it was a provision for cleansing.

And there is first a cleansing for our sin in the river. In his eventual obedience to God, Naaman, the proud Syrian general, was freed in the river from leprosy, the AIDS of his time. "Wash me thoroughly from my iniquity, and cleanse me from my sin," prayed a repentant David. "Wash me, and I shall be whiter than snow" (Psalm 51:2, 7). Into our guilty, chaotic, and defiled lives comes the river of God, cleansing and purifying. Our first contact with the river comes with the conviction that we cannot cleanse ourselves, and that we must be touched by His mercy: "Not by works of righteousness which we have done, but according to His mercy He saved us, through the washing of regeneration and renewing of the Holy Spirit" (Titus 3:5). The Bible also speaks of the Church being purified "with the washing of water by the word" (Ephesians 5:26). We walk through the world and we get our feet dirty. And in our day, the spiritual reality is the same. For our daily contact with a fallen world we need daily cleansing from the waterbowl of Christ.

Dignity

The second great accomplishment of salvation is the sense of value and specialness it restores to men and women. "You are a chosen generation," says 1 Peter 2:9, "a royal priesthood, a holy nation, His own special people, that you may proclaim the praises of Him who called you out of darkness into His marvelous light." A lame man has lost more than his legs; the loss of his mobility is also an assault on his dignity.

There is something about an external handicap that gets inside you; when you can no longer use your own limbs you tend also to lose your desire to do anything else.

John's Gospel records the account of healing of another crippled man (John 5:1–15). Jesus meets a man utterly powerless to move, someone unable to walk for 38 years. Day after day he has been carried there by others, perhaps even drags himself there to the sheep market pool, one small, lame part of the great crowd that hangs around Bethesda hoping for a miracle. I have friends who like this man have lost their ability to walk; I can know only something of the daily battle they wage with frustration and anger, the sense of uselessness, impotence, and helpless dependence such a crippling brings to the spirit. Thirty-eight years. "What more can we say about him," said Luigi Santucci, "once we know this about him? What is there to say about such a man apart from the number of years?"

And Jesus asks what must have sounded like a silly sort of question: "Do you want to be cured?" Cured? After being dragged here year after eternal year, always watching for the moving of the waters, scrabbling toward the rim of the pool at the troubling touch of the angel, but always being beaten to the edge by the man with the crippled hand but the healthy big elbows, the blind man with 20/20 hearing of water motion, or the deaf Olympic pole-vaulter?

Yet here is a Man with a question to ask that is not at all silly when you have been sick so long. "Do you want to be well?"

Sometimes you lose hope. One by one, your friends have gotten tired of carrying you around. They don't call anymore and you can't blame them. Nobody wants to look at you; they are afraid you will capture them with your naked stare of need. "I have no man" is your life summary now; you are all you've got but even you can't stand to live with yourself. And as for the angel who sometimes stirs these waters, how come he never notices you? You've been coming now year after year and here you are, still crippled while others have walked away free. Some healing angel! The angel must be blind.

But now suddenly a Face that does not look away; a gaze of utter and total attention; a look that will not let you go. Jesus is looking at you with those eyes that have eternity in them. And He is speaking, not to the crowd but to you. "*Do you want to be well?*"

Sometimes you forget what it ever felt like to feel good. You no longer remember what it is to be ordinary. You do not pray in faith because you have no remaining vision of what normal is. Your problem so fills the horizon of your daily life you have no room anymore for a surprise sunrise. Maybe you have been sick so long that now in your heart of hearts you actually find it preferable just to stay that way. You tried before; it never happened. It happened to others; it never happened to you. "*Do you want to be well?*" asks Jesus. "*Do you?*"

Responsibility

It is a frightening thing to be well. Ask the man in the asylum about it. Ask the habitual offender who is checked once again into his prison home how he handled the latest venture outside. It is sometimes easier to be sick. When you are well, people expect things from you. They expect you to help others. They expect you to carry your share of the burden, to be part of the solution and not the problem, to have something you can give for a change. When you are well, you are to be a healing force yourself in society; you are someone whom others may want to come to and draw from. It is a very serious question, this one Jesus asks by the edge of the water, as it reaches for our crippled ankles: "Do you *really* want to be well?" "It's not my fault," says the cripple at the edge of the pool. "I have no man." "*I am a Man,*" says the presence of Jesus. "*Rise, take up your bed and walk.*"

Mobility

Purity, dignity, responsibility. And when the healing river of God touches the lame man at the Gate Beautiful it gives him the one thing every person needs who cannot move: mobility. The man at the gate has much more than a divine healing; he also experiences a miracle. It is indeed a "notable" miracle because Scripture makes it clear that he has *never* walked. A man, around forty years old, instantly learning to walk? No tripping around, no crawling, no stumbling as a baby does? Just like that? A miracle indeed.

So comes the river of God to us in our powerlessness, in our weakness, in our helplessness, in our irresponsibility, having always to be carried by other people. The river touches us. It sets us on our feet. It sends us out with a message for a crippled world. It makes every Christian a missionary and everyone else a mission field.

When the priests bearing the Ark of God came to cross the Jordan into the Promised Land, the waters marking the beginning of their mission did not part until their feet touched the river (Joshua 3:7–17). And they stood on their feet in the middle of that riverbed with the waters rising "in a heap" in a faraway city until the whole nation had passed over to the other side. When the priests' feet then touched dry ground, the waters refilled the riverbed to overflowing.

This divine commission to move out may take us to some scary places. The water now washing our ankles will rise much more, and if we go where it is headed we will travel with it to a parched and dying world.

There is a mighty *GO* in the word *Gospel.* What cleansed, restored, and made you caring now needs to be taken to the rest of the world; the river brings healing and life wherever it flows, and a great draught of fish. Mobility. The Great Commission in our generation is a realizable goal. We know what it will take. We know what needs to be done. It can happen. We have begun to focus on the untouched places that are the last great frontiers of missions; God is looking for those who will go.

Maybe you never understood just what it meant to get involved with Jesus Christ when you first said you would follow. But He is out first of all to make you clean, to give you beauty for ashes, real love for others, and a global task to do that will not be over until you stand face-to-face before His throne.

What about the countries that are closed to the Gospel? "What about them?" says Brother Andrew. "There are no closed doors. Show me a country closed to the Gospel and I will show you a way to get in. I may not be able to tell you how to get back. But after all, Jesus just said, 'Go.' He didn't say, 'Come back.' "

All this and more is involved when the first innocent wave curls at your ankles. Are you ready for the rest of the river?

Prayer

Lord, we thank You for the bittersweet memories of things once deeply loved and shared that have now passed into history and the record of our walk with You. We thank You for each one of them—the places, the people, the circumstances and situations that became for a small, sweet time the reflection of Your great grace and provision for us.

We appreciate in each of them Your care; we acknowledge in all of them Your dear hand; we rejoice in what each taught us of Your beauty and Your bounty. And now that they are gone, moved with some sadness into the journal of what is now forever past, we ask for the grace to lift our hearts and our hands from what may never be again to what is yet to come. Our brook has dried up; the birds You sent are now gone, but we are not forsaken or forgotten. We hear again that still, small voice that calls on us once more to touch and taste and see anew the adventure that comes with Your friendship, our living and Creator God.

Thank You, then, Lord, for what is now past; we look to You in faith for the needs of the present hour in newness of expectation; and we say "Welcome" to the future as something under Your care, as that which has been filtered through the righteousness, care, and faithfulness of a God who cannot lie, who shall not fail, and who has promised never to leave or forsake us. We affirm again that nothing You give us can or must ever take Your own lovely place. You are our Father, and we are glad.

Level Two

Water to the Knees

"My Lord and my God." —Thomas surrenders to Jesus

Again he measured a thousand and led me through the water, water reaching the knees. Ezekiel 47:4, NAS

2

The Discipline of Limits

The river comes, secondly, to the knees. At this second level I can't help but think of an image from the wholly irreverent movie *Monty Python and the Holy Grail.* One unforgettable image from this weird flick is of the Black Knight protecting the bridge. He challenges King Arthur, who after a short scuffle promptly hacks off one of the Black Knight's arms. "Just a flesh wound," the Knight mutters and undaunted resumes the battle. Arthur then proceeds to systematically cut off his other arm and both his legs. Finally, there is left this man hopping precariously on his knees yelling: "*All right. Let's call it a draw.*"

It ought to be obvious. You can't fight when you are reduced to your knees. Resistance on this level is futile. The whole heart of the bowed knee in Scripture has to do with the idea of submission.

In the first stage of a standard spiritual conversion, a person goes from what Peck calls "chaos" to some form of "tradition," some structure, some limits. For example, you've been "doing your own thing" in some sophisticated or unsophisticated way. Then the river comes; it touches your ankles, it cleanses you and gives you strength. It puts you back on your feet. It makes you strong. Now you have some dignity; now you have some mobility. And with that dignity and mobility comes a danger. The danger is that now you've become a motivated person, you can easily become *self*-motivated. Now that you can move on your own, you may do just that outside of God.

The danger then of God's making us significant and responsible is that we now are tempted to do as we please. We can call it "the Protestant heresy" because it comes only to people who are free. We can be *too* free. Our liberty can degenerate into license.

That's why law is important and why tradition is important. That's why at weddings a bride doesn't usually come down in a purple dress with green spots, exchange chickens with the groom, and have a local dogcatcher conduct the ceremony. There is ancient wisdom, significant heritage embodied even in many of our traditional customs and rituals and ceremonies. There are principles. We need rules and limits and boundaries.

So the next thing is for the river to touch our knees. We now have to learn to do things simply because we're told, not because we personally agree, understand, or think that it's a good idea. We have to learn to obey even when the call comes against our own best intentions and our own good ideas.

Most conversions take place in this transition from chaos to tradition, nothingness to order. Even in the religious world that is not Christian, this is an observable stage of change: from dissipation to discipline; from doing our own thing to doing what we are told. The guy who's a drug addict takes up Zen Buddhism (with or without "motorcycle maintenance"). Before perhaps he was a vomiting, addicted transsexual; now he chants koans while people slap him on the back with wooden boards if he moves. The dissolute, indolent playboy who wouldn't give you the time of day before 11:45 A.M. now chants a mantra faithfully at his 4:00 A.M. devotions. Then after his sparse vegetarian breakfast he is off to sell magazines or flowers in airports.

This change is especially true in *real* conversion. What we get at this level are some limits and some guidelines. We all need rules. If we find the right ones (from God's Book and in God's world) and work with them, we are working with life as God designed it. And most times we're comfortable in this. The point to notice as the water laps around our knees is that now we do what we are told, rather than following our usual inclination to do what we think or feel. Previously, if people didn't like the way we were, then tough; we weren't in this world to measure up to their expectations and they weren't in this world to measure up to ours, and if by chance we met, it was beautiful. Now it's all changed. We are given rules, the limits, the way it's done; and we learn to bow the knee.

This surrender is, as we will find, a place of real security. We are told what to do by a trusted authority. We learn principles. We learn there are reasons behind the rules, and we learn the rules themselves and commit ourselves to God in them. We learn God's laws, His structures that govern relationships in the home and family and marriage, in business and government. We delight as a culture in seeing how God put things together and discussing why we think He did. Seminars that propose to show us these rules and relationships are a key part of our information-centered Western world.

But God likes people who do things because He told them to, not because they always understand why. Brother Andrew said he noticed one key difference between people who served God in the Bible and people who claim to serve God today. The people in the Bible disagreed with God quite vocally but still did what He said. Today we agree wholeheartedly with God, but *don't* do what He says.

The Bible God is the Ruler of the universe. All our lives are dependent on His care and guidance. He is under no obligation, save His love, to speak or reveal Himself to anyone. We, however, are dependent on revelation, and revelation is given only in trust. George Washington Carver, the man who found God's hidden treasures in the lowly peanut plant, said, "When you love someone or something long enough, it will reveal its secrets to you."

There is a divine order even to the *way* we receive truth from God. It goes something like this:

↓ *Revelation* — God speaks
Practical Service — We do it
Illumination — He explains it (maybe!)

This communication order is inherent in all of God's dealings with mankind; it is illustrated even in the order of the languages of Scripture. Hebrew, the language of the Old Testament, is a revelation/action language. Greek, the primary language of the New Testament, is one better suited to description and explanation. This is an order that promotes faith and develops trust with an ever-growing wonder.

The *maybe* in the above diagram is important. Explanation is not our own option. God never *has* to explain it. Obedience always precedes illumination. A. W. Tozer put it like this: "Obedience is the opener of the eyes."

It is true that we have to be sure it really *is* God speaking. It is biblically true that we are to "test all things" (1 Thessalonians 5:21), and to "test the spirits" (1 John 4:1). It is also true that the Christian life is supposed to be the wisest way, one that demands the commitment not only of the whole heart but also of the mind. God has not called us to some careless leap in the dark. God never said, "Be ye transformed by the removal of your minds."

But it is not true that God has to explain things to us before we can obey Him. It is not true that we have to know why before we must do it. God has an order in the way He communicates with us, and that order is always this: He speaks; we do it; He explains it—*maybe*. If we attempt to reverse this divine order we get into serious trouble.

Yet reverse it we do. We do it all the time. We do it especially in the Western world, with our rich heritage of thought from civilizations like those of Greece and India and millennia of philosophy, education, and science. It is the characteristic idolatry of our communication/information culture that our lust to understand has time and time again stood in the way of the clear Word of God. Our educational system, even in the majority of our best Bible colleges, fits this inversion. *FIRST we explain. Then we're encouraged to do. Later we are expected to become godly.* Yet somehow this "spiritual" goal keeps receding for many. They can't understand why the more they seem to learn, the less they seem to grow. In the desire to understand, we have become the victims of our own strength.

It is not the facts or the learning that is the problem. If the more we learn the less we grow in trust, then ignorance is indeed bliss. The less we know the happier we will be, and heaven is a final haven for all true idiots. If it is true that the more we know the less thrilled we are, then God Himself (with infinite wisdom) should rightfully be infinitely bored. If learning is an impediment to spiritual growth and excitement, then the Lord Jesus Himself who "increased in wisdom and stature" (Luke 2:52) as time went on should have become less and less committed to His task. Yet He was a man who lived by the hour, whose whole life was a testament of dangerous and infectious joy and of whom it was said near the end of His mission, "The zeal for Your house has eaten me up."

No, knowledge is not the problem; what we have is a *wrong priority*. Something good and right has been put in the wrong place and given false authority—a nice, approved, and eminently respectable idol, but an idol nevertheless.

What actually happens when we reverse the divine order is an eventual erosion of faith, a "rust" in our trust! The result of this inverted approach in our spiritual lives is that we become more cynical and rationalistic and fault-finding.

More than a hundred years ago, one of the great revivalists of history, Charles Finney, noticed the danger of a minister's explaining too much before calling people to obedience to

God. He said that this tendency would eventually result in a generation with a critical, proud, and rationalistic mindset that "either has no real faith or holds most loosely to Divine things that do not admit of a clear explanation" (*Reflections on Revival*). If God is not going to explain to our single brain cells why He made the universe, well, then, we're not going to do what He says.

The Western world (which leads in information and communication technology) has done precisely this. Part of God's work in our time is to restore divine order to our lives, to learn again how to follow when we cannot see.

This is exactly why God taught the leaders of His people in Bible days the central thought of *covenant*: that God and man may enter into a mutual pledge of faithfulness and commitment. In Genesis 15:18 and 17:4 the Lord covenants with Abram, promising his children not only the land from the rivers of Egypt to the Euphrates, but to make him "a father of many nations." To Noah and his family on the edge of the world's greatest disaster, God's covenants are the safety of the ark and His promise never again to destroy all life on earth by flood (Genesis 8:21; 9:11). His token of this was a rainbow (Genesis 9:13).

To "cut a covenant" in those ancient days in the cultures from which Israel came meant the forging of a mutual pact or oath made deeply serious by the slaying and sacrifice of an animal. This idea was inherent: "May my blood be spilled like this and my body cut apart if I ever break this promise to you." It also sometimes involved the sharing of a meal with someone; you would never harm even your worst enemy who shared your table.

What did covenant with God mean to Israel in Moses' day? It involved *blood* (Exodus 24:8), a *book* (Exodus 24:7), and a serious *bond* that was never to be broken. He told them, "If you will indeed obey My voice and keep My covenant, then you shall be a special treasure to Me above all people; for all the earth is Mine" (Exodus 19:5). They were warned not to covenant with the cultures around them, nor with their gods (Exodus 23:32). And for His part God promised that "before all your people I will do marvels such as have not been done in all the earth, nor in any nation; and all the people among whom you are shall see the work of the Lord. For it is an awesome thing that I will do with you" (Exodus 34:10). To this day Israel celebrates its Sabbath in honor of that covenant made so long ago (Exodus 31:16).

We have today in Christ by the "blood of the everlasting covenant" the promised help of the full energy of the Godhead for those who trust Him. This is the significance of the Lord's Supper when He took bread, broke it, and said, "This is My body which was broken for you," and poured out the wine with the words, "This is the blood of the New Covenant in My name." Jesus is committed to me by His blood, by His Book, and by an utterly serious mutual bond: God Himself has bound Himself to my happiness as I have bound myself to His.

Covenant also means this: It may be no great thing for me to give my trust and promises to God, but it is wondrous indeed that God would entrust His promises to me. My faithfulness to God will always be limited by my finiteness and humanity, but His faithfulness to me is without limit and without measure.

A classic example of faithfulness to God while enduring the discipline of limits is Joseph. If ever someone held onto a dream that seemed doomed from the start it was he. From his story, which we will explore in the next chapter, we will see that God is faithful beyond our understanding, that even when our dreams seem to self-destruct, God keeps His Word.

3

Joseph in Egypt: When Your Dreams Self-Destruct

There is a certain hard reality about getting your feet wet. Water can chill. And what happens to a high and lofty dream when it is hit by the cold water of reality? Those cold waves life's river throws at you can be devastating. How do the promises of God square with the failure of someone close to you whom you trusted, the pressures of seduction, temptation, and compromise, or, perhaps the hardest of all, to be apparently completely forgotten? What do you do with a wave that seems to leave you threatened in all the places you have just seen made strong—your dignity, your freedom, your purity, and your calling in God?

Years ago people used to sing a lot about dreams. In New Zealand we had a great deal of music from Europe and the United States. There were songs like Cliff Richards' "Theme for a Dream," the Everly Brothers' "Dream," and Johnny Burnette's "Dreamin'."

The last few years, things have changed and we don't hear so much singing about dreams anymore. Can it be that the world has lost its dreams? Many think the American dream has turned into the American nightmare. People used to write about utopias; they believed they would build a new world, a wonderful world where everything would be rosy. That's been ruined in the last few years. Wars ruined it. The Bomb ruined it. Ongoing sin ruined it. The Brave New World is still afraid and still the same.

Humanists used to go out with stars in their eyes and say, "Man will build a new world." Malcolm Muggeridge was such a person. He believed that given the right technology, the right education, people would be beautiful. He became bitterly disillusioned with his humanism and became a Christian. The world today is being broken and smashed in its dreams. The Optimistic Eighties have become the Nervous Nineties.

I once disliked witnessing to artists about Christ. I could speak to scientists because my background is organic research chemistry. I could share with musicians because I had a rock band for three and a half years. But I could not witness to artists. I thought artists were weird. I couldn't understand what they were trying to say.

One day the Lord spoke to my heart. He said, *Son, do you love artists?* I said, "Well, yes, of course I love artists. Thou knowest I lovest all men." So He asked again: *Do you love artists?* "No," I said. "Actually, I don't. I think they are all weird."

The Lord said, *I am an artist.*

"Well, all artists are weird—except You, Lord."

I began to realize there was an entire culture of people that I'd shut out because I didn't believe they could really be affected by the power of God like the other people I had seen. God convicted me of lack of love and concern for them. It's very easy to shut out an entire culture. Somebody's hair is longer or shorter than yours, or he has a safety pin through his cheek, and you say, "I don't know if God can save him."

So I began to pray. I took up photography—that's a science of optics and chemistry and yet an art, too. It helped link the world I knew with another world I didn't and bridged the gap. In a few months God began to open my eyes by visualizing through a camera lens some of the world of beauty He had made.

About a year later, I was sitting in San Francisco in a cafe. I looked on the wall and saw a painting. For the very first time in my life, I understood an artist. The artist had drawn a dry, barren world, with long grass that looked quite lifeless. Amidst that dead grass were two children; the grass around them was all short and stubbly. There was not a hint of green in the entire picture. The sky was dull and overcast, a brown, polluted yellow. The sun was only a big flat white penny spent in the sky; it didn't even shine, it was just there. There was a little girl standing in the grass and further back a little boy, almost lost in the grass. They both had these big eyes. The whole picture was brown—except for the blue in the kids' wide-open eyes. But instead of being a soft blue, the artist had chosen a hard, brilliant blue, like sapphire chips of glass.

Suddenly I understood what the artist was trying to say. "Here are two little ones; their eyes are wide open and they're seeing the whole world and it's dead. But you can see inside of them and they're dead, too. Just two little dead dolls stuck in a dead world."

And God spoke to me from that painting. He said, *When the dreams of children die, it's the end of the world.* When kids no longer have anything to believe in, they can't hope anymore. It's the end of the world.

In many people's lives, especially those who call themselves by the name of Jesus, there comes a time when dreams seem to die on you. People and circumstances and pressures conspire against what you are sure is God's calling. How can you handle the sins of others that affect your dreams? Take the story of Joseph.

> Now Jacob dwelt in the land where his father was a stranger, in the land of Canaan. This is the genealogy of Jacob. Joseph, being seventeen years old, was feeding the flock with his brothers. And the lad was with the sons of Bilhah and the sons

of Zilpah, his father's wives; and Joseph brought a bad report of them to his father. Genesis 37:1–2

Joseph is a simple guy, childlike, imaginative, uncomplicated. He is ingenuous. Do you know anyone like Joseph? Such people are becoming rare in our cynical, sophisticated, media-weary world. They are so naïve and straightforward that they can be embarrassing sometimes. They are the opposite of "cool," which is often a synonym for cynical, sophisticated, and cruel.

But Joseph watches his brothers blowing it and says, "Hey, you guys! That's wrong! Hey, Dad, they're doing some wrong things."

You can guess what his brothers think. They are disgusted with him. Everybody knows it isn't cool to rat on people in your family, even if they are doing wrong.

Some people say things and you have to ask, "Is that what he meant or did he *actually* mean this? Does he say that because he wants me to think that, but he really means the opposite? Or does he say that because he *really* means that and he means me to know that he means that?" We need to study body language manuals and take police interrogation courses to find out if people really mean what they say.

When you meet an ingenuous person, it's never like that. Such encounters can be embarrassing! Arthur Katz, who has a very regal bearing, visited our office and talked with my secretary.

She said, "You're Art Katz."

"Yes."

"I thought you'd be different."

"Really?"

She said: "I thought you'd be taller."

He laughed. She blushed. Ingenuous. It's wonderful to have a secretary like that around. Uncomplicated. Straightforward.

Joseph is like this. A person of integrity. Consistent. He

loves his father and his father loves him. This relationship is rare in the modern family.

One night God gives Joseph a dream. The next morning, having breakfast with his brothers, Joseph, in his simple but frank way, says, "Boy, did I ever have a neat dream last night. I can hardly believe it. Want to hear what it was about? We were all tying sheaves in the field and my sheaf stood up and all the other sheaves bowed before my sheaf." His brothers were not amused. "They hated him even more for his dreams and for his words" (Genesis 37:8).

It gets worse. He has another dream, and again uncool, ingenuous Joseph decides to share it with the whole family. "Hey!" says Joseph. "Remember that great dream God gave me? Well, you'll never believe it. Last night He gave me another one! Listen to this. You'll love it." And oblivious to the dark looks of his brothers he rattles on excitedly: "In this dream the sun and the moon and eleven stars bowed down to me. And, oh, Dad, the sun is you, the moon is you, Mom, and you guys are the eleven stars. Great, huh?"

Jacob, his dad, may not have been too swift, but he wasn't completely blind. Noticing the daggers in his sons' eyes, the father rebukes Joseph, saying, "What is this dream that you have dreamed? Shall your mother and I and your brothers indeed come to bow down to the earth before you?"

Who gives Joseph these dreams? *God* does. He shows him the same vision of his future in two different ways. There has never been a generation in history so visually sophisticated as this one. It is to this generation that the promise of God comes: "And it shall come to pass afterward that I will pour out My Spirit on all flesh; . . . *your old men shall dream dreams, your young men shall see visions*" (Joel 2:28, emphasis added).

A lot of people today are unable to distinguish between a call of God and religious fantasy. God speaks to the child heart, to the pure heart, to the heart set on seeking Him and loving Him. And if God gives you a dream, He will fulfill it.

I believe there are people to whom God has given dreams who today are wondering what in the world happened to them. God said to those people, "I have something for you that I am showing you," but then something seemed to go wrong and it's not clear exactly what. Look at Joseph.

His Brothers Betray Him

His father says, "Go take these peanut butter and jelly sandwiches down to your brothers." So along comes ingenuous Joseph with his sandwiches.

> When they saw him afar off, even before he came near them, they conspired against him to kill him. Then they said to one another, "Look, this dreamer is coming! Come therefore, let us now kill him and cast him into some pit; and we shall say, 'Some wild beast has devoured him.' We shall see what will become of his dreams!" Genesis 37:18–20

The oldest of the brothers, Reuben, hears these words and says, "Don't shed his blood, but cast him into the pit that is in the wilderness." Reuben thinks he might get him out later despite the murderous intentions of his brothers.

Did God really give Joseph a dream about everyone bowing down to him? If so, how come he's in a pit? How do you "bow down" to someone in a pit? What do you think Joseph thought?

Here is the first test of a dream: Can you handle it when even your own brothers (out of jealousy, envy, or just plain ignorance) oppose you and let you down?

An Ishmaelite trading party is going through on the way to Egypt. Joseph's brothers say to these Midianites: "Here's a good slave for you—strong and healthy. Make us an offer we can't refuse." They do. Reuben is away during that transaction but, perhaps out of fear, does not protest as the brothers kill an animal, dip Joseph's coat into the animal's blood, and take it back to their father who dearly loves his youngest son.

"This evil beast came and ate him up," they tell him. Jacob cries for a long time.

The most important thing to learn about a gift or calling of God is this: With great power always comes great responsibility. We all would like a dream from God, but are we prepared to handle the awesome responsibility that comes with it? We all would like the honor of representing Him, but are we prepared to be trained to think and act like Him? We talk about trusting God; can He trust us?

Only a godly character can survive the immense pressures a great dream brings with its promises. God is more concerned with how we handle pressure than with delivering us from pressure. Here are four false ways people respond when their dreams begin to evaporate:

1. Wildness (Intemperance). One of the most popular ways of dealing with the loss of a dream in the Western world is this: Go party it up and forget your sorrows. Joseph could have said to the Egyptians, "Give me a bottle of Nile Comfort. I never drank before, but since my world fell apart I may as well start now."

How do some people react to the apparent destruction of their dreams? They bury their pain in drugs. Grab themselves cans and bottles and get smashed out of their heads. Or shoot up. There are those pills that help them forget all ills. If they're short on cash, there's always a bag and glue.

The reaction of wildness is reaching new depths in our day, as so many young people are stripped not only of any sense of value or worth, but of hope. For some the answer is to immerse themselves in a continual round of parties, music, and fleeting "relationships" (nobody "falls in love" anymore). Life hurts. Things are going terribly wrong. Something must be done to take away the pain. If you were going to the dentist, would you refuse the novocaine? What sense does it make to "just say no" if what is offered seems to be the only way of taking away the hurt?

Others are driven into darkness; more and more young people are practicing demonic rites, hoping to find some measure of power over their circumstances. Now that the good seems hopeless, they turn to ancient evil. Satanism is the number one problem in many high schools in America today.

2. Withdrawal (Introversion). Another way of trying to handle problems in the West is to back out of everything. Pull out of the situation; create another little fantasy world where everything is neat and dreams are already true. Build a castle in the air, then try to move into it. This is the "Jonathan Livingston Seagull" answer. Fly through the rock, and you'll find it is not real; things are not the way they seem. Housewives get addicted to soap operas. Kids lose themselves in a musician, a rock star, adventure gaming. But a Christian Science approach to sin and misery always falls through in the Church. Hurt and sin and death are real. They do not have to be welcomed, but they cannot be ignored.

Joseph could have said, "I don't believe this is happening to me. It is not real at all. I'm not really on a slave caravan. I *can't* be! I'm supposed to have everyone bow down to me, not bow down to everyone else. I refuse to believe it. It is an awful nightmare. I'll wake up one day and I'll be safe in my nice little bed at home."

After a while, those who withdraw begin to go insane. They cannot confront the reality of what is happening. They don't accept the reality in a faith-filled way and say, "This is rotten, but I believe God anyway." It is trust in God that gives us the courage to deal with the hurts of life, because we know that ultimately He is just in all His ways and righteous in all His works, and no matter what comes down, He keeps His promises. The Christian is to be both a realist and an idealist. "He can be," said Peter Marshall, "he must be both."

Even clear, logical thinking that is based on false premises is destructive. Our world has tried to live out assumptions that are lies, and the results are all around us. When smart people see the results of their situations, when smart people try to face pressures in life they were never designed to handle on their own, they break down fast. The less quickly they see it, the slower it takes, but break down they will. That's why some men who originate destructive philosophies go crazy immediately. Those who follow them may not see the consequences as quickly (and sometimes it takes more than a generation to see those consequences), but when they do they all go crazy, too—at once. Bad things *do* happen to good people. Perhaps some terrible wrong happened to you, too, and it is just as bad if not worse than it seems. You can, of course, simply refuse to think about it, to ignore what happened, to try to put it out of your mind. But if you don't face it, you will go crazy.

I was in a city in southern California called La Puente and met a young lady after a meeting there. She said, "There's nothing real in the world. Only what you think is real." I said, "What are you saying?" She said, "For instance, what do you think that is?" She pointed to a piano. I said, "That's a piano." She said, "No, it isn't. It's a blue giraffe." I went over and played a few notes on the blue giraffe and said, "It sure sounds like a piano to me." She said, "You *think* it's a piano because you've chosen to believe it is a piano. But I believe it's a blue giraffe."

She was running away from reality. A girl who has totally blown the moral values of her life and she's trying to say, "This has not happened to me. It's only happened in my mind."

I asked her, "Are you saying there is no external reality other than yourself?" She said, "Yes, the whole world is what you make it."

(John Lennon once wrote a song called "Mind Games." That's what everyone is playing.)

I said, "You're saying nothing is real? Everything you experience is just the projection of your own consciousness?"

"Yes," she said, "that's it exactly. There is nothing real other than what we choose to believe in."

I pulled a Francis Schaeffer trick: I grabbed a pot of hot coffee and held it over her head. She said, "What are you doing?" I said, "I'm just going to pour this pot of hot coffee over your head. But you don't have to worry. If you don't *think* it's there, it won't burn you. I happen to believe it will."

Then I said, "Let's go up on top of this church and jump into the swimming pool." She said, "What swimming pool?" I said, "The one you can believe in on the way down."

Finally, I grabbed her nose. A nose is such a tangible thing. She yelled, "Let go of my nose!" I said, "I don't *have* your nose. You just *think* I have your nose."

Jesus calls us to confront the reality of our situation. He says, "It has happened. It is awful. You have to face it." When the problem is rooted in something we have done wrong we can come to Him and be cleansed, healed, and forgiven. When it is rooted in something others have done, we must forgive and release them from our temptation to bear grudges, hatred, bitterness. The way of denial, of withdrawal, is the way of madness. God calls us to face what has happened honestly, and to use it to throw ourselves more on His love and care.

3. Fatalism (Resignation). The third wrong way to cope with a loss of your dreams is the Eastern way, the way of acceptance. "Whatever is must be." It is *fate, kismet, karma.* Events are but the playing out of a movie; there are sad parts in with the good parts, but it is all at heart just illusion. People don't *have* dreams; they *are* dreams. There are no ultimate absolutes in the universe, and thus no opposites; no good and evil, no right and wrong, no life and death. The world is a *Tao;* reality is where darkness and light are one. God is good/evil, male/female, life/death, and reincarnation will recur until we merge into the Absolute. Everything we experience here is only a dream anyway.

"The truly wise man," said the Maharishi in his commentary on the Bhagavad Gita, "will never weep." Who cares about wars, disasters, destruction, murder? More than 1,700 years ago the Eastern philosopher Plotinus who recorded the ideas of Ammonius Sacchus, founder of the school of Neo-Platonism, put it like this:

> Still more what does it matter when people are devoured [by death] only to return in some new form? It comes to no more than the murder of one of the persons in a play; the actor alters his makeup and returns in a new role. . . . All human intentions are but play, that death is nothing terrible, that to die . . . is to taste a little beforehand what old age has in store, to go away earlier and come back sooner. Murders, death in all its guises . . . all must be to us but the varied incident of a plot, costume on and off, acted grief and lament.

Many people in the West also adopt this attitude, popularized by the New Age movement and spokespeople like Shirley MacLaine whose best-selling books are at heart twentieth-century updates of old and dark Eastern philosophies. Few in the West know what it is like to live in a culture dominated by such darkness; the human sacrifice, the burning of widows in suttee, the caste systems rarely spoken of in polite society in modern India. If all events are necessitated, if everything that happens in life is but the unreeling of film already recorded in the can, then accept we must, and resign ourselves we shall.

The old songs underlined it to previous generations. In the '50s Doris Day sang "Que Sera, Sera"—"Whatever will be, will be." The country-and-western singer of the '60s drawled "Born to Lose," and Steppenwolf in the '70s gave the Hell's Angels an anthem with "Born to Be Wild."

But the way of Christ is never passive acceptance of evil. It is not to admit its necessity or to resign ourselves to the belief that somehow we must learn to coexist with it. Jesus *hated* death, disease, and the rule of the demonic world in people's lives. He healed sicknesses, restored crippled limbs, opened blind eyes and deaf ears. He freed every demonized person He confronted. He never preached a funeral sermon. Instead He broke funerals by the simple expedient of raising the corpse from the dead and restoring the person to his family. Death, like sin and disease, is an enemy in the Bible (1 Corinthians 15:26). The shortest verse in the Bible describes Jesus' own response to the grief, death, and devastation in His poor, broken world: *"Jesus wept"* (John 11:35).

4. A Religious Answer. A fourth option of our time is that of the hurting religious person faced with the collapse of his dreams and the apparent failure of God's promises: It is to *blame God.* To call Him the devil in disguise; to distill all frustration into bitterness, hatred, and resentment and to unload it all on heaven.

That is the trouble with religious idealism when it becomes disillusioned: It quickly turns into radicalism. That's why Marxism could be properly called a Christian heresy. When people with religious backgrounds go sour, they can become the most dangerous people in the world. If our trust in God is inadequate, if we have given ourselves over to religious fantasy that is not founded on biblical revelation and spiritual reality, if we have followed a Christ of our own creation, we will be devastated when it dissolves. *If we have made up an imaginary God we will have to put up with the consequences of an imaginary salvation.* And when such religious idealisms collapse, "great is the fall thereof."

The hardest, most bitter people I have ever met are ex-church people who have turned sour. I can't think of a single atheist I have met in the Western world who has not first had some kind of church background. Most of the really dangerous radicals of our time are people who have given themselves to a religious cause that has been turned significantly to darkness. They become hostile, suspicious, mean. They love no one and expect no love from others. They trust no one and expect no trust from others. This bitterness toward God creates a callous attitude, a cold heart, and hatred not only of God and others, but even of themselves.

The religious person's answer to misplaced trust is often to distill all of his or her bitterness and pour it out on God; to say, in effect, "If *this* is the way it is going to be, God, then forget it. If this is what You had in mind by the dreams You gave me, then You are brutal and vicious and cruel. I trusted You, I listened to You, I believed You, and now everything has fallen apart. See if I ever do anything for You again. See if I ever believe You again. I'm against You, God. I will take my stand against You and I'll do my best to serve Your enemies to the limit of my abilities."

Joseph could have done this. He could have formed the "Egyptian Angels Chariot Club" and ridden around beating up people in border towns in the name of freedom. He could have become a hit man for Pharaoh or formed the S.L.A.—the Slavery Liberation Army. He could have planted bombs in Hebrew baby buggies and booby-trapped Israeli camels. He could have put the blame for everything that happened to him squarely back on the Lord and bitterly resigned himself to what was happening in a lifelong grudge against God.

This was the answer of *Jesus Christ Superstar* when the Judas of the '70s hit album and movie asks Jesus the question "What happened to Your dream?" And Rice and Webber have their Jesus answer: "Then I was inspired. Now I'm sad and tired." Their Christ blames God His Father for what is happening to Him. Like Judas, it is not His fault that things turned out the way they have.

Representations of this fantasy Christ come out in controversial movies like *The Last Temptation of Christ*. They are not new, but as old as every lost religious man's desire to shift the blame for what goes wrong in the world back to God.

But Joseph didn't do it. He refused to do any of these four things. He did not go wild. He did not withdraw. He did not resign himself to what had happened. And above all he did not blame God. Joseph knew he had a dream that was given to him *by God,* and circumstances don't alter divine destiny or dreams.

The classic movie *Ben Hur* explores the rift between two very close boyhood friends. Now adults, grown up apart from each other in two different cultures and worlds, Ben Hur refuses to give the names of some of the Jewish zealots to his Roman friend Messalah, and what begins as a touching reunion turns into a bitter confrontation. "You have no choice," says Messalah. "You are either for me or against me." "Then," replies Ben Hur, "I am *against* you."

Intensely hurt and angry, Messalah strikes back at his former friend, resulting in the destruction of his home, the arrest and imprisonment of his mother and sister, and Ben Hur's being sold into slavery. His world has fallen apart and all because he, like any good Jewish prince, has tried to preserve the religious dreams and ideals of his nation in its devotion to God. Beaten, broken, dying of thirst, with everything loved and secure stripped away from him, Judah ben Hur cries out to the God who seems to have forsaken him.

Then, from the first falling shadow of the Stranger who intervenes to give him water despite a centurion's orders to the contrary, to the final moving moments when he stands beneath the cross on which that same Stranger is dying for the sin and hurt of the world, the film is a statement of the faithfulness of God. There is healing for your hurt, for your betrayal, for your anger at what life has dealt you. Do not give up on God. "*His voice,*" says Ben Hur, "*took the sword out of my hand.*"

If God has given you a dream, nothing can stop that dream from coming true except your own sin. The Bible says, "If God is for us, who can be against us?" (Roman 8:31). If God has given you a dream, no demon in hell, no self-centered sinner, nobody in this world can stop that from coming true *except yourself.* If you don't learn to react the right way to adversity, if you fall into any of these four traps, then you will blow your dream. The only thing that counts is staying on God's side.

Joseph arrives. He's not blaming God, he's not getting mad or bitter. He's not vowing to himself, "If I ever get out of here I'll pay them back for every rotten thing they tried to do to me. I'm going to kill all my brothers one by one."

He thinks instead: "This is really a mess. My brothers have betrayed me, but *God* can keep me. *God* is faithful. *God* is the One who gave me my dream." So he goes to work as best he knows how in Potiphar's household in Egypt, and he does his work as "unto the Lord." And the funny thing that happens is this: The Egyptian is so excited about Joseph's faithfulness that he makes him head of the servants of the household. God gave him a dream that one day he would be a ruler, and though he is a slave, the pattern of the prophecy begins to be fulfilled.

Now if you were he you might say, "Glory to God! God said I would be in charge one day, and here I am." But fortunately (and unfortunately) that isn't the end of the story. God isn't finished with Joseph yet, and neither is temptation. Enter the femme fatale in the plot. Enter the second great test of his life. Enter the prototype of every *Woman in Red* and *Fatal Attraction* to come. Joseph now has to survive the attempted seduction of Mrs. Potiphar.

A Woman Sets Out to Seduce Him

The recent televangelist sexual and financial scandals that have rocked the church world are unique only in that we live in a world where bad or sad news can be passed on almost instantly. It has certainly become hard to sin in secret in our century. Jesus said, "There is nothing hidden which will not be revealed, nor has anything been kept secret but that it should come to light" (Mark 4:22). There was never a time when this could be made more literally true.

Sin in the Church is something both shocking and sad to God and to His children, but something we have always had to deal with from Bible times to our hi-tech century. Seduction is certainly not something new, but not all seduction is sexual. The love of money seduces; the addiction to pleasure seduces; the privilege of power seduces. A Mrs. Potiphar (whether female or male) is always around to waylay someone with a dream from God, and her determination to make the dreamer fall is frightening to behold.

I suppose she has her own reasons, and all of them make sense to her. Joseph is a slave and he is her husband's legal property. "What is his is rightfully mine," she could say to herself. Besides, there is something exciting about the planned seduction of an unspoiled, clean-living man fresh in from the country. He is no risk. He doesn't have herpes or AIDS and would no doubt be flattered that an attractive and sophisticated woman of power and wealth and position like herself would deign to pay any attention to him at all. So she brushes up on some well-thumbed passages from *The Sensuous Egyptian* and makes her opening gambits.

And to her intense frustration and rising fury, Joseph doesn't play along. For a while she probably thinks he is a bit thick and doesn't know what she has in mind. But after many days of doing everything but leap naked from the chandelier onto him she realizes this devastating truth: He isn't interested. Not only does he smile politely and pass by every approach, he even takes to going out of his way not to be found in the house alone with her.

Why *doesn't* Joseph succumb to temptation? He is young, no doubt anxious to please, and probably a bit lonely. He is far from home in a place where no one knows of or cares about his childhood commitment to God. This alluring woman is both willing and able to provide him with what seems to be an even greater level of security and power; in fact, to shun her attractive advances might be downright dangerous. If he looks only at his past disappointments, his present circumstances, and his future situation, surrender to this attractive seduction is a foregone conclusion. If Joseph at that point decides that his childhood dream is out of reach, we all know what the next lines of his story would be.

And all of us have been there, too. Perhaps not every seduction looks like his, but the name of the game is always the same. And perhaps if we had been where Joseph stood, the story would have turned out the way everybody would expect it to.

But it doesn't. Shockingly it doesn't. Joseph does something that seems so strange, so odd, so gauche in a modern world like ours that is without convictions, without absolutes, without ultimate commitments. He says *no.* He turns her down, not because he might get caught, or because he might get hurt, or because she isn't quite his "type." *He turns her down because he doesn't want to hurt God.* He has a dream God has given him to treasure, and he feels that God would never let down someone who loves Him. He trusts God, and rests his case in His hands. He looks to Him to meet his needs. And so he says to the greatest temptation he has ever had in his life, "How can I do this wicked thing and sin against God?"

If you haven't read the story you might expect that things go great from that moment on. Like: "Mrs. Potiphar breaks down and weeps, apologizes to Joseph for the madness that came over her, gets saved and recommits her devotion and marriage to her rightful husband. Then Mr. Potiphar is so impressed that he also gets saved and begins a church in his house attended by many of his soldiers, and pastored of course by Brother Joseph. A great revival eventually sweeps the Egyptian army and leads ultimately to Joseph's being returned to his homeland where his brothers are all so impressed by his achievements they welcome him home. . . ." And so on. . . . (Fade to black, Handel's *Messiah* or perhaps "Chariots of Fire" playing in the background; run "The End.")

But reality is different. What actually follows is even *worse* than before. Mrs. Potiphar, in a mad rage, rips off his clothes. Joseph becomes the world's first "streaker for righteousness." He barely gets out of the house with anatomy intact, let alone his dignity. And then in furious retribution for his deflating and humiliating refusal, to her husband she accuses him of rape. Only his previous knowledge of both his wife and his captured Hebrew slave's character (and perhaps the intervention of God) stops Potiphar short of killing Joseph on the spot. But it's into a dungeon for Joseph the dreamer, Joseph the man of God, Joseph the faithful. And *where is his marvelous dream now?*

From slavery to a prison? That's *down*, not up! Things are looking darker than ever for Joseph. Honestly now, would you have thrown in the towel? Would you? *Did* you? After being slung into a filthy hole seemingly to rot away for life, would you say, "O.K. That's it. I've about had it with this righteousness stuff. God, why in the world would You let her do that? Why couldn't You just have moved me on somewhere else where I would have at least had a chance?"

But Joseph is incorrigibly, embarrassingly *faithful.* (Some people never learn.) He says, "Glory to God anyway. I still have a dream." And he goes to work in the prison until he is made ruler of the prison. The most important thing we can notice right here is this: "But *the Lord was with Joseph* and showed him mercy, and He gave him favor. . . . Because the Lord was with him; and whatever he did, the Lord made it prosper" (Genesis 39:21, 23, emphasis added).

One day Pharaoh has a big tiff with his butler and his baker. They are unable to shred the evidence in time and both end up in prison under the care and friendship of Joseph. And one day they both have dreams. The butler says, "I had a big bunch of grapes on three branches and I squeezed out some wine for Pharaoh and he drank it. I wonder what in the world that means?"

Joseph is an expert on dreams by now; he's had one himself a long time that has never been fulfilled. In fact, he has thought about it every which way for years and is real sensitive spiritually whenever someone mentions "dreams." He says, "I know what your dream means. In three days you are going to be restored as Pharaoh's butler. Just one thing," he adds sadly. "When it happens (and it will happen) will you put in a good word for me with Pharaoh?"

The baker is encouraged no end by this interpretation of the butler's dream, so he shares his dream with Joseph, too. Unfortunately, not all dream interpretations turn out to be positive. Just as Joseph discerns, Pharaoh restores the butler but executes the baker. And the one last request that Joseph makes to the butler as he leaves the prison, "Remember me," is wiped away in the relief of his release.

A Friend Forgets Him

There is something even worse than being betrayed or tempted and that is to be *forgotten*. Many a man or woman of God with a dream has made it gloriously first through hurt and even through various attempts at seduction, only to lose the race at last with the finishing tape in sight, to fall to the creeping despair of being apparently ignored, shelved, consigned to oblivion. In betrayal you at least have something significant enough for others to be threatened; in seduction you have something important enough to be the target of temptation. But in oblivion you stand to lose everything that ever made you or your dream worthwhile. And Joseph has to face it, just as you or anyone else who has been given a dream by God will have to face it. What do you do if after all your faithfulness, everyone, even those you counted on as friends, *just forget you?*

Being forgotten: to go out with neither a bang nor even a whimper but only an emptiness; to have wanted to make some kind of splash in the lily pond of life but leaving not even a ripple, nothing more than the effect on the water an hour after you pull out your hand. "The central neurosis of our time," said a famous psychiatrist, "is emptiness." It is the ultimate terror; it is the final level at which faith is tried to see if it may be found finally true.

Days go by, weeks, months for Joseph as he waits in vain for a word from the grateful butler, but still no message comes. And as the months stretch out into a whole year, then another, it seems as if Job's wife had the final insight into the real running of the world: "Do you still hold to your integrity? Curse God and die!" (Job 2:9).

But Joseph does not. Doggedly, faithfully, determined to trust God to the day he dies, he goes on with his tasks, running the prison, loving God, serving to the best of his ability. Good old Joseph is still good old *ingenuous* Joseph. He hasn't become cynical Joseph, now-I-know-better, once-bitten-twice-shy Joseph muttering to himself as he clenches his teeth, "I've been umpteen years in this rotten place. Where is God when you need Him?" And the God who never forgets, who in absolute justice and absolute goodness rules the universe, is not finished writing this story yet.

The genius of the ingenuous one is his ability to work with reversals of the plan. And God is the greatest genius in the universe. He rules over what jealous, sneaky, or nasty people are up to. He takes the intentions of the wicked and weaves their ugly purposes into scenarios that one day proclaim to all watching worlds His greatness and His glory. God delights in overthrowing the evil schemes of men and devils and fulfilling exactly what He says He is going to do.

If God makes you a promise, you are going to see that promise come true. Who cares *who* says it "cannot," "will not" happen? If He says it will, it will. If He has to move heaven and earth to do it, He will fulfill His Word. He has magnified His Word above His name, and His name is Faithful and True, the God who cannot lie.

Joseph is in jail. The world is quiet, and Pharaoh has a dream. It terrifies him. It bothers him intensely. It is only a dream about cows, seven fat cows and seven skinny cows. And right on its heels another one, starring fat ears of corn and skinny ears of corn. The seven dream cows with anorexia take out the seven plump ones. The seven wind-blasted ears of corn cannibalize the seven Kellogg's pin-up ears. And Pharaoh hasn't got a clue as to what this deeply disturbing set of night revelations means.

"Pour me some of that wine, butler," he says. "I just had a dream that scared the living incense out of me. I know it's important, and I know it has something to do with the nation, but every charlatan I know has referred me to crystals, cards, and animal entrails and I'm not getting any joy from them at all. And you know what I do when I'm not happy with my staff. . . ."

The butler's hand shakes a little as he pours the wine. "So what do you think, butler? And don't talk to me about pyramid power. I built them myself and I know that's not going to show me what I need to know. If there were only someone trustworthy in the kingdom, someone who wouldn't want to use me or rip me off, *someone* who could tell me what these dreams mean. . . ."

And the butler says: "Uh-oh."

Pharaoh is the king of the known world, and God deals with him directly. You may not think about God much when you are busy running the world. You may not plan to fit Him into your schedule. You can fill your waking hours with business, pleasure, and everything else you can imagine to shut out His voice, but you can't get away from Him if He is going to deal with you.

The butler remembers. "There was this guy. Name of Joseph. He told me about my dream. Right on, he was. Never saw a man before or since who knew more about dreams."

"Where is he?"

"Prison, last time I knew."

"Prison! Get him out and bring him here."

And in minutes, pausing only for a shave and change of

clothes, Joseph goes from prison to the presence of the Pharaoh of the world.

"I know what your dream means," says Joseph. "There are coming seven years of plenty to this country and then seven years of famine. God has spoken twice to the Pharaoh and that means it's not only sure, it will happen soon. What you should do is appoint someone really wise and trustworthy to supervise storage during the plenty years for the coming famine. That's my advice to Pharaoh."

"That's incredible!" says the Pharaoh. "I can't find anyone in my kingdom made as smart and trustworthy by God as you. You're elected. You're my number one man."

Boom. From prison to number two in the world in an hour. That's what God does.

For seven years Joseph supervises food and stores grain and then the predicted famine comes. Joseph's family runs out of food and only Egypt has grain to sell. At Jacob's bidding, his sons make the long and risky journey to Egypt to seek the favor of this new ruler under Pharaoh. To get grain you have to go through him. If he cuts you off, you die. Everything depends on their making the right impression, as they are ushered into the audience of the awful presence that sits beside the throne of Egypt.

And then you know what happens. The brothers file humbly in, totally unaware of who it is they are bowing down before. Joseph is looking at them, and it is all he can do to stop himself from crying. He is thinking, *Glory to God. Glory to God.* He listens to them protesting for their lives and for their little brother's life and for their old dad Jacob back home waiting and praying the ruler of Egypt will show mercy to their family. Joseph is thinking about what his little brother looks like now, and what his dad looks like now, and finally he can't stand it. They are all sitting there whispering desperately to each other in Hebrew, not knowing Joseph understands, not knowing who he is, conscious only that they are at the total mercy of a man who could snap his fingers like that and have them all annihilated.

He tells them they must return again for food and bring with them their little brother Benjamin or be cut off from provision and die. How Joseph manages to go that long without revealing his secret I'll never know. But the time comes when he stands up before them, clears the court, and faces them all alone. Choking back the tears he asks them, "Do you know who I am?" His brothers look at him. They still feel the guilt of long, long ago. They are scared. They are worried. They *don't* know who he is. He's the second ruler in the world, isn't he? What does he mean?

"I am Joseph."

The dream. The dream comes true. Literally, in a way not even Joseph in his wildest child's imagination could have guessed, the God who gave him his dream fulfills it to the uttermost. And Joseph, unable to restrain the sobs, has the happiest moment of his life. It is God, wholly God, *God* who has worked with him all along. The betrayals, temptations, burials of the past are forgotten; nothing he has been through matters anymore. "God sent me before you to preserve a posterity for you in the earth, and to save your lives by a great deliverance. So now it was not you who sent me here, but God; and He has made me a father to Pharaoh, and lord of all his house, and a ruler throughout all the land of Egypt" (Genesis 45:7–8).

Nothing can stop a God-given dream. If you drop it, someone else will pick it up and run in your place. God will do what He has promised; but great dreams mean great trials and great responsibilities. And if you have a dream given you by God, you, too, are going to have to learn how to deal with the pressures set against that dream.

What to Do When Your Dreams Seem to Destruct

First, face honestly what happened. It may have been sin, it may have been yours, it may have been another's, but the damage has been done. If you have lost something precious tell the Lord: "It's gone and it will never come back. That's it. But Lord, You gave me a dream and somehow despite everything, despite my own weakness and inability and failure, You can find a way to glorify Yourself and fulfill Your promises."

Second, next time you must absolutely refuse to get bitter. You have no cause to blame God, and you must steadfastly refuse to harbor bitterness or grudges against those who have done you real or imagined wrong. If you harbor hurt, your prayers will only hit the ceiling. You *must* forgive. John Wesley met a man who said, "Sir, I never forgive." John Wesley said, "Then, sir, I hope you never sin." Unforgiveness is not an option in relation to a dream sent from God.

Third, you are going to have to use your present circumstances creatively. Use what problems you now face to practice your dream. So God called you to the mission field. But here you are stuck in some little Podunk place that doesn't look or sound like any mission field you ever imagined. Practice all you have in Podunk. Give Podunk your best shot. Don't get a vision for all of Africa until you have begun out of a full heart to evangelize your own "Pumpkin Holler." Serve where you are now in Jesus' name and gladly for His sake. The only thing you want to be *sure* of is that "God is with you." Learn to do what God calls you to do even in the limiting circumstances you may feel "in prison" with.

The late Peter Marshall, Sr., had a beautiful parable on an oyster. It is just lying there, innocent, opening its little shell and sucking in seawater to keep itself alive and a piece of grit lands right in its tender gut. Now faced with such a problem our oyster might say (if oysters could talk or think like us and with apologies to Peter Marshall), "There is no grit in my gut. I do not believe this. I will turn out from my saline consciousness any thought of grit."

Or he could say, "Why did God send me this grit? What did

I do to deserve grit? God, I can't believe You would do a painful thing like this to a faithful oyster like me."

Or he could just say, "Get me a stiff drink of seaweed. I'm hurting and it's not going away. I'm going to get thoroughly wasted and forget my pain."

Or he might say, "Well, that's the way it is with us oysters. *Que será, será.* It comes. It goes."

But the oyster doesn't say any of those things. The oyster, as Marshall said, is a "realist as well as an idealist." The oyster knows it has a problem that will not go away so it does something about it. It begins to coat that grit with a milky substance that it produces until finally it winds up with a pearl—in Peter Marshall's words, "A thing of beauty wrapped around trouble." And that's the way God makes His pearls.

Starting with problems that sinful people or the demonic world puts into your life, God turns them through your godly response by His grace into great treasure; He makes them ultimately into something precious and beautiful. Loren Cunningham says, "God delights in taking lemons and making them into lemonade." It doesn't ultimately matter what happens to you *as* a Christian as long as you truly *are* a Christian, a child of God, in love with God to the end. God can and will fulfill His dreams in you. The dream goes on and you can be there to see it.

Prayer

Lord Jesus, You are the One who went before us to taste the sting of both life and death for every man and woman in our world. We thank You we can speak with You as a man speaks face to face with a friend; for You Yourself became a man and lived among us and You know perfectly what it is to be human.

You know what it is to be brought before enemies and to have them mock You; to be with close friends and still not have them understand You. You know what it is like to be misrepresented and misunderstood; You know what it means to be despised and rejected, to be humiliated and hated, to cry real tears, and to know loneliness and grief and sorrow. Though You were God's own Son, You did not count equality something to be grasped after; You laid aside Your own rights in order to win the right for us to enter in at the throne of the Father in heaven.

Because You cared enough to die for us, we can ask in turn for ourselves to die to all self-seeking ambition; and because You live, we shall live also. Give us the courage to walk on from the dust of our past with all its failures and loss; to walk with our heads held high because of Your help and Your love;

to walk on with dignity as Your forgiven children without turning aside from this road You have already traveled on our behalf. We love You, Lord, and we believe; help Thou our unbelief.

Level Three

Water to the Loins

"Unless I see, I will not believe."

—Thomas to the disciples

"Again he measured a thousand and led me through the water, water reaching the loins." Ezekiel 47:4, NAS

4

The Challenge to Your Emotional Levels

When you hear the Ezekiel phrase *waters to the loins* in a sermon, some preachers will refer to the river's "touching your pockets" and the necessity of giving. Actually there are probably more primary meanings. Robes didn't have pockets in Bible times.

What do the loins signify in Scripture? These things: (1) the focus of power of your life, or your strength; (2) security; (3) the reproductive side of your life, or your creativity; and (4) the vulnerability and sensitivity of your life.

Strength

I asked a friend who is a legendary pro tennis player what physically goes first in competitive tennis. She said, "Your stomach." I said, "What do you mean, your stomach?" I would have thought your legs, your arms—perhaps as you get older and are still running around in the heat, even your brains—but no, her answer was your stomach. And a year later, playing for hours in a grueling tennis match, I suddenly found out what she meant. My arms were still there. My legs would still move. I still knew what I was supposed to be doing. The only trouble was, something in the very center of my body just quit.

You've probably noticed how weight lifters wear those wide belts. Why do they wear them? Here is one reason: If they sneeze at the wrong time, perhaps while power-lifting some megaweight, their bodies could give out there at its weakest spot. All the focus of our strength flows right through here.

The most vulnerable area of your body is the loins. That's why the Roman belt alluded to in the armor of God mentioned in Ephesians 6:14 was no little Gucci designer creation. It was a big, strong, broad belt. It was more than a support, something to hold up your toga; it was also a protective device. For the loins also represent your security.

Security

What are you really resting on? In what is your final confidence? Where is the ultimate base of your security? As we grow in grace, we learn some things in our walks with God that become life-messages to us, the central descriptions of our purpose in the world. We have some things that we consider very strong in our lives; they become areas we consider places of power, the focus of our God-given abilities.

And therein lies a danger. Our strengths can betray us. We can shift our reliance in subtle ways from trust in God, who gifts us, to trust in His gifts. We can lean on what He gave us and forget the Giver. But when the river rises to the loins, for the first time we realize that we are reaching a place where we can no longer dictate the situation.

Jesus is the only One I know who can look you in the eye, tell you how you are going to die, smile, and say, "Follow Me." He said it to Peter. "When you were younger," He told him, "you girded yourself and walked where you wished; but when you are old . . . another will gird you and carry you where you do not wish" (John 21:18).

There may come a time to you, too, when everything you could once do easily is threatened by the river; it moves to the place of your security and promises to carry you where you never intended to go.

The truth is we can't find ultimate security in any man-made institution. So much that we have relied on recently in the Church has dramatically failed us. We have looked up to and trusted people and they have failed, looked up to and trusted ministries and they have failed, relied on tried-and-trusted methods and approaches and formulae and, unaccountably, they, too, have failed. Our media are full of these failures in the Church; every day seems to bring a new exposé of people who have blown it one way or another in morals, in finances, in misused authority. The world is filled with hurt people who have trusted in someone or something that has gone badly astray.

Creativity

Another major area represented by the loins is, of course, the reproductive center of our lives; it is the focus of our sexuality, our ability to procreate, and thus the source of our initiating new life. And it is also in the area of our creativity that the waters will reach us, threatening all that we have been good at making and initiating and bringing into being. There may come a time when everything you have done well in now fails. You were once a wellspring of creativity; now, unaccountably, the spring seems to have failed. You were the one who had all the ideas; now they are gone. Our strengths are often the sources of our greatest weaknesses so God must also search us out here. What we have relied on outside of God Himself to carry us must fail, in order that we may learn again what it is to trust solely in Him.

Sensitivity

You may have noticed that writers in the King James Version of the Bible sometimes used the word *bowels* to refer to our affection, our compassion, the innermost being and emotional depths of our lives. (See Genesis 43:30; 1 Kings 3:26; Isaiah 63:15; Jeremiah 31:20; Philippians 1:7;1 John 3:17; etc.)

Here, too, the waters to the loins touch us. It is not until water gets to your waist that you really notice how *cold* it is. In almost every culture on earth, covering is placed around the loins. To be stripped naked is not merely something physical. It is also mental and emotional and spiritual, tied in since the fall of Adam and Eve (who once were "naked and not ashamed") with the whole core of our self-protection, self-image, and self-preservation. To be stripped naked is so fundamental a shame that it is given as a judgment in Scripture, one that touches us in the very deepest levels of our being. And when Jesus the Lord was hung on the cross, He was stripped naked Himself for our sakes. He was raked to the very depths for the covered-over secret sins of His fallen world.

Living in the communication-rich Western world has its unique advantages and its hidden consequences. We are continually exposed to the constant clamor of sophisticated media. It can result in what we could call "emotional shell-shock."

Faced with a constant barrage of demanding, exciting, scary, sad, painful, and frightening images, we learn in a way to live like someone in a war. If we have a choice, we get ourselves out of the danger, we switch off or disconnect the source. If we don't, we try to somehow dull out our responses; we steel ourselves to what is going on, and try to ignore our feelings. A person who has been badly shaken in combat one too many times goes over the edge into the rigid irresponsiveness we call "shell-shock."

A similar thing can happen to us right in our living rooms. Every day we can see hundreds of sophisticated commercials demanding our attention. We turn on the news; there are the headlines deemed currently significant, footage of new tragedies, of crimes or wars, brilliantly edited and presented as impending threats to our health, our family, or the entire planet. For entertainment we can watch close-ups of our favorite sports stars in the "thrill of victory" or the "agony of defeat," or see some multi-million-dollar dramatization, calculated by a team of talented professionals to make us laugh or cry or scare the living daylights out of us.

All these are vicarious; we are not really there and we rarely if ever share in the events we see. So we get to feel the feeling without actually having the experience. We experience reality secondhand. And the effect over a period of time is this: Either we learn to tune out deep emotions in self-defense or we need deeper and deeper levels of manufactured emotion to move us.

That's one of the reasons many modern kids like gory and scary horror movies. They have been exposed constantly to hurt and fear and shock. It takes something quite drastic now to move them. And drastic provision there is. Rock stars compete with ear-bleeding sound systems, outlandish stage acts, and more violent, mind-blowing, and extravagant sets. Music videos have to be full of drama, shock, and weirdness; metal singers have to scream for attention. There's a lot of competition for an audience out there and the ones who are noticed (any way they can be) are the ones who make the charts and the bucks. Listen to media-saturated kids today and you'll hear it. Their most common complaint and comment is this: "Boring, it's so-o-o boring." Emotional shell-shock. Either we turn it off (limit the input) or learn to turn ourselves off and limit our responses.

And this, too, has affected the Church in the West. We are not deeply moved by much. We have learned to carry our filters and screens and reservations around with us, to protect our deep levels of feeling from anything that may affect us profoundly. In consequence, we are often emotionally and in other ways shallow. We feel few things deeply. We are sheltered, secure, protected. We carry our defenses against mediated, secondhand feelings into the sanctuary and even into the inner court of God. We will not be affected, even by real events that demand real feelings. We are never caught naked and we are never ashamed. But that must change if we want to be serious with God. The river is rising. It is reaching for the depths of our emotions, and we will experience again reality firsthand.

Now it is in this area that we come to a major thing God is doing in the Church. There is unexpected danger in the comfort of inner strength, security, creativity, sensitivity. That danger is that we know the principle so well, we know the law, the rules, the tradition that have given us shelter so well, that we become entranced with the shelter and not with the Person who gave it.

God has a remedy for that. The water moves "up to the loins." We need something in our lives to threaten profoundly all our reliance on even the good things, the right, true, and proven things, the things we have learned to trust that have nevertheless moved us away from trust in God alone. We need to be stripped in a deep way. And this is where a whole new struggle begins.

5

Our Struggle with Doubt

Although everyone has experienced it, few people today have thought deeply about doubt. It is one of the most misunderstood problems in life. We always tend automatically to equate doubt with unbelief. It is not the same thing at all!

One of the few contemporary books on this theme was done by Os Guinness, a friend, teacher, and author who is an articulate and well-informed spokesman for the cause of Christ and for a biblical world view. I was first privileged to meet Os some years ago when he was teaching with Francis and Edith Schaeffer at L'Abri in Switzerland. I have always found his work both challenging and stimulating. Os put together one of the best overviews in print on the subject of doubt, one that certainly deserves more exposure. His book *In Two Minds* is a major source for much of what I have recast in simpler form here and is must reading for people who want to explore this area in more detail.

Os first of all defines doubt scripturally. Here are his five Bible words for doubt, and the first one is very easy to remember. It's in James 1:6 and it is "Don't waver." "He who doubts is like a wave of the sea driven and tossed by the wind." The Greek word is *dipsukos*, which means "to be chronically double-minded." A double-minded man is "unstable in all his ways" (James 1:8).

Next there is *diakrino*. It means "to discern," and is a stronger form of the verbs *to sunder* or *to separate*. It means that you are so torn between two options that you cannot make up your mind. It's used, for instance, in Mark 11:23: "Whoever says to this mountain, 'Be removed and be cast into the sea,' and does not doubt in his heart. . . ." (See also Matthew 21:21; Acts 10:20, 11:12; Romans 4:20, 14:23.)

There is a restaurant in northern California near Sabastapol where I used to live. It serves only three things: great steak, fish, and chicken. And the waitresses, I think, are trained to make a point of being rude to the customers about it. You see "Steak, Fish, Chicken" painted on the wall when you come in and sit down. There's no menu and you say, "Is there a menu?" "No," says the waitress, hand on her hip, "we don't *have* menus. Can't you read? Fish, steak, chicken. That's it! So *whaddya want?*" So before she really gets tough and punches me out, I say (in true character): "I'll take the chicken."

You know the good thing about a small menu? It makes it easier to decide. It's the multiple options of our society that have given people this looseness, this being in two minds, this being torn between this and that. That's one of the Bible words for doubt, *diakrino*.

A third word for doubt is the word from which we get the word *meteor*, *meteorizomi*. The word means "to raise up or suspend or to soar or lift oneself up." This idea is to be arrogant or proud. But another meaning, the way it's used in the Bible for doubt, is to be "hung up." We use that in the vernacular—to be "hung up," to be "up in the air" about something. That's what a meteor is—up in the air. To be hung up, to be unsettled, to be tense, doubtful. We also call it ambivalence. This is the word used in Luke 12:29: Jesus said, "Don't worry—don't be hung up—about these things." Don't be hung up about food and dress and where we're living. . . .

A fourth word for doubt is the word we get *dialogue* from, *dialogizomai.* The word means "thought" or "inner debate." "Should I do it? Should I not do it?" Talking to yourself. Dialogue. In Luke 24:38 Jesus said: "Why are you troubled?" In other words, "Why do questions arise in your mind? Why are you having this inner debate?" (See also Matthew 16:19; Luke 2:35, 5:22, 6:8, 9:46–47; Romans 1:21, 14:1; 1 Corinthians 3:20; Philippians 2:14; 1 Timothy 2:8.)

The last word, *distasia*, is found in Matthew 14:31. We get an account of the disciples who are out in the sea. A big storm comes up and threatens to sink the boat. They're scared out of their minds. Jesus is off somewhere on His own being spiritual, praying, and they're all going to drown. They just don't know what to do.

In the middle of it, here comes Jesus. He has no ground or sea transport available, so He just walks right across the sea toward the boat! Peter looks at this white apparition coming toward him, perhaps flapping in the howling wind and waves, and he is totally terrified. *There's something coming toward the boat walking on the water!* They are not only going to die; first they are going to be attacked by a ghost. All the disciples hide behind Peter. Then through the roar of the storm and the waves, in the licking of the lightning they hear these words: "Don't be afraid! It is I."

I know what Peter's thinking: "*Who* is I?" It *sounds* like the Lord. But most normal people don't walk on water, especially in the middle of a storm. So Peter the disciple with the foot-shaped mouth does it again. He says, "If that's really You, bid me come to You the way You are coming to us."

There's this pregnant silence. Then Peter hears what he probably never expected or wanted to hear: "Come."

Peter puts one foot out, then both feet. He even gets to take a few steps into miracle and mystery before remembering a lecture he heard at the University of Babylon on "Relative Density" and he goes under. A hand reaches down and grabs him and here's what Jesus says: "You of little faith. Why did you doubt?"

The word is *hesitate,* to hold back. "Why didn't you just keep coming?" It is the same word that is used in Matthew 28:17 when Jesus rose from the dead and they saw Him and they worshiped, "but some doubted." They held back.

If we put all of these five words together, we come up with what the word *doubt* really means. It is not the same as unbelief. Unbelief is "I don't care what God says; I'm not going to do it." Unbelief is a refusal to commit yourself to something seen quite clearly as true. Faith is "I see it and I'm going to do it." Doubt is "I am in two minds about it. I don't know what to do. I'm up in the air about it. I'm hesitating. I'm not sure." Doubt, says Os Guinness, is always a halfway house. There is no such thing as "total doubt." Doubt is always in between.

Actually, doubt is not the opposite of faith. When you doubt, it is not some cowardly betrayal of Jesus and a surrender to the wrong side.

The relationship between doubt and faith is more like the relationship between courage and fear. The opposite of courage is cowardice, not fear. Here's a person in a war who, though he's afraid, lets courage master his fear and goes ahead and does it anyway. Or take climbing a mountain. Healthy fear can be a good thing as long as it does not rule you in the hard or dangerous parts of the climb. So, likewise, faith doesn't mean that you will have no doubt. It just means that one overrules the other.

Doubt is never to be encouraged, of course, just as fear is not something given by God. Doubt is a transitional situation, something to be passed through and passed on. You can trust God in the middle of doubt just as you can be brave in the midst of fear. You come down on the side of what God says and you go on anyway. Like Peter, you put your foot down on the water despite everything that threatens you and you walk toward Jesus. Peter in the storm wasn't walking on the water.

He was walking on a *word*, and the word was from the One who made water, and the word was "Come."

Why does doubt devastate us so deeply? Because the bottom line of everything in life is trust. Without faith, it is impossible to please God (Hebrews 11:6). And when trust is threatened, betrayed, or put on the line, the wound is always huge because trust is the basis for everything between people. In every relationship—family, marriage, home, business, devotions, friendships—trust is the foundation.

God is a Person. Because we are made in His image, we are designed to draw our ultimate sense of personhood from Him. From His personality, we get the idea of our own sense of personality. To know God is to trust Him. To trust Him, then, is also to know ourselves better. That's why if we get our eyes off God we always have problems finding out who we really are.

The spirit of the world blatantly reverses that order. It says, "Express yourself!" or "Be yourself!" as if you were in real danger of becoming a carrot or something. But Jesus says, "Deny yourself." Try to find your value in other people, even in close relatives, and you will always be a loser. But give your life away to your Creator and you will discover why you were born. In other words, "He who finds his life will lose it, and he who loses his life for My sake will find it" (Matthew 10:39). And only an infinite God, expressing Himself in finite beings, can give us infinite diversity. None of us will ever be boringly alike unless we take our eyes off Christ as our prime focus and try to start cloning our visions and goals and character from each other. God's call to us is just: "Love Me. Don't try to be like anyone else. Just forget yourself and love Me." And in that uniqueness formed of trust, the closer you get to God, the more different you become from anybody else.

The more *un*like God you are, the more like the same mud of unsaved humanity you are. If you meet one drug addict, you've met them all. Meet one liar, you've met the prototype of all liars at all times. There are no new sins; there are no new, "creative" ways of wrongdoing. And the same is true in self-expression. Try to emphasize your own uniqueness, focus on "being yourself," and you usually wind up just like everyone else. Isn't it sad to see little kids all dressed up like Madonna or Rambo so they can be really different? That is why the "chief end of man" is to "glorify God and enjoy Him forever." That is why doubt is so devastating to us—because it attacks not only our trust, it attacks ourselves. It destroys our own ideas of what personhood is. Doubt is intimately linked with the matter of trust and trustworthiness.

To understand and react correctly to doubt will help equip us for two things. First, there is going to be a *radical apostasy* in the last days. (See 2 Timothy 3:1–5; 2 Peter 2:1–3, 12–22.) We know that. You have probably seen it. How many times do you hear, "I was once a Christian"? It is devastating in the West, where many people have given up their so-called "faith in Christ," or at least some professed form of Christianity. A lot of this defection, of course, stems from never really having come to grips with true Christianity; their contact with true faith is only a shallow thing. But some of it has to do with church people's going through some experience of not being able to handle doubt.

Doubt is common in one way or another to every child of God. Doubt comes to us all in different ways. And viewed correctly in the the light of God's purposes for us, doubt can even be a positive factor. Like temptation properly responded to, doubt can bring us into a better place with Christ.

Number two reason for the necessity of a time of doubt is *preparation for the years of testing.* I believe also that we in the West have entered a time of great testing. That decade of pessimism, of malaise and questioning, has already begun. It is not only happening; it is happening faster. Notice how everything is compressing? The consciousness generated by the '60s took about fifteen years; the '70s took about eight; the '80s took about six. We're already in the '90s. This is a time of serious testing, of pressure, of concentrated searching, and, if God's allowance of doubt has not done its work properly, some of us may not survive spiritually.

There is even something good that can come out of a time of pessimism. In good times, people often forget their source of blessings. It is harder to speak to a man who is lost and happy than a man who is lost and hurting. There is a shallow optimism that often rules in people's lives when everything is all right. They tend to take life for granted, not think much about the serious issues of life. But when times are hard, when there are days of darkness, when the bottom drops out of the stock market, when the nations shake and the world moves a step closer to total destruction, people begin to think a lot more. They ask questions, they wonder about their priorities, about what is really important. And while times of doubt are always times of shaking and uncertainty, they can lead to important changes in the way we think and feel and act.

6

Seven Kinds of Doubt

God is out to bring us to what we might call *radical trust.* What does that mean? It means, says Os Guinness, faith plus nothing. Not faith plus a good community of friends. Not faith plus ministry. Not faith plus people whom I can look up to. Not faith plus a lifestyle that happily enough agrees with the particular one I've presently chosen. Just *faith plus nothing.* Trusting in Him, that's it.

Final abandonment involves God's dealing with us even in principles we have trusted in—good principles, even godly principles that we have come nevertheless to rely on other than God Himself. That means that He is going to take all the things that we are so strong in and turn them under His careful hand into nothing. The things we know so well and are so reliable will fall apart. The house will leak. The business will fail. Your best bell-ringing sermon will be met with stony silence. Your joke will bomb, your singing voice will crack in public, your very best friend will blow it. The car, the equipment, the sound system, which has been previously flawless, will die.

Your strength is also your greatest weakness. And this necessary step when the water touches the loins must be death. Here is a summary of what Os Guinness sees as the seven different kinds of families of doubt. For details and much more content, get the book and read it carefully for yourself. Here my only concern is to introduce you to the problem on a very general level and relate it to the peculiar needs of our particular time. The first four levels of doubt have to do with a faulty *premise*, a poor or inadequate understanding of what it really means to be a Christian. This carries right into our Christian lives. The last three levels have to do with failure in the outworking of our Christian lives in *practice*.

Independence and Ingratitude

The first major cause of doubt Os examines has to do with *independence and ingratitude*. That's why we looked in our analogy of the river at the water rising to the knees. The danger of being made truly free in God is that you can move quite subtly from being free *under* God to becoming free *from* God. And in our four-level river analogy it goes like this: First, before it touched your ankles, you were a chaotic person. Now your needs are met and you have become resourceful; you are cleansed, given dignity and responsibility and perhaps even a ministry.

Take a kid, for example, who was a drug addict, in prison all the time, a real cancer in society. He gets saved. He sets his heart on loving God and people. Now he becomes in his own eyes significant. Now he realizes his value. He begins to preach. His ministry meets some needs. Large crowds come out to hear him. Now he's considered somebody important. There are a lot of people looking up to him for help, for answers, for an example. And now his temptation is different from when he was in the streets.

Similarly, when first our needs are met by Christ, we develop under Him some resourcefulness. The problem comes when that God-sufficiency begins to turn into self-sufficiency and, finally, independence. It's an independent spirit that wipes out more people than anything else. Satan didn't get in trouble trying to run off with some lady angel. His ultimate problem was an independent spirit. It's very subtle. No one would ever say, "Hey, I don't need Jesus anymore. I'm going to do this sort of stuff on my own." It never happens like that. It goes like this: We begin to focus on what we do well. We've got it down. And as we magnify in our own hearts how well we can do what we can do, we forget that what we have was given (John 3: 27). God does a slow fade.

What do you think God is really going to do at this stage? It's not something *bad* that is the idol of our lives; it may well be the gifts He has given us that are now becoming gods. How do you deal with the idolatry of a gift *given to you by God?* How do you deal with something given *by* Him that has taken His place? That's the situation of Abraham and Isaac. Isaac was given to Abraham by God (Genesis 18:11–14, 21:1–8). Now for Abraham to take that thing that was not only most precious to him but even given him in a miracle by God, to have to "deliver it to the death," to give it back. . . . It seemed just incredible. Yet God so tested Abraham, and the old warrior came through with flying colors (Genesis 22:15–18).

So here is really the heart of dealing with doubt on this level: "Blessed are the poor in spirit" (Matthew 5:3). Our antidote to ingratitude is many times spoken of in Scripture. It speaks of "*giving thanks*" (Ephesians 5:20), "*not forgetting*" (Deuteronomy 4:9, 6:12, 8:11; Psalm 78:7, 103:2; Jeremiah 2:32), and "*remembering*" (Deuteronomy 8:18; 1 Chronicles 16:12; Psalm 25:6; Ecclesiastes 12:1; Acts 20:35; Revelation 3:3). This is to be a genuine, unforced, and heartfelt response to God's goodness and provision. We can get so mechanical in giving thanks that that is all it is—a form and a tradition. Or we can get so loose over it that we forget. So thankfulness should be like a little bright thread that runs through all kinds of formal and informal occasions of giving thanks and remembrance.

In the Bible, Jesus said in one sad situation: "Were there

not ten lepers healed?" Only one came back to thank Him; the others were so excited about their miracle they forgot the God who made it possible (Luke 17:11–19). It is important that God is remembered and thanked. In Numbers 15:38–39 we read that the Israelites were even supposed to put special threads in their clothes to remind them to give thanks. They remembered God's salvation with unleavened bread (Exodus 13:3–10). They remembered His holiness by the censer altar plates (Numbers 16:40). And they remembered their deliverance and specialness as a nation on the Sabbath (Deuteronomy 5:15). They were not only to give thanks to God for *what* He did but to give thanks for *how* He did it (Deuteronomy 8:1–18).

We can call this the Pattern of the Prodigal Son. Come back thankfully. Come back conscious of God's mercy. To keep this in our lives all the time is an inoculation against the doubt of forgetting how bad it is to be lost. In 1 Chronicles 16:35, one translation says, "To make thy praise our pride." The thing we're to be really proud about is that God is so wonderful.

Doubt comes when we take our eyes off God. He will withdraw the sense of His presence and everything will fall apart.

A Faulty Picture of God

Doubt number two is *a faulty picture of God.* Now it is areas like this in which material like John Dawson's awesome little tract for Last Days Ministries, "The Father Heart of God," has been greatly used. So many people have poor pictures of God. Some come from the fact that they just don't know what He is like and need to learn. Some come from the fact that they have been hurt perhaps as children by an ugly and unworthy picture of God. We all need to learn more about what God is really like. Too often, as J. I. Packer points out, we'll hear people say, "I like to think of God as . . .," which is usually followed by some idiocy. Who cares what you or I "like to think" about God? God is who He is. We are not to try to fit Him into our warped or inadequate notions, but to let the revelation of who He really is keep on correcting our vision. The greatest need of the twentieth-century Church is a fresh discovery of the greatness, glory, and goodness of God.

Weak Foundations

The third kind of doubt comes from *weak foundations,* from a poor understanding of truth. You got saved, which at the time seemed the obvious thing to do. You understood that God was real and you were lost. You then had a real experience with Christ. You just trusted Him; it was wonderful. If anyone asked you, you could testify to meeting Jesus. You knew *that* you believed, even a bit of *what* you believed, but above all you knew in *whom* you believed.

At this early level of Christian experience "Christian apologetics" probably means to you telling people you are sorry you did bad things to them! You might not know the issues. You might not know there even *are* any issues. Your primary concern is that the Gospel works, and perhaps later with how it works; you may never have had to even think about *why.*

If Christianity is true, it is supposed to have real answers to the problems of life. When we are first looking for answers from anything, we usually carry in mind two simple tests: (1) Does it seem to work? (pragmatic, practical) and (2) Does it make sense from where it starts to where it ends? (logical consistency within its premises, coherency).

Now if Christianity is true, we should see (perhaps in someone else's life before our own) that it "works." We first find Christ a real answer for our felt and known needs. What we tried before did not last or did not satisfy. Our search for truth was on the basis of failed personal alternatives, not realized absolutes. Most of us meet Jesus on this first, pragmatic basis. We say, "I was into other things like ___ and ___ but my life was falling apart. Then I met Jesus and everything came together." Or, in the words of the old song, "I tried the broken cisterns, Lord, but, ah, the waters failed."

The truth is that Jesus is not only an "answer" to our needs. He is much more than even the real, sufficient, and only answer to *all* needs. First, Christ can meet our needs, but that is not why He is God. Jesus is much more than *an* answer, even more than *the* answer; He is the Lord of the universe, and we are to come to Him not just in needs, but in everything.

The second test, the "does it make sense?" question, usually isn't thought about until later. In this we come to the question of knowing who He is, and we can be freed from false pictures of Him by a growing, corrected revelation of His character that is both adequate and accurate. Here, when we have problems believing, we are dealing with doubt that comes from either being badly *taught* or badly *treated.* We can limit our vision of God and make Him too small, or we can live with a hurt that has damaged our idea of God and gives us a bad picture of Him. If our understanding of God's character is inadequate or inaccurate, incorrect or incomplete, we will experience doubt at this level.

But the facts that something "works" and "makes sense" within its premises are not the only tests for truth. There are after all a lot of things that seem both to "work" and to "make sense."

A devoted Buddhist lifestyle is a logical match for its philosophical tenets; a dedicated Muslim may live out the teachings of the Koran; even the hedonism and unabashed power-seeking of Satanism makes ugly, logical sense within its demonic premises. Hitler, too, accomplished things. Charles Manson made sense to his followers. Some things, like lies, are real but are not true.

So now we have to ask another question: *Is Christianity also true?* Does it make sense from where it starts to where it ends? Does it help? And now is it really true? We are going to be tested on that. We're telling other people in a world filled with competing ideas, principalities, and false gods that there is only "one Way" to heaven and only "one name under heaven" by which we may be saved. We are going to say to that world, "This is really true," so we are going to have to know something of the why. The bottom line is not that it "works," nor even that we can see how it "makes sense," but that it is true.

No matter how much we study or learn, of course, our knowledge of the "whys" and the "whats" of Christianity will never be exhaustive. We will never fully be able to know *all* the reasons; no finite being ever can or will. It does not mean that what we *do* learn is untrue; it just means there will always be more to learn, and there will be much more to the reason for what God says than we will ever know. Francis Schaeffer said we are like kids who've got our baby hands 'round the strings of a bunch of balloons. The balloons go all the way up. We don't have hold of the balloons; we have only the strings. We have no idea how many balloons are up there or what they all look like, but we really do have our fat little hands on the connections. What we have is true, even testably true, but not exhaustive. As eight-year old Anna of "Mr. God, This Is Anna," once said, "When you begin with the Answer, you can get a squillion questions right."

Why do we always have to put up with a partial revelation in which we always have to trust? Why doesn't God just come down and give us "no choice" but to believe? Why doesn't God just give us (as He no doubt could) overwhelming proof? Because that is not the rule of the game. "Overwhelming" is not the way God interacts with His children. Here's the God of the universe who knocks on your door. It is not: "Behold, I freak your head out and kick your door in." It is: "I stand at the door and knock" (Revelation 3:20).

It is in this area that we appreciate mystery because what we have is God who is utterly wonderful, yet reveals Himself in testable ways. I recently released a book on God that I've been working on for more than eighteen years. But it was not finished; it was *abandoned.* It never will be "finished." You never "finish" a book on God. In this world or the next, you will never stop thinking and learning about God.

So what if our basis for trust in God is not properly understood or solidly based? The best way to correct this kind of weak foundation is to do some reading and study. We must *do it,* not leave it for some expert or religious professional. Where are your own areas of inadequate or inaccurate vision? Find out for yourself. It will feed your faith to dig into some of the wonderful truths that await you. You will get excited to see just how powerfully the answers and evidences of the Gospel really are. There are many good books out today that deal with the facts and truth of the Christian faith. They deal with what we call "apologetics" or evidences for the truth of Christianity.

Josh McDowell has some excellent compilations in his writings on the truth of Scripture and the uniqueness of Christ in his best-selling books like *Evidence that Demands a Verdict*, *More Evidence that Demands a Verdict*, and *More than a Carpenter*. Michael Green and John Stott of England, John Warwick Montgomery, Clark Pinnock, Bernard Ramm, and Norman Geisler are just some of the scholars and theologians who have written powerful studies in apologetics that will be of help to you. Some of my favorites in this area are in the "Inklings," a small group of British literary figures who were also committed to Christ, like Dorothy Sayers, G. K. Chesterton, and C. S. Lewis. Thinkers from European ministries such as L'Abri like Os Guinness and the late Dr. Francis Schaeffer, men who minister in Eastern as well as Western cultures like Ravi Zacharias and the late E. Stanley Jones, have helped hundreds of thousands simply to reconsider the claims of Christ in the modern world.

Reading is an eternal investment, and study in this area will be deeply rewarding to you. If you are a parent, some of the most important and profound questions ever are not first mentioned in universities, but posed instead by your children. The best way to build truth into their lives is when they first ask, and you will find that you do not really understand something yourself until you are able to explain it to a child. On the job, important questions in life are always linked with the ultimate ones, and knowing some of the whys of Christianity will not only help you stay strong in your witness, but help you "give a reason for the answer that is in you." If you are an artist, a poet, or a musician, this will help develop your vision; you have a responsibility not just to be creative and moody, but to think deeply, too!

Sometimes people use Abraham and Isaac as an illustration of faith not involving any thinking, but that isn't true. It is precisely *because* Abraham knew *who* God was that he could trust Him in the dark when he didn't understand the *why*. He didn't know why, but he knew why he trusted God who did know why.

Faith without truth can pass as fantasy. How do you know that what you have is not fantasy? Perhaps this thing called Christianity is only a wish-fulfillment. What if you're just part of some sociological trend, some religious reaction to the emptiness, barenness, meaninglessness of our time? Truth is the answer to that. Faith without truth seems like fantasy. That is why a lot of kids are so cynical. They have no basis for trusting anyone or anything. In a *Roger Rabbit* world, when people are no longer able to distinguish between fantasy and reality, your best corrective after putting on display some working models of love and wisdom is a solid dose of truth.

Our Failure to Really Commit Ourselves

A lot of doubt begins here at this fourth most common cause of doubt. Commitment cements belief into conviction.

You only really believe something when you commit yourself to it. Have you ever met ex-church people who have dropped out? They will sometimes blame their defection on what they did or didn't believe, but that usually isn't the problem. The problem is, they don't want to commit themselves to what they found out was the truth.

I once talked to a young Red Guard who was actively promoting radical Communism in the West at a time when the Cultural Revolution in China was in its heyday and Chairman Mao was really hot news in the world. This guy had the armband, the button, the whole thing. He apparently once had some sort of church background, but had thrown it all away and embraced instead *The Little Red Book* and *The Thoughts of Mao*. For some reason he came to a service in which I spoke about commitment and happened to mention in passing the Red Guards. He came up to see me afterward to say what it meant to him to be a Mao follower. He said, "I don't believe in Jesus Christ. I don't believe in the Bible."

I said, "Have you read the Bible?"

He said, "Yes."

I said, "If you knew the Bible was true and that Jesus Christ really was God, would you have to make some major changes in the way you're living?"

He said, "Well, yes, I would."

I said, "It's not a question of whether you believe in Jesus and the Bible or not; it's a question of whether you really want to commit yourself to what you know. That's right, isn't it?"

He got very quiet. His eyes filled with tears and he said, "You don't understand. I train young people for Maoism in this country."

I said, "I really want to change the world, too. If Jesus were not who He said He was, and the Bible were not what it claimed to be, if there were no God and I was sure, I would probably be a Marxist or a Maoist like you. But the simple fact is that I cannot ignore the truth. I must deal with Christ. You know why it is easier to be a Marxist than to follow Jesus?

Because you can keep your selfishness and be a Maoist, but Jesus calls you to die."

Marxist thought requires unselfishness for revolution but cannot deliver it.

Failure to commit ourselves. We are to take truth and personal convictions seriously. How do you know if you really have convictions? You have to have an invisible sign hanging around your neck. (Mine reads, for instance: "This ministry is not for sale.") No conviction is truly your own unless you're prepared to hold it even if all others are against it.

I've sometimes told young Christians, "You need to follow Jesus even if everyone you know who is supposed to be a Christian turns his back on both Him and you." Here is a test of whether or not you really do hold a conviction. Can you say it succinctly, put it into a sentence? If not, it's just some vague idea. Can you put into a single statement, "This is what I am prepared to covenant with God"?

In Joshua 24:15 Israel's young leader calls the people to conviction: "Choose for yourselves this day whom you will serve." This was a situation of doubt for Israel, in which the people were called to make a decision. "Why," says Joshua, "do you stagger about between two things?"

Today we are called to make up our minds, and "put our money where our mouths are."

Daniel 3:16–18 gives us another wonderful insight into Christian doubt. Three boys are about to be thrown into a blast furnace. The king has had a sell-out concert. Everybody who was anybody in the whole Babylonian world was there, all the big bands were combined for this concert, and there was not an empty seat in the house. Everyone had to stand until the band played. Then everyone was supposed to bow. And they all did—all except three Hebrew guys who despite their extensive royal training did not seem to understand plain Babylonian.

They stood there alone and upright in the crowd and the king called them out. He said: "Don't you understand? If you don't bow, I'll throw you into this furnace!" (It's an extremely hot blast furnace, probably fired with bitumen and oxygen.) Nebuchadnezzar goes on. "You may be my favorite helpers, but this is embarrassing. You had better bow or you are going to burn. I am the king of the world and unless you show that you worship my statue along with everyone else I really will permanently take care of you."

What would you do? Would you smile and, so as not to offend, go ahead? Would you bow (certainly not enthusiastically) and mutter to yourself: "Well, God knows I am not really bowing 'in my heart.' After all, He has gone to all this trouble to put me in a place of some leadership and influence with these ungodly pagans and He certainly wouldn't want all that to come to an end now because of some silly little external show. I'll bow (outwardly only, of course) just to please the king, but God knows that it is all only an outward appearance. In my heart of hearts, am I not still following God?"

These boys didn't have the benefits of our modern understanding and could not adequately conceptualize some sort of contextual, cross-cultural, relational, and situational posture of influence. They had apparently also not yet learned how to spell *compromise* in either Hebrew or Babylonian. And this is what they said:

"If it be so our God whom we serve *is* able to deliver us. . . . But *if not. . . .*"

That *if not* is a Christian affirmation. It's doubt. It says, "I don't know if He will or not. I know He *can*. I *don't* know if He *will.*"

These boys knew who God was. They knew something of His wisdom, His character, and His power. They knew what He could do. They also knew some way or other, in life or by death, they would shortly be out of the king's power. They knew God could intervene. But they did not know, for them, for then, if God *would.* And knowing the king as they did, knowing that he would do exactly as he said, knowing fully the consequences of a polite but firm refusal, *they refused any-*

way: "But if not, we will not bow down." That's conviction. It has to do with commitment—even if you don't understand the whole thing, even if you don't know what's going on, even if you don't know what is going to happen to you. As Os Guinness says, weak convictions act on the drive train of faith like a slipping clutch.

Lack of Growth

Number five on the list of what brings on doubt is *lack of growth*. We have seen now the early reasons for experiencing doubt—having faulty *premises* as a Christian. The next two types of doubt have to do with our daily *practice* as Christians. This is not a problem of holding onto wrong ideas; it has to do with loss of freshness. One of the major reasons God will allow doubt in our lives is because we have not grown. Thirty years at one devotional level is not going to be sufficient if we hope to take on demons in a nation.

We're not talking about a deficiency in understanding about becoming a Christian but a deficiency in actual practice. Basically, it is this: We must always be developing a Christian world view. Ordinary living is a reality test for faith. This is why young people sometimes get wiped out spiritually even in a Bible college. They are not in the normal situations of life; they are often isolated from ordinary living. They don't meet real secular people who would challenge their small, smug answers and send them weeping back to God for something more. They don't run into people who have absolutely no concept about God and could not care less. If we want to win the world, we have to live in it and know both why and how it is lost. We need to rub shoulders often with people who, like ourselves once, are outside of God.

Some people are innocent in their rottenness. They have no great battles with spiritual claims. To them "*Jesus*" is only a swear word. They plow on in life apparently blind to spiritual reality until it hits them in the face. And often they are the easiest to win. Jesus really loved lost people who knew it, the drunks, the hookers, the rejected street people of His time. What He *said* and what He *was* struck them like spiritual lightning. It was said of Christ that He taught "as one having authority, and not as the scribes." He *lived.* He was full of goodness and compassion and excitement. Jesus did not seem to be religious; He was real.

Recently I was having lunch with a friend in a small Washington, D.C., hotel coffee shop. Out of the corner of my eye I noticed a man near us at a single table who seemed to be listening to our conversation, which revolved around some of the fun things God was up to in our lives. I didn't look at him, but from that point on I cut out of my vocabulary any specifically religious buzz words and kept on talking. The man finally finished his lunch, paid the bill, and left. But just minutes later he returned to his table and ordered a glass of water! He sat there sipping, ostensibly studying the door of the coffee shop, but gradually he moved his chair more and more around, until he was all but sitting facing us. Finally he could stand it no longer, and just plain interrupted. "Excuse me," he said, "I'm sorry to interrupt, but, hell, this is the most exciting thing I've ever heard!"

It turns out he was a businessman, a totally secular engineer with no spiritual background at all. He had known nothing about God and cared nothing about Him until his wife (who had apparently become a Christian) was killed in a car accident leaving him with two boys to bring up alone. It suddenly hit him that he had been relying on his wife to give the boys something spiritual; now that she was gone it was up to him. This man had never (as far as I was able to find out) been to a church; he wasn't going to one now. He knew less about God than the average seven-year-old Sunday school kid, but he had just gotten hold of a Bible and was reading it day and night. He was excited out of his mind with what he found. And this was the first time he had ever heard anyone else talking about it. God is constantly at work in His world.

What keeps you fresh? For me, it is keeping myself exposed to reality. Life is a reality test case. I've been out there 25 years saying, "Jesus is the answer." When I first said that, I didn't even know what the questions were. It's one thing to *say* something like that when you start, but it is quite another thing 25 years later still to be able to say the same thing, with ever-deepening conviction: "Jesus Christ really *is* the answer."

That answer must be practical, fresh, and contemporary. We either grow or we retreat. One reason doubt can creep in is that we're lazy. We don't want to grow. We're stuck where we are and contented. We're not constantly exposing ourselves to new risks, new ideas, new challenges. If you don't practice truth, after a while you begin to think that perhaps it is impractical. And truth that is impractical will soon be discarded as being untruth, and that's where doubt comes in.

Runaway Emotions

This sixth pathway to doubt is one most of us have faced but not understood. Doubt can come from *runaway or depleted emotions*. And I'm not just talking about Christians. There are Buddhists with runaway emotions who have doubts. There are atheists with used-up emotions who have severe doubts about atheism. It's a human problem, not a peculiarly Christian one. Everyone has doubts at times that stem from runaway emotions.

Doubt can sometimes be a good thing, because we live in a world that is fallen. This means that not everything is true though it often purports to be. Doubt doesn't buy at face value. So doubt doesn't have to be all bad; it can sometimes be good. The idea of *skeptic* comes from a word that means "to check it out," to investigate to find out if it's true or not.

But some doubt comes from emotional reaction and is not a mental or philosophical difficulty at all.

Let's look at a classic biblical example. We see Elijah (in 1 Kings 19:4) as a suicidal ninth century B.C. prophet. Imagine this: You have the most awesome experience of your entire life. A giant confrontation between God and Baal. All the priests of Baal come out. They're all there in force and there's just you (and Jehovah). There's the altar they built. They're dancing and cutting themselves with knives and crying out to Baal to answer by fire. Nothing is happening. People are getting a bit bored, so you provide a little side entertainment with suggestions like: "Better yell louder! Maybe your god went on a vacation. Perhaps he's on the toilet somewhere."

That's what Elijah yells to them all day . . . but they have no fire, nothing. They're ticked off. They've slashed their nice Sunday clothes to ribbons and nothing has happened. Then it is Elijah's turn. He rebuilds the altar of the Lord, digs a trench, and soaks the sacrifice in barrels and barrels of water. (There is always the skeptic in the audience who nods and says, "Ah. It was a rather hot day and rather dry wood. Spontaneous combustion. I've heard about it.")

Then Elijah prays a small prayer: "Lord, let it be known, I've done this according to Your word. Hear me that these people may know You are God." The fire falls, on the rocks, the bull, the water—everything. The fire licks up the bull, the rocks, the water in the trench, leaving just a big smoking hole, a lot of shocked Baal-worshipers, and a lot of very impressed Israelites. The people who are quite swift at recognizing the supernatural in this sort of thing all say: "The Lord, He is God!" (1 Kings 18:20–40).

After this supernatural act—the most awesome experience in Elijah's whole ministry—what do you think he is like from now on? A giant of faith? Far from it. This woman Jezebel puts a contract on his life and Elijah splits. When we find him, he's under a tree praying to die.

Isn't that the way it often is? *How is it that after the greatest experience of your whole life you suffer the greatest doubts and the greatest temptations?* Why is that?

The answer is simple. When you carry a huge amount of emotional intensity and then suddenly it drops, something snaps. It can be successes or failures. It can be after the greatest miracle of your life, or it can be when you're exhausted or lonely or tired or undernourished. Perhaps it's when you've suffered from a long illness, and an accident happens to you or a bereavement. Maybe you've gotten really angry over something, or something doesn't turn out as you really wanted it to, or perhaps the problem is a battle with deep feelings of jealousy. All those things use emotions.

And when those emotions ebb, as they must, you can't handle it. There is this sense of numbness, of coldness, of loss. You feel empty, but cannot really see why. There is apparently no logical reason why you feel the way you do, but what you may lack in facts in this area at this time you can make up for in drama and imagination. There are no apparent reasons why you should be like this, but in your own mind you come up with one: "God is dead. Or if He is not dead, He has probably abandoned me." Your world has fallen apart. You can behave totally irrationally at this point, but it all makes sense to you . . . somehow!

Have you ever been in that situation? Isn't it a weird thing? There's apparently no reason for it. Something just snaps. You'd think after such an awesome demonstration of the power and presence of God in his life that Elijah would say, "Nobody is going to put out a contract on me! Fire fall on you, Jez." But here he is, the man of God, the one full of faith and power, asking for a quick death at the hands of God.

What is under fire here is not the *truth*, but individual *faith*. The facts are not the issue, not *what* you believe or *why* you believe it, but *how* you believe. Your own perception of truth is being challenged. The facts of what God is and what He says are not at all determined by what you know of Him now. It's not God's faithfulness, but your own faith that is in the fire, and in this case it is because your emotions have simply unloaded on you.

What is God's prescription for this? A refresher course on systematic theology, Divinity 1? A list of all the Scriptures that promise divine protection from demon-possessed queens in authority? Perhaps some stirring up of the prophet, something to keep him firmly reminded of his task and holy calling? Something in the order of:

"Elijah? What in the fat are you doing out here? Don't tell me after all I've done for you that you're afraid of one 'devil woman.' Get off your tail, cut out this pity-party, and get your act together. You get back to work. And, oh, Elijah, remember the fire that fell on the mountain? I can do that again, on anyone. Anytime I want to, remember. . . ."

No. You know what God does? *He bakes a cake for him* (1 Kings 19:5–8).

You sit down and pray that He will kill you and He brings you a cake! He says, "Have a little rest, all right?" What kind of God is this?

The answer to this kind of doubt from shattered emotions is not to increase your religious activity, but just *rest and relax.* Take a break. Play. If you're doubting because you're tired, the answer is not to pray more, but to sleep. Overwork may not need a spiritual heart search but a day off at the beach—maybe three days off at the beach.

There are ministers who have driven themselves to burnout because they feel the responsibility of always being spiritual for other people and no longer have time to enjoy being saved themselves. There are housewives who suffer a crisis of faith. They cannot understand why they feel the way they do about God. The fact that their new baby is crying at odd hours of the night and their two-year-old is wrecking the house does not have anything much to do with it. It's just that their weekly requests for prayer at the ladies' luncheon (sent in by proxy because they are too tired to go) do not seem to be relieving the pressure. But the answer here is not intensified religious activity but relief of the pressure and relaxation.

It always amazes me how much material Charles Haddon Spurgeon put out. From the time he was seventeen he just churned out words. My Spurgeon library in New Zealand takes up an entire wall of thick volumes, with thousands of sermons in his *Metropolitan Tabernacle Pulpit* alone, not to mention his *Treasury of David, Lectures to My Students*. . . . He just preached and preached. Yet I hear that every summer he went down to the beach and snorkeled and lay around in the sun. Then he went back to his pulpit full of fire and fresh zeal and put out all this material that is still ministering to people a century after his death.

It is as much a command of God that we *rest* as that we do not commit adultery. Yet sincere and godly people who would not think of lying or stealing or dishonesty, let alone murder or immorality or blasphemy, habitually and regularly violate this divine provision. They are to be found grim-lipped and devout, continually pushing themselves beyond their human limits, meanwhile quoting to themselves and others various sacred imprecations like "I'm not going to rust out, I'm going to burn out . . . for God."

The "for God" is always added for its devotional overtones. Without it, the drive might be recognized for what it often is: ambition, guilt, or religious fantasy posing as spirituality. Burn out, not rust? Go ahead. The only difference between rust and fire is time. Both are the results of oxidation; one just goes quicker than the other. When the wick in a lamp starts to burn, the lamp is running out of oil. And the solution is not more fire, or a lament for the wick, but more oil. Sons and daughters of God are led, not driven.

Sometimes we lose it all because we are wound up and overburdened and this becomes a major crisis in our faith. We say, "I don't know what to do. Heaven is blank." Have a sleep! Eat a cake! And after a couple of treatments of this, God shares some things with Elijah that will help put him back on the track to finish his course.

The rest and food first. This is not the final or only answer, of course. We must learn as well to recognize this sort of doubt and learn to retrain our emotions so we don't get overwhelmed in situations like this. When this happens, we have a short-term answer: Take a break. But we can also work on a long-term answer: Learn not to trust your feelings and thoughts in such situations, as they often run wild. Understand that when it comes, as it came to Elijah, that emotional overload may be the reason for your doubt. Learn that you can have those times.

They Doubted For Joy

This last one is probably the hardest of all to handle. When the disciples saw Jesus return from the dead, Scripture (Luke 24:41, RSV) says: "They disbelieved [doubted] for joy." What does that mean? It means this: You want so much to believe in the unexpected good news that to discover it isn't true would just totally destroy you. It is a doubt that comes in the very area you most want to believe, because of some hurtful experience in the past.

They saw Him die! For a long time it was just talk. Jesus said: "I'm going to be taken. I'm going to be crucified." They said to themselves: "Oh, yes. He'll be crucified but at the last minute the nails will come out by miracle, the messianic reign will begin, and we'll, of course, be there to share in it."

And then He didn't do it. He didn't fight. He let Himself be laid down and the Romans did nail Him up and He really did die. The soldier put the spear into His side and the blood really came out and He really was dead. And the disciples wrapped His body themselves and they laid Him in the grave. Talk about doubt! They were devastated. I'm sure some of them thought about packing it all in and going back, somehow, if they could, to their old lives.

But suddenly there on the shore was someone who looked awfully much like Jesus and they couldn't believe it. They wanted so much to believe it was true, but they couldn't. They couldn't believe it because they knew it was the very thing they most *wanted* to believe. What if it turned out only as another crazy wish-fulfillment fantasy, like the one they just had followed? Jesus had said He was the Messiah. They had seen the miracles and the love and the power and they had believed He would rule the world. But then they had seen Him really die and all their dreams had come crashing down in the dust.

Now there was someone standing on the shore that unaccountably looked like Him and sounded like Him, but how could it be? Their fresh scars were in danger of being ripped again, this time for good.

That is probably the hardest one of all. In all of our lives there is usually one place that still hurts. There's one place still sealed. There's one place where final healing has not been allowed, one place that we keep away from complete openness. We would love to believe it. It is the one thing *we most want* to believe out of anything and everything we have ever wished. But what if with all our hopes at their highest, it doesn't turn out to be true after all? It would be the final devastation. It would hurt so much we would never recover. So we don't want to think about it. We don't want to talk about it. Leave us alone, okay? We don't want to look at that figure on the shore. We're not able to receive.

And what have we done? We have let a problem take God's place and become the controlling principle of our lives. So our problem becomes our idolatry. And in the best of polite, sad, well-chosen spiritual words I may say to myself: *Well, I'd really like to believe that. It's true, I suppose, for some people, but I can't look because (though I'd never tell another living soul) I'm afraid it won't be true.* So the problem becomes god to us. We look at God through the eyes of the problem instead of looking at the problem through the eyes of God. We won't let Him be God in the situation, and it becomes the secret, absolute center of our whole lives.

What is the answer to this last sort of doubt? First of all, get that doubt out in the light. Perhaps write it down on paper so you know exactly what it is. You've lived with it hidden too long. Articulate your doubt; make sure you know clearly what it is and what it isn't. "This is what I am most afraid of. I really wish this were true, but I don't know if it is." Identify it so that it's not some lion lurking in your subconscious ready to pounce on you.

When C. S. Lewis went through that terrible time of watching his wife, Joy Davidman, die, he went through real doubt. He said that during that time of doubt, it wasn't that he doubted that God wouldn't turn out to be there after all, but that maybe God would not turn out to be the God that Lewis had always thought he was. "Sooner or later," he said, "I must face the question in plain language. What reason have we except our own desperate wishes to believe that God is, by any standard we can conceive, 'good'? . . . I wrote that last night. It was a yell rather than a thought. Let me try it over again. Is it rational to believe in a bad God? Anyway, in a God as bad as all that?"

Lewis went on to say in *A Grief Observed* that too-human pictures of God forged during hurt and grief leave no room for "something older than yourself, something that knows more, something you can't fathom." In the preservation of mystery there is hope. If by some sort of "extreme Calvinism" our fears of God being unreasonable, vindictive, vain, unjust, and cruel were urged on us as "actually true but count as virtue in Him," we would lose all our basis of thinking and living. Then reality is in its very root meaningless, and "what is the point of trying to think about God or anything else? This knot comes undone when you try to pull it tight."

"The doubt of joy" is a hard one because we want so much

to believe that God is really the way that He says He is. But what if He really isn't? What if I trust in that area and am devastated again?

What does Jesus do? It's a beautiful thing. He's there on the beach doing the most ordinary thing. He is cooking breakfast! He does something so simple, so common, so natural. He doesn't glow with light from another world, float out toward them in the boat, and speak with a voice enhanced by heavenly echo chamber. He eats breakfast. *Ghosts don't eat fish.* What He does is give them a whole fresh context, and that's what you need for this final area. You've got to step out of the circle of your own pain for a moment and see things in a totally different light. In the disciples' minds, it can't possibly be Jesus. He's dead. This is a ghost, some alien.

Yet He stands there and says, "Have you had breakfast yet?" And He eats. And something shifts deep inside and they suddenly see. "He really is alive! He really is!"

7

Elijah at Kidron: When the Brook Dries Up

Elijah was a man taken care of by God when the land was under His judgment. Although drought and famine filled the nation of Israel, Elijah was fed supernaturally. Although Christians may share to some extent in the consequences of a judgment that comes on a nation because of sin, God's provision and care continue for the individuals, in this case the prophet.

Then the brook dried up.

Why did it happen? And what do you do when supernatural provision stops?

Henry Sloane Coffin looked at this theme in his 1930s message *Inspirations that Fail.* If we were to paraphrase and amplify that message in the light of the situations of our time, it might look something like this: God has a course for His children. Everyone's curriculum is different. The only thing that remains the same is its *aim:* to keep you confident in *depending on resources outside of yourself.*

Elijah was a man who knew how to hear from heaven. He was a man we recognize as the greatest of all the prophets of the Old Testament. He knew how to talk to God, and he knew how to listen. A bad king gave a series of bad calls, and Elijah's response under God was to face that king with the consequence of his sin and to tell him that God was going to bring judgment (1 Kings 16:30–32, 17:1).

Judgment on the Nation

Elijah's word to the king was that the heavens would give no rain and though, as James says, he was a man of "like passions as we are," he "prayed earnestly . . . and it rained not on the earth by the space of three years and six months" (James 5:17, KJV). If we do not listen to His Word, God has, of course, other ways of getting our attention. There are four major ways in which God can bring up judgment on a country (Ezekiel 14:13–23).

First, through the economy: He can "cut off the supply of bread." Money gets tight, food and water are in short supply, essentials get scarce. Sometimes people start thinking seriously about God only when things start going wrong.

Second, through ecology: He can "cause wild beasts to pass through the land." God is sovereign Ruler of the whole creation. Even one small creature let loose in the judgment of God can fell a ruler. For Pharaoh it was frogs, lice, flies, and locusts; for others it might be a wasp, an ant, a medfly. It could be a change in weather, in the relationship of the sun or (in Elijah's case) the dew and the rain. The worldwide concern over the greenhouse effect may not just be about fluorocarbons and exhaust emissions. When the very air and weather begin to change in unpredictable ways, people start thinking about their own personal behavior. For Egypt, the pests were a testimony to the fact that something was supernaturally wrong in their land. For Israel in Ahab's day, the drought was a sign of the displeasure of God.

Third, through disease: He can "send a pestilence." When God removes His hand of protection from a nation something too small to see begins to bring sentence on whole cities. There are yet more dangerous plagues possible than AIDS; sometimes people begin to take eternity seriously only in the face of incurable illness. In Naaman's leprosy he sought God; in Herod's death great fear came on the court.

Fourth, through civil or international war: He can "bring a sword on that land."

It has happened in history before and it can happen again. When we do not listen, the judgment of God can "bring a sword"—that is, He removes His peace from a country and allows another nation to invade or go to war with the land.

Elijah was a man who lived in a nation, like some of us today, under divine judgment. People were hurting financially. Jobs were lost, crime was on the rise, people were struggling. There was political division, collapse of leadership, bad public examples, murder, and suicides. The land was in famine; but through it all Elijah was personally taken care of. God faithfully provided food and water every day; He commanded the ravens to bring meat, and the river kept running (1 Kings 17:3–6).

No one has all he needs in himself. Elijah needed the brook and the birds. And no one can live a truly independent life. Besides basic physical needs like food and water and shelter we all have other needs. "Blessed are the poor in spirit," Jesus said, "for theirs is the kingdom of heaven." A genuinely *poor* person has no resources in himself to meet essential needs. And no one, especially not a man or woman of God, has all the required wisdom, abilities, and means. As John Donne wrote, "No man is an island."

We tend to focus on people or situations or things that seem to meet those needs: friends, teachers, books, ideas, a place, a work, a church. A *friend* can stimulate our minds, satisfy our hearts, and stir our souls. A *teacher* can catch our admiration, awaken our appreciation, push open a mental door for us to new realms. A *book* we come across might capture our imagination, reset our priorities, restructure our whole world view. A *place* we live in can become a home, a castle, a refuge, a security that sends us out armed with determination and courage and welcomes us back to rest and sympathy. Our *work* can be the dominant drive of our lives, giving us a reason to get up in the morning with purpose and vision. Our *church* might be the focus of our hopes and ideals, the friendship and encouragement of others much like us who are learning life together. Or we may be gripped by a *great idea* that lights up our whole world with a vision of what can be done. All these and more may be to us as a river of God full of water.

When the Brook Runs Dry

Imagine what it was like for Elijah. Each day his every need had been met. He never had to worry like the rest of the nation where his next meal was coming from. God was in charge of things, God was going to take care of him. All he had to do was trust and pray and wait. And then one day the brook dried up.

What happened to Elijah can happen to us. Things or people we relied on, depended on, built our lives around suddenly change, move on, or move away.

Your *friend* is still your friend; but somehow, insensibly, you have grown apart and now it seems irreversible. It is not that you have quarreled; it is just that now your paths are moving in different directions. You may see him or her almost as much as before, but somehow it now seems less. It is sad and it wrenches at something deep inside you, but there is really nothing either of you can do. Just like the brook, the water you once drew from in your friend's life has dried up.

You still get to hear your *teacher*, but the man at whose feet you sat in wonder at twenty you may have outgrown at thirty or forty. It is not that what he says is now no longer true; it is just that you judge things more critically now. You have grown. You see things somewhat differently with the passage of the years.

That *book* moved you once, and perhaps it still does; but

you do not care to read it over again and again. Many like it have passed from dominating your thoughts and attention into pleasant and sometimes quaint memories; like old songs they have moved into nostalgia and history.

Maybe you return to the *place* you loved and remembered before but to your surprise, everything is changed. Someone else lives there now and he has made it almost unrecognizable. Perhaps the house where you lived is gone, or it has become, by neglect or disaster, a ruin. Or circumstances have changed and you must move somewhere else, find another home, change everything you were always so contented with: The brook dries up.

The *work* you are still doing but is it the same for you now? Maybe you can keep on doing it until you die; some do. But then again, perhaps the brook here, too, has dried up. Perhaps your job is gone now. They did not need you any longer. Either someone else has filled the ranks instead or you can no longer do what you did before.

The *ministry* you were given: Is it coming to an end?

And your *church*, the place that was such a haven for your spirit: What has happened there? It is not as if it had to split or fail; it may still be as before, perfectly able to meet others' needs. It may be simply that *for you* it has somehow lost its appeal. The water from which you drew has been diverted to other side channels. The people you were close to have moved, the pastor has changed, the ministry you previously relied on has begun to dissolve or disband. It hurts, it is uncomfortable to think about, it bothers you deeply, but the outcome is certain: The brook has dried up.

But you, like Elijah, should know this could happen to anyone. It can happen over anything we try to count on always being close to us. It happened *even to Jesus*. There was a time when He couldn't rely on His friends, His family, His ministry, His home church, or even His best and closest disciples.

There were things happening to Him that weren't in the

Book He knew and loved from childhood. Of His ministry He said, "My meat is to do the will of Him that sent Me and to finish His work," but there were times when even He could do nothing.

He had grown up going to the synagogue. He had been the central focus of the teachers there when He was only twelve. Then later, giving His first personal message, what He said came into violent conflict with the elders and they "cast Him out."

There came a day even to Christ when His family seemed to fail Him, when He was misunderstood and interfered with, when even His relatives told people that He was out of His mind. There came a time when He said, "The foxes have holes and the birds of the air have nests, but the Son of Man has nowhere to lay His head."

And there came an awful hour when He could not rely on even His closest friends. The disciples went to sleep during His agony of prayer and the man He had called "friend" sold Him to His enemies for thirty pieces of silver.

There was even that one frightening moment when it seemed as if the Great Vision that moved Him all His life hung in the balance. In Gethsemane He prayed, "Father, if it be possible, let this cup pass from Me." And on the cross He cried, "My God, My God, why have You forsaken Me?"

If it happened to Elijah, if it happened to Jesus, it will no doubt happen also to you.

No One Should Possess a Private Brook

All the land is drought and famine but Cherith is still flowing when Israel is dry. What would have happened to Elijah if the stream had kept on flowing?

(1) His blessings would have become a barrier. Elijah "was a man of like passions" but it certainly doesn't seem like it. This man is like something out of a fantasy movie—some holy

Lawrence of Arabia figure, twice as large as life, not your average Christian! The brook *had* to dry up. God was behind it. That is what happens; people need to be reminded they are ordinary after all. The godly especially sometimes become inhuman. They find the invisible so satisfying they are hard on their fellow mortals.

What might have happened day after day sipping from the cold stream when all the land was parched and dying? Elijah might have lost his prophet's sympathy for people. He might have been tempted to take the attitude, "People are starving and thirsty, but they deserve it. If they would only learn, like me, to trust God they wouldn't be in such a mess."

(2) His privileges might have turned to pride. Elijah had a high standard for his own life. Like all prophets he knew what is expected of the godly. As a child he had great dreams. He had no doubt set his heart as a boy to be the very best he could be. To fail that calling in any way is for an Elijah utterly devastating. Later in his life Jezebel put out a contract on his life and Elijah the fearless prophet ran away. The sense of failure so overwhelmed him that he wanted to die.

His words reveal the danger of a high self-set standard that is somehow compromised: "It is enough! Now, Lord, take my life, for *I am no better than my fathers!*" (1 Kings 19:4). Did he really think he was? The brook *had* to dry up. Elijah had to be reminded that the only thing that makes us special is that we are made in God's image, and the only thing that sets us apart is the grace of God.

(3) His rest might have made him a permanent recluse. We all need time to recover from the pressures of life; it is part of both the design and commandment of God to take off from daily labor. Jesus told His disciples to "sit by the well and rest." "Come ye apart," the old adage says, "or ye will come apart." But too long in the safety and shelter and security of Cherith may have worked to hurt him instead of help him. Elijah may have become content to stay near Horeb supplied by God and quit the battle. God is out to do three things, said

an old writer: "Get us out of the world, get the world out of us, and then send us back into the world." No one can live forever at Cherith.

Elijah Driven to Zarephath

Here is a man who has challenged the might of kings, a solitary man who has stood alone unaided by anyone except God. All through his life and ministry he has been dependent on no one but God, and needed nothing but God's word. But now that word comes to him and calls him to a place of embarrassment: He is to go to a home for shelter and sustenance where a widow and her son are about to make their last meal before they starve to death.

Sometimes your Cherith must fail in order to force you to hurt with other people. If the brook had kept on flowing Elijah might have counted on it and forgotten the God who gave it. *The means by which God maintains us are always in danger of becoming the barriers that shut us out from Him.* Cheriths can't be permanent.

Now, more than ever, we live in a future shock world. Nothing seems to last. People change; friends come and go; the world keeps shifting gears. Best-selling books are now in bargain bins. Ideas change as fast as rock stars and we are wholly not the same people we were ten years ago. Thomas Hardy wrote: "It is the ongoing of the world that makes it sad. If the world stood still at a happy moment there would be no sadness in it. The sun and moon standing still on Ajalon was not a catastrophe for Israel but a type of paradise."

But a stationary heaven or earth would become dull at last. All change is risky, but some change must come. God has given us seasons. Without the winter, summer's warmth would not be as welcome; the reds and golds of fall set off the coming green freshness of spring. And so with the seasons of our spirit; each is necessary for all the colors and flowers of our lives.

Don't mourn your Cheriths. *In the growth of your spirit, the next is always better*. Thank God for what they meant to you as reminders of His love and move on. You will one day see the hand of God in the drying up of your brook. The dwindling of the stream will mean in time not only help for you, but help for others. Elijah left Cherith for Zarephath, not only to save a mother's life, but to learn something more of God's love. A brook and birds don't show you as much of God as a mother and a child. And though you may miss your brook, you will not miss God; your new course will take you all the way from the valley to a foretaste of Bethlehem.

Prayer

O Jesus, we thank You. We thank You for the river that rises, touching our loins, and we thank You for the river we are going to hit that we can't swim in anymore. It will carry us. We can't carry it. It is a river not only that we can't pass over, but that cannot be passed over. We thank You for calling us to abandonment to You, to being swept along, not in chaos, not in the same thing we were in long, long ago, but in a sense of abandonment to the purposes of the river. We believe out of this river will come healing wherever it goes.

So we pray that You will take our own doubts, our own struggles and suffering, and translate these into life. Feed this river, we pray, with our own suffering and our own struggle for the help of others who may face probably the scariest time in our century with courage and joy and faith.

Prayer

Level Four

Waters to Swim In

"Blessed are they that have not seen and yet have believed."
—Jesus to Thomas

Again he measured a thousand; and it was a river that I could not ford, for the water had risen, enough water to swim in, a river that could not be forded. Ezekiel 47:5, NAS

8

Abandonment to Mystery

And now the last stage of the river—the scariest stage of all. All the while the river is rising, first flowing under the door, to the *ankles*, to the *knees*, to the *loins*. And now, at last, to the very limit; it is no longer something you can carry, it is something that must carry you. The last step in God is one that takes you beyond your own control.

Our Call to Abandonment

We all should know what it means to surrender to Christ, but *how deep does that surrender go?* Ezekiel faced something that was finally beyond his limit. The previous measures into the river were all right; they could be managed, handled, accommodated. But now this was the end of wading. He knew he could not ford this crossing; it was now bigger than he was.

Do we really know our limits? A characteristic of our Western culture is our deep need to be able to control our own lives, to be able to get a handle on everything we meet. In the U.S. Bill of Rights every citizen under the government of this nation is guaranteed protected personal rights; but in the Bible mandate, every citizen of heaven under the government of God is called to give up the self-protection of his or her rights and come wholly under the provision, care, and shelter of Another. We are not used to being unable to control things; it bothers us intensely when things happen that we cannot manage. But to meet and follow the living God is to deliberately hand over the reins of your life to Another. As the bumper sticker says, "If God *is* your co-pilot—switch seats."

Ezekiel's call to the last level was not, however, a situation of despair. It was too high for walking, but it was high enough now to swim in. God always calls us, as Catherine Marshall said, "beyond our selves." Nothing of faith is ever quite safe.

We have a habit of looking at things out of our depth as barriers instead of possibilities, as signposts of discouragement instead of opportunities to trust and learn. We firmly resist things we have never attempted: "No, thanks; I can't do that." But there is so much that God wants us to do that we cannot do ourselves. When we run out of our natural resources, God is ready to show us His supernatural ones. And risk, challenge, adventure are the heart of all growth and life. It is in the early shallows of the river that our first tests come; if we are not found faithful there, what will happen to us when the river really rises? Whether we like it or not, situations and circumstances will come to us like Ezekiel's river, in which we will either have to learn to swim or drown.

> "If you have run with the footmen, and they have wearied you, then how can you contend with horses? And if in the land of peace, in which you trusted, they wearied you, then how will you do in the flooding of the Jordan?" Jeremiah 12:5

A. J. Gossip was a famous preacher at the turn of the century. Like his congregation, he too had his share of shock and the unexpected floods of life; yet in the midst of his own great personal grief and hurt, he was still expected to minister and be a comfort and blessing to others. In 1927 after his beloved wife died, Gossip preached a message from this text in Jeremiah that he called "But When Life Tumbles In, What Then?"

It is one thing, Gossip said, to complain to God about the bewilderment of life when all you have faced are the "little rubs and frets and ills of life that fall to everyone."

> [But] if these have broken through your guard, pushed aside your religion, made you so sour and peevish and cross toward God—God help you. What will happen when sudden as a shell screaming out of the night, some one of the great crashing dispensations bursts in your life and leaves an emptiness where there had been a home, a tumbled ruin of your ordered ways, a heart so sore you wonder how it holds together? If you have caught your breath, poor fool, when splashing through the shallow waters of some summer brook, how will you fare when Jordan bursts its banks and rushes as far as the eye can see, one huge wild swirl of angry waters and you, your feet caught away, half-choked, you are tossed nearer and nearer to the roaring of the falls and over it? . . .
>
> Do you think Christ always understood or found it easy? There was a day when He took God's will for Him in His hand and turned it round and looked at it. And, "Is this what You ask of Me?" He said and for a moment His eyes looked almost incredulous. And another day, puzzled and uncertain, He cried out, "But is this really what You meant that I should give You, this here, this now?" Yes and another still, when the cold rushing waters roared in a raging torrent through His soul; yet He would not turn back, fought His way to the further bank, died still believing in the God who seemed to have deserted Him. And that is why He is given a name that is above every name. . . . You people in the sunshine *may* believe the faith,

but we in the shadow *must* believe it. We have nothing else. . . .

[And when] standing in the roaring of Jordan, cold to the heart with its dreadful chill, and very conscious of the terror of its rushing, I too, like Hopeful, can call back to you who one day in your turn will have to cross it: *"Be of good cheer, my brother, for I feel the bottom and it is sound."*

9

A River that Could Not Be Passed Over

Notice how much this last level in our scriptural lives looks like the first; we are not in control of ourselves. At the level of chaos we are at the mercy of our own lusts; at the level of mystery we are at the mercy of the Lord Himself. At the first stage of chaos we are borne along by something we cannot control; like Paul we can say, "What I will to do, that I do not practice; but what I hate, that I do" (Romans 7:15). Our lusts are lord of our lives. The river rises all the time, from chaos to principle to doubt and now to mystery; and now at this last stage, too, we are no longer in charge. We are about to be carried along by someone who has a far higher and better purpose than just letting us do what we want.

And as Ezekiel noticed, it "*could not be crossed.*" It was not just something beyond his own personal limits—"I could not pass over"; it was something beyond anyone's personal limits. What God has in mind is not for some special saint, some rare individual with unique gifts and calling. God is out to bring His people all to the end of their limits; this is a river no one can pass over.

This stage takes you beyond your own control of things. It not only answers the questions, it takes you beyond the questions because it is touching something more than you can comprehend. It is called *abandonment*. It is the level of loving service that all the great saints and lovers of God sought and many experienced over the centuries that made them strong in the face of great hardship and difficulty.

A Thirst for God

A book was published centuries ago called *The Cloud of Unknowing*. It was written in the Europe of the fourteenth century, a time of great distress, social unrest, and violent insurrection. There was famine, war, and terrible plagues. In England the Black Death killed multitudes, including many of the clergy and ministers of that time, spiritually impoverishing the world.

Yet this terrible century produced at the same time some of the greatest contemplative Christian saints and mystics of the Church, who not only "possessed their souls in peace," but wrote of their experiences with God with profound thought, vivid expression, and contagious enthusiasm.

Richard Rolle, Lady Julian of Norwich, John Tauler, Henry Suso, and St. Catherine of Siena were some of the greatest devotional writers of the Church. They all lived joyously, even radiantly through this same time. They were not just a few odd hermits and recluses; they were practical men and women with active lives and sometimes major responsibilities in leadership and society.

Not all the depths they explored are recommended or even advised for everyone; they took pains to point out that God calls people into a work, that the effort itself depends on God, that it is "never gotten by study, but only by grace," and that it is a mistake to imagine all Christians are to apply themselves in the same way. Indeed, most of them were at a loss to explain or recommend methods, principles, and approaches to others, as it was their conviction that God alone would provide for each individual.

"He is a jealous lover," wrote the author of *The Cloud*, "and suffereth no fellowship; He liketh not to work in thy will unless He be only with thee by Himself. He asketh no help but only thyself. He wills thou but look on Him and let Him alone." They knew only that the key to entering into the mystery of God Himself was to set the heart on loving God past our human limits of understanding Him, that this devotion should not be "artificial or violent, but spring gently and sweetly from love to love."

They all shared this one thing in common: a thirst for God and a depth of desire for Him that is largely missing in our shallow century. Their writings show us that "in spite of all this, and perhaps because of all this—a man could possess his soul in peace and that there were many more like him. They are evidence that through all difficulties there persisted a Christian life which was superior to secular disturbance . . ." (from the introduction of *The Cloud of Unknowing*).

Into the Depths of Mystery

Mystery. The Bible is full of it. The *Kingdom of God* operates in "mystery" (Mark 4:11). *Lawlessness* is called a "mystery" (2 Thessalonians 2:7) and so is *godliness* (1 Timothy 3:16). The *Church* is a mystery (Ephesians 5:32). The *Gospel* operates in mystery (Ephesians 6:19; 1 Corinthians 1:17–25). The *resurrection* is a mystery (1 Corinthians 15:51) and *God Himself*, our Uncreated Triune Creator, is the ultimately Mysterious One (Colossians 2:2).

But *mystery* in the Bible does not mean quite the same thing as it means to most people today. *Mystery* in the dictionary primarily signifies something hidden, withheld, strange, or secret; Oxford defines it as a "hidden or inexplicable matter." Mystery, of course, does mean this, but it means something more in the Bible; it is spiritual truth divinely revealed. Although mystery is something only God can show us, it is something He *can* show us. Mystery is indeed a secret; but in the revelation of God, it is an "open" secret.

Mystery, says Vine's *Expository Dictionary,* simply denotes "something outside the range of natural unassisted apprehension." Mystery is something you can't grasp with just personal study, effort, and training; mystery is something you cannot know at all unless God shows you "in a manner and at a time appointed by God and to those only who are illumined by His Spirit. . . . In the ordinary sense, mystery implies knowledge withheld; its Scriptural significance is truth revealed" (*Expository Dictionary of New Testament Words*).

In mystery, the divine plan is concealed from all until God's time and even then revealed only to His chosen; but He does show His purpose to the right people at the right time. And what is the foundation, the secret, the heart of receiving any such divine revelation? Not knowledge, but *love.*

"He who has My commandments and keeps them," said Jesus, "it is he who loves Me. And he who loves Me will be loved by My Father, and I will love him and manifest Myself to him" (John 14:21). Notice: *A manifestation of Christ to the soul follows the obedience of love.* Not knowledge first, but love. Not information as a start, but devotion. Not understanding to begin with, but abandonment. Indeed, without that love, even an exceptional degree of religious insight is worthless. "Though I speak with the tongues of men and of angels," said Paul, ". . . and though I have the gift of prophecy, and understand all mysteries and all knowledge . . . but have not love, I am nothing" (1 Corinthians 13:1–2).

God, who is the Maker of both the power to love and to know, says the unknown author of *The Cloud of Unknowing,* is to the knowing power alone "ever more incomprehensible": but to the loving power "He is, in every man diversely, all comprehensively to the full. . . . One loving soul, alone in itself, by virtue of love, may comprehend in itself Him who is sufficient to the full—and much more without comparison—to fill all the souls and angels that ever may be.

And this is the endless, marvelous miracle of love, the working of it which shall never have end; forever shall He do it and never shall He cease for to do it. See who so by grace may see; for the feeling of this is endless bliss and the contrary is endless pain."

It is, he says, *the work of the soul that most pleases God.* All the saints and angels "have joy of this work and hasten them to help it with all their might; all friends be mad when you do thus, and try to defeat it in all that they can. . . . Have no wonder that I stir thee to this work. For this is the work . . . in which man should have continued if he had never sinned. And to this working was man made, and all things for man to help him and further him to it. And by this working shall man be repaired again. And for want of this working a man falls ever more deeper and deeper into sin and further and further from God."

Learning How to Swim

I learned to swim in a New Zealand primary school. At least, I was *supposed* to learn. What actually happened is that I splashed impressively with my arms, kicked with one foot, and hopped along the bottom with the other; it looked like swimming and it passed for it as long as we were in our shallow little school paddling baths. Fine, as long as there was a bottom I could always feel and touch.

Then one day my aunt took my younger sister and me to a country swimming hole. A narrow ledge of rock went out from the bank for a few feet before a big drop-off into the dozen-foot-or-so-deep hole. I was hopping along this narrow ledge kicking and saw a long branch lying near me in the water. I thought, *I can probably hold onto that stick and float with it.* So I grabbed the stick and continued kicking along the ledge until I suddenly ran out of rock. My foot went off the end, I lost the branch, and went under. The next second I was drowning.

I didn't know how to swim. I had had the illusion of swimming as long as I had one foot on the bottom, but now it was the real thing. There was nothing left to stand on. They say your life passes before you die; I was only little, so mine passed very fast. The next thing I remember was being pulled out of the water by one of my aunt's boyfriends, who had just happened to notice me going under for the last time.

And you—have you had the floor pulled out from under you? In this area of mystery, God takes the ledge away from us in order to bring us into reality. Like children, we have hopped too long with one foot on the bottom, secure in the illusion that we were really swimming; now there is no bottom to touch in this river, and we find out just how much of our splashing around was only a show. The river is rising, and we are not to be children forever.

"Right well have you said," noted the author of *The Cloud*, " 'for the love of Jesus.' For in the love of Jesus shall be your help. Love is such a power that it makes all things to be shared. Therefore we love Jesus, and all things that He has are thine."

This love, of course, is not a feeling; it is an act of will. *Agape* love in the Bible is an unselfish choice for the highest good; of God first, and then His creation. You can love with this love when you do not like; you can choose when you cannot feel; and you can set your heart on pleasing God when you cannot comprehend.

"For of all other creatures and their works—yea, and the work of God Himself—may a man through grace have fullness of knowing, and well can he think of them; but of God Himself can no man think," reports *The Cloud*. "And therefore I would leave all that thing that I can think, and choose to my love that thing I cannot think. For why, He may well be loved, but not thought. By love He may be gotten and holden; but by thought neither. . . .

"And although it be a light and a part of contemplation, nevertheless in this work it shall be cast down and covered with a cloud forgetting. And thou shalt step above it stalwartly, but listily [with pleasure or delight], with a devout and a pleasing stirring of love, and try to pierce that darkness above thee. And smite upon that thick cloud of unknowing with a sharp dart of longing love; and go not hence for aught that befalleth."

10

All-Out Faith

What does it mean to trust Christ? Blondin (Jean-François Gravlet) was a famous acrobat and tightrope-walker in the nineteenth century. His most famous achievement was crossing Niagara Falls by tightrope, usually without a safety net. He did it many times in different ways: blindfolded, in a sack, on stilts, even sitting down to make and eat an omelette and make a cup of coffee with a primus stove and water drawn up from the river!

Perhaps one of his most daring feats was to push a wheelbarrow loaded with a heavy sack of cement across the wire. With all that weight, the slightest overbalance could wrench the barrow out of his hand or twist him off the wire and into the river. But Blondin, the supreme showman of that time, was the master of the high wire; he took the wheelbarrow all the way across without a hitch.

After one such successful stunt, Blondin asked an impressed reporter: "Do you believe I can do anything on a tightrope?" "Oh, yes, Mr. Blondin," said the reporter, "after what I've seen today I believe it. You can do anything."

"Do you believe, then," said Blondin, "that instead of a sack of cement, I could put a *man* in this wheelbarrow—a man who has never been on a tightrope before—and wheel him, without a safety net, safely over to the other side?"

"Oh, yes, sir, Mr. Blondin," said the reporter, "I believe it."

"Good," said Blondin. "*Get in.*"

It is one thing to give mental assent; it is something else again to "get in." When you "get in," that's faith, and faith, of course, is a doing word. It is not something you discuss, it is something you do; it is not just something to learn, but something to live.

We are not told what happened to the reporter, except that he probably suddenly remembered an urgent appointment elsewhere. To put your life totally into the hands of others on the bare record of who they are and what they have done is faith indeed.

But that is not the end of the story. Blondin did, I understand, finally find some daredevil willing to ride in his wheelbarrow. He tipped out his sack of cement, put the man in the barrow, and started across.

Wagers were flowing on both sides of the Falls. One man in particular had tendered a very large bet Blondin would not make it. Blondin set out, wheeling the man carefully on the tight wire, who you can imagine was white-knuckling it all the way, clinging to the sides of the barrow and not daring to look down. Blondin breezily passed the halfway point on the 1,600-foot rope.

The man on the other bank who had made the large bet knew that unless something drastic happened he was surely going to lose a fortune. Surreptitiously he slipped away. He went to one of the support ropes that kept the main tightrope taut and stopped it from all side-to-side movement. And when no one was looking, he cut it.

Twa-ang! Suddenly this tensioning rope flew free. Blondin still had his man in the barrow, with many feet to go. There they were, 160 feet above the water, with Blondin's tightrope vibrating violently like a plucked bowstring. The wheelbarrow pitched crazily from side to side. Any moment now, the rim of the wheel would come off the rope. With no safety net both men would be pitched into the raging grave of Niagara Falls below.

Blondin's brave passenger was now out of his mind with fear, screaming bloody murder, and they were only seconds away from death. Then Blondin spoke, and his voice snapped like that of a military commander.

"*Stand up!*" he commanded the terrified man. "Stand up! Grab my shoulders!"

The man stared at him in unbelieving desperation.

"Let go and stand up! Let go the wheelbarrow! Do it or die!"

In total terror, the man somehow let go and fought his way up from the rocking barrow.

"Your arms—'round my neck! Now, your legs—'round my waist!"

What choice did he have? This was life or death; whether Blondin was right or wrong, he was all he had. It was obey or die. He threw his arms around Blondin's neck; he wrapped his legs around Blondin's waist. Blondin took the strain and stayed balanced there, every trained and honed muscle in his body reacting desperately to the singing, swinging wire under his feet.

The wheelbarrow, empty and abandoned, somersaulted down more than sixteen stories into the Falls and smashed into the water to be swept away. For all I know, it is down there still.

Imagine the sheer terror of this man. He had nothing left to cling to now but the man with the power and skill, the expert who had dared the rope before, time and dangerous time again, and still lived. Blondin somehow was still standing on the crazily swaying rope, arms stretched wide and shifting every second for balance, with his passenger now locked in a death grip around him. And it was then he heard Blondin say the final thing that saved his life.

"Hold on," said Blondin. "But don't fight. If we are going to make it alive, you must not fight me. You must move when I move, give when I give. You must become one with me. *For just this little while, you must become Blondin."* And in the reality of that command, he carried him safely to the other side.

You and I, too, have a long and dangerous journey to make. There are some who bet we will not complete it. And they may be right. Indeed, they are surely right if all we have to make it with is what we are. Martin Luther understood the situation very well when he wrote:

> Did we in our own strength confide,
> Our striving would be losing;
> Were not the right Man on our side,
> The Man of God's own choosing.

The danger is real; the fall is real.

But we are *not alone.* There is Someone with us, and it is Someone who has crossed the rope—over the waters—before. Our hope, our only hope, is to hold on so tightly to Him that to all intents we share in what He is, and become part of His purpose. *Faith is not something you hold, but Someone who holds you.* We can trust Him; we *must* trust Him. And He will carry us safely to the other side.

11

The Darkness of God: Trusting When You Cannot See

I am no prophet nor the son of a prophet, but I do believe we are headed for some very dark times in this decade. I really believe in some places it is going to be rough to be a Christian. In other nations believers have already faced trouble and pressure. But what I want to look at here does not come about from the persecution of the world. This is a problem that will happen to every single Christian who wants to be involved in the work of God, or to any ordinary Christian who has set his heart on pleasing God. This is not just a problem that comes from other people; neither is it necessarily a problem that comes from the demonic world. It can very well come to Christians from God Himself.

> "Who among you fears the Lord? Who obeys the voice of His Servant? Who walks in darkness and has no light? Let him trust in the name of the Lord and rely upon his God. Look, all you who kindle a fire, who encircle yourselves with sparks: walk in the light of your fire and in the sparks you have kindled—this you shall have from My hand: you shall lie down in torment."
>
> Isaiah 50:10–11

When I first read this passage, I assumed it was written to an unbeliever. After all, it deals with darkness. I knew in Scripture of only three kinds of darkness and, well, everybody knows that darkness comes only to unbelievers. Perhaps it meant the darkness of *sin*. After all, the Bible does say: "Men loved darkness rather than light, because their deeds were evil" (John 3:19). And again, "What communion has light with darkness?" (2 Corinthians 6:14). God has called us to be a "chosen generation, a royal priesthood, a holy nation, His own special people, that you may proclaim the praises of Him who called you out of darkness into His marvelous light" (1 Peter 2:9). "If we walk in the light as He is in the light, we have fellowship with one another, and the blood of Jesus Christ His Son cleanses us from all sin" (1 John 1:7).

Secondly, there is a darkness in the Bible that is really *ignorance*. The opposite of this darkness is the word *light*. This is one of the most basic statements of God in the entire Scriptures: "God is light and in Him is no darkness at all" (1 John 1:5).

Now this word *light* as used in the Bible means "that which is most wise." The Bible word *light* used of God says that He is the total criterion, the ultimate standard and example of all that is most wise and most holy in the universe. When the Bible says that "God dwells in the light," it means God lives perfectly according to that which is most wise and most intelligent. And when He asks us to "walk in the light," God is asking us to live according to the highest intelligence.

The Christian life calls you not only to be good but to be wise. One of the meanings of the word *darkness*, then, is "ignorance," not really understanding the ways of God.

Then, thirdly, *demonic power* is sometimes referred to as "the power of darkness" (Luke 22:53; Acts 26:18; Ephesians 6:12; Colossians 1:13). So the satanic world is sometimes involved in the word *darkness*. I've done battle before with darkness that was demonic.

But the darkness Isaiah spoke of is none of those things. The strange thing about this verse and this kind of darkness is that it happens only to people who are walking with God, who love God, who are not messing around with sin, and who are not ignorant. There is a darkness that can come to men and women of God that has nothing to do with sin, that has nothing to do with lack of wisdom, and has nothing whatsoever to do with the devil. And the tragedy is, when this darkness comes upon certain people of God, they don't understand what it is and it nearly wipes them out.

Everyone who has set his heart on serving God will have this darkness come at some point. When this happens we must learn to recognize it and deal with it.

Fears the Lord

Let's look at the person to whom this verse is addressed. God says, first of all, "Who among you fears the Lord?" *The fear of the Lord is the awesome reverence of God.*

I have often prayed that God will reveal Himself to me. When I was a new Christian, I wanted God to talk to me in an audible voice! I didn't know what I wanted Him to say, I just wanted Him to say something. I had been saved about six months so I said, "O Lord, how come You have never spoken to me? You've spoken to some of these people in the Bible. You spoke to Your Son."

I had forgotten that, as far as we know, Jesus lived thirty years before his Father spoke to Him in an audible voice. And there I was, a six-month brat, who wanted God to do all kinds of audible, supernatural things for me.

So late one night in a Christian campground I said: "God, I'm going to fast and pray. . . . I'm going to die unless You come down and speak to me. Amen."

Then I got my Bible and my sleeping bag and went out into the woods. I started to pray, "Lord, come down." I was yelling out in those woods at two o'clock in the morning. Suddenly I realized that all the crickets had stopped chirping. All the birds and owls had stopped hooting. Everything had stopped. It wasn't just that I was making a racket. I was on my knees with my Bible in front of me and I thought, *Why is everything so quiet?* So I shut up a minute. It was very, very still right then. I think I stopped breathing. And then, without turning around, still on my knees on the sleeping bag, I very slowly looked behind me. And it seemed to me that Something white was standing there.

Do you know what I did? I did not turn around. I did not dare. Without looking back, I picked up my Bible and my sleeping bag. I headed straight for my bed, got in, closed my eyes tight, and went to sleep immediately. I never prayed that prayer again. I realized that when the God of the universe appears, you don't have anything to say at all. When He comes down, the whole world shuts up. Nobody talks. Before, I had had all these questions I was going to ask God. In the morning all the answers were right there in my Bible.

This Isaiah verse is addressed to a person who "fears the Lord," who has this awesome reverence for the Lord. This isn't a cheap, shallow, one-time-in-the-presence-of-God person. This is someone who has reverenced His presence. The Bible also tells us "the fear of the Lord is to *hate evil.*" Since the fear of the Lord is to hate evil, and "the fear of the Lord is the beginning of wisdom," the one to whom *this* darkness comes is not someone living in sin or ignorance. This is a person whose life is set against evil, who does not want to do evil. This person already knows some things about God, someone perhaps who has already had a long walk with God.

Habitually Obedient

There is a second thing we know about this person: The Bible says this one will "*obey the voice of His servant.*" The great Servant of servants is Jesus Himself. We may be justified here in capitalizing "His Servant"; the passage refers ultimately to someone who is obeying Christ Himself. This person is not lost; this person is a true believer. The one this verse is talking about is somebody who is an obedient follower of Jesus Christ.

This is not someone habitually living in disobedience to God. People sometimes say they are "pretty much a Christian" or "fairly Christian." You can't be half-Christian any more than you can be half-pregnant. You can only be "in Christ" or out of Him. There's no moral halfway in Scripture. God says, in effect: "There's a big, wide freeway that leads to destruction. There's a narrow little road that leads to life" (Matthew 7:13–14). There's no middle-sized motorway for people who can't make either. The Bible says, "No one can serve two masters; for either he will hate the one and love the other, or else he will be loyal to the one and despise the other" (Matthew 6:24). You can't fool around in sin or live to please yourself and still match what the Bible says when it describes a Christian.

I remember one time when I was in San Francisco. I was witnessing in Golden Gate Park. I met a young lady there who was reading something with a bunch of hip kids around her. She was smoking grass, rolling a joint. I approached. The place was so blue with smoke I was afraid I'd get high just standing around and talking. I noticed that the book she had was the Bible. That was not too unusual in those days in San Francisco. A lot of kids would do drugs and see if they could get into the imagery of the book of Revelation with all its dragons and things.

"I see you're reading a Bible," I said.

"Yes."

"Do you enjoy reading the Bible?"

"Oh, yes, I love it."

"Do you know about receiving Jesus?"

"Oh, yes, praise God, I'm a Christian."

"How much of the Bible have you read?"

"Oh, a lot of it."

"You're reading Revelation. Are you aware of the word there that is translated 'witchcraft,' the word *pharmakia?*" (Revelation 18:23).

She said, "Yes, I know that word."

"Do you know the meaning of the word *witchcraft* there? It means to induce a religious experience through the use of drugs."

"Oh, yeah, someone told me that once."

"Do you know that this is expressly forbidden in Scripture?"

"Yes, I know that."

"Then you know that using drugs is a sin?"

"Oh, of course."

I was looking at the joint in her hand that she was blowing. I said, "Then why in the world are you smoking that grass?"

She said, "You don't understand. My *body* is sinning, but my *spirit* is worshiping God."

I couldn't help but wonder which part of her was talking to me.

What is this darkness? It is something we are rarely made aware of in this hi-tech hungering for hi-touch century; it is something that the old saints and mystics often spoke about as an essential element in the development of the depth of the spiritual life. It has been largely neglected, untreated, or unknown in twentieth-century evangelical speaking and writing. It is something that comes from the hand of God.

Has it happened to you? You wake up one day to find all spiritual feelings gone. You pray and nothing seems to happen. You read your Bible, and you understand the words, but there is no light. You search your heart and find nothing to match what you are going through. You rebuke the devil, you ask others for prayer, you go to hear your favorite Christian guru—and nothing happens. No counsel seems to help; no answers answer.

St. John of the Cross called it "the dark night of the soul." Tozer called it "the ministry of the night." Spurgeon preached about "the child of light walking in darkness." The author of *The Cloud of Unknowing* wrote:

> For the first time . . . thou findest but a darkness, and as it were a "Cloud of Unknowing," thou knowest not what save that thou feelest in thy will a naked intent unto God. This darkness and this cloud . . . is betwixt thee and thy God and hindereth thee, so that thou mayest neither see Him clearly by light of understanding in thy reason nor feel Him in sweetness of love in thine affection. And therefore shape thee to bide in this darkness as long as thou mayest, evermore crying after Him whom thou lovest. For if ever thou shalt see Him or feel Him as it may be here, it must always be in this cloud and in this darkness.

Each writer dealt with this differently and on different levels, but the experience is common. It is not the darkness of wrong or guilt or demonic oppression. It is not sin; it is instead an inexplicable sense of loss, uncertainty, perplexity. It is above all a *withdrawn sense* of the presence of God.

Now it is natural to live in His sunshine. We believers don't have to sing "Don't Worry—Be Happy." We take for granted that "in the presence of God is joy and at His right hand are pleasures for evermore." Yet a lot of heaven's journey must be made at night. Happiness is not always the test of holiness. It is possible to be happy and not holy: "As the crackling of thorns underneath a pot, so is the laughter of fools," said Solomon. "This also is vanity." There is a false laughter and an empty lightness of heart that the Bible calls the sin of levity—foolishness and shallowness in the things of God and life and reality. And this is a characteristic of much of our public popular image today: Christians are often perceived as happy idiots, like people in some asylum, who are happy only because they have lost the ability to live in reality.

But God never designed real life to function in an artificial environment. Without doubt, conversion often takes place with an accompanying jolt of pure joy. In the glow of that first meeting with Christ, you get a taste of an excitement and release that seems as if it will last forever. When you first get saved you think it will be all music, dancing, and steak on the hoof. You come home like the Prodigal and there is the welcome party. But it doesn't take long at home before you hear from your elder brother who is getting mad at all the excitement over your return. The party is fun, you get a new set of clothes and a ring; but the morning after the party there'll be dishes to wash, a room to clean, and a farm to run.

St. John of the Cross, in his classic work *Dark Night of the Soul,* spoke of two levels of this darkness. The first, and the one we focus on here, deals with our attachment to the world of sense; the second, on a deeper level, with our spirit. The first dark night, which is "bitter and terrible to sense," he wrote, "is common and comes to many; these are the beginners." Even this kind of darkness, so basic to elementary solid Christian growth, is little understood today, let alone the second dark night, something "horrible and awful to our spirit" that John said is "the portion of very few. . . ."

These men and women of God are walking with Jesus. They "obey the voice of His Servant." Nothing matters to the Lord Jesus like obedience. They know this. They live in it; they love it. Then out of the blue this awful thing happens to them. Right in the middle of much glory and praise of God, there comes an inexplicable darkness. Suddenly all the lights go out in their Christian experience and nothing they do seems to change it.

What Does Darkness Look Like?

The first thing that happens is this: There's a *strange sense of emptiness* in your life. There's no sign of God. You sit in services, take your usual notes, and the message is great; but this time there is no answering chord of response in your heart. When everyone else is feeling something, why don't you feel anything?

So you pray; you get on your knees and tell God you don't feel so good. Prayer usually "changes things," it is said, but this time there seems to be no light from heaven! You go to hear teaching that has always excited you; you sit down like an addict needing a fix, stick out your arm for a Gospel shot—and nothing! You walk out of the service in which everyone else "touched God" and you say to yourself: "What in the world have I done?"

Perhaps, you think, it is *unconfessed sin.* You get on your knees and have a big response session. You apologize to everybody. You write letters of confession to your grade school teachers. You forgive your cat. You go through everything you can possibly think of, but it's all still the same. Nothing.

Then you think: "Ah ha! Of course. It's the *devil!* I haven't taken my authority in Christ." So you do. And? Still nothing.

"Well, I think I'd better go check with a Christian brother who can help me." So you go to the local godly authority on everything. . . . "Brother, can you tell me what's happening to me?" And horrors—you know what? He can't help either. He's counseled you for two hours, prayed, given you Scripture—and still you have the same darkness.

By now you are getting seriously concerned. What if you are in some really deep deception? So deep you can't even see what it is? You pray quite intensely, even desperately now: "God, *show me!* What am I doing wrong?" And again—nothing.

What you are going through is not new. It came to every major man or woman of God in Scripture. It came to Abraham when he stood waiting for God to accept his sacrifice (Genesis 15:12). It came to Moses on the mountain waiting to receive the Commandments in the "thick darkness" where God was (Deuteronomy 5:22). It came to Job when he "looked for good" and "evil came" (Job 30:26). It came to David when the bottom seemed to drop out of his world. In the middle of great trouble, when all of his enemies seemed to rise up to mock him, "deep called to deep" in David. All the flood of the waves and billows of God seemed to go over him and he cried out in agony and anger to the God whom he knew as his Rock: "Why have You forgotten me?" (Psalm 42:9). "O God," said the psalmist, "why have You cast us off forever? . . . We do not see our signs; there is no longer any prophet; nor is there any among us who knows how long" (Psalm 74:1, 9).

It came to the prophets and they wept. It came to the godly kings and they humbled themselves. One dark day it came even to Jesus the Son of God Himself. And if you set your heart to seek God, this darkness will come also to you. You will not be exempt. You will not escape it. It is the essential factor in a deep and thorough Christian experience.

Even in nature you know it's true. Nothing can live in unbroken sunshine. There must be the cycles of the night, the days of clouds and rain. Light and darkness alike are essential for plant growth; nothing but sunshine makes a desert. What is true in the seasons of nature is also true in the seasons of the spirit. Summer is beautiful, but winter must always come. Don't be surprised at the darkness. Jesus will help you walk in it sooner or later.

Satan will perhaps come and use this opportunity. A world of scoffers may surround you and taunt you as they taunted other men and women who trusted God. Your own failures and weaknesses and temptations may rise up out of nowhere and you will face a time of testing to the very roots of your life.

Dealing with Feeling

An unsaved girl who had been attending a Christian college once asked me a profound question. It is just the kind of question we need to ask for the time of great trouble and testing that faces our world now. It is the question that centrally has to do with this unique kind of darkness.

She said: "Do Christians really love Christ or do they just love the good feelings that come from loving Christ?"

Good question. Do you love Jesus or do you love the results of loving Jesus? Or put it another way: Would you still love Jesus if you could feel or sense no immediate benefits?

How do you wean a generation away from its love of pleasure as an end in itself? How do you teach a person to endure hardness, to practice patience, to handle suffering and loss victoriously, to lose something precious in order to accomplish a much greater goal of good in the end? If you were God, how would you teach your child what trust really is?

Job faced the same question when his world fell apart and God did not seem to answer. Sheltered in the personal care of God, he had walked secure in the knowledge that God his Friend was also his Provider and Protector. He, too, was a man who feared the Lord, who walked in obedience, who trusted Him. Satan's challenge to God over Job was simple. He said, in effect: "Sure Job reverences you. Why not? You are his celestial Santa Claus. Take away the presents and he'll be just the same as one of my crowd" (Job 1:8–12). So God let Satan test Job. And Job came through—but barely.

Do Christians really love Christ or do they just love the fringe benefits of obedience?

Saul, the proud and brilliant Pharisee with a driving ambition to be the most holy man of his time, faced the same awful dilemma: How do you covet holiness when covetousness is sin (Romans 7:7–13; Philippians 3:4–14)? Or to put it still another way: Babies always want to see that their parents are there, but they have to grow up one day and that means there has to come a time when they learn to realize their parents still love them even when they can't see them.

And so we have the special darkness, the darkness that is the most fearsome of all to the child of God. Not the darkness of sin, not the darkness of ignorance, not the darkness of the demonic, but the divine darkness, the darkness of the *with-*

drawn sense of the presence of God. God simply takes away the feeling of His nearness. He is always there; the omniscient, omnipotent, omnipresent Lord never sleeps, and His ear is always open to our cry. But He is a God who hides Himself, a God who dwells in darkness (Isaiah 45:15; 1 Kings 8:12). Divine darkness comes in different levels and at different times in each believer's life; but it is necessary and it accomplishes much that nothing else can do.

12

Tests of the Divine Darkness

First, it tests your courage. There is something universally scary about dark. When I was little my parents managed a shop. Friday night in New Zealand was late shopping night. They put us kids to bed early in our house behind the shop with the radio on in the darkness to keep us company until they came home again about 10:00 in the evening.

My younger sister usually dropped off to sleep right away, but I was always a night owl. Lying awake in a totally dark house was fine with the radio on quietly tuned to a classical easy listening program. But this particular night the station changed its format.

There I am in bed, trying to get to sleep, when the announcer introduces a new horror show: "Blood On the Cat"! It opens with the purported taped account of a reporter who has been murdered while spending the night on a dare in the darkness of a waxworks museum. The show opens with a courtroom full of people listening to his last recorded words. He is giving his impressions of the room in which they found him dead with the tape still running.

For the first five minutes he is full of bravado, thinking out loud. And there I am, also alone in my totally darkened room.

The reporter is looking at the wax statues: "There is Frankenstein's monster," he says. "There is the axe-murderer. Over there in the corner is Jack the Ripper."

Now I have lived in my bedroom a long time, but tonight it has become the Twilight Zone. The man is talking terror, and now everything in the room is starting to look strange.

"Funny," says the doomed reporter. "I know I'm here alone, but these things look almost alive."

Twenty seconds of silence. . . . You can hear the hiss of the tape. Then: "What was that?"

Silence. . . . "Is anyone there?"

The radio is only in the front room, about twenty paces away from my bed, but to get to it I have to cross Jack the Ripper darkness, get past Frankenstein's curtains, and make it safely past the axe-murderer doorway. So do I do it? Not on your life. I lie there and listen while my heart does handsprings and tries to climb right out of my mouth.

"You're crazy," says the reporter to himself. "There's nobody here with you." A nervous little laugh. "It's only your imagination. . . ."

Ri-i-ght, ri-i-ght! I think desperately to myself. *Imagination!*

More silence. Then, in the darkness, a tiny, almost imperceptible sound. Is it on the tape or is it in my room?

"Hello? Hello?" says the about-to-be-murdered man. "There *is* someone here!" It seems like forever before finally he screams.

My parents come back home a little later on to look in on me. They find a rigid, boy-shaped board in bed instead of a child.

There is something universally scary about the dark. Things always look better and safer in the light. It is one thing to be out in the jungle wilderness or an unfamiliar lonely city street in the day; it is something else again to be there when darkness falls. And so it is with your soul. The darkness tests your courage.

Second, it tests your convictions. When the darkness comes down, the first thing you do after you've tried everything else is begin to wonder what you really believe in. The first test comes to your convictions. You say to yourself: "I learned some principles. They are biblical. These principles work. You do this first and then this result happens. Now I've done this and nothing has happened." So you say to yourself: "Did I learn something or didn't I?"

How does God deliver us from a love for what He gave us? How do we deal with a *biblical* idolatry? How can we be freed when we are so entranced with the beauty of an idea *from* God that we are in danger of forgetting the God who yet has all kinds of new ideas to share that we cannot see?

We have all these things we know about God, and we try (as we have many times before) to put them into action. What if nothing happens this time? What if, inexplicably, the reliable thing does not work? Everything we have ever heard or thought about God comes under question.

Darkness has power to magnify not only fear but also dread—what we call *angst*. It isn't what we see that bothers us in *angst*, but what we don't see. In the light it is easy to be sure. In the light it is easy to be strong. In the light it is easy to have convictions. But when darkness comes down on our hearts and souls, we start to question everything we have and even are. "Do I really believe what I think and say I believe?"

You have said some things with utter conviction. You have said, "This is what I *know*, and I would die rather than deny it." You have been utterly sure of some things, and you have said that no matter what happens, you will never change those convictions. Indeed, that is the test of a true conviction: It is something you will not change no matter what. And then the darkness comes—and what is this? You find yourself questioning everything you were once so sure of. The worst thing is, you can't even judge your own conduct in the dark.

Third, it tests your calling. You had a sense of purpose when you met Jesus. You were chosen, you were called, you knew whom He wanted you to be and what He wanted you to do. But now comes your day of darkness; and suddenly everything is unaccountably unsure!

You ask yourself, "Did I really dedicate everything I have to God or not?" Something is happening to you that you can't track down. There is just no communication with God. No answering chord of response. "Did God really call me? Do I really have a ministry? Am I really in the right place?" The darkness comes down, and what was once clear is now hard to see.

Much of the conduct of young Christians, said John of the Cross, "has much to do with their love of self and their own inclinations. . . ." God desires to lead them further. He seeks to bring them out of that ignoble kind of love to a higher degree of love for Him, to free them from unworthy and unbefitting sensation-hungry pathways of devotion and lead them

> to a kind of spiritual exercise wherein they can commune with Him more abundantly and are freed more completely from imperfections. For they have now had practice for some time in the way of virtue and have persevered in meditation and prayer; whereby, through the sweetness and pleasure they have found therein, they have lost their love of the things of the world and have gained some degree of spiritual strength in God. This has enabled them to some extent to refrain from creaturely desires so that for God's sake they are now able to suffer a light burden and a little aridity without turning back to a time which they found more pleasant.
>
> When they are going about these spiritual exercises with the greatest delight and pleasure, and when they believe that the sun of Divine favor is shining most brightly upon them,

> God turns all this light into darkness, and shuts the door and the source of the sweet spiritual water which they were tasting in God whensoever and for as long as they desired.
>
> And thus He leaves them so completely in the dark that they know not whither to go . . . their inward sense being submerged in this night and left with such dryness that they not only experience no pleasure and consolation in spiritual things . . . but, on the contrary, find insipidity and bitterness. For . . . God now sees they have grown a little and are becoming strong enough to lay aside their swaddling clothes and be taken from the gentle breast; so He sets them down from His arms and teaches them to walk on their own two feet, which they feel to be very strange, for everything seems to be going wrong with them.

The very ministry you have seems at stake when the darkness comes on your life. All kinds of strange thoughts may come in during this time; these may very well be satanic. Suggestions may come: "I told you this Christianity business was just a big laugh. You should have listened to me the first time. Now you've become a Christian and it's a joke. If you had stayed with me you would have gone to hell, but at least it would have been fun on the way some of the time. So what have you got now? Nothing."

So you begin to question: "Did I really have a call from God? A ministry? To what?" You really begin to wonder.

Fourth, it tests your consecration. Left in the darkness long enough, the questions get deeper and even more searching: "Why won't God speak to me? What is wrong with me? Why can't I get an answer? I've tried everything I know and still there is nothing but silence. Am I really right with God?" You begin to ask serious questions about what you are supposed to be doing.

How do we know it is the darkness of God and not the darkness of guilt and sin? One key sign is this: You not only find no pleasure in the things of God; you find no pleasure in anything else in creation either. Not so with the one who has his heart straying back to the world; he finds greater delight in it. And if you are truly in the darkness of God, your mind and heart are centered on Him during the whole bitter experience. You are still thinking deeply about your relationship with God. This is not the mark of a backslider.

Fifth, it tests your conversion. The deep treatment of the darkness can go further. There may come a day when you get desperate on a level you never knew before—a level that strikes at the root of your very spiritual security. It has come to all the saints before you. If you have set your heart to be like Christ, it will come to you.

The question for you is now no longer one of being brave for Jesus, or being faithful to the truth, or being obedient to a call. The question for you now is more basic, more elemental, more foundational: "Exactly what does it mean to be a Christian? Am I really a Christian? If Christianity is true, do I actually 'have' it, or have I been living in some religious fantasy? *Am I really saved?*"

Sixth, ultimately it tests your commitment. The final stage of darkness searches you to your very depths. It shakes everything that can be shaken. It is the absolute bottom line. You are no longer asking questions about Christian obedience; you are now asking the ultimate question:

"Is there a God? How can I be so sure that there is? Is that God really Jesus Christ? And if so, do I really know Him?"

When your sonship is in doubt, the darkness is darkness indeed. When a clear sense of God's love is gone from your heart, the night that follows looks as if it will never end. You feel as though your heart is stone—dull, dead, stupid, unfeeling—when once you could jump for joy. You read the Bible and the promises don't promise. You try to pray, but your prayers seem to bounce back off the ceiling. And your favorite Christian counselor has nothing whatever to say to you that can help you now.

So here you are, as Spurgeon said, a "child of light walking in darkness." Clean as you know how to be, you have set your heart on pleasing God, and you are alert for spiritual war. But here you are, still in the darkness; there has been no word from God for a long time now.

Cheer up, child of God. You have not been abandoned! We have not been left comfortless. God has given us a word.

13

What to Do in Darkness

"Who among you fears the Lord? Who obeys the voice of His Servant? Who walks in darkness and has no light? Let him trust in the name of the Lord and rely upon his God."

Isaiah 50:10

What can you do to get out? Answer: *Nothing*. Nothing at all. There is nothing you can do to get out of the darkness if it is *God* who put you into it. That is why all your usual remedies will fail, all your counselors draw a blank, all your frustrated attempts come to an eventual exhausted end.

The darkness of God is given by Him, and it will not lift until it has accomplished its work in your soul. Jacob was "left alone" in the darkness "and there wrestled a Man with him until the breaking of day" (Genesis 32:24). You cannot escape it, but you can surely live through it, and God has told you what to do when you go into it.

If chosen men had never been alone
In deepest silence, open-doored to God,
No greatness ever had been dreamed or done.

First, do your duty nevertheless. What do you do when you are going through the darkness? The funny thing about this is that in this darkness, you can't get any guidance. That's the worst part of it. You say, "Lord, I know that this is a hard place. But what shall I do?" Nothing. Silence.

"Well," you say, "at least show me what to do." Nothing. Yet what is this person in our text, Isaiah 50, doing? Look carefully: He is *walking*.

What is the first thing that happens to us when all the lights go out? Imagine yourself walking out of an auditorium with a crowd of people and all the electricity goes out—every single light. It is pitch-black, outside and inside. What do you do?

What is the first thing we ever do when darkness drops suddenly on a familiar path? We stop. We freeze. We do not want to move. A moment before we saw the way in the light, and it was simple, straight, and clear. Nothing was ahead to trip or interrupt us and our path was plain. Now the darkness has fallen and we have stopped.

But notice the description of this child of light in the midst of darkness: He or she is *still walking*.

And that's what you will have to do. The first thing you must do when the darkness comes is to do your duty, to keep going in the same direction you were going when the darkness came. You must continue your daily routine. A. W. Tozer has a very heavy thing to say about this in his book *That Incredible Christian*, in what he called "The Ministry of the Night":

> If God sets out to make you an unusual Christian, He is not likely to be as gentle as He is usually pictured by the popular Bible teachers. A sculptor does not use a manicure set to reduce a rude, unshapely piece of marble to a thing of beauty. The saw, the hammer and chisel are cruel tools, but without them the rough stone must forever remain formless and unbeautiful.
>
> To do His supreme work of grace within you, He will take from your heart everything you love most. Everything you trust in will go from you. Piles of ashes will lie where your most beautiful treasures used to be. . . .
>
> While in this state you will exist by a kind of blind will to

> live. You will find none of the inward sweetness you had enjoyed before. The smile of God will be for the time withdrawn or at least hidden from your eyes. Then you will learn what faith is. You will find out the hard way but the only way open to you that true faith lies in the will, that joy unspeakable is not itself faith but a slow-ripening fruit of true faith, and you will learn that present joys will come and go as they will without altering your spiritual status or in any way affecting your position as a true child of your Heavenly Father. And you will also learn, probably to your astonishment, that it is possible to live in all good conscience before God and men and still feel nothing of "peace and joy" you hear talked about so much by immature Christians.

So what did God say to you *before* you went into the darkness? What were you supposed to do when the path was filled with light? What was your call, your command when the voice of God was clear? Then do it still. Do not stop because it is now dark. Keep on walking. Nothing has changed on the path except your perception of it. Do what God said for you to do before the darkness came. Do your duty nevertheless, and determine to keep walking in His previously revealed will regardless of the fact that now you cannot see. Keep walking even when the lights go out.

Second, trust in His name. We are to "let him who has no light trust in the name of the Lord." Notice: It is not to trust *in* the Lord; it is to trust in the *name* of the Lord.

And what is the Lord's name? Moses asked that question, too. This was God's answer out of the bush that burned with fire: "I AM THAT I AM."

His name is descriptive of what He is, and He is there. He is the uncreated, unchanging, unshakable God. He is what He always is. He has not changed in the darkness. He is not missing because you cannot see Him. God is committed in everlasting covenant to you. He is faithful and will remain faithful, regardless of your character or circumstances, "the same yesterday, today, and forever" (Hebrews 13:8), the One who bids you "be still, and know that I am God" (Psalm 46:10).

God says, "You are to trust *in My name.*" The most basic thing about God is that He is always there and He always will be. Even if you don't feel He is, *He is!* You say, "But I don't know where I am." It doesn't matter. He knows where He is! Trust in the name of the Lord. "The name of the Lord is a strong tower; the righteous run to it and are safe" (Proverbs 18:10). "Those who know Your name will put their trust in You" (Psalm 9:10).

You're to get on your knees and say: "O God, I don't feel You. I don't get any zap from You. I don't feel Your presence. But You're there nevertheless because Your Word doesn't change. Amen."

"If we believe not," said Timothy, "yet he abideth faithful: he cannot deny himself" (2 Timothy 2:13, KJV). "God may not give us an easy journey to the Promised Land," wrote Bonar, "but He will give us a safe one."

Third, remember who God is. Here is something else you can do: In this time of darkness, go over in your mind what God has already done. Those things aren't just little dreams in the back of your head. They really did happen; God really did do them. Now you are going to have to remember them.

Those things may seem very far off to you at this time, but now is when you're going to have to remember. Go back in your mind. Say, "God, You've done this before. You were like that before. You're not going to change now."

Remember what His character is like. When you can't see the way, open the Book and see again what He is like. F. B. Meyer said, "There is nothing indeed which God will not do for a man who dares step out upon what seems to be a mist, though as he puts down his foot he finds a rock beneath him." Others before you have walked in the darkness; they, too, have found that *faith is not something you hold, but Someone who holds you.*

Recall what God has already done in your life. What have you seen of God in your own experience? Then you said, "I will never doubt Him again. I have seen His hand, I know what He is like, and I am committed to Him forever."

Now, did you mean it? If you don't trust Him now, you will have cause to suspect whether you ever did. If you don't trust God in the dark, it would seem your faith is in light or in your own eyesight. Unless we trust in God and in God alone, we don't trust Him at all.

People in Bible times sometimes built memorials to the mighty acts of God in their history. They put up stones of remembrance, built permanent records in rock that would serve as witnesses to their children and to their children's children as to what God had done for them. Christians in the past often kept journals, diaries of their spiritual experiences with Jesus. From the records of both Scripture and Church history, we know that the God who acted in times past still acts today, no matter what we presently feel.

Fourth, there's a time to stay, a time to lean. What else do you have to do? Stay—or lean. What does that mean?

Years ago one of my friends and I went out to fish off the coastal waters of a place called the Great Barrier Island in New Zealand. We went out in a little rowboat and, ridiculously enough, took our wives with us.

It was the first and last time we ever did that. Our wives are great to have along except on a fishing trip, for three reasons: First, they knew even less about rowing than we did; second, we had two extra passengers in a very small boat; and third, they talked the whole time we were trying to fish.

Faye and Kathy were having a great time fellowshipping while Tony and I were having a greater time learning how to row. We took our boat out to the middle, threw our lines over, and waited for some fish to come along. The fish were a lot smarter than we were; we didn't catch anything except colds. For over an hour we sat there while the girls talked and nothing happened. Finally we looked up and saw all these dark clouds.

Tony and I looked at each other.

"Shouldn't we go back?"

"Sure."

The wind by now had started blowing offshore out toward the sea, so we started rowing back to shore. We rowed for fifteen minutes before we realized we were in exactly the same place. Our efforts had just balanced out the wind. Out there was only open ocean, and once we ran out of rowing steam, the next stop 1,200 miles away was Australia. It was getting darker and starting to rain. We had to take a break and then make a full effort to get back to shore.

Do you know what we did?

In the boat there was an anchor. What do you do with an anchor when a storm is blowing and you have to stay in the same place? You don't throw that anchor on deck where you can see it; you throw it out into the deep where you can't see it. You let it hook onto the unseen reality of the rock at the bottom of the ocean. Then it grips and there you stay until the storm blows over.

We did that. Hours later, wet and shaken, we were able to row back to safety.

And here is *an anchor for your soul in the day of darkness*. Here is a permit issued specially to you. It allows you to trust God in darkness. It is a command. It is an order. It is to be obeyed to the hilt. God says, "*Lean.*" You can take this word in your hand and say to the Lord: "This is all I have. Here will I rest my case. You said it, and I will lean on Your love like a child." You have said you would trust Jesus forever. Now you get your chance.

What do you do with your faith? You can't see it. It's too dark. You have to send it out where you can't see anything. Let it touch the great I Am. Lean on His arms. Say, "God, I can't feel anything. But I just lean on You." Your song is going to be that old chorus: "I'm leaning on Jesus; contented am I." You're going to sing that every day until the darkness comes off.

You have taken Him to be your God; He has taken you to be His own. "Let him stay upon his God." This is His covenant, said Spurgeon; lean on it. You are not dealing with a liar. It is bought by blood. It is sealed by an oath. You can say, "Lord, I cannot be overconfident in what You have said. I do not know and I cannot see; but I can trust You and I can lean."

Nothing you go through in this darkness is outside of His love; everything is filtered through His careful, caring hand. "Who is this," said the biblical writer "coming up from the wilderness, leaning upon her beloved?" (Song of Solomon 8:5). Paul Pastnor put it like this in his beautiful poem:

> "Child of My love—lean hard,
> And let Me feel the pressure of your care.
> I know your burden, child. I shaped it;
> Poised it in Mine own hand;
> Made no proportion in its weight
> To thine unaided strength.
>
> "For even as I laid it on, I said,
> 'I shall be near, and while she leans on Me
> This burden shall be Mine, not hers.'
> So shall I keep My child
> Within the circling arms of My own love.
> Here, lay it down—not fear
> To impose it on a shoulder which upholds
> The government of worlds.
>
> "Yet closer come: thou art not near enough.
> I would embrace thy care;
> So I might feel My child reposing on My breast.
> Thou lovest Me? I knew it. Doubt not, then;
> But loving Me—*lean hard.*"

14

The Purpose of Darkness

Why is God doing this to me? Why this darkness? And how long will it last? How come when I talk to Him He doesn't answer? Why am I not getting any revelation in my life?

Probably because this is the only way God has of teaching you some very important lessons. And those lessons are basically these: Will you obey Him whether you feel like it or not? Will you do what He asks you to do? Will you hold onto the truth He's given you, whether you feel He's there or not?

You say, "Of course I will!"

How about with no sense of His presence?

It's easy for us to say, "O God, what I've just learned is so exciting that I'll never doubt it, never, never, never. . . ."

God says, "I heard that. You feel good now. You *say* you believe this; you *think* you understand it. We'll see."

You learn the principle. Now the problem comes. You use the principle but this time there is no flash. You say, "Hey, what *is* this?" When the Prodigal Son returned home to experience forgiveness, after all, he got a new suit, a ring, and a steak dinner. If he had gone out to the harlots and the pigs again, he would have been lucky to get a fast-food hamburger.

God doesn't want us addicted to the joy of returning. But does the fact that we can't feel it as before change the principle? We have to learn that. It's easy for someone to tell us, but it's a lot harder when we're going through it.

Some of you have *convictions* that God has written and locked into your heart. You think these are so strong, so unshakable that you will never, ever doubt them. Then the darkness comes and you start asking questions. Are these convictions really true or not? What you will find out is whether you really do believe them. The darkness will test your convictions. And the only thing left when the darkness lifts from your life is what you really do believe.

How about your *consecration?* You had a wonderful experience, perhaps in a service one time. A totally incredible, miraculous, fantastic thing happened. You wish you had a movie so you could play it back every day of your life. On that day you said, "Lord, I know You've called me. I'm giving my life to You. This is it. Hear me, Lord. I dedicate my life to You. Amen. I'll never turn back."

Then darkness comes.

Do you still trust Him when you don't feel Him? Suppose you have been praying for a miraculous confirmation of a *call.* Perhaps you have even asked God for a "fleece." A brick falls out of the sky, hits you on the head. There's a text on it: "Go to Africa." The very next week the sky lights up with lightning. The swirling clouds spell out a message in the sky: *Africa.* You come home from work and there is a spear embedded in your door. Engraved on the shaft are the words *Come over and help us.* And so you say, "God, I think I know where You want me to go."

Now it's only a few months away from getting the tickets and the darkness comes down. And you wonder, "Was it Africa or Australia?"

What about your *conversion?* Remember the day you got saved? You may have been reared in a loving Christian family who taught you how to love Jesus from the time you were a kid. You may have come from a family that was rotten or just plain nuts.

Or perhaps you know what *lost* means. You were once really bad yourself. You ran around chopping people up; you rode with Bonnie and Clyde. You shot fifty innocent citizens before you got saved, and those were just your friends! You had quite a cosmic change take place in your life at your conversion. Then you said, "I got so saved you won't believe it. I'm going to make Billy Graham look like a backslider!"

That's what you said. Then, the darkness. How are you doing now?

We say: "Salvation is not dependent on feelings." We tell young converts: "Now understand, it doesn't matter how you feel. Take it by faith." You said that to others; now you've got to live it yourself.

How long will the darkness last? A week? Maybe not. Maybe more. Maybe a year. How long will it last? *As long as it takes God to confirm those four things in your life.* And no amount of resisting the devil, searching your heart for sin, praising God, or any other normal thing that is supposed to bring release will ever do it, until God is finished with you.

When the darkness has finished its work in you, everything that can be shaken will be shaken, and only what is firm, real, and solid shall remain.

15

Benefits of the Darkness

First, you will learn what you really know about God. We live in an age in which communication technology has given us the most advanced methods in history of gaining access to knowledge. We have cassette tapes, tracts, books, videos, radio and T.V. programs transmitted by satellite. We have church meetings, seminars, teaching crusades, and home Bible studies. We have scores of different translations of Scripture and access to all kinds of lexicons and word study books; we can now disobey God in Hebrew, Greek, and Aramaic.

There is danger in much light; it is not the same as spiritual sight. It is perfectly possible, especially for us in the information age, to learn spiritual truth without ourselves becoming spiritual. As A. W. Tozer wrote in *That Incredible Christian:*

> Spiritual truths differ from natural truths both in their constitution and in the manner of their apprehension. . . . The truths of the natural sciences, for instance, can be grasped by anyone of normal intelligence whether he is a good man or a scoundrel. . . . A man may study philosophy for a lifetime, teach it, write books about it and be all the while proud, covetous and thoroughly dishonest in his private dealings. The same thing may be said of theology. A man need not be godly

> to learn theology. Indeed I wonder whether there is anything taught in any seminary on earth that could not be learned by a brigand or a swindler as well as by a consecrated Christian.

The difference between "light" and "sight," said Tozer, is in the revelation ministry of God the Holy Spirit. In "light" we can learn *about* God, but only when we learn *of* God are we given "sight." Spiritual light is a discoverable fact, and we can get as much of it as we want by close attention to reading, work, and study. But spiritual sight is a *gift of God,* and it comes only in humility of heart. Again, Tozer (from *Born After Midnight*):

> To find the way we need more than light; we need also sight. . . . Between light and sight there is a wide difference. One man may have light without sight; he is blind. Another may have sight without light; he is temporarily blind.
>
> . . . Religious instruction is not enough. It brings light, but it cannot impart sight. . . . There can be no salvation apart from truth, but there can be and often is truth without salvation. How many multiplied thousands have learned the catechism by heart and still wander in spiritual darkness because there has been no inward illumination? The assumption that light and sight are synonymous has brought spiritual tragedy to millions.

Because of our particular strength in the West in communications and information access, we are exposed through many means to much religious content. We know all kinds of things *about* God. But what do we really know *of* God? What are the actual realities He has imprinted eternally on our souls? What is revelation and what is just information? In the darkness, all we are left with is what we *really* know. Darkness teaches us the difference.

Second, you will be humbled. Are you the one with such a history in Christ that you are used to being the source of all the helpful and practical answers? Are you the one with the light and the way and the truth? You may be a leader, a challenger, an intercessor; perhaps you are used to telling people what to do and what is wrong. And it has been a habit of yours to give help and counsel to those less fortunate or blessed than you. Possibly you no longer ask for help yourself much anymore; you have spiritually "arrived." As John of the Cross said:

> As the beginners feel themselves to be very fervent and diligent in spiritual things and devout exercises from this prosperity (although it is true that holy things of their own nature cause humility), there often comes to them through their imperfections a certain degree of secret pride which they come to have with their works and with themselves. And hence there comes to them likewise a certain desire, which is somewhat vain and at times very vain, to speak of spiritual things in the presence of others and sometimes even to teach such things rather than learn them.

How can you tell the difference between what you have really learned and what you have simply passed on as information to others that you have enjoyed without embracing? You need God to show us what is truly yours in Him and what is only mental assent. And so, the darkness. You are in real need yourself now; but now you don't know what to do or what to say. The "one with all the answers" has no answer for his or her own life. Darkness comes to reveal our need of God and God alone. Don't fret over your helplessness, your emptiness; they will be riches to you. God says, "I will give you the treasures of darkness" (Isaiah 45:3).

There is more than one kind of fast in the Bible. There is also the fast in which we set our hearts under God to cut ourselves off from religious unreality, to determine to act in truth and compassion, and from the brokenness of our own lives feed others. "If you extend your soul to the hungry and satisfy the afflicted soul, then your light shall dawn in the darkness, and your darkness shall be as the noonday" (Isaiah 58:10).

Third, you will learn again the feelings of the lost. Do you remember what it felt like when you were lost from God? Perhaps you don't. Some of us have been saved so long that we don't know anymore what it's like to be lost. We have nothing now to say to a broken, hurting street kid. People may be dying in front of us, but we've forgotten what it felt like.

How is God going to teach us what it's like to be lost? What does a sinner go through each day? No conscious sense of the presence of God. God is going to have to teach us compassion, and the darkness of God will teach us well. When it is finished, we will learn again the feelings of those outside the Light of the world. And next time we talk to a lost man we'll be able to say, "I know what you feel like. I really know."

I went to work for a summer years ago at Teen Challenge in New York. I had grown up in New Zealand near a beach—a really beautiful country. A murder in New Zealand when I was a child was something nationally shocking that we seemed to hear about once in a blue moon. A generation ago, New Zealand hotels rarely even had locks on the doors.

Can you imagine coming from New Zealand for the first time to a big city like New York? I mean inner-city, run-down-ghetto, gang-warring New York in the summer. There was a murder every eighteen hours in the city then, a major robbery every three minutes. Like many a huge metropolis with gangs, drugs, and violence, New York was Paranoia City at night.

And there I was trying to minister in the heart of the city's worst crime districts. You went up to somebody to ask directions and they thought you were going to mug them. Nobody looked at you on the street; everyone walked fast in case you were a panhandler, a lunatic, or a desperate drug addict.

A friend of mine from New Zealand once visited New York.

He parked his car outside a police station, put his camera underneath the seat, locked the doors, and went in to ask directions. When he came out just a few minutes later, there was a hole smashed in the back of the car window and his camera was ripped off. In horror he ran back inside and exclaimed to the officer, "Hey, my camera got stolen! I had it under the seat of my car parked right outside."

"Too bad," the policeman said.

"What do you mean, too bad? Aren't you going to find it?"

"You've got to be kidding."

Then my friend snapped, "I demand to see the chief of police."

But when he eventually got to see him, the chief of police said the same thing. My friend got so angry he stormed out—only to discover someone had stolen his car.

So there I was in the middle of New York, feeling I just couldn't take it anymore.

I remember walking one hot, dangerous night in all this filth and I said to God: "Lord, this is ridiculous. I can't stay in this place. I can't even breathe here without eventually dying. I'm used to home with beaches and blue skies and white clouds where you can lie down right on the grass . . . no snakes to bite you, no human snakes to jump on you. And you don't get beaten up or mugged just because you have change in your pocket.

"Lord," I said, "this is it. New York is a filthy place. I can't stand it."

And then this poem I had heard one time came burning back into my mind:

> I said, "Let me walk in the fields."
> God said, "No, walk in the town."
> I said, "But there are no flowers here."
> He said, "No flowers, but a crown."
> I said, "But the sky is black.
> There is nothing but noise and din."

But He wept as He sent me back;
"There is more," He said,
"There is sin."

Do you remember what it was like to be cut off from the love of God? To wake up each morning without a sense of God's forgiveness, of divine purpose and security and hope? Perhaps you met Christ years ago. It has been a long time since you felt the wonder of that first love. You have said you want to have His compassion for unsaved people. Perhaps you have prayed that God would give you a heart for the lost.

And then came this darkness. You cannot feel or sense the presence of God anymore. You wake up in the morning without any conscious sense of His nearness and His care. You no longer are sure He is speaking to you.

Do you know what it's like to be without Christ? Darkness will teach you. You will learn what you really know about God. God can come at the end of darkness and comfort you in an incredible way, but during that time you will have learned what you really know about Jesus. You'll learn the difference between feeling and doing, feeling and obeying. Nothing matters to Christ like obedience. You had forgotten what it was like to be lost, but now you know again.

The darkness of God teaches us to care.

Fourth, you will prove the power of prayer. "If you always have bread," said Spurgeon, "you'll never know the power of the prayer 'Give us this day our daily bread.' "

If a man sneers at prayer and tells you the name of a dozen cynical philosophers who say they prayed and God did not answer their prayer, *believe it;* God doesn't have to answer the prayers of professional cynics.

Jonah, the prophet, like all of us, knew something of perfunctory prayer. A man of God, he no doubt dutifully put in his daily devotional time. Then one day God told him to "arise and go to Nineveh." He arose and went, all right (so far, so good!)—to Tarshish. (Not so good!) After a short and scary voyage in a vessel targeted for divine interruption, Jonah was pitched overboard and got to spend three days and nights in the belly of Jaws Five. You can bet he really learned to pray! The last thing he remembered as he dropped beneath the surface of the sea was a rush of water, a huge open mouth, and a certain sinking feeling that he was really out of the will of God.

Thank God for obedient whales. The fish didn't say to God, "O God, you know I can't stomach preachers!" And Jonah went down whole. When he finally woke up he was in a place that was dark and hot. Can you guess what he was thinking? "I knew I was a bad preacher, Lord, but I didn't know I was this bad!"

Scripture records the essence of his prayer: "Out of the belly of hell I cried, and You heard my voice." And with weeds wrapped around his neck he *really* learned to pray. For three days and three nights he prayed. He did nothing but pray—past "short" requests and "important" requests and "quite urgent" requests into *absolutely desperate* requests, the sort of life-or-death agonizing that the impending destruction of an entire city is all about. And in the School of the Whale's Stomach Jonah probably learned more about reality in prayer than he ever had in Bible college.

His eventual obedience resulted in the largest recorded awakening in the Bible: an entire city humbling itself, repenting and turning to God.

Fifth, you will come out into a greater light. Darkness often follows great light. The darkness of God often comes immediately after some of the best teaching and deepest revelation you have ever had. Like the fact that your greatest time of temptation sometimes strikes right after your most wonderful time in the things of God, spiritual darkness follows hard on the heels of a time when you have learned much.

As children my sister and I sometimes rode into town with

our relatives by train. Earlier New Zealand railcars had no lights on in the daytime. When one entered a short tunnel, the carriage where children sat became for a brief time totally dark.

You know what happens in such darkness. The pupils of your eyes, which in the sunshine had shrunk almost to pinpoints, now expand wider and wider in the darkness. And when the train suddenly bursts out of the other side of the tunnel, the brightness of the world outside is astonishing.

And so with the darkness of God. We do not know or appreciate the brightness of the light we already walk in until we enter this discipline of God. We have absorbed so much that our spiritual perception has shrunk to a pinpoint. We have been given so much that we cannot appreciate what has been shown us. And then God puts us like children onto His train and runs it into the darkness.

This darkness you are in is only a tunnel. The train is on a sure journey. It is headed without fail to the place you need to be, and the Engineer knows all of the way. The tunnel is not eternal. You will not remain in darkness forever. And you will come out of the darkness into a greater sense of light than you had when you went in. "Unto the upright there arises light in the darkness" (Psalm 112:4).

The Danger of False Fire

I want to show you what God can teach you in darkness, and then give you a beautiful promise. But first a *warning*.

"The way in which they are to conduct themselves in this night of sense," said St. John of the Cross, "is not to devote themselves to reasoning and meditation, since this is not the time for it, but to allow the soul to remain in peace and quietness, although it may seem clear to them that they are doing nothing, and are wasting their time, and although it may appear to them that it is because of their weakness that they have no desire in that state to think of anything. The truth is that they will be doing quite sufficient if they have patience and persevere in prayer without making any effort."

Isaiah 50 contains a solemn warning. You cannot take matters into your own hands. If God does not bring you light, you must not make your own. Some have tried to do just that. "If God is not going to speak," they say in anger, "then I am going ahead anyway. If He won't show me the light, I will make my own." What they are saying is, "O.K., God, if You're not going to guide me, I'm going to guide myself."

"Sparks," says the Lord. What you have then is an extremely brief and temporary light; it cannot last and will only leave you blinded. Don't do it. Don't make the foolish and futile mistake of lighting your own fire. If God has put you into the darkness, let it do its work in your soul. He got you in; you can trust Him to take you out. If you light your own light, your little match, and go and do your own thing, you will see in that manmade light a destruction of much that is beautiful that God had for you.

You cannot afford to do your own thing if you do not feel the presence of God. Walk in what God has already given you to do and remain faithful until new light comes. Light your own path and you can expect nothing but grief. You say, "No light. O.K. I'll light my own fire." Then this will be your swan song: "I did it my way."

The Bible has a word for you: "Walk in the light . . . you have kindled—This you shall have from My hand: *You shall lie down in torment*" (Isaiah 50:11).

Wrote St. John:

> Spiritual persons suffer great trials; not so much of the aridities which they suffer, as of the fear which they have of being lost on the road, thinking that all spiritual blessings are over for them and that God has abandoned them since they find no help or pleasure in good things. . . .

> These souls turn back at such a time if there is none who understands them; they abandon the road or lose courage; or at least they are hindered from going further by the great trouble which they take in advancing along the road of meditation and reasoning. Thus they fatigue and overwork their nature, imagining they are falling through negligence or sin. But this trouble that they are taking is quite useless; for God is now leading them by another road. . . .
>
> It is well for those who find themselves in this condition to take comfort, to persevere in patience and to be in no wise afflicted. Let them trust in God, who abandons not those who seek Him with a simple and right heart, and will not fail to give them what is needed for the road, until He brings them into the pure and clear light of love.

God is the One who dwells in thick darkness (Deuteronomy 5:22). The darkness and the light are alike to Him (Psalm 139: 12). There are treasures that can be found only in such darkness and He will show you there things about Himself and about yourself that you will never learn any other way.

And the things you will find in that darkness! You will hear the voice of God at the end of the tunnel saying, "Well done, you good and faithful servant. Enter into the joy of your Lord." You will go through it, beloved; make the most of it. He will speak to you in that very silence.

We must ask God for courage to go through the darkness ahead. This is necessary because God is going to prepare His people to obey no matter how they feel. And we must have it. Christians are going through this darkness now.

On my grandfather's wall for many years hung a small plaque. I was not a Christian when I first read it, nor then was my grandfather. Many years later, on that first night Granpoppy came to hear his oldest grandchild preach, he responded to the invitation to surrender everything to Jesus. Only a short time later he died. His house was eventually sold. I don't know what happened to that little plaque, but I still remember what it said:

I said to the man who stood at the gate of the years,
"Give me a light that I may walk safely into the unknown."
He said to me, "*Go out into the darkness*
And put your hand into the hand of God
And He shall be to you brighter than a light
And safer than a known way."

Prayer

Heavenly Father, we praise You for the light of God. We thank You for Jesus Christ, the Light of the world. We thank You, O God, that on a rainy day the sun has not vanished, just gone behind a cloud. We thank You also, O God, for the night, because plants need the darkness as well as the light to survive.

Father, we forget that we're the planting of God. We want sunshine all the time and we forget that nothing but sunshine makes a desert. Teach us, dear God, the meaning of the darkness. We don't care, Lord God. You can run us through as much darkness as we can possibly bear so long as it's not from the devil and it's not from sin. Prepare your saints, O God, for the dark times that will come by giving them a taste of what it's like not to feel Your presence and yet obey. And we thank You that we can learn a lesson of faith that will last for eternity.

Dear God, we pray for those right now who are going through times of darkness and have not understood. They have lit their own lights and gone out their own way and seen much destruction and sorrow. We hear the awful warning of Your Word: "From My hand: You shall lie down in torment." We pray, O God, that You will minister to those. Give them another chance, O Lord, and this time encourage them to go through in faith.

We pray, O Lord, for those going through times of darkness—who have felt no blessing, experienced no excitement. Nothing seems to move them, yet they've checked their hearts again and again to see if they have walked away from You and found nothing. Dear Lord, encourage their hearts. Give them a great and mighty challenge to go through this time and to learn their lesson from You.

In the name of Jesus we pray. Amen.